PARADOX

To Joe and Victoria
With best regards

PARADOX

This is a work of fiction. Names, characters, places, and incidents are a product of the author's imagination. Locales and public names are sometimes used for atmospheric purposes. Any resemblance to actual people, living or dead, or to businesses, companies, events, institutions, or locales is completely coincidental.

I hasten to add that I have enormous respect for all our fine men and women at the service academies. Nothing in this fictional story is meant in any way to denigrate their service nor demean the prestige and honor of their mission.

With apologies for the salty language. The intent is not to offend but rather maintain authenticity.

www.wynnestevens.com

ISBN-13: 978-0-9848199-4-2

Fiction / Romance / General Frequency

To Allan

Acknowledgments

It is with extreme gratitude that I acknowledge those who have helped and supported me along the way.

First, and forever foremost, Andrea—the light and love of my life.

Jim Gormly, for whose support and assistance I shall always be grateful. Jim is an awesome friend who has helped me for years as I struggle through the writing process.

Dick and Mary Ellen Meryhew who lent their proofreading skills with such meticulous professionalism.

And, as always, Jack Roberts, without whose early encouragement, this book might never have been written.

"I saw courage both in the Vietnam War and in the struggle to stop it. I learned that patriotism includes protest, not just military service."

John F. Kerry

Contents

Chapter One 7
Charlie
Chapter Two 27
Melinda
Chapter Three 38
The Naval Academy
Chapter Four 65
History Lessons
Chapter Five 102
Christmas Leave
Chapter Six 121
Kacie
Chapter Seven 161
Eli and Arlo
Chapter Eight 187
ONI
Chapter Nine 225
Decisions
Chapter Ten 242
St. Johns College
Chapter Eleven 271
Drafted
Chapter Twelve 337
Home

CHAPTER ONE

Charlie

1948

A shower curtain separated the space between the living and dining rooms.

An elderly assistant suddenly appeared from somewhere in the back. She looked indifferently at the young woman. "Do you have the money?" she asked.

"Yes," Melinda answered softly.

"Give it to me."

Melinda reached into her purse and removed a roll of twenties. She handed it to the assistant who quickly counted it. She then disappeared back behind the curtain.

Melinda stood and nervously paced while she waited for the assistant to return. She was both curious and frightened. Behind the curtain, someone coughed. A slit in the curtain allowed a thin shaft of light to fall on the floor. Through the slit, she could see preparations underway.

It was, indeed, the doctor's dining room. A sheet lay over the dining room table. The assistant was laying out an array of scary looking surgical devices along one side.

Melinda closed her eyes tightly. Tears ran down her pale cheeks. She clenched her fists and asked God if she was doing the right thing.

A child-like voice whispered softly in her ear.

"Hey! Don't do this! I worked hard to get here! Do you know the odds I overcame?

Melinda *knew*. This wasn't right.

Her hands pressed against her head as if to ward off the demons. She ran out the living room and through the entry door, into the misty gray darkness of the cold night.

Present Time

Dumb ass!

Unbearable grief lay upon him. With one hand, he leaned unsteadily on the squalid bathroom sink and scrutinized the blue-gray eyes in the mirror before him—eyes that had witnessed much over his seventy-two years.

The old man's hand twitched uncontrollably. His time in Vietnam had polluted his DNA with deadly chemicals. He suffered from Parkinson's disease—a direct result of exposure to Agent Orange.

His mouth formed a snarl as he spat out the words.

"Fucking Agent Orange!"

"Fucking Vietnam!"

However, it wasn't Agent Orange that ruined his life. It was anger. It ruined his life and those whose lives were touched by his.

The eyes before him softened with sadness. His old heart ached for what might have been. These eyes looking back once belonged to a handsome young man, so talented and optimistic. He knew the handsome young man still resided somewhere deep within his consciousness, crushed and beaten almost to death by bad choices and overbearing personalities.

The eyes in the mirror once belonged to a fearless teenager who disdained authority and conformity.

He was once that teenager so many years ago; those eyes were his eyes.

He looked at what he had become and turned away angrily.

The old man longed to be that rebellious teenager again. This time, no one would dominate him in futile attempts to mold his character. This time, he would ignore the narrow-minded judgments of a few.

No one would ever tell him that he wasn't good enough; that he didn't measure up.

June 1969

Charlie McDaniels pushed away wrinkled sheets with his foot, struggling to sit upright on the edge of his bed. His older brother stood over him, flushed and uncharacteristically excited, waving a white envelope.

Charlie squinted angrily while shaking off the grogginess. He snatched the envelope from his brother's hands and turned it slowly towards him. As his eyes focused, his demeanor weakened; his right hand trembled slightly as he read the return address.

"Office of the Superintendent, United States Naval Academy"

Immediately, he knew what was inside. It was the response to his application for admittance to the Naval Academy.

"Open it for God's sake, Charlie!"

Charlie knew it would be a rejection—one that would further diminish him in the eyes of his father and brother.

"Hang on, goddamnit, Frank!" he yelled back. You just woke me up, for christsake!"

Frank jumped back, surprised at his younger brother's anger.

Charlie flipped the envelope over and back. He was procrastinating. He didn't want to open it. He wanted to throw it away.

Who cares? My application to the Naval Academy was ridiculous—nothing more than a laughably futile exercise to please my father. I met none of the academy's high standards.

It would be another rejection, another unfavorable comparison with his older brother. He stalled and looked at the floor.

"Come on, Charlie! What the fuck are you waiting for?"

Charlie wanted to punch him.

Instead, he looked up from the envelope and eyed his older brother. "Get out of here, Frank. I need some privacy. I'll be down when I'm ready."

"I don't get it. Aren't you curious?"

"Not at the moment."

"He knows you have it."

"You told him? You can't keep a fucking thing from him, can you?"

"Of course not," Frank answered indignantly. He's our *father*."

"Oh, that's right. Of course. The 'little general'."

Frank glared at Charlie's irreverence. "Don't talk about him like that."

"Go! Come back in half an hour." Charlie said. "I want some time to myself."

"Dad will want to know soon."

"I don't care. Shut the door on your way out."

The door slammed. Charlie stood slowly and looked on the floor for his jeans and shirt.

Once dressed, he walked across the room and stood at his old dresser, diminished with age and abuse. His eyes traveled over meaningless trinkets acquired through the years. He sighed and shook his head.

"What's the point?"

He looked in the mirror. He showed no enthusiasm or expectation. His bright blue eyes reflected uncertainty and indifference. Like an unwanted toy, he tossed the envelope on the dresser and turned away.

However, as he stared at the Potomac from his window, his curious side began to chatter. He had to know for sure.

Open the fucking letter! Get it over! Just go down and tell him you didn't make it. He knows what it takes to get in a place like that. He knows you don't have it. What's one more of his belittling looks?

He returned slowly and deliberately to the dresser. He hesitated before retrieving the envelope. He flipped it back and forth, waiting.

With a single grand gesture, he savagely ripped one end open.

Inside, he could see a single sheet of fine linen stationery. He extracted and opened the letter tentatively. His eyes focused on its words.

"Congratulations. The Selection Board awards you a Presidential Appointment to the United States Naval Academy, Annapolis, Maryland. Should you accept this appointment, you are instructed to report to Tecumseh Court at the entrance to Bancroft Hall no later than 1300, 19 June 1969."

Charlie's jaw dropped; he was stunned. He read the letter a second time and looked up with wide eyes.

Accepted? What the hell?

Charlie steadied himself on the dresser. He looked at the letter in a state of shock and disbelief. This *had* to be a bad dream.

Shit. How is this possible? Didn't anyone look at my high school record?

Charlie's first thought was of his father. He pictured him downstairs waiting, assuming rejection and ready to issue yet another verbal put-down.

Charlie threw the letter on the dresser. His mind continued to spin. His reality twisted grotesquely with the understanding of what lay ahead.

This dilemma was now many times worse than enduring a few verbal barbs from the old man. He *never* wanted to go to the Naval Academy. He had his *own* life to plan.

This was not supposed to happen!

He looked over at the two guitars hanging on the wall—a Martin and a Fender. Charlie played each at a level no one could match—not Frank, not his father, not anyone. Music was the source of his power and respect.

He slowly flexed the fingers of his left hand, fingers that effortlessly created beautiful sounds.

I'd have to give up the gigs... and the girls.

How could he tell his father he wasn't interested? Who turns down an appointment to the Naval Academy?

The old man would have a legitimate shit-fit.

Charlie's father was GeneralByron McDaniels III, commander of the National War College at Fort McNair, U.S. Naval Academy,

Class of '42.

Charlie dreaded his father's anger. He had seen it before — many times. He could take the yelling, but he couldn't take the ridicule… the disgust and disappointment in his eyes.

General McDaniels fancied himself the quintessential symbol of manhood and bravery, the demanding disciplinarian operating in a family cult of military idolization. It was a cult of fear that no one dare challenge or deny. His aura of superiority was powerful and intimidating.

Charlie was trapped. He had inadvertently betrayed himself. He'd never considered that the Naval Academy might *accept* him. It was absurd.

I guess the joke's on me.

❋

Charlie grew up strongly influenced by the general's ideology of strength, toughness, leadership, and authority. Of course, Frank was the better athlete, more outgoing and authoritative in manner. Academically, he was first in his class — the classic all-American youth. He even *looked* like his father — shortly cropped dark hair, barrel-chested frame, and bushy dark eyebrows. Frank loved his father's military ideology and wanted to be just like him.

Charlie considered his brother an insufferable ass-kisser. Besides, how could he possibly compete with Frank who was president of the senior class in high school and captain of the varsity football team?

Charlie was a singer in a rock and roll band. It goes without saying that, in his father's eyes, he did not compare well with Frank.

Charlie looked nothing like either of them. His tall, lean frame and masculine features belied a sensitivity that neither his brother nor his father shared. His penetrating blue eyes were soft and affective — a gift from his mother. He was the quiet one, the shy one.

His father disdained such personal traits, believing them

unbefitting a "real" man. He thought Charlie soft and weak and told him so regularly, forcing Charlie to question his own developing manhood. Was he weak and effeminate as his father often insinuated?

His father's eyes ridiculed Charlie in a way that made him feel different, inferior. The message he received was that he was a loser... he didn't measure up. These perceptions carved deep wounds in his young ego.

Only his mother provided an occasional safe haven for Charlie. They were real friends and kindred spirits. She knew that being a teenager is tough. She understood social pressures and the need for acceptance.

Charlie was her favorite, their bond special. She wanted him to find himself on his terms.

Yet, she was powerless to guide him through the awkwardness of teenage years. When her husband was home, she became a passive observer to whatever example he chose to model. She remained silently in the shadows, never interfering or challenging his brand of discipline.

With little support at home, Charlie looked to like-minded friends, friends who were the antithesis of his father's ideals.

⁂

Charlie put his hands on the dresser and leaned toward the mirror. He smiled as his mind traveled back to those times when he was close to rock bottom in Hawaii.

I was fourteen and in Virginia when the family moved to Hawaii. Frank was a plebe at the Naval Academy and I had just barely finished ninth grade.

It was a tough first month at that new school. Coming from the East Coast, I thought I was a cool dude, dressed in a white tee shirt, jeans and blue suede bombers—suede loafers with one-inch soles. Ugh!

The girls were hot and pretty much occupied my fantasies. I told them I played the guitar. They were impressed.

The guys, however, thought differently. They repeatedly drug me into the bathroom and beat the crap out of me until I conformed to the local dress code and lightened up on the swagger. Eventually, I made friends with most of my assailants. They invited me to join their gang. They were tough; I followed their lead and gained their acceptance

If they smoked, I smoked. If they went joyriding with a case of beer, I was right with them. I took on outrageous dares to ensure their continued trust.

My father hated my friends—called them "delinquents" because of their long hair disrespectful attitudes. One of them lit up a cigar right in front of him!

I didn't care what he thought. They were my friends. So what if they were the "wrong crowd"; so what if they were juvenile delinquents?

My father and I had no functional father-son relationship in Hawaii. We rarely talked. Each time I disobeyed authority, he reminded me how much better Frank was than me. He knew nothing about how I was doing or how I liked school…until the first report card arrived and he saw how poor my grades and attendance record were.

"Where the hell have you been this semester?" he yelled like a drill sergeant. His round little face was the color of a ripe tomato. Spit flew from his mouth.

I had skipped school thirty one days that semester. I was on the verge of failing. I waited for the inevitable comparison with Frank.

"Stand at attention while I'm talking to you!" he yelled as if I was a recruit at boot camp.

I listened to him go on about "cutting the mustard" and becoming a man…the same old shit.

Mom stayed in the kitchen. She never intervened when he was disciplining me.

✵

CHARLIE

The sound of his father's booming voice downstairs interrupted Charlie's thoughts.

"Chuck, what the hell are you doing up there?" he bellowed.

Charlie winced at the nickname.

"I'll be right down soon, Dad," Charlie yelled back. "I'm getting dressed."

Then, he heard his mother's voice from the living room. "Charlie, it's okay if you weren't accepted. You have other talents. Come on down."

"Thanks, mom. Another five minutes please."

Charlie turned away from the dresser and sauntered to his only window. Rain beat steadily against the glass panes. In the distance, the turbulent waters of the Potomac River churned, darkened by mud and debris.

Charlie chuckled as he thought back to those days in Hawaii. He looked at his right forearm and admired the amateurish tattoo he had created at the age of fourteen. He kept it covered with makeup, it was barely visible to any casual observer, including his father.

*

God, I remember the day I came home from school with that tattoo. I had skipped school that day to work on my new inspiration with friends who were happy to show me how to do it.

I did it myself with a needle and a bottle of India Ink. It took hours to pierce my skin with a sewing needle wrapped in thread. Sure, it was a handmade job, but when completed, I thought it looked pretty good. I had designed an unfurled, albeit shaky, banner with the name "MOM" on it. It covered a two-inch by five-inch area of my forearm about five inches below my elbow.

I had a real tattoo! I was quite proud.

When Mom saw it, she laughed—told me tattoos don't wear off, that I'd be looking at my masterpiece for the rest of my life. "One day," she said, "your tattoo will be wrinkled and adorned by long, gray hairs."

She told me my father had a low opinion of tattoos on officers and gentlemen—thinks they belong only on enlisted men and others of lesser rank and stature.

Mom said she wouldn't tell him. It was up to me to keep Dad from seeing it.

Well, I didn't.

They were the first words he spoke to me in over two weeks. "Get rid of those drawings on your arm, son," he said at dinner a few weeks later. "Men don't need to decorate their bodies."

I told him it wouldn't wash off.

He leaned over the table and grabbed my right arm, putting his elbow in the Brussels sprouts.

"It's a tattoo honoring Mom," I said as if that would help.

"You're honoring no one!" he roared. "Let me see that goddamned thing!"

His eyes bugged out. For a minute, I thought they would roll out of his head and into the casserole. His face turned bright crimson.

"What the hell have you done?" he bellowed. "Tattoos are for enlisted men, not officers."

He looked at Mom. "Did you know about this?"

She shrugged her shoulders. "Nothing we can do about it now."

Dad banged his fist on the table with such force the plates bounced. "I'll tell you what we can do about it. We're going to have the goddamned thing cut out! Make an appointment at the dispensary first thing tomorrow!"

You cold-hearted bastard, I thought. Are you serious?

He was.

Mom really came to bat for me. She was as pissed as I'd ever seen her. She put her foot down. "Franklin," she said, "if it's so important, you take him to the doctor!"

That night, they got into a terrible fight. Even though my bedroom was on the other end of the house, I could hear their muffled shouting. The old man kept on about some "agreement"—that's all I could hear.

Finally, it was quiet.

I thought she had refused to take me to the doctor—wouldn't do it. However, a few days later she told my father that she had made an appointment to have the tattoo removed. He grunted.

The next day, we got in the car and drove off. Instead of going to the dispensary, however, she drove a few blocks before pulling over and parking under a large coconut tree.

"What're we doing?" I asked

Yanking the emergency brake, she informed me with a wink, "We're faking the surgery."

I started laughing. I couldn't believe Mom would take a chance like that for me. I had no idea how she could pull this off.

"Give me your right arm."

She took my arm and started putting iodine then gauze around it. In five minutes, I had a proper-looking surgical dressing over my right forearm where the tattoo was.

Then, we went shopping for guitars.

When the old man saw the dressing, he looked satisfied. He thought Mom obeyed his order. He dismissed the incident from his mind.

Mom later gave me a jar of her makeup and demonstrated how to conceal the tattoo to the casual observer.

"Stay out of the water when he's around," she winked.

Mom enabled me to keep that stupid tattoo. What she did took courage. Dad never knew.

The secret Mom and I shared from Dad brought us closer. I had renewed respect for her and realized that I barely knew who she was. I wanted to know more.

⁂

Charlie found a respectable shirt to wear. He brushed his hair and applied makeup to his right forearm.

He continued to procrastinate.

Charlie moved back to his dresser. His gaze returned to the

mirror's reflection. He thought about his other crazy stunts in Hawaii.

Charlie smiled as he thought about his old room in Kailua—the one with a back door.

It reminded him of another experience—spending the night in the Juvenile Detention Center.

❋

I'll never know why they gave me the back bedroom in that old house they rented in Hawaii. My room had an outside door—my ever-present portal to freedom.

Anytime there was a late-night party, I waited until the lights went out, stuffed a few extra pillows under the sheet and crept into the darkness outside.

Since I was restricted to home in the day, I looked for fun at night. There was always a beach party somewhere. We sat around a fire and got shit-faced on Country Club Malt Liquor. They were the best parties ever, sometimes lasting all night.

The fun ended around three one morning after a long party. I had a long way to go and decided to hitchhike home. The first car to stop was the Kailua Sherriff. He wanted to know what I was doing out so late. I was only fourteen and in violation of the curfew. He told me to get in and drove me to the sheriff's office. I sat silently in his small office while he called home.

Dad answered. Shit!

I could hear the old man screaming on the other end of the phone. The sheriff held it back from his ear.

When the sheriff hung up, he looked at me strangely and shrugged his shoulders.

He told me we were going to the Kailua Juvenile Detention Center.

I couldn't believe it. For curfew violation? Come on!

The sheriff didn't want to lock me up. However, that's what the son of a bitch told him to do. The sheriff had no choice.

I guess my father wanted to teach me a lesson. He thought it would scare the shit out of me. It didn't.

The sheriff and I arrived at an old building on the other side of town surrounded by barbed wire and lit up like a stadium.

This was not a place one could leave by normal standards.

The sheriff took me past a security checkpoint. We entered a small lobby at the entrance—just a caged office and small waiting area with a chair that looked like a reject from the Thrift Shop.

I remember the large Hawaiian behind the cage. He had jet-black hair and a pockmarked face. The sheriff called him "Sugar".

"Sugar" looked at me. The sheriff told him I violated the curfew. Sugar got really pissed. Said he didn't have room for curfew violators. They talked some more.

Finally, Sugar said I could stay in the courtyard until someone picked me up…assuming someone would. I still had my guitar. He wanted to take it. I asked to keep it.

Sugar didn't care. Said it might come in handy as a weapon. He told me young haole kids are not popular in a place like this.

When the sheriff left, he shook my hand and wished me well! We had gotten along pretty well.

Sugar led me into a large grassy lanai surrounded by cells. He pointed to a rusty column and told me to stay there. Said to me he couldn't protect me; wasn't responsible for me.

That was unsettling.

So I sat on the grass, leaning against the post with my guitar beside me. The night was still. I wondered what morning would bring.

I must have fallen asleep. When I looked up, fifteen or so of the toughest-looking dudes I had ever seen were standing around me. I stood up quickly.

The group had a leader, an enormous Hawaiian guy wearing standard prison garb—baggy khaki pants and a short-sleeved shirt.

His arms were massive and terribly scarred. He had decorated himself with a sharp knife. It was both ugly and awe-inspiring. A kid like that must be capable of anything, I thought.

The guy's name was Marko. He wanted to know why I was here. I told him curfew violation. He didn't believe me. I tried to cooperate. I sure didn't want any trouble from these guys.

"My name's Charlie," I offered.

They didn't care what my name was. The circle of inmates around me tightened. Sugar was nowhere around. Marko grabbed the guitar, surveying it carefully. He called me Elvis.

"Do you play, Elvis?" he asked with a leering smile.

"A little," I said.

He gave me a hard push that almost knocked me down. I regained my balance and faced him. I looked into his dark brown eyes. I couldn't imagine what those eyes had seen. I didn't want to know.

Next thing I know, he shoved the guitar back to me.

"Play," he grunted.

I assumed they were going to make fun of me before they beat me up. The gang told me that, if I weren't good enough, they'd cut a finger off.

I hastily began to play one of the current pop hits.

I watched the group as I played and sang. They were moving with the rhythm I established. Thank god, they liked my chops.

As I finished, some even smiled. The guy named "Marko" told me to keep playing. I played and sang all the current hits until Sugar found me. Dad was here to pick me up.

He didn't say a word to me—just grabbed me by the arm and dragged me out to the car.

It was an awkwardly silent ride home.

The old man refused to talk to me for months after my night in the detention center. He just ignored me as if I no longer existed. That was all right with me…kind of. He was a master at passive aggressiveness.

Charlie's experience that morning with the juvenile inmates taught him that his music had power. As he played for that group in the grass lanai, he saw their eyes change from anger to something else—something far from aggressive.

Charlie had the rare gift of communicating through voice and rhythm in a certain way that could touch emotions. He looked wistfully again at his guitars. How could he give them up now?

❋

Charlie frowned and looked outside. The rain was subsiding; rays of light danced on the backyard patio. He returned to the mirror. He was running out of time, he had to go down.

Charlie glanced down at his right forearm and casually ran his hand over the tattoo. He had perfected the art of cosmetic concealment. It was barely visible.

Suddenly, there was a loud knock on Charlie's door.

"Come on in, Frank."

"Dad sent me up to bring you down—now!"

"I know my time's up. All right; I'm ready."

"Have you opened the letter yet?" Frank asked suspiciously.

"Yeah, I did."

"Well?"

"I'm in."

Frank's face changed to a look of shock and surprise. "What? Are you accepted? Seriously?"

"Yes. The academy accepted me. Can you believe it?"

"No shit! Congratulations. We'll be classmates this year!"

Charlie's crooked grin returned. "Oh, won't that be swell?"

Frank ignored the irony. "Wow! You only have two weeks before you ship out."

"Don't get ahead of yourself, Frank. I haven't accepted yet."

"You *will* accept, I assume?" he asked.

"I don't know. I still think it's a mistake."

"Those people don't make mistakes. You know that."

"No, I don't! Listen, Frank, I don't have the grades or the leadership skills to get in a place like that. Hell, I was *expelled* my sophomore year in high school—twice. It makes no sense."

"Jesus, Charlie! You *have* to accept!" Frank said, mimicking their father's authoritative tone. "The Academy is one of the best schools in the country. You can't ignore this appointment—you can't just walk away from it!"

"Fuck you, Frank. Stop telling me what I have to do. Come on, let's go downstairs."

He was right though. I had to accept.

Charlie opened the door and followed Frank downstairs. He knew it would begin a journey into uncharted waters.

Charlie's mother and father were waiting for them in the living room, a large area at the front of the house. Its ornate trim and expensive embellishments created a tastefully colonial décor. An equally stylish dining room adjoined, formed by white columns on each side of its entrance.

A large picture window at the front of the room looked over on an immaculately landscaped and expansive front yard. Sturdy white oaks shaded Azaleas and Dogwoods.

Charlie hesitated on the landing. He turned toward his family feeling embarrassed and self-conscious.

"What the hell have you been doing up there, Chuck?" the general said with slight irritation. "We've been waiting for you."

"Sorry, it was a late night."

Frank settled in one of the matching rockers by the picture window. He had a half-finished bourbon on the small table. His mother sat alone on a sofa.

His father stood and smiled smugly. His mother looked at Charlie with from the couch with a sympathetic smile. Her heart was heavy knowing the rejection would be hard for him.

"Well?" the general demanded. "Are you in or not?"

"Looks like I'm in. The letter says I'm accepted."

His father smiled. There was no shock or surprise on his face. His mother put her hand to her mouth. She gasped.

"Oh, Charlie," she cried running toward him, "Really?"

Charlie hugged his mother. He saw the confused look on her

face smile. He smiled in acknowledgment. They both shrugged their shoulders.

"Well done, son," his father echoed loudly. He stood and extended his hand for a rare, knuckle-crushing handshake. "I'm proud of you."

"Thanks, everyone," Charlie said, mustering as much enthusiasm as he could.

"This calls for a drink," the general proclaimed. Melinda, get Charlie a beer and another double Jack on the rocks for me.

"I don't need a beer, dad. I just woke up."

"You shouldn't sleep so late, son. You're having a beer to celebrate with us."

"Yeah," Frank echoed. "When you're a plebe at the Academy running around with guys screaming at you, you'll remember these good old days."

"Good old days?" Charlie asked cynically. "Having a beer forced on you at eleven in the morning?"

"Listen to your brother, son. He's older and wiser. And be careful," he added with a wink. "In two weeks, he'll outrank you."

Frank was loving the moment.

Fuck both of them!

Charlie's mother returned with their drinks on a silver tray. The general grabbed his bourbon and proposed a toast.

"To Charlie," he said raising his glass. "May he one day wear the proud uniform of a Marine officer."

Tell him you're not interested! Think of your future! Get it over with; take the hit now and move on!

Charlie wouldn't listen to his inner voice. He had no way to say no, no way to defy the general's proud moment.

Charlie looked around and held up his mug. With complete and utter disregard for his well-being, he mouthed the prerequisite response, "Thanks, dad. I'll do my best to become that proud Marine officer."

"Here, here!"

"Sit down, Chuck," his father thundered. "Enjoy the celebration.

It's in your honor for a change. It's not every day a man learns he's going to the Naval Academy."

Charlie sat politely next to his mother while his brother and father went on about military life. They never seemed to run out of stories about the Naval Academy.

Charlie shifted uncomfortably on the plush sofa. His mind wandered. He couldn't concentrate.

Will I like the Naval Academy? Can I grow to like it? How hard will that be, I wonder.

"Chuck! You're daydreaming again. This is supposed to be a party!"

"Sorry, Dad, I drifted off for a moment."

"Frank and I are talking about the Academy. You should pay attention."

"Yeah," Frank chimed in, "We're wondering how you'll fare during Plebe Summer. It was the toughest three months of my life. We're picturing you being chewed out and having to keep your mouth shut."

"That's a lovely image, Frank. Thank you."

The general missed the sarcasm. "Well, let me tell you this, Chuck. I think you might just have the balls to get through Plebe Year."

Charlie fought to tone down the cynicism. "Thanks, Dad," he said. "That's a real compliment coming from you."

The general smiled and raised his empty glass. Rattling the ice cubes to get his wife's attention, he said, "Melinda, another round."

When Melinda left, the general looked at Charlie, his expression serious. "You know, Chuck, you have been given the opportunity of a lifetime."

Charlie nodded pensively. "I know."

"It no longer matters that you were a complete fuck up during high school," he slurred. "You have a clean slate, a fresh start. The Naval Academy will teach you to become a man…just as it did your brother. Those who make it through Plebe Year are the toughest, most disciplined and respected of all."

Of all what? Tell him you changed your mind, for chrissake!

Maybe if he gets drunk enough, it won't matter.

Charlie knew this was wishful thinking. He had to show some enthusiasm to underscore his bazar fortune. Looking at his brother, he asked, "So what's it going to be like now that you're a senior, Frank?"

"First Classman, not senior—that's for civilian schools."

Whatever. Tell me how great it'll be, how much more you'll be able to crawl up Dad's ass.

"Sorry. Go on."

"I can't wait, Charlie. The privileges of a 'Firsty" are significant. You have to earn them."

"What a 'Firsty'?"

The general jumped in. "It's a casual way to refer to a First Classman. I'm surprised you don't know that."

Fuck you.

"Are there, like 'Secondies' and 'Thirdsies'?"

Melinda giggled. The general stared back with an angry look. "You may feel you can make fun of all this now, Chuck. I guaran-damn-tee you in two weeks you won't."

"Plebe year will completely change you, man," Frank said. His voice carried military authority. "You'll go from a smartass to a well-disciplined midshipman."

"Hey, I'm not making fun. I really don't *know* what the different classmen are called."

No one looked satisfied with the answer.

Charlie continued, "What's been your favorite subject so far?"

"Oh, definitely Navigation. I loved the Nav classes.

"What did you like about it?"

"I loved learning how to use the sextant.

"What's a sextant?"

The general rolled his eyes.

"A sextant is a device that allows you to navigate by the stars. Every officer must know that skill."

"So you loved the sextant."

"Yes, and all the other tools as well."

"Such as?"

"The Maneuvering Board for one."

The what?"

"Maneuvering Board. It's a device about the size of a slide rule. We use it to compute course and speed."

Charlie forced himself to ask another question. "Do you get to keep all the tools the Navy gave you for navigating?

It was a lame question; the best he had.

"Of course. I still have my Maneuvering Board."

"I bet you have it hanging on your wall upstairs, huh?" Charlie shot back with his crooked smile. He saw immediately in Frank's eyes that he guessed correctly.

"Go ahead; make fun now," he lashed back. "You'll get it when you grow up."

"And wipe the smirk off your face," the general added.

Charlie's Mom joined the conversation to change the subject. She looked at him with a sympatric smile. "How will the band take your leaving them in two weeks, Charlie?"

The depressing weight of leaving his band weighed heavily on his shoulders. "Not well, I suppose," he said. "We have several gigs planned this month."

Frank interrupted and smiled with satisfaction, "From now on, you can kiss your guitars goodbye, man."

"Can't I take them with me?"

"And what would you do with them? Start a plebe band?" Frank snickered.

"Of course you can't take them with you," the general added. "Rock music and dancing have no place where you're going."

Swell.

CHAPTER TWO

Melinda

Present Time

For a moment, the old man thought about his mother. He rarely did.

Their relationship was confused and awkward. There were times when she was his best friend and other times when she ignored him.

Finally, he just gave up; he didn't matter to her, she didn't care about him.

He hadn't seen her in forty years; he didn't go to her funeral. He couldn't bear it.

Absently, he rubbed the fingers over the ugly scar on his right forearm. It served as an eternal reminder of the control by a narcissistic father and a mother who could never shelter him.

Even now, he felt the rage of helplessness.

1942

Before meetingMcDaniels, Melinda was a Julliard-schooled pianist and guitarist. She would graduate with distinction in June. Her potential was limitless. Music brought her joy.

She had deep blue-green eyes and blonde hair. Her personality was bright and cheerful. She knew herself well; she held life in her hands.

In 1942, Melinda drove from New York to Annapolis to visit

friends. Though the Naval Academy is located in Annapolis, she had little interest in visiting tourist destinations.

She drove through the quaint city on a sunny Friday in April. The following day, she had a few hours to herself while her friends had to be out. Melinda decided to use her free time walking through town. She wandered from State Circle to Maryland Avenue and peacefully walked from shop to shop.

Maryland Avenue stopped at a gated entrance guarding a large institution. A six-foot wall next to the gate displayed the name of the school in brass letters.

United States Naval Academy

Founded 1845

Melinda paused to watch the activity around her. Tourists took pictures of the entrance; others moved freely to and from the campus through a pedestrian gate. An ornately designed wrought iron gate blocked vehicular traffic.

Melinda crossed the street and approached the pedestrian entrance. The beautiful grounds on the other side sparked her curiosity.

A young Marine corporal stood formally in uniform beside the gatehouse on the other side of the road. He smiled and politely nodded as she passed through.

She stood for a moment trying to figure out which way to go. Ahead were the sculpted and manicured lawns of the Academy's campus, or Yard. White Oak trees, in a new canopy of leaves, shadowed brick walkways that led through the grounds. Azaleas were in full bloom—rivers of colors weaved between the statues and monuments.

Melinda blended with and followed the visitors. They seemed to be moving in a particular direction. She looked at her watch—five minutes until noon.

Bancroft Hall stood in the distance like a great castle of stone. A crowd was gathering at the entrance to Tecumseh Court—a grand cobblestone courtyard protecting the main entrance.

She merged with the growing crowd, edging her way toward the focus of interest. The tourists were lining up along a barricade of white rope along the outer limits of the court. Beyond the barricade, uniformed men were occupying positions throughout the courtyard.

"What's going on?" she whispered to the woman beside her.

"Saturday noon formation," she said. "Midshipmen line up by company before Saturday liberty call."

"Midshipmen?"

"They're the students."

"Oh, thank you."

Melinda looked across at the woman's husband whose left hand casually rested on the rope barricade. On his ring finger was a thick gold ring. "Did your husband graduate from here?" she asked.

"My fiancé," she corrected, "but, yes, he did, just before the war."

Melinda watched the courtyard continue to fill with midshipmen. Several hundred yards ahead, a grand portico, supported by six marble columns, guarded the main entrance to Bancroft Hall. Broad steps led to three entry doors below the portico. The grandeur and pageantry advertised a significant event in this formidable military institution.

Midshipmen had now filled the entirety of Tecumseh Court. They formed perfectly aligned groups, or companies, molded to fit precisely within the confines of the courtyard. Soon, the entire brigade, consisting of thousands of men in dark-blue uniforms, assembled for noon formation. Melinda guessed this was why the crowd had formed.

As the formation of Midshipmen solidified, all activity ceased. Each man stood at attention in his assigned spot. All talking stopped. The only sounds were the chirping of birds from the oak trees behind.

Melinda's attention shifted to a triangular group of six senior Midshipmen marching in unison toward her. They stopped only ten yards from the tourist barrier.

At the front of this perfectly formed triangle was a barrel-chested, dark-skinned man with many gold stripes adorning the sleeves of his uniform. He wore white gloves and carried an unsheathed silver and gold sword held tightly against his right shoulder.

"Who's the guy with all the gold?" Melinda whispered.

"Brigade Commander. The 'Top Dog'; he's the senior man in the whole brigade."

The Brigade Commander barked an order. His staff of five halted in perfect unison. The commander stood ramrod straight with eyes fixed ahead. For a split-second, his eyes shifted to Melinda, long enough to make fleeting eye contact. While he paused, flashbulbs popped around her.

The commander issued another command. "Staff, about face."

The staff reversed itself so that the commander could address the brigade.

At that point, the leader issued other commands; his voice echoed throughout the buildings. Immediately, Melinda heard a series of reports from battalion and regimental commanders within the formation. Swords flashed in the bright sunlight; flags waved in precise coordination. When the reports ended, a military band began to play *Stars and Stripes Forever.* It was the cue for the commander and his staff to march toward the entrance of Bancroft Hall.

She watched each company turn and sequentially follow in lockstep toward the center of the courtyard, turning once again in the direction of the entrances to Bancroft Hall.

In less than a few minutes, the great courtyard was empty. The show was over. An enlisted man removed the temporary barricade so that the visitors were again able to enter the courtyard again.

Melinda smiled at the young woman beside her. "What happens now?" she asked.

"Liberty Call," she answered. "In a minute, this place will be swarming with guys. Get ready," she added with a laugh.

Suddenly, the doors opened beneath the portico. Melinda saw hundreds of Midshipmen in navy-blue uniforms descending the stairways and moving in two's and three's toward Tecumseh's statue and beyond. The weekend had officially begun.

Melinda retreated from the rush of men. She walked to the nearby bronze bust of a Native American—Tecumseh. Visitors waiting to meet midshipman occupied several benches surrounding the pedestal.

She looked up at the statue of the celebrated Native American. He was enormous. His marble pedestal featured a plaque inscribed with a brief description his life.

While hordes of young men passed by, she read Tecumseh's inscription. As she read, a voice behind her said, "That's Tecumseh, an iconic Native American folk hero who sided with the British during the War of 1812."

"Why do you honor a traitor?" she answered coyly without turning.

He laughed. "Tecumseh's our good luck statue," he said. "We shower him with pennies during exam week."

Melinda turned. She stood face to face with a man she recognized immediately—the Brigade Commander. He acknowledged her as well. To Melinda, he looked splendid in his blue uniform, decorated with silver and gold.

He introduced himself as Frank McDaniels.

"So you're the top dog?"

He laughed. "Yeah, I guess you could say that."

"Did you wink at me back there?"

He blushed. "I did. Hope you're not offended."

"No, flattered actually. I'm Melinda."

They shook hands formally.

"Can I buy you a coffee in town?" he asked.

Melinda hesitated and looked at her watch. "I only have an hour before I meet my friends."

"Let's make the most of that hour then."

Frank escorted her through the grounds back into town. They found a small coffee shop just outside the gate. Although a brief encounter, Melinda knew that she would be willing to see this guy again, assuming he would ask her.

They chatted over coffee for half an hour. Frank was a good conversationalist. She relaxed into his smooth, self-confident charm.

After forty-five minutes, she looked at her watch. "I suppose I should go. My friends are probably back by now."

Frank rose immediately. "It's been a pleasure talking with you, Melinda. Will you be here next weekend?" he asked.

"I live in downtown New York; it's a four-hour trip away. What are you proposing that would make the trip worthwhile?"

"Do you sail?"

"Never been on a boat."

"Would you like to give it a try? We can go out in the Chesapeake. I'll show you the ropes."

So began Melinda's relationship with Frank McDaniels, dashing military charmer. Geographically, it was logistically awkward. Nevertheless, they made it work

Frank was infatuated with Melinda's alluring beauty. Her dark blue-green eyes always seemed to be questioning, probing for the facts. They worked well together as long as neither discussed politics.

Frank's principles were conservative while Melinda took a progressive view of life. Their opposing political viewpoints provided several playful and sometimes animated conversations. Frank took it in stride…it was all in fun.

When Frank was in New York, he accompanied Melinda to off-beat cozy venues where she occasionally played to a packed house. Her celebrity was a source of pride as he sat close to the stage.

Three months later, Melinda and Frank were married in the Naval Academy Chapel. Frank wore the traditional Marine Blue Dress, and Melinda wore the long white gown of her fantasies. After the ceremony, they exited the chapel under an arch of crossed swords.

It was a storybook beginning. Melinda was in love with the most handsome man she had ever seen and couldn't wait to start a family. She looked forward to a happy relationship.

Frank began his new career in Quantico, Virginia, at The Basic School, a twenty-eight-week indoctrination course for newly commissioned Second Lieutenants. Quantico was a long way from the excitement and glamor of New York. Nevertheless, Melinda did her best to adjust to the new environment. In truth, she was bored.

This is only temporary. It'll get better after Frank's first duty assignment.

After graduating, Frank's first duty assignment was in Hampton Roads, Virginia, on an Amphibious Assault Ship. His ship was often at sea, sometimes for extended periods overseas.

By the end of her first year as a Marine wife, Melinda was even more bored. She lived on a military base in a run-down housing project. Frank's friends and their wives were unbearable conservatives. She had no friends of her own. No one shared her values.

Also, she was pregnant.

When in port, Frank worked long hours and became a heavy drinker. The Marine Corps changed him from charmer to controller. Melinda became lonely and isolated in a community of people too rigid for her progressive tastes.

However, the weekend parties attended by junior officers were often a wild ride. They gave Melinda the opportunity to practice her charm and wit. She flirted, told great stories and danced like a professional.

Frank looked at these parties as an opportunity to advance his standing with his senior officers and advance his career. Melinda dutifully stood at his side at these parties using her charm and grace to enhance her husband's reputation.

Notwithstanding Melinda's value to his career, Frank became increasingly aggressive and authoritarian at home. Alcohol clouded his emotions; it slowly chipped away at his soul

Slowly and painfully, Melinda realized that she had made a terrible mistake. She had let the glitz and glamor of the uniform conceal the real character of the man.

When Frank Junior was born, the joy and happiness temporarily returned. Frank Senior was, at first a doting and devoted father. Melinda vowed to hold the marriage together.

As Frank Junior grew, however, her husband became a harsh

disciplinarian, insisting on full command and control of raising his son.

"Go fuck yourself, Frank," she yelled back one night. "I don't want our son growing up to become like you…ever!"

Frank was now a captain and eager for the challenging assignments that warranted quick advancement up the chain of command. The recent promotion brought him an eight-month assignment overseas. When he left, Melinda was alone with a son just learning to walk. She thought about moving back to New York.

I don't know what to do. New York City is no place for a one-year-old.

She decided to stay in Hampton Rhodes and devote the time to her new son. He was all she had. Were it not for Frank, Jr. she would have returned to New York. Instead, she stuck it out on the Marine base.

Frank returned from his overseas deployment two weeks before Christmas. For a while, the relationship was better, Frank Junior was at the adorable age, and his father was fascinated with his firstborn. Frank and Melinda coasted for a while, a short while.

Charlie was born later that year.

Melinda's bond with Charlie was immediate and unique—in a way not experienced with Frank Junior. She saw in Charlie sensitivity and creativity. He quickly became her favorite.

Charlie was not the athlete his brother was. It infuriated her to see Frank Jr. ridicule Charlie for being clumsy. She remained silent, however. She always did.

Not having a mother who could protect him from his father's ridicule and military authority was equally confusing for young Charlie. He needed balance; he had none.

Melinda trudged on, remaining the career wife and mother—charming, engaging and, at home, silent. She couldn't wait for his next overseas assignment when she could have Charlie to herself.

Melinda waited until Charlie was old enough before giving him her greatest gift—the joy and creativity of music.

When Charlie was ten, Frank Senior deployed overseas for a full year. Shortly after he left, she brought out her old guitar. She rarely played anymore. Frank wouldn't allow it.

His absence gave Melinda the opportunity to strengthen the bond with her younger son. The first thing she did was buy him a guitar of his own so that she could teach him how to play.

When Charlie heard his mother playing and singing one day, he was instantly mesmerized. He stopped and stared with surprise and appreciation. "Holy cow, Mom. That's cool! I didn't know you could do that!"

Melinda smiled and stopped. "Thank you, Charlie. Want to try for yourself? Here. Sit. I'll coach you with some basic chords."

Charlie dropped his books on the nearest table and eagerly joined her. She handed him the guitar and showed him how to hold it.

"That's right," she coached. "Now, let me show you the E chord."

At first, Charlie's left hand felt awkward as he attempted to find the right strings and frets. Soon, however, muscle memory took hold and the awkwardness dissipated. His mother showed him more chords. He learned quickly.

The sounds and feelings he could create through music fascinated Charlie. Even as a neophyte, he adapted well to the challenge.

He was a natural—a child prodigy as Melinda once was. From that moment, all Charlie wanted were his creative talents in music.

Within months, Charlie had the skills and knowledge to play most of his mother's favorites. They played together every chance and were soon jamming like real musicians.

Their duets grew better and better. Charlie learned vocals as easily as the guitar. His voice was pure; their harmonies exact.

"Charlie, you have a real gift for this!" she told him. "It could be your calling."

"Thanks, Mom. Playing with you is a hoot."

Melinda laughed. "Same here; keep practicing."

Charlie needed no encouragement to practice. He devoted the all of his free time to practicing the guitar.

Melinda treasured these times with her son. Their musical sessions sustained her throughout a loveless and frustrating marriage.

Music saved Charlie's life by giving him an outlet for his anger and frustration over the judgments from his father and brother. With his father away, Melinda became his rock, his island of sanity.

Melinda was secretly sympathetic to the growing anti-war movement simmering throughout the country. Though only in its infancy at that time, folk music inspired by artists' such as Bob Dylan and others became the foundation of her tutoring. She taught Charlie every song that came from the peace movement.

Frank watched Charlie's playing and singing with disdain, laughing at him and calling him a pussy.

Charlie once asked his mother, "Mom, why is it that you don't ever want Dad to hear our performances? I think we sound pretty good."

Melinda sighed, "Your father doesn't like music."

"What? He doesn't like *music*?"

"No."

"Then why did you marry him?"

"You're too young to understand, Charlie."

Charlie sensed that his mother was trying to tell him something. However, whenever his father was around her demeanor changed. She became quiet and withdrawn.

This confused Charlie. There had to be a reason for his mother's puzzling behavior. What changed her in the presence of his father? She no longer came to his aid; never questioned her husband's authority nor stepped in to take Charlie's side.

Confusion and insecurity intensified for Charlie after the family moved to Hawaii. When he needed her the most, she was silent.

It broke Melinda's heart to see her son drift away, to see him become angry and rebellious. She knew Charlie couldn't understand. Worse, she knew she was partly responsible for his outrageous behavior at Kailua High School.

Melinda screamed inwardly every time her husband shoved Charlie around. She was infuriated whenever he ridiculed Charlie's identity as a person. Charlie was a good soul; he didn't deserve this treatment. To her, toughness was overrated.

The pressure on her continually increased. Every maternal instinct cried at her to come to her son's aid—regardless of the consequences.

Melinda snapped the night Frank Senior told the sheriff to lock Charlie up. She thought he must surely be insane.

Melinda was wide-awake and furious. She shoved her husband roughly, preventing him from going back to sleep.

"What the hell are you doing, Frank. You can't have our son put in jail! He'll never get in college with a police record."

"Our son?" the general responded angrily. "He broke the law. That's how the system works! It'll teach him a lesson he'll never forget. Now, shut up and let me sleep."

Melinda got out of bed and grabbed her bathrobe. She tried to call the sheriff's office back. Her husband had taken the phone off the hook and put it under his pillow.

She looked for the keys to the car. She would drive down to the Sherriff's office herself.

"If you're looking for the car keys, don't. I have them in a secure place."

She had never felt such anger, such disgust with her husband.

It was time to reassert her independence. It no longer mattered what her husband would do. From that moment, Melinda changed. She hoped it was not too late.

CHAPTER THREE

The Naval Academy

Present time

The old man continued to reflect on his wasted life. Four failed marriages and seven grandchildren that hardly knew him. What's the point?

"Stop stalling and get it over with!" he mumbled.

He studied his gray and unkempt beard. His silver-gray hair likewise was dirty and bedraggled, lying across his shoulders and partially covering his right eye. He shook it away.

The trailer in which he lived was equally untidy. What did he care? He never had company. The trailer and his retirement benefits were all he had. Most of his monthly check went to his ex-wives.

He barely had money enough to buy liquor.

He shook his head slowly and sighed. On the stained counter was a bottle of more than fifty Ativan pills that he had hoarded over the years. He knew the effect of this powerful anti-anxiety drug; he knew he had enough in the bottle to kill him.

Trouble was all the old man knew. It followed him everywhere, due in large part to his own self-loathing, anger and revenge.

He never knew love. He never knew how.

Alone in a dilapidated trailer in a run-down park, he had only himself; he didn't enjoy the company.

He was forgotten in a world that had little patience for the elderly. It was time to end this unfulfilling life; he was ready to go. There was no future worthy of inspiring or a single friend with whom to share this future.

A loner all his life, he refused to speak up when it mattered. Instead, he coasted along on whatever path best suited his self-interests. Rules were anathema; he disregarded them regardless of consequences.

Sorrow and pain brought him ultimately to this moment. Continuing life would only bring more suffering.

"Screw it," he said to his forlorn reflection. "It's time to say goodbye."

June 1969

At 12:45 PM, Charlie stood with over a thousand nervous young men in Tecumseh Court, each ready to assume a new identity. Individuality would be gone. From this point on, teamwork, loyalty, and blind obedience would become the standards of achievement.

Today was induction day for the class of 1973. At one o'clock, the entire assembly of new plebes would raise their right hands and pledge their allegiance to an institution with which they were only vaguely familiar. Once they uttered the words "So help me God," the Navy-owned them and would for the next four years and beyond.

The early summer sun highlighted a colorful collection of civilian outfits from sports coats to tee shirts and shorts. Excited conversations buzzed and echoed within the broad limits of the courtyard.

After saying goodbye to his parents, Charlie walked self-consciously into Tecumseh Court and joined his future classmates. Wearing khaki pants, a beige pinstriped shirt, and white sports coat, he felt conspicuous and uncomfortable. Charlie shuffled his feet on the worn cobblestone and looked around at a sea of unfamiliar faces.

He waited silently, wondering what lay ahead.

Just behind the cordoned-off area in front of the courtyard, a large crowd of family members and friends stood to watch the ceremony. Their sons were leaving home for a long time. Several mothers wept openly; fathers stood proudly taking pictures.

Charlie's father and mother stood with them. Today was, indeed, a proud day for Frank Senior. Recently promoted to general, he felt he had served the family legacy well. He knew his own father would be proud were he still alive.

The general, himself, had stood in that very courtyard twenty-seven years ago to say farewell to his parents. Today, his second son would follow his noble example.

The circle continued. The general could now brag that he had two sons serving their country as officers in the United States Marine Corps. He reflected complacently at his achievement.

Precisely at 1300, or 1:00 PM civilian time, the microphone on the top landing of the entrance to Bancroft Hall squealed. A row of officers and senior midshipmen flanked the Commandant of the Naval Academy as he prepared his welcoming speech. The accompanying band picked up their instruments smartly and began the Star Spangled Banner. Every man in uniform stood at rigid attention saluting the flag hanging limply in the hot summer air.

The crowd of civilian inductees looked around. Some put their hand over their heart; others stood respectfully while the Anthem played.

A short welcoming ceremony followed. The Commandant, attired in formal dress whites, approached a podium to address the new inductees. He pulled the microphone closer and began a short speech about the honor and opportunity each new midshipman will receive.

"You are members of a rare and elite group, the commandant began. "In a moment, you will become the Class of 1973, Brigade of Midshipmen, United States Naval Academy. You should all be very proud."

Following his remarks, the Commandant ordered each inductee to raise his right arm and recite the oath. It would pledge each man, some as young as seventeen, to honor and defend the Constitution at whatever cost.

The band played *America the Beautiful.* The Commandant and his staff departed into Bancroft Hall. The induction ceremony had ended. Soon, the conversation level increased as the men looked around wondering what to expect next. Each was officially a midshipman, a plebe, subservient to all.

Second-class Midshipmen began to mingle with the new plebes. A select group of high achieving juniors was given the responsibility of training over a thousand plebes. By the end of August, each plebe would be thoroughly indoctrinated to the Navy way of life.

Charlie felt uncomfortable and out of place as he waited with the new class. He was embarrassed as he looked around at his new classmates knowing each was in the upper one percent of his high school class. Charlie barely graduated. He felt phony, disingenuous.

It was his choice, though. He felt no sense of purpose and self-determination. Charlie's freedom and individuality no longer existed. It was as if the door was shutting on a critical time of Charlie's life. He had rather enjoyed the life of a rebellious teenager. That time was gone.

Charlie's mother stood silently while the crowd of parents dispersed. She had seen the ceremony before with her first son. She knew what lay ahead for Charlie and felt the same sense of loss that he did. Unlike that of Frank, this would be a more difficult journey for him.

❋

Many more Second Class leaders were in the courtyard now, segregating the new plebes into smaller, more manageable units of approximately forty to fifty men. Each group became a company. Sixteen companies formed the summer brigade.

Charlie belonged to the Eighth Company. One of the second classmen directed his company to stay together and follow him up the wide marble steps and into Bancroft Hall. Charlie shuffled along with his group into the central foyer, a massive domed rotunda with polished tile floors and bright marble walls. Busts of distinguished graduates from the past stoically surrounded the domed walls.

The group quickly moved on. They continued up two flights of stairs to the second deck landing. Charlie looked down into the rotunda below. He could see another company enter through the large bronze portal.

Charlie followed his company through wide hallways lined with rooms. They crossed an open bridge from the Second to the Fourth Wing.

A quarter of the way down the hallway, they stopped. Several of the men continued to talk and laugh, waiting expectantly for the next command. Like others in his company, Charlie slouched slightly trying to look unrattled. He stood in a group of strangers. His classmates would form a close bond through the long and arduous summer ahead.

Two Second Classmen began reshuffling plebes into a reasonable semblance of order. Soon, the new Eighth Company plebes stood shoulder to shoulder in three rows. One of the Second Classmen came to the front of the company and spoke loudly with authority.

"Gentlemen, listen up," he barked crisply and loudly. "My name is Midshipman Second Class Brewer. I want to see only precise military bearing from this point on. You're in the Navy now; act like it! I will be in command of this company during Plebe Summer. You will address me as either 'Mr. Brewer or 'sir' *only*."

Brewer paused as if waiting for a response.

"When I issue an order, I expect a reply. Is that clear?"

"Yes, sir," the group chanted incoherently.

"Goddammit it, is that clear?" he screamed. His face turned red, and his expression was intimidating.

"*Yes*, sir!"

Brewer shook his head in disgust and continued. "On my port side is Midshipman Second Class Walker. He is second in command of this company. One of us will be on duty during the day to supervise and oversee your progress."

Walker was a ruggedly handsome young man with sharp gray eyes and a steely stone face. "Stand at attention!" he ordered. "Remember your position. You are the Eighth Company, and you *will* make this the best company in the Summer Brigade. Is that clear?"

"Yes, sir."

"The proper response to an order is Aye, Aye, Sir. It is the *only* response to an order."

Walker continued, "Stand at attention. That doesn't mean grab-assing and looking around! You will remain silent with eyes fixed straight ahead! Do you understand?"

"Yes, sir!"

Midshipman Walker proceeded down each of the three rows of plebes, readjusting the position of several plebes as necessary. He glowered at them as if they were derelict.

For over half an hour, Walker inspected each man, He asked each for a name and origin.

Charlie stood at attention, waiting for his turn. When Walker reached him, he grabbed his shoulders and moved him slightly to the right. He stared at Charlie for a long time before he spoke.

"And who might you be, Skinhead?" Walker asked.

Charlie looked into his eyes and started to speak.

"I'm…"

"Keep your eyes in the boat, Mister!" Walker interrupted.

Charlie returned his eyes straight ahead. "Charles McDaniels, sir," he answered.

"And where are you from, Skinhead?"

"Washington, D.C., sir."

Walker shouted, "Keep your head still and eyes in the boat, Mister. I'm not telling you again!"

Charlie could feel drops of spittle hit his face. He raised his hands to wipe it away.

"Put you goddamned arm down. You're at attention."

"Yes, sir," Charlie answered.

Managing personal attacks and insults would become familiar soon for Charlie. He couldn't take it personally.

This is only a game, he thought to himself.

Walker detected a faint grin on Charlie's face. "Do you find this amusing, scum?"

"No, sir."

"Drop for fifty, now!"

"Yes, sir."

"Aye, aye, sir." Walker corrected.

Charlie dropped to the floor and began counting push-ups.

"Count louder!"

After he had finished, Charlie jumped back to his place in line. By then, Walker had moved on to the next plebe.

After the initial inspection, Walker returned to the front of the company, nodding to Brewer. "Gentlemen," he shouted, "from now on, whenever you are in any passageway in Bancroft Hall, you will walk at attention, braced up. I want to see each of you only in the center of the passageway, and you will square each corner when you turn. Is that clear?"

"Aye, aye, sir," most answered.

"What? I can't *hear* you! Louder!"

"Aye, aye, sir," all the plebes shouted.

Walker briefed his company on every aspect of Bancroft Hall. He told them about the mess hall, laundry, barber shop, phone booths, the Midshipman Store and a variety of other facts and requirements.

Brewer took over, "Gentlemen," he said. "Pick two of your classmates to be roommates."

Charlie looked to his left and motioned to the next two in line with a questioning look. They nodded with a smile; Charlie now had roommates.

The three men shook hands quickly. Charlie's new roommates introduced themselves as Brian Kennedy and Stuart Medora. Charlie would later learn that Kennedy was an All-State basketball player; Medora carried a perfect 4.0 average through high school. Both were presidents of their high school class.

Charlie kept his resume to himself.

Kennedy had curly blond hair covering his ears and friendly, engaging eyes. Charlie liked him immediately.

Medora sported shoulder-length dark hair and a neatly trimmed beard. Though his eyes were dark and cold, his mannerism was friendly.

Walker gave each group of roommates a room number. "Fallout, gentlemen. Find your rooms and stow your gear. You have five minutes."

After several wrong turns, Charlie and his roommates found their room. It was small—smaller than an average motel room. Bunks and metal lockers for each man stood neatly on each wall. In the center of the room, three desks faced inward. A single window overlooked McDonough Hall in the distance.

Charlie chose a locker and bunk along the east wall. The gray locker would provide storage for all his military possessions. Each piece of equipment and clothing he received from the Navy would soon fill the six-foot gray cabinet, each component in its proper place and frequently inspected for neatness and compliance.

As three roommates started to get to know one another, the loud and grating public address system reverberated through the hallways.

"Attention all hands. Fall in."

What does that mean?" Brian asked.

"I think it means we go back out and stand in line again," Charlie answered.

"Swell," Stewart said with a sneer. "This place is already starting to bug me."

Outside, the men of Eighth Company stood milling around in the hall, waiting for some direction.

"Fall in, men. This isn't a social break," Brewer shouted. He seemed to appear from nowhere.

"We are going to the barbershop. Feel those curly locks for the last time."

It was a brief walk down a wide stairway to the basement. Charlie would learn that the basement was a major utility area.

Around one corner was the mess hall, accessed by a set of double doors. Charlie looked briefly through the glass inserts. The room inside appeared to go on forever.

Charlie's company waited in line outside the barbershop. It was a large facility with fifteen chairs in front of a continuous mirrored wall. A barber stood behind each chair waiting to go to work.

Slowly, the line began to move. By the time Charlie entered the room, piles of hair were ankle deep around each chair. He watched the barbers move quickly and efficiently as their shears moved expertly across each head. Curley locks, some of which had taken years to grow, disappeared unceremoniously in piles beside each chair.

In the days ahead, Charlie did everything with his assigned company. They traveled as a group down to the tailor shop where an army of tailors measured each man. The tailors' cloth tape measures moved quickly and fluidly around each new torso. In a few weeks, each plebe would own a full ensemble of Navy uniforms.

Charlie's first ensemble consisted of three pairs of white cotton pants with drawstrings and a thick cotton pullover. A white hat with a blue stripe around its circumference completed the outfit. Each plebe also received Navy-issue underwear, dark socks, and marching boots.

Walker gave each man name tags and showed them specifically where to locate it on their uniforms.

"You will wear these nametags with every uniform," he said. "Failure to do so will result in a Form-2."

A man in the first row asked, "What's a Form-2?"

Walker ambled over to the man and stood before him menacingly. "How will you address me?"

"Sir."

"Drop for fifty."

"Yes, sir."

"I gave you an order!"

"Aye, aye, sir."

"If any of you men have questions you will first ask permission. Is that clear?"

Charlie quickly learned that the Naval Academy is a military enclave within the small town of Annapolis. Bancroft Hall was a city of and by itself. It had a hospital (and sickbay), a bookstore, a laundry/dry cleaner and even a cobbler shop—everything needed to sustain the new plebes through their training.

❋

As evening approached on that first day, Charlie's company reformed for dinner. He and his newly clean-cut classmates dressed in their recently issued working uniforms. They stood uncertainly waiting for instructions. Everything was new, completely different and unfamiliar. It would take time and resilience to adjust to what, in essence, was summer boot camp on steroids.

At exactly 1800, Walker and Brewer appeared in front of the Eighth Company.

"Fall in, men! Stand at attention!" Brewer bellowed. "We will march to the mess hall now."

Walker led the Eighth Company down three levels and through a door into King Hall.

"This is your authorized entrance to the mess hall," he said. You will sit at tables thirty-one through thirty-seven. Find this section and occupy a place at one of the tables. This will be your permanent seat for the duration of the summer."

Charlie's company entered the mess hall and looked around in a state of wonder. A thousand other new plebes were filing in from all access points. The entire contingent of the new class still occupied just over a quarter of the mess hall space. The remainder of the mess hall was in darkness.

Charlie found one of the tables assigned to the Eighth Company and stood behind the chair with his arms on the backrest. His table filled quickly; each man looked around at their tablemates. He looked around the mess hall. It was enormous, containing over 55,000 square feet with 400 tables.

Brewer and Walker stood in the central aisle and watched.

"Eighth Company," Brewer yelled loudly. "You are to be at attention at all times and places, including the mess hall."

Walker added, "You will remain at attention when seated. You are to occupy only the first three inches of your seat. You will stay braced up for the duration of the meal. That means shoulders back with eyes straight ahead. You will not sit until given permission to do so."

When Walker gave the order, chairs scraped on the concrete floor as the men sat. Charlie had a place away from the aisle. There was one empty seat at the head of the table. Walker found it and joined Charlie's table.

He looked at Charlie's nametag. "McDaniels."

"Yes, sir."

"Are you looking at me?"

"Yes, sir. Sorry, sir."

"Shove out!"

"Sir?"

"Move your goddamned chair back! I want you to sit on air. No part of your ass is to touch that chair."

Charlie moved his chair back as instructed. Only his leg muscles now supported his entire weight. It quickly became very uncomfortable.

After five minutes in the "shove out" position, Charlie's legs started to complain seriously. Nevertheless, he remained motionless as an army of Filipino stewards delivered steaming platters of food to each table.

Sweat trickled down his brow and into his eyes; his thigh muscles screamed.

"McDaniels!"

"Yes, sir," Charlie answered, his voice hoarse and strained.

"How do you feel?"

"It hurts, sir."

Walker banged his fist on the table plates rattled. "Are you a pussy, McDaniels?"

"No, sir."

"Then your response to my question will be affirmative the next time."

"Yes, sir."

"McDaniels!"

"Yes, sir."

"How do you feel now?"

"Fine, sir."

"Better."

❋

Plebe Summer was designed to mold civilian teenagers into the proper image of Academy midshipmen so that they would be fit to join the full Brigade when it returned in September. It was a notoriously difficult three-month period. It was, in short, Hell.

Reveille was at five a.m. commencing with a five-mile run, rain or shine, around the Yard. Charlie learned how to scale ropes, stay afloat in the pool for hours, clean his government-issued M-1 rifle and a wide range of other military skills.

He learned the proper way to salute, how to carry a rifle and tie every imaginable knot. It seemed an endless succession of uninteresting skills.

Each day, the entire plebe brigade assembled on one of the parade fields in the Yard. Charlie stood at attention for hours in the unbearable August heat. His company practiced marching maneuvers endlessly. Despite his discomfort, he became an expert at marching and holding his M-1 rifle.

Standing at attention with his company, he could see homes and yards on the opposite bank of the Severn River. The world he used to know was close but no longer reachable. Charlie thought he was condemned to hell. He despised every second of Plebe Summer. The Second Classmen bullied and harassed him continuously. It seemed he couldn't do anything right. All he wanted was to get out; this was *not* the place for him.

Charlie had to stifle his misgivings. It was too late.

Quitting was never an option no matter how deeply he grieved his loss of freedom. His father hated quitters. To him, they were worthless— too weak and afraid to stand up to the challenge of the military way of life.

According to the general, Plebe Summer would weed out the "lesser" men—the weaklings who had no place in military society.

Charlie envied those who had the courage and common sense to resign. He would never begrudge their decisions. He suspected each of those who resigned would return to temporarily disappointed friends and family. Eventually, however, they would find other, more suitable paths and merge comfortably into other learning institutions.

The last weekend of August marked the end of Plebe Summer. It was a celebratory time and, most importantly, the first opportunity plebes had to leave the academy grounds.

Charlie's mother and father drove to Annapolis to see their son for the first time since June. He had not spoken to either since the induction ceremony.

Attired for the first time in heavily starched dress whites, Charlie inspected himself in the mirror. He put on his cap and looked closer.

With his deep blue eyes, broad shoulders and square jaw, he could be the poster child for *Shipmate* magazine. He couldn't help smiling at the transformation. He was now a real midshipman, complete with visored cap and stripeless shoulder boards. He survived Plebe Summer. Now he belonged.

He briefly looked down at his left hand. Fingers that were once hard and calloused from the steel strings of his guitar were now softer, well-manicured. He now had the hands of a gentlemen as his father would say.

The first liberty call of the entire summer sounded at noon that Saturday. As Charlie walked out the entrance to Bancroft Hall and down the marble steps, his heart swelled with the unfamiliar joy of freedom.

There, next to the ever-present statue of Tecumseh, father and mother looked expectantly at the surge of white uniforms passing them.

They hardly recognized him at first. He waved to attract their attention. His mother waved back excitedly and ran to him.

"Charlie, I've missed you so much!" she cried, holding him tightly. "You've lost weight."

His father, dressed in full uniform, greeted Charlie with a firm handshake. "You look good, Charles. I can see a positive change in you already."

"Thanks, Dad."

As they walked through the streets of Annapolis, his father received salutes from other Plebes nearby. Charlie wanted to hide.

Why does he have to be in uniform? Couldn't he find a nice sports coat?

The general had made reservations at one of the finest restaurants in Annapolis near the water in the town's center. Known as the Harbor View Restaurant, it overlooked the quaint fishing harbor at the end of Main Street.

Once at the restaurant, the general opened the door and expertly ushered Charlie and his mother into the packed foyer. "Wait here," he yelled above the noise.

He pushed and shoved his way to the maître 'd and interrupted gruffly, shouting loudly in his best command voice, "General McDaniels. Reservations for three."

"Yes, sir. One moment, please."

Immediately, the maître'd escorted them to a table by the window.

My father in action.

Charlie sat across from his parents in a booth next to a large plate-glass window. His father waved his hand and immediately ordered a drink.

"Double Jack Daniels on the rocks—with a splash."

"Yes, sir," she answered. "And for you, Madam?

"She'll have a scotch and water," the general interjected, "And bring my son a diet coke."

Here we go. Try to stay sober, Dad.

After the drinks had arrived, the family continued their conversation. The restaurant was crowded but surprisingly quiet.

"Well, Charles," his father began, "tell us how you like it so far. Were we right?"

"I like it fine, Dad," Charlie lied. His tone belied his words.

"You'll like it more after the Brigade returns next week. That's when the *real* Plebe Year starts."

"It gets worse?" Charlie asked with a trace of mockery.

"Of course not," the general corrected "*Better*. You'll have many more men to instruct you."

Charlie glanced at his father's tumbler of bourbon. It was half-empty.

Slow down, Dad.

"How are you feeling, Charlie?" his mother asked. "You look thin."

"I'm in good shape, mom. The Academy is a very physical place."

"It's the rite of passage from boy to man," the general interjected. "You must be physically strong in combat. Strength will serve you well in this or the next war.

What next" war? Isn't Vietnam enough for now? And who the hell said anything about combat?

"So tell us what you've learned, Charlie," his mother asked warily. "I know the academy is about more than just strength."

As Charlie went on, his father seemed to be losing interest in the conversation. His glass was empty. He waved it in the air.

"I've learned quite a lot, mom. I can tie knots, sing the alma mater, salute, sail and a lot more."

His mother could read the sarcasm in his son's eyes. She smiled at him.

"Sailing!" his father exclaimed, loudly reentering the conversation. Charlie was sure half the restaurant could hear him. "Now that's what I loved the most. Picture a man at the helm with a beautiful girl by his side and a strong wind in his sail."

"Your father and I used to sail out into the Chesapeake Bay on the weekends. It's fun but a lot of work, too."

"Really, Mom? You sailed? Did you ever take the helm?"

Don't go there! Don't egg him on.

"Of course not," his father answered. "Sailing is a demanding sport. Takes strength to handle the boom and rudder."

Melinda winked at her son with a warning look.

"What's your favorite activity here, Charlie?" she asked quickly.

"I'm on the boxing team, Mom," Charlie replied.

"You know I was the Brigade Heavyweight Champion, don't you?"

You've told me a hundred times, for god's sake.

"Yeah, I know, Dad."

"Keep after it, son. Knowing how to fight will serve you well."

Really?

Melinda looked at her husband and put a finger to her lips. Her husband ignored her and ordered another drink.

"We had Frank with us for the last week," his father thundered. "Back from the sea. The young man is becoming a splendid officer."

"That's great dad." Charlie's voice was flat; he could muster little enthusiasm.

The waitress arrived to take their order. Melinda went first; Charlie picked one of the specialties.

"Crab cakes for me," the general said while rattling ice cubes in his empty glass.

Lunch was quite pleasant. Charlie's mother was able to maneuver the conversation away from inflammatory subjects. She was good at it.

Charlie's father remained quiet for the most part, staring pensively out the window with his hand securely around his Jack Daniels. The general had consumed enough alcohol to make the average man throw up. He barely showed it. Its only effect was withdrawal into a pleasant, although irrational disposition. He contributed little more to the conversation.

After lunch, the three strolled through town and toward State Circle. Puffy white clouds against a deep blue sky kept Charlie lighthearted. It was a beautiful day for late August.

At four o'clock, they were back at his parent's car.

Charlie said to them, "It's after 1600. I should be getting back."

"I know you do, Charlie," his mother said. "I can't tell you how good it is to see you again."

"Me, too, Mom. Next time will be Christmas."

"You'll see a hell of a change in the boy then, Melinda. He's on his way to becoming a fighting machine."

"Let's go, Frank," she urged, "Let Charlie get back."

Charlie hugged his mother and whispered, "Love you, Mom." She could feel the emotion of his loneliness engulf him. "I'll try to write," he said. "You know we can't use the pay phones."

"Be patient, Charlie," she whispered back. "Hang in for as long as you can. We need to talk privately soon—perhaps over Christmas."

He shook his father's hand firmly, struggling to hold back tears.

"Buck up, son. Nice to see you becoming a man."

Charlie turned quickly and headed back to Bancroft Hall. Back to hell.

As he joined the throngs of white uniforms returning to Bancroft Hall, he pondered his mother's last words.

She wants to tell me something.

THE NAVAL ACADEMY

❋

In early-September, the remainder of the Brigade of Midshipmen returned to Bancroft Hall. The passageways echoed with greetings and laughter.

Charlie and his roommates sat quietly at their desks watching and listening. They watched men of every class milling about in the wide hallways.

The plebe brigade disbanded and integrated with the other classes in one of thirty-six companies. Charlie and his gear moved to the Eleventh Company in the Third Wing. He acquired a new room and roommates in the move. Richard and Don were friendly guys. They liked Charlie's laid-back personality. It was a good fit.

Frequently, upperclassmen entered curious to see the year's new plebes. Charlie and his roommates jumped to attention at each visit. Some of the upper class who came by were friendly, some curious and some downright mean.

The door banged again.

"Attention on deck," Charlie yelled.

A heavyset, short third classman entered with a swagger. He surveyed Charlie and his roommates with an arrogant stare. His nametag said "H. Dorfman".

"What are you looking at, plebe?" Dorfman sneered contemptuously.

"Your name tag, sir," Charlie answered.

"Keep your goddamned eyes in the boat!"

"Aye, aye, sir."

Dorfman was a new third classman. He had been a plebe, himself, only three months ago. Now he was ready to test his new authority and power.

"What's your name, plebe," Dorfman demanded

"Charles, sir."

"Do you go by 'Charlie'?" There was sarcasm in his voice. It was not a friendly question.

"Yes, sir."

To his surprise, Dorfman extended his right toward Charlie. Charlie moved to shake it. As he did, Dorfman pulled his hand back out of reach.

"Dumbfuck!" he laughed. "Did you think I would *spoon* you?"

"Yes, sir," Charlie replied.

"I will *never* spoon you, plebe!"

"Yes, sir."

Dorfman inspected Charlie quickly.

"You having fun here, Charles?" His voice was sing-song and sarcastic.

"Yes, sir."

"Really?"

"Yes, sir!" Charlie answered again. His eyes remained impassively fixed on the opposite wall.

"Don't bullshit me, plebe. Drop for twenty, now!"

Charlie fell to the floor and did twenty push-ups. Dorfman lost interest in Charlie. He was busy harassing his roommates.

❋

Later that afternoon, Charlie was sitting casually on his bunk reading a new textbook. Suddenly, he heard "Attention on Deck!" from Don.

Charlie looked up and saw his brother standing in the doorway. With a wide grin, he moved to shake hands.

However, Frank remained stone-faced and unresponsive.

"Attention, plebe!" he ordered. There was no feeling in his voice.

Charlie's eyes narrowed with anger. He ignored Frank's command and stared back with an incredulous look on his face.

Charlie stopped. "Jesus, Frank. You're not going to fuck with me, too, are you?"

Don't pull rank on me, damn it. Don't act like the old man.

"Have you learned the proper way to shove out yet, Charlie?

Huh? Have you?"

"Yeah. Does that make you happy?"

"Do you still laugh at the system, Charlie?"

"Man, you can carry a grudge for a long time."

"You'll have to do as I say," Frank smirked.

"Go fuck yourself, Frank. It's been great seeing you again. I've got work to do."

"Come on, Charlie. You *need* a friend here. How 'bout if I spoon you now?"

"I have plenty of friends, thanks."

Frank shrugged his shoulders and disappeared.

"What was that all about?" Don asked.

"My brother," he answered indifferently.

"You have a brother here?" Richard asked.

Charlie nodded with a shy smile and shrugged his shoulders.

"Pardon me for saying this," Richard added, "but your brother's a bit of a jerk."

Charlie nodded glumly and returned to his textbook.

❋

Charlie quickly forgot the incident with his brother. He was not going to be the friend he had hoped. Why should he? Afterall, he never had been.

He had, in fact, little time to think about anything. There was no place to hide.

The Eleventh Company had a reputation for being particularly tough on plebes. Charlie worked hard to learn new names and routines. He memorized volumes of useless data and phrases. He was continually on guard.

Charlie had a full academic schedule as well. The Navy dictated what he would study. Every plebe took on the same heavy academic load that included naval history, advanced calculus, thermodynamics, weaponry, and others. He hoped he would find something of interest.

⁂

The first evening meal with the full Brigade was a memorable experience. To see the entire mess hall filled was an impressive sight.

Charlie ran to his newly assigned table and stood motionless behind the chair at his appointed place. Three other plebes, one a roommate, joined him simultaneously.

The plebes shared the table with eight upperclassmen. Charlie sat braced on three inches of his seat with eyes fixed ahead. The balance of his table filled shortly. An excited din of conversation and laughter pervaded the huge space.

The plebes sat quietly, forbidden to speak unless asked. Across from Charlie, four third classmen talked loudly while they found their seats. Two first-classmen sat at the head of the table; two second-classmen sat at the other end. Charlie would grow to know each man well over the course of the year.

The upper classes discussed casually and informally throughout dinner. They were more interested in discussing their summers. No one said a word to the plebes…except for Harry.

Charlie looked at the heavyset man across from him, shifting his eyes ever so slightly to read his name tag. "H. E. Dorfman".

"Are you looking at my name tag again, plebe?" Dorfman asked. "You're not queer for me, are you?"

"Yes, sir. No, sir."

A few at the table snickered. Charlie felt an uncomfortable energy from Dorfman. He hoped he would not become an enemy.

⁂

Every plebe had a first classman assigned as a personal mentor, a "go-to" senior in the event of trouble. The "Firsty" took a plebe under his wing, providing a sanctuary of sorts—a personal interface between reason and insanity.

Charlie's Firsty was Pete Hartwick, Company Commander, with a reputation for being tough but fair. Hartwick had little time for silly antics and routines that plebes were forced to follow. Rather, his motivation was to fulfill his role as mentor, by example and direct counseling when needed.

Pete and his roommate, Dave, were the two seniors assigned at the head of Charlie's mess table. A day later, Pete began to scrutinize the four plebes on his right. Something about Charlie intrigued him. Here was a good-looking young kid who responded well to others at the table. He possessed a certain grace and ease despite constant challenges. Charlie's military bearing needed a lot of work. However, that would come. Charlie displayed a freshness and innocence that Pete picked up at once. He saw in Charlie a natural likeability, an individual personal enthusiasm. He wanted to know him better.

Later that evening, as Charlie was relishing the quiet during the study period, a knock on the door interrupted the silence. Pete casually walked in wearing a West Point bathrobe.

"Attention on deck," Charlie announced. Everyone rose quickly to attention.

"Mr. McDaniels, front and center," Pete directed.

"Aye, aye, sir!"

Charlie stood before Hartwick at attention, waiting.

"You have a Firsty yet?"

"No, sir."

"You have one now. Come around to my room at 2000 for a briefing."

"Yes, sir. Aye, aye, sir."

Hartwick turned and said to all, "Carry on, gentlemen." When he left the room, the roommates relaxed.

"Wow! Nice going, Charlie," Don said. "The Company

Commander is your Firsty!"

Charlie shrugged. He didn't know if that was good or bad.

Just before 2000, Charlie knocked on Pete Hartwick's half-open door. "Request permission to come aboard, sir."

"Come on in Mr. McDaniels," Pete answered.

Charlie opened the door and stood at attention just inside the room. Pete's roommate, Dave, glanced at Charlie indifferently before returning to his studies.

"Where you from, Mr. McDaniels?" Pete asked.

"Washington, DC, sir.

"Well, you're close to home anyway. Are you a Navy junior by chance?"

"Yes, sir. Marines, sir. My father is stationed at Fort McNair."

"Is he an officer?"

"Yes, sir."

"What does your father do at Fort McNair?"

Sir, he's the base commander." Charlie answered.

"So your father is a general, I presume."

"Yes, sir."

"That should give you an advantage here. You already know what *real* military life is like."

"Yes, sir."

"You plan to be a marine when you graduate?

"There is some pressure for me to do that, sir."

"Any siblings?"

"I have a brother, sir. He's a first classman.

"Really? What's his name?"

"Franklin McDaniels, sir. He's in the Twenty-First Company."

"Oh yeah, I know Frank. He and I met during some staff meetings. He seems to be an okay guy, good military bearing. I'm betting he'll be our brigade commander next semester."

"Yes, sir."

"How well do you get along?"

"Not well, sir. We never have."

"That's unfortunate," Pete said. "Why not—if you don't mind me asking."

Charlie related the incident earlier with his brother as an example. Pete shook his head but said nothing.

"I suppose your brother wants to go to Vietnam."

"Yes, sir."

"So you have pressure from two fronts—your dad and your brother? That's sure a shit sandwich, isn't it?"

Charlie smiled wryly. "Yes, sir."

"If you're under that kind of pressure, start thinking now about Vietnam. Many of our guys are dying. It's a hell of a mess as far as I'm concerned."

Charlie was surprised. He hadn't expected disparaging remarks. "Yes, sir."

"How much do you know about the conflict in Southeast Asia, Mr. McDaniels?"

"Very little, sir. Just what's on the news, sir."

"I think you should learn more about this war, Mr. McDaniels. If you feel pressure to go to Vietnam after graduation, you should have all the facts to support whatever decision you plan to make."

"Yes, sir."

"You deserve the privilege of personal choice, here and after you graduate, you must choose, based on knowledge and understanding. Know your own truth."

"Yes, sir. Thank you for saying so, sir." Charlie would never forget these words.

"Okay. Here's the deal then. I get a newspaper delivered outside the room every morning a half hour before reveille. Sometimes, I'm not able to read it as thoroughly as I want to."

"Yes, sir."

"I want you to read my paper every morning. Read the articles on Vietnam before reveille. I want a report on the headlines on the war at breakfast. If your report is good, the men at our table may learn as well."

"Yes, sir."

"Don't be limited by what's in the paper, however," Pete added. "There are a lot of resources here about Vietnam. You should study them as well."

"Request permission to ask a question."

"Sure."

"Does that include historical information, sir?"

"Yes. *Especially* the history. You can't understand the present without knowing the past."

"Aye, aye, sir."

"Become an expert on *all* aspects of the Vietnam War. I challenge you to motivate all of us at the table to be better informed. You must be objective and, above all, accurate. Learn to filter out the politics."

"Aye, aye, sir."

"Okay. You know you can call on me if you have a problem or a question, I'll be available to help you. However, I'm not going to bail you out for your mistakes—you're on your own for that. But I will ensure you're treated fairly."

"Yes, sir."

"I also want to be kept current on how you're doing with military and academic training," Pete added. "Report that weekly. Should you have a problem, come to me first—anytime."

"Aye, aye, sir."

"Any questions?"

"No, sir. Thank you, sir."

"You're welcome. You're dismissed."

"Aye, aye, sir."

Pete reflected on his conversation with Charlie. Dave looked briefly up from his book. "Seems like a good kid."

"Yeah," Pete answered thoughtfully.

❋

Charlie began the following day at 5 a.m. just outside Pete's door. The dimly lit halls were vacant and silent as Charlie waited patiently at parade rest. Soon, he heard the sound of newspapers dropping randomly on the floor—each hit echoed through the empty passageways.

The civilian delivery man walked to the end of the hall and, when seeing Charlie standing against the wall, handed him the paper. Charlie thanked the man and opened the newspaper immediately. It was the *Baltimore Sun,* an excellent paper with a reputation for accuracy.

Standing in the dim glow of the nearest wall light, Charlie read every article that pertained to Vietnam. On the first page, below the fold, was a story announcing the death of Ho Chi Minh, leader of the North Vietnamese government. The story included a brief biography of Ho. Charlie memorized it.

Later at breakfast, as the platter of scrambled eggs passed from man to man around his table, Pete looked toward Charlie, sitting on the edge of his chair two places away.

"Mr. McDaniels."

"Yes, sir."

"What's going on in Vietnam today?"

"Sir, Ho Chi Minh died."

Really?"

"Yes, sir."

"And who is Ho Chi Minh?"

"Sir, Ho Chi Minh is recognized as the founding father of the Democratic Republic of Vietnam, a communist, one-party state."

Charlie recited the newspaper's summary verbatim.

"Okay, good. Sounds to me like Uncle Ho Chi Minh was a really bad guy. What do you think?"

"Sir, he was the leader of North Vietnam. That would make him our enemy."

"Did you know we were his ally at one time?"

"No, sir."

"Look at the history of our relationship with Ho Chi Minh. You'll find it politically interesting."

"Aye, aye, sir."

"So, be prepared. I may ask you in the future. *Know* the history of our involvement."

"Aye, aye, sir."

Pete turned his attention elsewhere, giving others the opportunity to badger and haze the plebes.

CHAPTER FOUR

History Lessons

Present Time

One more drink to celebrate his departure; a drink to toast the courage to end his life.

A half bottle of cheap bourbon rested on the toilet tank.

The old man grabbed the bottle by the neck and drank heavily. Liquor always took him to a better place. The warmth of the alcohol expanded through his system. He paused gratefully, acknowledging its calming effect on him.

His reflection looked back with glassy and judgmental eyes – eyes that berated him for his poor choices in life. He had the chance to break free once, the opportunity to stand up to the little dictator.

He didn't do it; he was afraid of the reaction, afraid of the judgment. Instead, he allowed himself to remain stuck in an incompatible way of life.

He looked down at his left hand, resting beside the bottle of Ativan. The old and battered school ring still decorated his fourth finger. Its inscription read "USNA class of 1973". The ring was one of his few remnants from the past—that and the hideous scar on his right arm.

The old man remembered the talented musician he once was. He had a rare gift and could have done so much. Instead, he threw his love of music away; threw it away for country.

For what.

He could have gone to Canada and avoided it all, but he didn't have the guts back then. Instead, he relented to the dictates of others whose power he feared. He was afraid of their judgment.

Had he only stood up to that son of a bitch, things would be a lot different now ... wouldn't they?

The faded blue eyes stared at him evenly. There was no answer.

1969

Charlie dutifully reported the headlines from the *Baltimore Sun* each morning as directed by Pete Harkins. Most reports contained stories of death and destruction of a culture ten thousand miles away. Over time, Charlie would form his own opinions on Vietnam.

Now in October, Charlie had faithfully reported news of Vietnam for almost six weeks. He had also spent considerable time in the library researching the origins of the war. No one asked him about Ho Chi Minh's background.

This morning, the lead story news was of an "unprecedented" anti-war movement in Washington and other places throughout the country. The youth of America seriously questioned the U.S. role in Vietnam. Nixon was losing support.

Charlie's expressionless voice repeated the story that morning at breakfast. To the men at his table, the peace demonstrations were repugnant, un-American. None wanted to hear of the thousands of "cowardly" collegiate anti-war protesters who defamed military service.

It was an un-American affront to the brave men who serve with honor in Vietnam.

"We don't want to hear about hippies and peaceniks, McDaniels," Harry interrupted and turned to Pete. "If that's all he's got, Pete, we don't want to hear it."

Pete looked at Harry. Though he was merely doing his job, Charlie was the bearer of bad news. The angry expressions around the table confirmed that Charlie was the unwelcome messenger.

"Do you mind, Pete?" George asked.

Pete nodded. "Of course I don't mind, George. Don't take bad news out on Mr. McDaniels. He's only doing what I asked of him."

The men watched Pete as he spoke. A couple shrugged their shoulders; a few looked down at their plates. None displayed enthusiasm.

"Sure, Pete," one said. "You're the boss."

"Mr. McDaniels," Pete said, "this morning we'll go somewhere else. Tell us about the Ho Chi Minh and his history in the war."

"Come on, Pete," Harry complained. "This guy doesn't know shit. Who is he to give *us* information?"

"I still want to let him try, Harry. Listen to what he says. Maybe you'll learn something. If not, we'll do something else."

"Go ahead, Mr. McDaniels," Pete said evenly.

"Aye, aye, sir."

"You have two minutes."

"Sir, our relationship with Ho Chi Minh began during World War Two. Vietnam was part of French Indochina. During the war, the Japanese army invaded Vietnam and expelled the French.

"Ho Chi Minh and his army were a valuable counterforce for us during the war. Ho called his army the Viet Minh or League for the Independence of Vietnam. They disrupted Japanese supply lines, provided intelligence on Japanese troop movements and rescued downed American pilots.

"We established an alliance with Ho Chi Minh and the Viet Minh during World War Two. In exchange for Ho Chi Minh's help, we gave him whatever money and arms he needed."

Harry's head jerked up. "What? You're telling us we supported that gook bastard? That's bullshit!"

"See, Harry. I told you that you might learn something," Pete interjected with a smile.

"Yes, sir, we *did* support him, Mr. Dorfman. The U.S. shaped and strengthened the very army it now fights in the jungles of Vietnam.

The Viet Minh army became the Viet Cong."

Harry looked at Charlie as if he was crazy.

"Sir, it was our aid during the war that legitimized Ho Chi Minh," Charlie continued. "He became an influential and popular leader, a symbol of Vietnamese liberation and freedom."

"How long did our alliance with Ho Chi Minh continue, Mr. McDaniels?"

"Until the end of the war, sir. When Japan surrendered, France brought its old Emperor back to Saigon and reinstated him as the 'lawful' head of Vietnam."

"I don't suppose Ho Chi Minh took kindly to having the French back?" Dave stated with a grin.

"No, sir. Ho Chi Minh became an anti-French activist. He opposed and harassed the French government's efforts to again impose its culture on the people of Vietnam. In defiance, Ho Chi Minh took over Hanoi declaring it to be the capital and declared Vietnam a free and sovereign country. He called his country the Democratic Republic of Vietnam."

"And did we continue to give him arms?" Dave asked.

"No, sir. France was our ally. We abandoned Ho Chi Minh and discontinued our aid to him. Ho Chi Minh was left holding the bag with no support."

"Well, isn't that tough shit," Harry said sarcastically.

"Sir, Ho Chi Minh was trying to free his country from French domination, sir."

Pete cringed. *Don't argue, McDaniels.*

He quickly interrupted, "Okay, that's enough for now, Mr. McDaniels. Good job."

"Thank you, sir."

"We'll continue the story another time. You've told us the French came back to Saigon and Ho Chi Minh staked out Hanoi. Continue from that point the next time I ask."

"Aye, aye, sir."

HISTORY LESSONS

❋

The following morning Charlie continued.

"Ho Chi Minh led the Viet Minh in opposition to French efforts to reoccupy his country. He and his army were powerful now. He had the weapons we once gave him. He had the loyal following of half a million soldiers skilled in jungle combat."

"But he no longer had our support."

"No, sir."

"So you think we should have continued our aid to Vietnam rather than France?" Dave asked.

Charlie paused.

"Mr. McDaniels," Pete said slowly, curious to see how Charlie would respond. "Answer the question. Should we have supported Ho Chi Minh?"

"Sir, Ho Chi Minh was the most popular leader in all of Vietnam. He wanted freedom — to rid his country of French occupation. The French were foreign aggressors, sir, unlawfully occupying his homeland.

"Sir, our country supports freedom and independence. Free choice is the cornerstone of our Declaration of Independence," Charlie continued carefully.

"So your answer is a yes?" Pete asked cautiously. "We *should* have supported Ho Chi Minh."

"Sir, Ho Chi Minh was a Communist... but he wanted *freedom*."

Charlie had exceeded his allotted two minutes. He was a good storyteller. Many were curious how the story would end despite their irritation. Harry and others were more interested in seeing Charlie hamstring himself with another personal comment.

"We have a few more minutes, Pete addressed his group. Anyone object if Mr. McDaniels continues?"

No one spoke. The three plebes next to Charlie loved him. They were able to eat in relative peace while Charlie continued talking.

"Okay, I'll give you another minute, Mr. McDaniels," Pete said.

"You have implied that Ho Chi Minh was left 'holding the bag' as you put it."

"Yes, sir," Charlie answered. "We abandoned Ho Chi Minh after his declaration of independence from the French. For what he believed a noble cause, he was confident the U.S. would assist him."

"But we didn't assist him, did we?" Dave said.

"No sir."

"Should we have?"

"Sir, I believe we turned our back on a friend."

"This isn't a church, mister," Dave responded. "We don't care what you believe."

"Yes, sir, we did turn our back on a former friend and ally," Charlie replied cautiously. "In retrospect, a negotiated separation with Ho Chi Minh would have been more productive, possibly even preventing the war we find ourselves in now."

Pete held up his hand and quickly stepped in.

"Okay, okay, we're done. No more speculation, Mr. McDaniels. All I want are the facts. We'll decide who we should have supported and how."

"Aye, aye, sir."

"Be objective if I ask you again to speak, Mr. McDaniels. Otherwise, there will be no further discussion on the subject."

Charlie was crestfallen. "Aye, aye, sir," he answered. He feared that he had both let Pete down and alienated the rest of the table. No one wanted to hear about the old self-serving politics and arrogance that engulfed the U.S. in this foreign war. To them, America was exceptional among the world's countries. It was the moral and righteous leader of the free world. It always did the right thing.

He had to be careful.

❋

Pete stopped by Charlie's room that evening. Charlie and his roommates rose to attention.

"Carry on, gentlemen," he said as he sat informally on the edge of Charlie's desk. Charlie looked back expectantly.

"Mr. McDaniels," he said, "excellent work this morning. You have obviously spent a lot of time on my assignment. You speak well. I believe some of the men at our table were genuinely interested in your presentation."

"Thank you, sir," Charlie said, feeling better about his performance.

"However, the majority resented a plebe suggesting that our country did not act honorably. You *have* to stop interjecting personal feelings when you speak. I can't emphasize that enough."

"Aye, aye, sir."

Charlie considered Pete's warning. He had reported the truth this morning even though it to put him at odds with America's moral principles. How else could he speak of the war's history?

"Sir, request permission to speak."

"Go ahead."

"I'm only reporting the facts, sir."

"I know you are. It's your *tone* that worries me. Your descriptions are laced with cynicism and condescension. Your ad-libbed comments imply disapproval. I heard someone today suggest you're sympathizing with the Communists. Believe me; you don't want that reputation."

"No, sir."

"Okay. Try to speak with an even, objective voice the next time. Your opinions are just that—opinions. You need to assemble all the facts before accusing the U.S. of backstabbing a friend."

"Aye, aye, sir," Charlie answered.

Pete's right. Second-guessing the politics is easy. I need to acquire more facts.

Pete stood up to leave. "Okay, gentlemen," he said with an easy smile. "Get back to work."

After Pete had left, Don was the first to speak. He sat beside Charlie at the mess table and knew what Pete Harkins was saying.

"Charlie," he said, "Mr. Harkins is right. I thought you were critical of our foreign policy this morning. You must be nuts! I'm glad he warned you."

Charlie looked skeptically at his roommate. "What would you have done?" he asked argumentatively.

"Well for starters, I'd never tell eight upperclassmen that we turned our back on an ally."

"But we did, Don."

"I think I would have left that part out."

"Okay, I hear you. But if I ignore facts detrimental to the U.S., how the hell will we ever know the real truth?"

"Okay. I hear you. Do what you think is right. It's your funeral."

Charlie nodded absently and looked down at his textbook. He reflected on Don's caution. He was right in the sense that Charlie's first goal was to *survive* here. Pete had put him in this precarious position. Why?

Charlie felt frustrated. The more he learned on his own; the more his positions turned against the war in Vietnam.

❋

Harry Dorfman sat with his feet propped on his desk. He stared at the bright ceiling light above, carelessly blowing smoke rings into the air. His roommate was engrossed in the latest issue of *Playboy*.

Abruptly, Harry sat up and declared, "That McDaniels sounds anti-American, don't you think?"

Bruce looked up from his magazine. "Yeah, why's Pete's plebe telling *us* about Vietnam?"

"He's company commander. I guess he thinks he can protect him."

"Pete can do what he wants, Harry. You'd be stupid to fuck with his plebe at the mess table."

"Yeah, I know," Harry said. "But he can't hide *all* the time. We need to take him aside to remind him he's only a fucking plebe."

"What's on your mind?" Bruce asked.

❋

The brigade formed three times a day before each meal. With the onset of winter, most formations were in the hallway under more forgiving fluorescent lighting. Occasionally, on the rare unseasonably warm and sunny day, the brigade would form outside. Standing in bright sunshine revealed every uniform discrepancy, especially lint. Outside formations required plebes to work twice as hard to look good. Charlie hated outside formations.

Plebes, the first to arrive, scurried in every direction toward preassigned locations. They stood at attention, waiting for inevitable inspections and critiques by others. Upper class walked between the rows of men, randomly inspecting plebes, looking for any infraction from stray lint to scuffed shoes.

Each formation lasted about ten minutes and was the primary source of information about all aspects of Brigade life. Afterward, the companies marched as a unit down the stairs to the mess hall.

As Charlie stood waiting, Harry stepped into his field of view. He stood there for a long time, inspecting Charlie, looking for any infraction, no matter how small. Harry resented Charlie and his seemingly unflappable persona. Charlie was a plebe who thought he knew more than he did. It fed his sense of low self-esteem.

Harry wanted badly to break through Charlie's calm façade. He wanted to make Charlie fear him, to cower before him and enhance the tough-guy image Harry so wanted. He saw in Charlie qualities that he envied.

Harry looked around to make sure Pete was preoccupied at the head of the company formation. He whispered to Charlie with cold, dark eyes, "McDaniels, you faggot, you look like shit!" Harry whispered with a sneer. "When are you going to resign and make our home here a better place?"

"Never, sir!"

"Never? I think we can make you change your mind."

Charlie said nothing. He looked passively ahead, eyes fixed on the back of the man in the row ahead. He accepted unflinchingly the barrage of insults directed at him.

"What's for dinner tonight, shithead?" Harry asked softly.

"Sir, the menu for tonight is chicken pasta primavera, tossed salad, fruit, and milk."

"How about dessert, dummy?" A friend asked.

Charlie froze. He couldn't remember dessert.

"I'll find out, sir." It was the only permitted answer to an unknown question.

Harry smiled. Charlie could smell his hot breath as he moved inches away from his face. "Well, well," he hissed to no one in particular, "Seems McDaniels here doesn't give a shit about his responsibilities. Is that right, pussy?"

"No, sir."

"Come around, you fuck up."

"Aye, aye, sir."

❋

The "come-around" period was during the half-hour period of relative quiet before evening meal formation. Most plebes were required to visit or come around to various upper-class rooms for any military infractions committed during that day. Harry normally had a whole roomful of plebes.

At one minute before 1800, Charlie and several other plebes stood at parade rest just outside Harry's door. At precisely 1800, Charlie snapped to attention and knocked loudly on the half-opened door.

"Request permission to come aboard, sir."

Harry looked up from his magazine. "Get in here, McDaniels.

Stand against that wall," he said pointing with his finger.

Charlie and the other plebes were fully dressed and prepared for evening meal formation. Harry was still in his skivvies. As he stood and swaggered toward him, Charlie was able to see his large, hairy gut. A radio on the desk was playing rock music.

Harry dismissed the other plebes who gratefully exited the room, leaving Charlie alone and unprotected with his antagonist.

Charlie stood, waiting for another barrage of insults.

Harry looked up and gazed at Charlie indifferently. "McDaniels, you think you're hot shit, don't you? Professor of Vietnam history."

"No, sir."

"Tell me, pussy. You really think you can make it here?"

"Yes, sir."

Harry stared back with contempt and self-righteousness. Charlie could see through the cruelty in his eyes and saw only a somewhat overweight and insecure comrade trying to frighten him. Charlie displayed no fear, however; no "deer in the headlights" look. He stood silently and impassively for the next command.

Charlie's refusal to flinch bothered Harry. He wanted to see fear.

"I bet you think you're some kind of stud, don't you, McDaniels … Pete's golden boy. You can't help sucking up to him, can you, you miserable ass kisser."

No, sir. Mr. Hartwick is my Firsty."

"Hartwick's a douche bag." Harry spat the words. "He couldn't lead his way out of a gunny sack."

Charlie remained silent; his eyes focused briefly on Harry to let him know his swagger did not intimidate him.

"Do you have anything to say, McDaniels?" Harry screamed at him in frustration. Charlie was sure his voice was carrying down the passageway.

"No, sir."

"Drop for twenty."

"Aye, aye, sir.

Charlie found an uncluttered area in the room and proceeded

to do twenty push-ups effortlessly.

"Twenty more, you maggot!"

"Aye, aye, sir."

Harry continued this game until Charlie had completed over two hundred push-ups. His arms began to ache and tremble.

"Keep going! Faster! Let's see if you're man enough to make two fifty."

"Aye, aye, sir," Charlie answered with a strained voice. A pool of sweat formed on the deck below his face.

At the two hundred and forty-first attempt, Charlie's arms refused to extend anymore. No amount of effort would do what his physical body would no longer allow. He lay exhausted on the floor, breathing heavily.

Harry stood over him with feigned contempt. He never knew a plebe who could do over two hundred pushups. He kicked Charlie in the ribs, careful not to break anything. Pain shot into his chest accompanied by sharp anger. Charlie prayed for self-control as he lay in a pool of his own sweat. He channeled his anger inside, creating the will and energy to keep going. With a short burst of strength, he reached two hundred and fifty push-ups.

"Get up, McDaniels."

"Aye, aye, sir," Charlie answered. His voice cracked as he struggled to get up.

Charlie remained braced against the wall as Harry put on his pants and began to dress for evening meal formation. He looked at Charlie one more time and said quietly, "Get out of here. Change your shirt. And don't you mention our little interlude this evening to Hartwick."

"Aye, aye, sir."

Charlie left quickly and returned to his room to prepare for another formation. He couldn't understand what he had done to make Dorfman so angry. He was grateful that this come-around was over. He knew there would be more.

HISTORY LESSONS

❋

At breakfast three days later, Pete asked Charlie to continue the history of the Vietnam War. Charlie stood rigidly at attention behind his chair and waited for the upper-class to sit. Harry sat across the table with a sneer over his round face.

The plebes sat in unison and braced on the very edge of their chairs. During breakfast, a cacophony of sounds from bowls of scrambled eggs banging on each table to the yelling and screaming at plebes from every table

Harry remained unusually reticent this morning. He seemed more interested in stuffing his mouth with honey and biscuits than joining in the hazing.

After the pancakes had gone around the table, Pete tapped on his milk glass with his spoon. Conversation stopped.

"Mr. McDaniels!" Pete commanded.

"Yes, sir."

"What happened in Vietnam today?"

"Sir, a company of South Vietnamese suffered heavy causalities today in a conflict with Communist forces near Cambodia."

"Any of our guys hurt?"

"Sir, the company was led by Green Berets. No U.S. causalities reported, sir."

"Good. Anything else?"

"We are continuing our sweep into the DMZ to remove the two North Vietnamese divisions positioned there. Over six thousand Marines were airlifted into the DMZ. B-52s continue to bomb suspected targets."

"Causalities?"

"Sixty-five Marines killed and seventy-seven wounded, sir."

"What about the VC?"

"Sir, 742 North Vietnamese are reported killed."

"Another victory for the good guys, right, McDaniels?" Harry interjected.

"Sir, such loss of life is no victory for either side."

Harry growled back "Don't question me, you little shit!"

Pete held up a hand, "Stop baiting him for an opinion, Harry. Let him continue."

"I don't care what he thinks."

Pete ignored Harry's petulance and turned to Charlie. "Mr. McDaniels, what happened in Vietnam after we changed sides and supported the French? How did we help France?"

Charlie lay his fork quietly on the side of his plate and took a deep breath.

"Sir, by 1952, the U.S. was funding 80% of the French in its war against the Ho Chi Minh's National Liberation Front. By 1954, we had invested over two billion dollars propping up the French puppet government in Saigon."

"Two *billion*? That's a lot of money, isn't it Mr. McDaniels?" Pete commented.

"Yes, sir. However, Russia and China stood with and backed Ho Chi Minh's Democratic Republic of Vietnam. Both countries were supplying aid and arms. Both countries were our enemies.

"Sir, China had become a communist country. We worried about the spread of Communism to Vietnam and beyond—the Domino Theory, sir. It was a huge deal at the time, sir."

"Why?" Dave asked.

"America thought of Communism as an evil force that would undermine democracy in countries nearby—especially Vietnam."

"And what do you say?" Harry taunted.

"That doesn't matter, Harry," Pete said tersely. "He's not required to provide editorial comment."

"Sir," Charlie continued while Harry sulked, "the French democracy represented what we believed would serve as a barrier to further Communist expansion from the north. We supported France even though it's colonial empire represented oppressive control of a sovereign country.

"We knew Ho Chi Minh was a fervent and popular leader, sir.

Nevertheless, we supported French colonialism as the lesser of two evils. We assumed that with enough arms and money France could eventually overpower Ho Chi Minh in the end.

"However, in 1954, sirs, at the battle of Dien Bien Phu, French military forces were soundly defeated by the Viet Minh. France realized it was fighting an unwinnable war and retreated, eventually leaving Vietnam altogether.

"Who was left?"

"Only us, sir...and the remnants of the French puppet government, the Republic of South Vietnam."

"So what did we do?" Dave asked.

"Sir, when General Eisenhower became president, he decided to prop up the old French Republic, empowering it with more arms and other military aid. We assumed that we could make it strong enough to defeat Ho Chi Minh and the Viet Minh army."

"Wait a minute," Dave asked. "Didn't we give the Viet Minh a shitload of arms before the French took over?

"Yes, sir, we did. We once were the Viet Minh's main supplier of arms—the same arms now used against us."

"What about two billion we gave the French? That buys a hell of a lot of firepower."

"There's not much accounting for it, sir. Most of the weapons likely fell into the hands of Ho Chi Minh."

"Do you have a problem with that, McDaniels?" Harry asked.

"It's just a fact, sir."

"Go ahead," Pete said. "What about South Vietnam's government?"

"Sir, the government was corrupt and unpopular with the local people. A lot of American financial aid wound up in politician's' hands. The president, Bo Dai, and his cabinet bribed their way to popularity. Friends, supporters and relatives all occupied prestigious and lucrative positions in Bo Dai's government."

"Fuck that!" another blurted. "We should have bailed. What was the point?"

"To defeat communism, sir."

"We should have nuked Hanoi then. That would have stopped them."

"That would have started World War III, sir."

"How do you know that?"

"Russia and China are formidable opponents, sir."

Pete interrupted. He didn't want Charlie in an unwinnable argument.

"Let's stop there, Mr. McDaniels," he said. "We'll continue the subject later."

"Aye, aye, sir.

Pete looked around the table. No one spoke. It was hard to guess what they were thinking. Regardless, he intended to ask Charlie to continue tomorrow.

Two days later, Charlie finished another summary of the war headlines. Pete waited until everyone was served before tapping the side of his water glass.

"Guys, I'd like to have Mr. McDaniels continue with the history of the war. We'll keep it short."

The table returned a collective shrug. Charlie's reports had become almost routine by now.

"Mr. McDaniels."

"Yes, sir."

"A couple of days ago you left us with the impression that we were in bed with some banana republic ridding the world of communism."

"Sir, we propped up the South Vietnam government for years. China and Russia propped up the north. It was a stalemate.

"In 1954, the Geneva Accords divided Vietnam into two zones—North and South. Ho Chi Minh controlled the North; Ngo Dinh Diem and his government were given jurisdiction in the southern zone."

"Seems like a fair compromise for starters," a second classman ventured.

"Yes sir, in theory. But Ho Chi Minh didn't want half the pie. It would be like us giving everything west of the Mississippi to another country."

"No personal analogies, Mr. McDaniels," Pete cautioned.

"Aye, aye, sir. Ho Chi Minh wanted *all* of Vietnam. He was fighting a patriotic war."

"So, what?" A Third Classman named Sam said.

"Sir, the division of Vietnam was to be temporary. Free elections were to determine which government would assume power.

"Nothing wrong with that, is there?" Sam asked.

"No, sir. Except we knew that there was no way Diem could defeat Ho Chi Minh in a free election. Diem was corrupt; our aid never reached the local people. The country remained weak and unenthusiastic about democracy.

"Ho Chi Minh on the other hand, sir, was the most popular leader in all of Vietnam. We knew Diem could never beat him. The whole country would become communist if left to the people."

"So, what was the outcome?"

"The U.S. intervened, sir. The CIA stalled and ultimately prevented elections that would likely bring Ho Chi Minh to power."

"That's bullshit, McDaniels," Craig said. "We wouldn't do that!"

"Were the elections ever held?" Pete asked.

"No, sir."

"Are you suggesting the CIA intentionally block free elections?" a Second Classman asked. "That's pretty hard to believe, you know."

Charlie heard the anger in his voice—anger directed at Charlie for even suggesting manipulation of the voting process by America, the country these men pledged to serve.

"Sir, I'm not suggesting," Charlie answered carefully. "The elections never happened. The CIA played a part in stopping them."

"Where are you getting this info?" Dave asked.

"In the library, sir."

"Listen, mister," Harry spoke out. "We do what we have to do to defeat communism. Do you have a problem with that?"

"Sir, it isn't our right to interfere with the free will of the people, regardless of who they support. We lead by example, not by interfering with the rights of a sovereign country."

"So, you're sympathizing with the Communists again?" Harry asked scornfully.

"I disagree with the ideology of communism, sir."

"Answer the fucking question!"

Charlie had trapped himself by speaking his mind. He couldn't help himself.

"No, sir. I'm not a Communist sympathizer."

"That's enough, for now, Mr. McDaniels," Pete interrupted. "We'll continue this discussion later. Continue your research, the more you learn, the better you'll understand our policies and decisions. Don't second guess or make judgments without having *all* the background info."

"Aye, aye, sir."

After the table had emptied, Charlie sat alone picking at leftovers. He hadn't made any friends this morning.

❋

The vivid composition of colors fall had brought to the campus was fading. The huge oak and maple trees that lined Stribling Walk discarded their leaves everywhere. Charlie walked to class each day as leaves gently fluttered around him. It was a beautiful time of the year.

He longed to be somewhere else.

Charlie's schedule grew even more demanding. With classes, sports and the demands of upperclassmen, Charlie had little time for much else—except his research on Vietnam.

In his room, Charlie was subject to spontaneous visits and

inspections from upperclassmen. There was no place to escape.

Charlie pushed through a heavy academic load—courses through which he struggled continually. Most were of little interest to him. To combat boredom, he recalled happier days with his old band. He wondered if they were still together. Had they found a replacement for Charlie?

Each day followed the one before with the same monotonous routine. Charlie found ways to cope. He had to.

Charlie knew there was no way out. He felt trapped; he *had* to stick with it.

He had let others shape and direct his path. Were it not for his father and brother, Charlie would have been long gone, happily attending some co-ed college. It was a favorite fantasy.

His frustration and anger grew—anger at himself.

❋

The table was in a good mood this morning. Navy had beaten Notre Dame Saturday. The Army game was only two weeks away. Charlie continued his research and reporting of ongoing war facts.

On a rainy Monday morning, Charlie sat stiffly on the edge of his chair and stared straight ahead while his table filled for breakfast. Filipino stewards hustled back and forth; wheeling out trays of platters filled with pancakes and hash-brown potatoes. He and his fellow plebes waited patiently to see what remnants of the main course were still available.

Pete sat at the head of the table and watched Charlie answer questions directed at him by others. He handled himself well under pressure despite his adversaries. It was time to continue with Charlie's report. Pete was curious to see how he would conduct himself in the presence of increasingly adverse news from the newspapers. He wanted Charlie to continue with the war's history.

Pete tapped again on his water glass to gain attention.

"Excuse me, gentlemen. I'd like Mr. McDaniels to continue reporting on the history of Vietnam. Can I have a few minutes of silence?"

Several around the table nodded and the conversation stopped.

"Mister McDaniels."

"Yes, sir."

"So, France was gone, defeated by Ho Chi Minh. We were in bed with a dysfunctional puppet government. What happened next? You have five minutes."

"Five minutes?" Harry whined.

Pete glared at Harry briefly before continuing. "Are you prepared, Mr. McDaniels?

"Yes, sir," Charlie said as he lay his fork on the table.

"Proceed."

"Aye, aye, sir. President Eisenhower gave the Republic of South Vietnam as much military and economic aid as Congress would permit. Our allies believed the U.S. was containing communism and pledged their support. We began a nation-building program in the South Vietnamese regime."

"Did our allies participate?"

"No, sir."

"What did we do?"

"Sir, we kept sending arms and money."

"Did we make progress?"

"No, sir. The Chinese and Russians countered by sending aid to the North.

"Ho Chi Minh had declared a 'People's War' to defeat South Vietnam and reunite his country. He had broad support from his countrymen in the north. The People's War went on to become the Second Indochina War and, as we became more involved, the Vietnam War.

"The Soviet Union proposed a permanent solution by dividing the country into North and South Vietnam. China went along with the idea."

"I assume Ho Chi Minh was forced to go along if he wanted aid from China."

"Yes, sir. It was an effort to contain Communism to a relatively small area in the North."

"So, what happened?" Sam asked from the end of the table.

"We refused. We didn't want *any* more communist countries in the region."

"You don't sound very happy, McDaniels," Harry said. "I bet you'd like to see another Communist country, wouldn't you?"

"No, sir."

"Bullshit!"

"That's enough, Harry," Pete said and nodded toward Charlie to continue.

"We were committed to defeating communist expansion. President Kennedy sent 400 Green Berets to South Vietnam in 1961. Military advisors and helicopters followed to transport and direct South Vietnamese troops in battle. We soon had 16,000 military advisors involved in the conflict."

"Do you think we should have pulled out then and let Ho Chi Minh's Viet Cong take over the country?" another asked skeptically.

"In retrospect and with hindsight, yes sir, I do. We were taking combat causalities. Our international reputation suffered. A lot of deaths could have been prevented had we been more willing to negotiate with Russia and China."

Harry raised his head and glared at Charlie. "No one here cares what you think, McDaniels. You're too stupid to give any of us your opinion!"

Pete interrupted at once. "He's only answering the question, Harry. He hasn't volunteered anything."

"Yeah, but he's telling us our country was *wrong*, for chrissake, Pete!"

Pete signaled the table as a referee. "Hey guys, let's hear some reasons why Mr. McDaniels is wrong. Does anyone here disagree with the facts as he has presented them?"

After a pause, Pete looked at Charlie carefully. "Okay, let's wrap it up, Mr. McDaniels," he said. You have one minute left."

"Aye, aye, sir."

"With the approval of Congress, the United States became heavily invested in Vietnam in the sixties.

"At first, we had the popular support at home. Soon, we were spending two million dollars a day to oppose Ho Chi Minh."

"That's bullshit, plebe, a Second Classman interrupted. "Where are you getting this information?"

"Sir, from the encyclopedia."

"Go ahead, Mr. McDaniels."

"Despite all the aid and combat support, the forces of South Vietnam could not push back Ho Chi Minh's guerrillas. We continued sending aid, believing, at some point, with enough money and arms, Ho Chi Minh and the Viet Minh would fall, and democracy would be restored in all of Vietnam. The more money we sent, the more South Vietnam wanted. It was a vicious circle; we were sucked into a conflict that made no rational sense."

Harry shot back, "McDaniels you better keep your opinions to yourself. You sound like a fucking pacifist again."

"Aye, aye, sir."

Pete held up his hand, "Harry's right. 'Pacifist' is a dirty word around here. Be careful."

"Aye, aye, sir. I was second-guessing. Sorry."

"Go ahead."

"When President Johnson came in office in 1963, the American public was becoming disenchanted with the war. We had little to show for the aid we were giving South Vietnam and the American lives lost in the process.

"President Johnson asked Congress for increased funding and ground support. However, the Senate, responding to public criticism from their constituents, refused to go along.

"The President's support for the Vietnam War dwindled. He hadn't the political capital to continue sending men and money to the war. A growing number of politicians wanted us to walk away and cut our losses."

"Obviously, that didn't happen. What changed?"

"The Tonkin Gulf incident, sir."

"Let's stop here, Mr. McDaniels, Pete said.

"Aye, aye, sir," Charlie answered appreciatively.

Pete looked around the table. "Should we let Mr. McDaniels report on the Tonkin Gulf incident another day?"

The majority nodded.

Pete would wait a while to let emotions cool.

*

As the cold November winds, rushed across the Chesapeake Bay, Charlie continued to survive the rigors of Plebe Year. Time crawled. Only the upcoming Army-Navy game and Christmas leave provided relief from the depressing routine.

Charlie's breakfast news briefing continued. For two minutes, he recited stories and statistics as reported in Pete's *Baltimore Sun*—from battles and casualties in the field to political developments at home.

Charlie described every air strike and ground campaign—every victory and every defeat. He reported U.S. casualties that continued every day. It depressed him.

The loss of so many young men, most poor and uneducated, drafted with no recourse of their own. Meanwhile, the "fortunate sons" found ways to avoid service.

Fifty thousand American men had died attempting to stop North Vietnam and the spread of Communism. Was there any rational justification for the tremendous loss of life? He couldn't find it.

To Charlie, it was an exercise in futility. No one at the Academy cared whether the actions of their country were right or wrong. Most only wanted to join the fight. They were staunch supporters who cheered the troops onward to a victory they considered inevitable.

Over five hundred young men died each month, most in dense jungles in an insignificant country. These were lives tragically ended. With each life lost, dreams and hopes vanished. The lives of mothers, girlfriends, wives, and children—ruined.

Charlie read that reported enemy losses were over twice the number of American deaths. He pictured the young Viet Cong who experienced the same horrendous tragedies; so many who likewise left loved ones behind to defend their country from outside invaders. At least they had fought intensely and proudly for their just cause.

They died for a reason, Charlie thought bitterly.

His increasing scope of knowledge created more judgment and disillusionment. Charlie could see that his growing understanding of the Vietnam conflict could lead him down the road of cynicism and disapproval. As his attitude shifted, it was inevitable that he would become more isolated.

He wanted to be done with further history on Vietnam. His reputation was in trouble. He *had* to be careful. He was wandering into a trap, a no-win situation. Surely Pet could see where this was leading him.

Charlie would occasionally express his negativity to his roommates. They wanted no part of Charlie's ideology, however. Like his tablemates in the mess hall, Don and Steve refused to question the war in Vietnam. Blind obedience and faithful acceptance of their military and political leaders dictated their attitudes.

❋

Pete Harkins sat in his room with his feet propped on his desk. Staring into the night, he thought about Charlie's situation. He had grown fond of his young plebe despite the fact that he struggled with military bearing. Charlie was a smart guy out of his element.

He admired Charlie's resolve to question why—a rare quality

in a young officer. However, Pete knew the consequences Charlie faced each time he expressed negativity. The more he understood this quiet and engaging young man, the more he wanted to help him.

How would Charlie resolve his internal conflicts? He probably knew more about Vietnam than anyone at the academy. Pete thought about canceling the Vietnam reports for the sake of Charlie's reputation. Charlie had to make the decision himself. No one would do it for him. Does he stay here and remain silent or express his views and risk washing out on military demerit.

Pete decided to force that decision.

Tomorrow, he will ask Charlie to continue the history report.

❋

"Mr. McDaniels," Pete said at breakfast the following day.

"Yes, sir."

"What was the Tonkin Gulf Resolution and how did it affect the course of the war in Vietnam?"

"Sir, it was a resolution passed by Congress that authorized increased military action in Vietnam."

"What precipitated it?"

"Sir, on 31 July 1964, three North Vietnamese torpedo boats attacked the *USS Maddox* twenty-six miles east of the North Vietnam coast near Than Hua."

"What was the *Maddox* doing so close to the coastline, Mr. McDaniels?"

"Sir, the Maddox was supporting covert actions along the North Vietnamese coast."

"What kind of actions?"

"Sir, the CIA was blowing up bridges and roadways in the north. The *Maddox* was inside Vietnam's territorial waters, aiding and directing CIA commando forces."

"Come on, McDaniels, that's a crock of shit!" Sam said at the end of the table. "Where are you getting this crap?"

"From the library, sir. I've read the microfilmed news accounts in the papers for several days after the incident sir."

"What else did you find?" Pete asked

"Sir, the attack on the Maddox was reported as unprovoked. It angered the American people and became a rallying cry. Until then, President Johnson had been unable to obtain the support from Congress needed to escalate the ar."

Charlie paused for a sip of water.

"What happened next, Mr. McDaniels?"

"President Johnson retaliated. He had the support he needed at home. We sent sixty-four fighter planes in to bomb Hanoi. Two were shot down. The first American POW was taken, sir.

"It was the Tonkin Gulf Resolution that gave President Johnson virtually unlimited authority to go to war. No one questioned the attack on the *Maddox*. It was assumed to be true."

"What do you think, McDaniels?"

"The Maddox posed a threat to the Vietnamese people. The attack could have been defensive. It's what we would do if the Russians were patrolling our sovereign waters."

"Are you saying the government lied to the American people?"

"Enough!" Pete quickly interrupted before anyone could react.

Pete looked in the eyes of those around the table. Reactions ranged from anger to confusion. He would give Charlie time now, over the Christmas holidays and beyond.

❋

Later that afternoon, Charlie was in Pete's room for his weekly status report. Breaking tradition, Pete rose from his chair and made direct eye contact as he spoke.

"Mr. McDaniels, let's cool it with the history lessons. No one around the table is comfortable with what you say and the way you say it. You've become the subject of criticism. We can't have that if you want to get through this year."

"Yes, sir." Charlie felt the slow creep of the demon of disapproval. He shook it off.

"We've talked about this before. I understand your need to speak your truth. I admire that you say what you mean and won't back down."

"Thank you, sir."

"Maybe after Christmas, we can continue."

"Yes, sir."

"Keep reading and reporting the headlines from my paper. If you see something that bothers you about the war, bring it to me first."

"Yes, sir, I will."

❋

Charlie didn't speak with his brother until November. One Saturday, he just appeared as Charlie and his roommates were shining shoes. They heard the distinctive sound of an Academy ring knock softly against the door's frosted glass.

Charlie's looked up to see Frank standing in the doorway. Charlie remained seated with his feet on the desk as his roommates stood at attention.

"Hello, Frank," he said with no emotion. "It's been a while. What brings you here?"

Frank sat on Charlie's bunk after shaking his hand. "Carry on, guys. I'm just checking in with my little brother."

"Where've you been? It's been two months."

"I know, I know," Frank said with some embarrassment. "Dad told me not to interact with you for a while—said you needed time to grow without your family's influence and help."

"Really? I thought you were going to be my mentor?"

"I can't, man."

"Why not?"

"Dad wants me to keep a low profile."

"Is that what you want to do?"

"It doesn't matter what I think. Dad calls the shots."

"No, he doesn't. You should be able to think for yourself, shouldn't you?"

"Look, man, you're in the Navy now. Dad wants you free of any coattails, any advantage. He wants to see how well you survive on your own."

"Well, take a look around. What do you think?"

"You've lost weight."

"No shit. I'm starving half the time."

For the first time, Frank laughed. "Yeah, I lost fifteen pounds myself plebe year."

"Tell Dad I'm really gung-ho. I want to set this place on fire."

"That's the spirit!"

"No. I mean *really*."

Frank laughed. "I've been there. It'll get better, believe me."

After chatting briefly about the Academy, Charlie brought up his research on Vietnam.

"You want to *go* to that place, Frank?"

Frank was stunned. He looked at Charlie as if he came from another planet.

"Man, you better not talk like that around Dad."

"Let's hope the subject doesn't come up then."

Frank shrugged and stood. He was uncomfortable with Charlie's attitude.

"Look, I've got to go. Don't *ever* criticize the war around here. Seriously!"

"Don't worry. I'm not stupid," Charlie said. "Thanks for stopping by."

✵

On a dark and gloomy late November morning, Charlie stood in the passageway next to Pete's room. He unfolded the Baltimore Sun and scanned the headlines as he had done for the last three months.

It was a slow news day in Vietnam. The only relevant news Charlie noted was a story published by the Navy Public Affairs Office regarding the defoliation program. The *Sun* reported that American officials in Saigon released the Navy's final study on the environmental impact of its chemical arsenal. No humans or animals would be in any danger from exposure to the chemicals.

What chemicals?

He hastily finished reading and returned the newspaper to Pete's door.

What the hell is Agent Orange?

❋

In the library, Charlie learned that President Kennedy authorized the use of the chemical defoliants in Vietnam in 1961. Called Operation Ranchhand, its objective was to destroy the jungle that provided cover for the Viet Cong. The defoliant was called Agent Orange because Dow and Monsanto delivered it in fifty-five-gallon drums with an orange stripe on the side.

Enough chemical defoliants were dropped by B-52's to destroy one and a half million acres of jungle and rainforest.

One and a half million acres! That can't be right.

Charlie researched the chemical compounds in Agent Orange. What he found was unsettling. He learned that half of Agent Orange consists of a chemical called dioxin. Dioxin is a poison.

Something told Charlie to keep digging—to find out how lethal Agent Orange was. The library had little information on the subject. Charlie would ask his chemistry professor this afternoon.

Charlie had a free period later in the day. He stood at attention in the offices of the Chemistry Department, hoping his professor was free.

Luckily, Professor Stone walked in a minute later. He was a kindly civilian professor in his late fifties. He peered at Charlie through thick spectacles and recognized him at once.

"Mr. McDaniels," he greeted, "what brings you to the Chemistry Department?

"Sir, I'm trying to find out about a defoliant called Agent Orange. Can you tell me about it?"

Professor Stone's eyebrows rose. "Come into my office. Do you have time?"

"Yes, sir."

Charlie followed Professor Stone to his office. It was a small and cluttered room with a lone window looking towards the Severn.

"Move those books on the chair, Charlie, and have a seat."

"Thank you, sir."

Professor Stone sat at his desk and folded his hands.

"No one's ever asked me about dioxin, Charlie. Why do *you* want to know?"

"I'm wondering why we're using it in the war."

"Ah, good question. I take it you don't approve."

"I don't know, sir. I was hoping you could tell me more about it."

"Dioxin is a man-made organic compound, a byproduct really. It's one of the most deadly toxic chemicals we have ever produced."

"Then why would we use it against another country?

"It's classified as a 'defoliant', Charlie—not a chemical weapon. That's how we justify its use."

The professor removed his glasses and wiped them absently. He had to be careful how he addressed this bright young midshipman.

Professor Stone looked into Charlie's eyes. "There are many forms of dioxin. The dioxin in Agent Orange is fifty times more deadly than typical agricultural herbicides."

"Fifty times?"

Professor Stone nodded. "Agent Orange is over half dioxin. You can imagine its effect when dumped over a village from a B-52."

"It's said to be harmless, sir."

"Do you believe that?"

"Not anymore, sir. Where does it come from?"

"Dow Chemical…and Monsanto. It used to be a waste byproduct. Now, these companies sell it to the government. It's quite profitable."

"What about the environment, the farmland, the wildlife, the civilians?" Charlie asked. He was stunned.

"We're at war, Charlie. Collateral damage is inevitable."

"Will the rain forests grow back?"

"Perhaps," Professor Stone answered. "Not in our lifetime though—not for generations. The environmental balances of the rainforests have been destroyed. It remains to be seen whether they will ever come back."

Charlie could only shake his head.

Where's the outrage? Don't people realize what we're doing over there?

"Are we using other chemicals over there, Professor Stone?"

The professor shifted in his chair, reflecting quietly on Charlie's question.

"I suppose you know about Napalm? It's another chemical compound we use over there."

"No, sir, I don't."

There's more?

"Napalm is also a chemical defoliant, a mixture of plastic polystyrene, hydrocarbon benzene, and gasoline. It is a substance with the consistency of jelly, usually sprayed from B-52's. When ignited, Napalm sticks to anything and can burn up to ten minutes."

"So we're using both chemicals over there, sir?"?"

"Yes. Both are powerful defoliants, Charlie. Napalm burns at over two thousand degrees. It sticks to the skin and is unbearably painful, usually causing death. It'll defoliate a rain forest instantly."

"And the civilians. Do they get sprayed with Napalm?"

"Only if they're in the way."

Charlie stood, visibly shaken.

"Will you excuse me, Professor? I have to go now."

"Of course," he answered standing and extending his hand. "I know plebes rarely have much time to themselves."

"Thank you for taking the time to explain this to me."

"You're welcome."

Charlie shook his hand and thanked the professor once again.

Professor Stone watched him leave. He liked Charlie, even if he wasn't one of his best students. To his knowledge, he was the first midshipman to question the use of chemical defoliants in Vietnam. He appeared upset.

Charlie walked into the gray misty air and headed back to Bancroft Hall. He had a navigation class in fifteen minutes.

I have to see Pete.

However, what Charlie learned the following day eclipsed his disgust about the use of chemical defoliants.

❋

The following day, 28th of November 1969, would mark a turning point in Charlie's life. That day, the *Baltimore Sun* disclosed horrendous facts and photographs that would forever sour him on American policies and its purpose in this small country.

The Government, he read, announced that a Lt. W. Calley was indicted for killing 107 Vietnamese civilians in cold blood. It was the lead story. The photographs sickened him.

He couldn't avoid the story. He would have to report it at breakfast this morning.

In the mess hall, Pete casually asked Charlie how he was doing.

Charlie's turned and looked at Pete. Turmoil and confusion clouded Charlie's blue eyes.

"Eyes in the boat, mister," Pete commanded halfheartedly. There was something in Charlie's expression that had never been there before.

"Aye, aye, sir."

"Something bothering you?"

Charlie sighed and hesitated. He didn't *want* to go on.

Pete poured a cup of coffee and waited.

"Mr. McDaniels. What going on with you? Are you all right?"

"Sir, it's the news today. The lead story in the paper is about My Lai."

"Where's My Lai?"

"Quang Ngai province, sir—near the coast."

"Okay. What happened in My Lai, Mr. McDaniels?"

"Sir, the Army has announced the general court-martial of a Lieutenant William Calley," he answered, stammering and looked down at his plate.

"You're at attention, plebe!" Harry interrupted.

"Wait a minute," Pete continued as he held his hand up. "Get your head together, Mr. McDaniels. Who's Calley and what's he charged with?"

"Sir, Calley killed one hundred and nine civilians, women and children in cold blood."

Pete's expression was one of disbelief. "He killed women and children? Are you sure about that?"

"Yes, sir. The lieutenant is charged with premeditated murder."

The table was silent. Everyone was looking at Charlie. No one wanted to accept his words.

"What the hell?" Harry finally responded. "What else, McDaniels?"

'Sir, the Cleveland Plain Dealer has published pictures of women and children lying in a ditch along a dirt road. U.S. soldiers gunned them down. The *Baltimore Sun* picked up the story as its lead. I read it this morning."

"When did this happened?" Dave asked skeptically. "Yesterday?"

"No, sir. It happened a year and a half ago."

"Oh, come on, McDaniels, surely someone would say something about that when it happened. How could something like that be concealed?"

"The Army apparently covered it up, sir."

"You can't be serious."

Pete shook his head sadly and looked at Charlie "This just can't be possible."

Once again, Charlie had brought them ugly facts about the war. However, no one would shoot the messenger this time.

⁂

Over the following week, Charlie learned more about the *My Lai Massacre*. There was much more.

"Reports surface that the My Lai massacre of March 1968 was carried out by 60 to 70 U.S. soldiers who killed some 100 Vietnamese men, women and children in less than 20 horrific minutes. The incident ranks as the most serious atrocity yet attributed to American troops in a war that is already well known for its particular savagery."

The same chilling black and white picture published by the *Sun* accompanied the short article. Charlie looked again at the lifeless and innocent mothers and children by the side of the road. He felt he was going to be sick.

How in the hell could soldiers commit such an atrocity?

Is this what war represents? How can this happen in the United States Army?

Someone suppressed the incident.

But how?

There must have been eyewitnesses—a whole platoon was involved, and no one spoke up? Had the upper command concealed incident? Did they think the story would go away?

What about the honor code?

⁂

Charlie needed support. That evening we visited his brother's room for the first time.

He knocked on Frank's door.

"Charlie! Come in. What brings you here all of a sudden?"

"Can I sit down?"

"Sure. What's on your mind?"

Frank's roommate watched Charlie sit on his brother's bunk. Thankfully, he decided to go somewhere else so they could talk privately.

"It's about the news over the last two days."

"My Lai?"

"Yeah."

"We don't know all the facts yet, Charlie. Don't get your skivvies all bunched up. I'm sure there are more facts coming out. The press can be overzealous about such things—let's wait until there's more follow-up from the media."

"Follow up? Look at the fucking pictures, Frank!"

"Hey, calm down, Charlie. Let's give it some time before you do something drastic. Dad will have a shit-fit if you mouth off about that."

"Do you think I care?"

"I said relax man. Don't talk like that. Think of Dad before you say anything crazy."

"I don't want to think about Dad!" Charlie's voice was rising. "You know what really upsets me?"

"Go ahead," Frank replied, his voice heavy with condescension.

"It took a year and a half before the Army admitted there ever *was* a massacre—and that was only after a guy sent letters and photos to Congress. The company and battalion commanders must have known about it. It was a major operation in Quang Ngai province. They *had* to know."

"I'm sure there's a valid reason."

"Yeah—to cover their asses."

"Careful," Frank cautioned with an authoritarian stare. "These are superior officers you're talking about."

"Superior? Not to me they're not."

"Damn it, Charlie. Show some respect or leave. That's an order."

"Don't give me that 'order' shit, Frank!"

Frank stood angrily and pointed angrily to the door. "Get out, Charlie, before I put you on report!"

Charlie stood and walked quickly toward the door. He bristled at Frank's lack of sensitivity. He grabbed the doorknob and looked back coldly before he left. "You know what, Frank?" he said. "This place and West Point treat the Honor Code as if it was the holy grail. How could West Point graduates conceal this for so long? Where's the morality? Where's the honor?"

"Dad will have a plausible explanation," Frank said.

"Plausible? Look, he'll whitewash it the same as his buddies did."

"He's been a Marine for a long time," Frank said. "Don't underestimate him."

"Bullshit!

"I said get out, Charlie. Don't make me put you on report. I'll have to, you know." Both men were shouting at each other.

"Go ahead. Put your own brother on report." Charlie shot back sarcastically.

Frank took a deep breath, struggling to gain his composure. "You've always been a screw-up, Charlie. Maybe if you listened more closely to Dad, you'd think differently."

Charlie was close to the boiling point. "He doesn't have *all* the answers, you know."

"I'm not listening to this," Frank said. "Get out—now!"

❋

In the weeks that followed, My Lai and Calley dominated the headlines. The subject was inescapable in the news media.

The irony of Nixon's words played over in Charlie's mind.

"North Vietnam cannot defeat or humiliate the United States. Only

Americans can do that."

The subsequent photos in *Time* and *Life* magazines were chilling and heartbreaking. Someone had taken a picture of a group of four adult Vietnamese women and three small children, huddled together just before members of Calley's platoon murdered them.

The look of terror on the old woman's face as her family huddled behind her was one he could never forget. She looked like she was pleading with the soldiers—to no avail. Moments later, they were dead.

CHAPTER FIVE

Christmas Leave

Present Time

The old man hesitated. What are you waiting for?

He emptied the bottle of Ativan into his left hand and clutched the pills tightly so as not to spill any.

His right hand shook spasmodically. He slammed it on the dirty vanity with all the force he was able to muster.

The pain was sharp. It traveled instantly to his wrist, arm, and shoulder. Was his reflection mocking him? He looked down to avoid the eyes that would judge him one more time.

His throbbing hand picked up a well-used paper cup. He filled the cup with warm water from the rusty faucet.

This was it.

The demons laughed at him.

1969

Christmas leave arrived at last. It was a joyous moment when the doors to Bancroft Hall swung open at noon allowing a mass exodus of excited midshipmen. Charlie joined the throngs and headed for the bus station as fast as he could. He assumed his brother was doing the same — they would likely meet at the boarding platform for the next bus to Washington.

Charlie spotted Frank in the terminal and approached tentatively with his characteristic crooked grin.

"Look, Charlie," he said, "let's bury our differences for now. I don't want to screw up Christmas for Mom and Dad."

"I couldn't agree more. No arguments," Charlie said. "Let's call a truce over the holidays."

Frank looked at him and extended a gloved hand. Charlie smiled and shook his brother's hand.

With that, they boarded the bus.

"Be nice if they would pick us up," Charlie mused as the bus left the station and turned on West Avenue.

"You know Dad."

Just before dusk, the Greyhound pulled into the Washington, D.C. station. General and Mrs. McDaniels waited in the adjacent parking lot. Frank spotted their car from the bus window and made sure he was the first off when the bus stopped. Charlie paused, thinking.

How hard would it have been to pick us up in Annapolis?

He knew not to second-guess his father's motives, however. He left the bus and joined the happy reunion in the parking lot.

His mother broke into tears when she saw him. She hugged him tightly and said, "Charlie! You're so skinny! I need to fatten you up before you go back."

"You boys look magnificent!" she added, surveying them together.

"They're men, not boys anymore, Melinda," the general corrected. "Get in the back seat, you two! Let's go!"

Charlie wished his father had not worn a uniform. Christmas lights reflected from his medals and insignia. He found it intimidating.

Charlie opened the sedan's passenger door for his mother and slid into the back seat with Frank. The general started the engine and pulled out of the bus station parking lot and onto New York Avenue.

Charlie couldn't believe he was free from the dark and oppressing institution he now called home. It was surreal—as if all a dream, as if the nightmare of last six months never happened.

Their father expertly negotiated the heavy traffic until they reached the freeway. Ten minutes later, they crossed the Anacostia River and entered Fort McNair where the Anacostia meets the Potomac.

Entering the base, they stopped briefly at the main gate. The two guards on duty recognized the general's car and executed flawless salutes. They turned on to Second Avenue at the Officer's Club and followed it up a row of modest officers' housing on the Potomac side. The neighborhood changed as they drove, the houses became larger and statelier. These were the houses reserved for generals and admirals.

At last, they pulled into the driveway of the familiar home with the full front porch. It had been home to Charlie for the last year. He was glad to be back.

The brothers grabbed their gear and headed for the front door. Inside the living room, the furniture was the same as Charlie had left it six months ago. He dropped his duffel bag at the foot of the stairs. His mother rushed to him and hugged him again fiercely.

"I'm so glad to have you back, Charlie. I've missed you so much."

"Me, too, Mom. You can't imagine how much!"

"Put on some comfortable clothes for a change."

Charlie nodded with a smile and lugged his duffle bag up the stairs to his old room. He found a pair of old jeans and a sweater. It felt good to wear civilian clothes again. When he returned to the living room, he felt like a new man.

Everyone sat around in the living room. Frank had decided to leave his uniform on for a while longer. Charlie thought he was nuts. It was so good to be a civilian again!

His father scowled at Charlie's informal dress but said nothing. His mother beamed and said, "That's better. You look much more comfortable now."

"You know, Charles," the general commented with a frown, "officers should look their best—even when not in uniform. In my opinion, jeans are not acceptable attire for dinner, or anywhere, for that matter."

"For god's sake, let him relax, Buzz," Melinda said. "I told him to get comfortable."

The general scowled at her but said no more.

A steady rain had developed over the afternoon and into the early evening. Charlie said little during the cocktail hour. He drank several beers, watching Frank and his father dip wholeheartedly into the Jack Daniels. His mother sipped a glass of wine.

Abruptly, their father stood and proposed a toast, "Here's to Charlie's new chapter in manhood as a Midshipman Fourth Class at the Naval Academy." The general's volume increased as he spoke and raised his glass. The bourbon was kicking in.

"Thanks, Dad." Charlie cautiously replied. "It's good to be home again."

With any luck, it would not be a lengthy cocktail hour.

The general rattled the ice cubes in his tumbler. By habit, Charlie's mother rose to take his empty glass.

"Another, beer Charlie?" she asked.

"Yes, please, Mom. I can get it."

Why don't you just bring me a six-pack? This situation is way too awkward to withstand soberly.

"Get another bourbon for Frank, too," the general commanded.

Charlie hated how his father treated his mother, ordering her around like a servant. He stood to join her.

"Where are you going, Charles?"

"Just to see if I can help."

"Sit down. Your mother doesn't need any help."

Charlie ignored him and walked deliberately towards the kitchen. His mother urged him to return. She could already feel the friction between her husband and son. Nothing had changed.

"Go on back, Charlie. I'm all right," she said softly.

The general eyed Charlie sternly as he sat back down, but said nothing.

Frank spoke up to break the tension. He had a special announcement to make. "Well everybody," he announced with pride and smug authority, "I learned just a few days ago that I'm going to be the brigade commander for the winter set."

His father looked back with smug gratification. Genetic superiority flashed in his eyes.

"That's terrific news, son!" he said. "You'll be wearing six stripes. Well done! I was the Brigade Commander in 1942. I've known from the moment you signed on that you had it in you."

Frank beamed with happiness at the compliment. Charlie looked at both of them in their glory. He had about as much chance of being a six-striper as Harry Dorfman. To Charlie, it was just another unfavorable comparison.

"Well, Charles, aren't you going to congratulate you brother, too?"

"That's cool, Frank; nice going," Charlie answered. His tone was flat and expressionless.

A few cocktails later, dinner was ready. Everyone moved from the living to dining room. The general sat at the head of the table while Melinda busily brought bowls of mashed potatoes and vegetables from the kitchen. A bottle of red wine went around the table.

Charlie sipped his wine and looked at his family. He saw his brother and father differently now. Their gung-ho attitude about the war in Vietnam made no sense to him. Charlie's four months of research gave him an insight into the war that he doubted his father nor brother understood.

"Just imagine, son!" the general slurred with bravado. "In less than a year you'll graduate and be on your way to Nam. If you're lucky, you'll be a platoon leader—right in the middle of the action. Combat experience will toughen you even more and set you on the right career path. I can see you now, wading through the rice paddies. It'll be the best experience of your young life. Can't wait, can you?"

"No, sir. It'll be an honor defeating the spread of Communism in

Nam. Maybe Charlie and I can serve together over there one day."

Charlie looked back at his brother curiously.

When pigs dance, I will. Stop kissing dad's ass, Frank. You can't really buy into all that nonsense, can you?

"What about you, Charlie?" Frank asked his brother. "Do you think the war will wait for you to graduate?"

Charlie shrugged his shoulders. "Probably, at the rate it's going." There was undeniable sarcasm in his voice.

The general stared at Charlie peculiarly for an instant.

"Those young soldiers are so brave," Melinda quickly added. "You must be very proud, Buzz, to have such fine sons ready and willing to do their duty."

Big Frank nodded and took another long pull from his bourbon. He sensed hesitation from his youngest son as if he were holding back.

"You don't sound terribly enthusiastic, Charles," the general observed. "I would expect you to be grateful for the opportunity to serve your country after it put you through college."

At that moment, something snapped in Charlie's mind as if some profound awareness entered his thinking. He had to let it out; screw the consequences. He would no longer hide anymore.

"The Vietnam War isn't about liberation and defeating communism—it's about politics and power."

The general seemed stunned for a moment, as if at a loss for words. His face turned red. His response was punctuated with a fine spray that flew across the table.

"Goddamnit, Charles. I want to hear some respect!"

"This is not a respectable war, Dad," Charlie answered cautiously. "What about My Lai? Our guys just murdered women and children—in cold blood! It was a massacre. Where's the honor?"

There was dead silence around the table—a proverbial perfect storm simmered. Charlie looked at each of them. His mother looked down; his brother looked back with smug condescension.

"Sorry, Mom," Charlie amended. "This My Lai thing has upset

me."

After an awkwardly silent ten seconds, the general spoke, first quietly and steadily before exploding in anger. Charlie had ruined dinner.

"Never question the actions of your government," his father began, "*Never*! Do you understand?" He banged his fist on the table. "Jesus Christ, kid," he continued. "Those gooks were communists, Viet Cong waiting to kill us. That guy, Calley, should receive a Silver Star."

Charlie shook his head in disbelief. "Sure, Dad," he said with more than a trace of sarcasm. "Let's change the subject please."

His brother saw the frightening change in his father's eyes and stepped in quickly.

"You going out later, Charlie?" he asked.

"Not tonight. Tomorrow. I'm rehearsing with the band. We have a couple of gigs scheduled this week. I'm a little rusty. We need to practice."

The short interlude gave their father time to settle down. He set his tumbler slowly on the table and looked coldly at Charlie.

"Son, we're going to talk more about Vietnam. I want to see the same fire in your eyes as in Frank's. I'll set you straight, believe me."

"Sure, I'd be happy to talk about it."

Thankfully, the general backed away from the subject of Vietnam and made a surprise announcement of his own. It shifted the tone of the conversation away from Charlie.

"Well, everybody," he said forcefully, "*I've* just learned that I will receive orders soon for another tour in Nam. There's a promotion involved as well."

Charlie disliked the word "Nam"—it was a catchphrase as if Vietnam wasn't a real country.

"A promotion?" Frank exclaimed excitedly. "You'll be getting another star. That's great news, Dad!"

Charlie remained silent.

"When are you going?" Frank asked.

"Less than a month. I'll be over there when you graduate, Frank. Sorry I'll miss it. Maybe I'll see you there before my tour is up."

Charlie decided he needed to show some enthusiasm despite privately acknowledging that his father was only a tool of a government, hell-bent on destroying the whole country if need be.

"Where will you be stationed, Dad?" he asked.

"Twenty-Seventh Marines in Da Nang," he answered. "Do you know where that is, Charles?"

"I do. Will you be in command?"

"Of course."

"Will you spend much time in the bush?" Frank asked.

"As much as I can, son. I need to be with the action. It's who I am."

Charlie drained his wine glass and asked for a refill.

❋

And so went the Christmas holidays of 1969. It was a time of ostensible good cheer and relaxation in the McDaniels family. Although supposedly on vacation, the general went to his office every day. Charlie wondered why. He assumed his father was having an affair. He didn't care where his father was as long as it kept him out of the house.

Charlie decided silence was his best tactic.

Keep your mouth shut. Think of Mom.

How do I do that when my father thinks Lt. Calley is a hero?

Charlie felt ungrounded; he had difficulty concentrating. Rehearsal with the band wasn't what he had hoped it would be. Charlie was lead guitar and now, quite rusty. The band was never the same after he left for Annapolis. He doubted it would stay together much longer.

While the general pretended to be at work, Charlie was able to spend time alone with his mother. They talked, they laughed, and they jammed.

"You've changed, Charlie," she said one day. "I can see it. Something's not right, is it?"

"It's the war, Mom. I know too much about it to support it anymore. I wouldn't go if the Navy ordered me there."

"Choices. So many in life, Charlie, every one a crap shoot. Go with your instincts, go with what feels right inside. Don't let *anyone* tell you otherwise."

"And you've changed as well, Mom."

Melinda smiled. "I feel free for the first time in many years. I'm no longer obligated to cater to your father's ridiculous thinking."

"Obligated? Why?"

"It's getting late now, Charlie. Let's talk more about this tomorrow. We need to be alone."

"This sounds serious."

"It is. Perhaps after your father leaves for work."

"Sure. I'm curious, but I'll wait," Charlie said and asked, "Do you think he's working?"

She smiled. "Who knows; who cares?"

Charlie wouldn't get the chance to have that talk.

❋

Shortly after eleven that evening, Charlie returned from a night with his old friends. He opened the front door slowly and quietly. It was quite dark inside; he closed the door behind him and searched for the banister.

As Charlie grabbed the handrail, a small lamp in the living room switched on. His father was sitting alone in the dark, waiting.

An open bottle of Jack Daniels rested on the small table beside his recliner.

"Charles, come in here," he said. "I want to talk to you—man-to-man."

Charlie changed direction. "Sure. What's up?" he said. "I thought you'd be in bed by now."

He walked across the living room and sat in a chair opposite his father. He crossed his legs, looking calmly and expectantly into the general's brown eyes.

"Drink?"

"No thanks," Charlie answered warily. "Where's Frank?"

"I suspect your brother has turned in. Unlike you, he's an early riser."

Charlie ignored the insult. "Where's Mom?"

"Out somewhere. She's not here so don't expect to hide behind her apron strings."

What the fuck does that mean?

"Okay. What's on your mind?"

"I've been watching you for the past few days—ever since you two returned. You've made disparaging remarks about our country. It troubles me."

"I spoke what I believed to be true. It's my opinion. I know a lot about the war now."

"You're too young to know shit! You're still a teenager for god's sake."

"I'm old enough to read and ask questions."

"Where's your *enthusiasm,* man? Where's your enthusiasm for the Naval Academy? Enthusiasm like Frank has. I don't see any passion for the military career you've chosen."

Do you really think I wanted it? Get the hell out of here!

"I'm learning as fast as I can. Bear with me while I sort things out in my mind."

"No! I will not bear with you," he replied angrily.

"I'm doing the best I know how," Charlie responded calmly.

"Not good enough. I expect to see the same fire in your eyes that your brother and I have. I want to see that same fire in your belly. You're privileged to have such an opportunity before you. I want you to act like it."

Charlie returned his father's gaze unflinchingly. "And how would you propose I act?"

"Like a good soldier, goddamnit! You need to man-up and stop complaining."

At that precise moment, Charlie felt something shift within him. He didn't know from where it originated, nor why it chose this moment. Where there should have been fear, there was none. Strangely, he felt nothing as he stared evenly into his father's eyes.

Charlie sighed. *This is it. I'm done. Lord, don't let this be a shit show.*

"Like a good soldier?" Charlie asked steadily. "With enthusiasm? With pride? With respect?"

The general took a long pull from his tumbler, belched and stared back defiantly. "You have a problem with that, boy?"

"I have a big problem with it. I have no respect for a war that sucked us in. We were blind. What I've learned gives me a totally different take. I've tried to be positive; I can't."

"Then try harder!" the general shouted back. He was drinking straight from the bottle. Not a good sign.

"Listen," Charlie said evenly, "fifty thousand American men have *died* in Vietnam. For what cause? Our government appears to have no coherent policy for ending this war."

"Of course they do! You must be reading that liberal rag, the *New York Times*. For God's sake, did you not hear the President's speech last month? We will stand with our allies against Communist aggression."

"I didn't hear it, but I read it. Nixon wants to stop the demonstrations by suggesting we have a path to peace. He blames the war on Johnson and Kennedy. He said we're going to 'Vietnamize' the war, turn it over to South Vietnam so we can get out. *Peace with honor*? He wants us to *believe* that."

The major flushed with anger. "And you don't?"

"Of course not! We're in the process of destroying that country, killing god knows how many species of wildlife in the process. For all the military power we've thrown at the Viet Cong and all the men we've lost, I don't see where we've made much progress at all."

"Goddamnit, I didn't raise you to question authority. I raised you to obey!"

"Obey? Like Calley claimed in his defense? He said he killed civilians because he was *following* orders from his superiors. That's crap and you ought to know it."

"You think you know it all, don't you?" his father yelled. "Well, let me tell you. You don't know shit. How can you claim to have insight when you've never even *been* over there?"

"I read the papers."

"I read the papers too! We have an important commitment to defeat the spread of Communism. Many a brave lad is fighting in support of that cause. To question is to deny the sacrifices of our battle troops."

"I don't deny those sacrifices. However, Communism isn't really a threat to capitalism, is it? It's an ideology incapable of sustaining itself in the end. Let it run its course. If Communism is such a grave threat, why are we the only ones in Vietnam? Nixon says we have an obligation to defend our allies. What about NATO? Why don't more countries support us?"

"Our country does the right thing regardless. It's who we are. It's why we're such a great nation."

"What about My Lai?" Charlie asked. "What about Agent Orange? What about Napalm? I don't believe we're such a great country anymore. Great countries don't commit atrocities."

General McDaniels paced back and forth in front of Charlie. *No one* had ever questioned him like this. Charlie knew he had gone too far but didn't care. It was time to stand up to him for once. Perhaps the Naval Academy had given him the confidence to do so. Whatever—he had facts—much more than his father.

The general paced silently for another minute before turning to Charlie. He was drunk by now. He swayed as he spluttered his next words.

"Those gooks Calley shot were all VC sympathizers. "You *know* they had to be killed."

"Even the small children?" Charlie asked.

"This is war!" he shot back. "You sound like a goddamned pacifist!"

"Call me whatever you want."

"Are you a pacifist?"

"Of course I am. We should all be for peace."

"You were always the weakest. I should have known."

Charlie was on his feet as well. "Franklin right, fine. Whatever. Talk to me about Agent Orange, Napalm, and the cluster bombing? Do you know we've destroyed an environment over there the size of Massachusetts? This country is in violation of the Geneva Convention. We're war criminals, for Christ sake! War or no war, what gives us the right to use our power just because we can?"

At that point, the general exploded inside. He was losing the argument to a son who seemed to have lost respect. He paused while waves of anger and indignity poured over and through him.

Struggling to remain calm, he said slowly, "Charles, I think it's best that you return to school."

"What? Are you serious? You want me to give up five days of Christmas leave for speaking my truth, giving you my honest opinion? Why should an honest opinion condemn me to return to the Academy early?"

"Go anywhere you want then! Find some hippie peaceniks and hang around them. You're all just a bunch of fucking cowards as far as I'm concerned. Don't come back until you're ready to support our country. Go back to the Naval Academy and hope that it can drill some sense into your cowardly attitude. I hope when you graduate, you're sent to become a platoon leader yourself—just like Calley!"

"Say whatever you want. I disagree with you! Get used to it. It's who I *am*!"

"I said go!"

Charlie shrugged "Alright; I'll go. It's your house."

Charlie rose slowly and started toward the stairs, stunned that his father could treat him like that. He shook his head slowly and walked up to the stairs without looking back. Quickly, he repacked his duffle bag and changed back into uniform. He looked around his room quickly. On impulse, he grabbed the acoustic guitar that he played so beautifully. He put it in its case and collected a few more things. Five minutes later, he was back in uniform walking down the stairs.

The general remained seated in his chair. Charlie glanced at him briefly from the foyer. Neither man spoke as he opened the door. He walked into the night and never looked back.

❋

Half an hour later, Frank stumbled up the steps to the front porch. Inside the foyer, he spotted his father still sitting in his favorite chair – drunk and angry. Something was wrong.

His father was good at holding his liquor. Something had upset him enough to drink half a bottle of Jack Daniels.

Taking the same chair that Charlie had occupied earlier, he looked at his father and asked carefully, "What's wrong, Dad? Isn't Charlie back yet?"

The general looked back at Frank with sullen, bloodshot eyes. "Charles won't be coming back," he slurred. "He's no longer welcome here."

"What happened, sir?" Frank tried to look sincere and concerned, inside he felt smugly satisfied. He always felt that way at Charlie's expense. The juxtaposition only enhanced his image in his father's eyes.

"Charles has gone back to the academy early. He needs to get his head screwed on right."

"It's about the war, isn't it, sir?"

"Yes, your brother sounds like a pacifist. There's no room in this house for such an attitude."

"I agree, sir. I don't like the things he says about our country either. I must say I'm not surprised, though. He has no military presence.

I still don't know how he got in."

The general ignored the question in Frank's eyes. "At least I have one son with integrity. I still have hope the Academy will make Charles see the errors in his thinking."

⁂

Charlie stepped onto the front porch and down the walkway. He turned at the wet sidewalk and looked back at his former home with sadness and confusion.

Mom stood up to that son of a bitch! So did I!

Charlie felt something different in his consciousness. He had never stood up to his father as he had this evening. Perversely, his defiance felt good—empowering in a new way.

That's it! Empowerment! I don't seem to give a shit anymore about what he and my brother think…what anyone thinks. I'm on my own, and it feels good!

The only family he knew discarded him for his beliefs. With no resources of his own, Charlie either went back to school or became homeless. The Navy provided room and board at no cost.

He strolled along the sidewalk in the direction that would take him to the main gate. He lifted the collar of his overcoat for protection against a chilly, moist breeze. Rain was forecast later in the night.

Charlie's footsteps echoed softly on the pavement. He passed neatly maintained lawns with homes decorated colorfully for the holidays. A brightly lit sign on the lawn ahead proclaimed the message of Christmas— "Peace on Earth, Good Will To Men".

With every step, Charlie reflected on his "eviction" from home. It felt right to stand up to him as if all the pent-up anger of adolescence exploded at once. The purging of insecurity brought liberation and freedom.

It was wonderful!

He saw the strength of his mother for the first time. She was remarkable. He knew she would go the distance to back him.

His mother was solidly on his side. She never looked stronger.

Ahead, the lights of a car appeared, moving slowly down the empty street. For a moment, he thought it might be Dad or Frank coming to get him, to bring him back home and out of the cold.

The car stopped when alongside. Charlie shielded his eyes while reading the insignia on the side—Base Security. The driver rolled down the window and addressed him kindly.

"It's pretty late, mister, you all right?"

Charlie stepped over to the open window and looked inside.

"I'm fine thanks, Sargent. Just heading to the bus station."

"That's a hell of a walk from here. Get in. I can take you as far as the main gate. You can get a cab from there."

Charlie gratefully opened the passenger door after stowing his gear in the back seat. "Thanks. I appreciate it he said extending his hand. "I'm Charlie McDaniels."

"Joe Forrester. Pleased to meet you."

As he accelerated, Joe asked, "Are you General McDaniels' son?"

"I am."

The driver looked at him curiously. He was a staff sergeant and knew all the officers well. "Mind if ask what you're doing walking to the bus station at this time of night?"

"Long story. My father and I disagreed. We decided it best if I return to school early."

The sergeant looked at him sadly. "What?"

"Yeah, but I'm all right," he answered with a broad smile. "Better than ever."

"Well, I sure hope so. I'd take you to the Greyhound station if I could."

Five minutes later, they were at the main gate. Charlie opened his door and walked around to the driver's side. "Thanks so much, Joe. Merry Christmas."

"And to you as well, sir" he answered. "You look like a good kid.

I wish you the best."

They shook hands again, after which, Charlie removed his stuff from the back seat and stepped onto the curb. Joe drove off with another wave.

The guard on duty at the gate saluted. "Do you need a cab, sir?"

"I'm good thanks," Charlie replied. He had to conserve the money his mother gave him. "Are there any buses that stop here?"

"Yes, sir. But not this late."

"Okay. I'm in no hurry. I can hoof it for a while."

The guard saluted again as Charlie picked up his bag and guitar.

It was a long walk to the bus station. Charlie didn't care. He was in good shape and needed time to think.

Two hours later and with the help of two kind souls who took him part way, Charlie stood at the entrance to the Greyhound Bus terminal on New York Avenue. The neighborhood was poor and run down. Homeless people—men, women, and children huddled together for warmth along the avenue.

It occurred to him what a fine line it was between security and homelessness.

Charlie opened the main door and entered the terminal. At two o'clock in the morning, the lobby was empty. The warmth and solitude felt good.

Charlie walked to the ticket office at the main desk. It, too, was unoccupied. He rang the small bell on the counter. After a short wait, the door opened. An agent appeared from the back and grudgingly faced Charlie at the ticket counter. The agent had apparently been sleeping. He surveyed Charlie and remained silent.

"Ticket to Annapolis, please."

That'll be $19.50.

Charlie handed over a twenty and asked, "What time does it leave?"

"Not until seven. You've got five hours."

Charlie set his gear on one of the benches near the back where large plate-glass windows offered views of the terminal platform.

Only a week ago, he stood with his family at this very spot, filled with happiness and optimism. Now, he was alone—alone in a new reality. He had much to contemplate.

What about Frank? My own brother —asleep in a warm, comfortable bed. Wouldn't he wonder where I was? Wouldn't he try to find me?

He'd be here now to take me home—if he gave a shit.

Charlie strolled around the terminal. His buzz of new energy would not allow him to sleep yet. That was fine with him; he had lots to ponder.

The automatic doors to the boarding platform opened as he walked by. He looked out at the vacant concrete loading platform and decided the relatively fresh air might help him think.

Charlie stepped through the doors. It was fairly warm thanks to several well-placed heaters along the benches lining the outside wall.

At night, after midnight, the homeless occupied the seats at the far end of the platform. The terminal night manager looked the other way as long as they remained quiet.

Charlie set his bag and guitar case on a bench away from the door. He was alone but relatively warm where he sat. He opened his guitar case and removed the old acoustic guitar. Music always calmed his soul.

He took off his gloves and quickly tuned the instrument.

He thought of the songs his mother had taught him—folk music primarily.

He strummed the guitar softly, searching for an appropriate song. The words and chords from Bob Dylan appeared.

Charlie closed his eyes and sang softly in the quiet night, absorbed in what he loved. Each melody and rhythm healed wounds and brought him peace.

Charlie relaxed into his natural being, keeping eyes closed while peacefully inside himself.

When he finished the first song, Charlie was surprised to hear soft applause. He opened his eyes quickly and smiled. A small family of homeless stood around him. Charlie acknowledged them smile with a soft smile.

"Thank you," he said. "Hope I didn't wake you."

"No, man," a tall guy dressed in military fatigues answered. "Can you play some more?"

"Sure," Charlie grinned at this circle of four. "Any requests?"

A small child peeked out from her mother's dress. "Play *Frosty*!"

"The snowman? Sure," he said. "Can you help me with the words?"

She nodded shyly but enthusiastically.

Charlie began *Frosty The Snowman*. His voice captivated the child. She beamed and applauded when he finished.

For the next hour, Charlie performed an impromptu concert of Christmas songs while the homeless sang along. It would become one of his most treasured memories.

CHAPTER SIX

Kacie

Present Time

He wondered if anyone would miss him. Surely none of his past wives. He had mistreated them. He was sorry. It was too late for apologies, however.

He thought of one who might mourn his death. The one who had captured his heart when he was nineteen.

He could see her in his mind as if it were only yesterday. So bright, joyful and talented. She had that smile that could paralyze him. He adored her. Still.

It was fear that caused him to leave her—his father didn't like smart women. She dressed differently and spoke her mind. He was afraid of her and told him to find a proper military wife, one with credentials, grace, and sophistication. Not some anti-war hippie.

The old man wondered where she was now, whether she was even still alive. He had no idea.

Fear overruled his heart; his only love lost. The rest is a blur of misery and unhappiness.

That son of a bitch!

The old man steadied his left hand while methodically emptying the Ativan pills into his dirty palm. He picked up the paper cup and brought the pills to his mouth. Without warning, his hand spasmed causing the pills to spill onto the cracked linoleum floor.

Cursing, he bent over to retrieve them one by one.

1969

Kacie Mitchell awoke with a start when the bus stopped. She looked out the window and saw that it had arrived at the station. She glanced out the window before grabbing her bag. Something moved and caught her attention; a young man and his small audience of the homeless.

Holding her bag in her lap, she watched and smiled. A clean-cut guy in a dark suit was playing the guitar.

That's a little odd at this time of night.

She studied the guitar player while the bus emptied

He looks like a midshipman. What's a middy doing here at four in the morning?

❋

The PA system intruded on the concert with the announcement of the bus from Annapolis at Gate 7.

Charlie's fingers were cold and stiff. He looked up when the bus approached. The concert was over.

Charlie put his guitar away and shook hands with each member of his small audience. To his surprise, the young child put a quarter in his hand. They quickly disbanded into the shadows at the end of the platform.

The coach made a full turn and gracefully slowed into the parking stall. Charlie felt an odd curiosity watching the bus approach.

A bus from Annapolis…at four in the morning?

He remained in place as the air brakes hissed and the coach came to an easy stop six inches from the curb. The front passenger door opened and the driver jumped out to open the baggage compartment.

Charlie slipped on his gloves and watched the arriving passengers begin to depart. Most looked weary; several looked at him and his uniform curiously. Feeling a little conspicuous, he turned around and faced the plate glass window behind him. The overhead lights reflected a perfect image of the remaining passengers stepping onto the platform.

He shoved his hands into his overcoat pockets as luggage was picked up and dragged out. Soon, the sounds were gone. Charlie assumed the bus was empty and prepared to return to the terminal waiting room. Suddenly, he sensed another presence behind him, another passenger. His eyes were drawn back to the glass reflection on the terminal window.

One of the last to exit was a young girl carrying a small backpack. When Charlie saw her reflection, he froze—at once, mesmerized as she stepped on the platform. He swung around as if propelled by some unknown force.

There she stood beside the empty bus, less than ten feet from him. She was looking at his uniform inquisitively. He could *feel* her energy.

Around her head, long dark braided hair bounced off her shoulders. She shook her head slightly and donned a flowered headband. Her dress and clothing suggested she might be a hippie.

For a fraction of a second, they locked eyes. Something mysteriously beautiful filled Charlie as he stared back.

He wanted to speak but couldn't. He had to say something before she was gone but remained frozen instead. It was no use.

The young girl briefly acknowledged him with a smile and flashed the peace sign. Her uniquely beautiful smile gave him shivers. Charlie felt paralyzed—dumbfounded. The rest of the world dimmed to a soft blur.

Charlie's spell was abruptly broken by the appearance of a lean, bearded man who emerged from the dark interior of the bus. He moved quickly down the steps and on to the loading platform. Long black hair bounced down his neck as he slung a backpack over his shoulder and put his free arm around the girl's shoulders, steering her toward the terminal entrance. As they moved away, the man glanced at Charlie's uniform disdainfully and gave him the finger. The couple entered the terminal, laughing as if they had no cares. Charlie watched them walk away in spellbound fascination. In an instant, they were through the terminal and into the darkness outside.

Charlie watched them for as long as he was able. He would never forget this brief moment in time. Something about the young hippie girl filled him with deep longing and overwhelming loneliness. Though she disappeared into the night, he would remember her always. Sadly, he knew he would never see her again.

Wait a minute! Don't let her get away, Charlie! You can either stay and lose her for sure…or take a chance and go after her. Your choice.

Charlie lay his bag and guitar on the bench and raced into the terminal. He rushed through the main entrance and into the cold night, looking up and down New York Avenue. They were at the next block apparently looking for a cab. He began to run with a sense of urgency compelling him to hurry.

Just before reaching them, Charlie saw a cab pull over beside them. "Wait!" he called.

Both turned around with surprise.

"My name is Charlie," he blurted.

"Beat it, buddy," the man said with a threatening look. Charlie stopped and watched the cabbie open the rear cab door. Just before getting in, the young hippie girl looked back at Charlie with a demure smile.

"Kacie."

Charlie stood awkwardly on the sidewalk and watch the cab pull away. Soon, it disappeared in in the early morning traffic. He returned to the bus terminal, out of breath but elated. He knew her name! Fortunately, his bag and guitar were still on the bench outside. He brought them in and sat happily on an old wooden bench waiting for the bus to Annapolis.

KACIE

❋

At six thirty, the PA system announced that the bus to Annapolis was ready for boarding. a line began to form on the platform outside. Charlie joined his fellow passengers outside in the dark and gloomy morning.

Charlie walked down the aisle and eased into one of the seats. As the bus began to move, he closed his eyes and immediately fell asleep.

Two hours later, he awoke with a start, confused and groggy. He was in Annapolis, back to his alternate reality. Exiting the bus, he found his duffle bag and guitar on the platform. A gray sky greeted him as he started walking. Flakes of wet snow drifted across his path.

At the end of Maryland Avenue, he passed through the main entrance to the Academy. The ever-present marine guard stepped out of the gatehouse and waved Charlie through. He was back.

The experience was surreal. The Yard looked bleak, empty and silent. The snow fell more heavily now.

His were the only footprints in Tecumseh Court. The fortress remained solidly intact. He felt no welcoming energy as he walked up the main steps—no happy return "home."

Inside the rotunda, Charlie brushed the snow from his uniform and approached the office to his left. At the desk, a single midshipman sat and looked at Charlie quizzically.

"Midshipman fourth class Charles McDaniels, reporting back from Christmas leave, sir."

The duty midshipman swung his chair around and gave Charlie a written brief that described his status for the duration of the holidays.

"Here's everything you need to know until the Brigade gets back. You're free to come and go whenever you want. There are no formations or inspections to attend. You may carry on anywhere in Bancroft Hall."

"Thank you, sir," Charlie said as he took the briefing sheet. He turned and walked into the shadows of Bancroft Hall.

The dimly lit empty corridors echoed his footsteps. He was one of very few midshipmen in Bancroft Hall. Only those on restriction for grave violations of conduct shared the space with him.

Charlie arrived at his room and opened the door. He threw the duffel bag on his bunk and lay his guitar carefully on the desk. Outside the small window, snow swirled in lazy white vortices between buildings.

He wanted to scream.

A father too pig-headed to openly discuss and question the war had thrown him out of his home. He realized that the military reshaped a man's thinking. Its goal: blind obedience under fire. America always did the right thing.

A sense of utter depression crept into his consciousness. He fought it off by opening the guitar case and retrieving his old friend. Just holding it made him feel better.

Removing his overcoat and jacket, Charlie played a few chords absently. He could play anytime for the next four days—until the Brigade returned. No one was around to hear him, no one cared.

Charlie picked on the strings to form melodies while softly voicing lyrics. He closed his eyes and saw the image of the young girl, Kacie. She would not leave his thoughts.

He thought back to his audience of homeless and smiled. Here he was, virtually alone in the massive dorm with nothing else to occupy his time. He knew he had to call his mother later, but would wait until he was sure his father had left the house. He knew she was worried. He was worried about her as well.

He had questions.

As he played, he pondered his father's behavior when bombarded by facts.

That's what really pissed him off. I knew more than he did.

The foundation on which Charlie's need for approval rested began to shift. He was a smart guy with all the facts. Surely, he could rid himself of the demons standing in his way.

For the moment, however, he was too exhausted to do any serious planning. He returned his guitar carefully to its case and lay down with his feet propped on his duffle bag. As his eyes closed, he pictured the hippy girl once again before he drifted into a deep sleep.

❋

Charlie slept for twelve hours. When he opened his eyes, the room was pitch black and silent. No sounds echoed from the hallways. He had slept through the day.

For a moment, he didn't know where he was. He sat up and looked at his watch. It was ten thirty in the evening. The mess hall was closed until the following morning.

He had to find something to eat, however. After a quick trip to the head, he descended to the basement level in search of the vending machines.

Charlie carefully negotiated the dark stairways past the phone booths. Only the sound of his footsteps penetrated the stillness.

Shit! I didn't call Mom.

He found a bank of vending machines near the laundry and slid a dollar into the change maker.

The selection was limited. No one had replenished the machines over the holidays. His only choice was a small bag of salted peanuts or a Twinkie.

Then he remembered that he was free to come and go as he pleased—anytime.

Screw this. I'm going to town. I'm wide awake. There are restaurants still open.

He returned to his room and shaved quickly. Donning his wrinkled uniform, he left for the outside world in Annapolis.

A thin blanket of wet snow covered the front steps to Bancroft Hall. He bounced down and across the dimly lit courtyard. It felt surreal leaving the Yard at this late hour.

The night was clear and cold. As Charlie's eyes adjusted to the dark, he looked up and saw the Milky Way extended across the horizon. Never had he seen it so clearly, so massive and awe-inspiring.

The streets in town were quiet but well lit. Headlights from a few cars traveled intermittently in the night ahead. He could hear his footsteps along the narrow sidewalk. Condensation from his breath swirled around him.

Buddy's Deli was still open on Main Street. Charlie walked in and found a booth by the window. The place was almost empty.

From behind, a young waitress spoke. "Hi there, captain. You just made it. We close at midnight."

Charlie looked back with a smile.

"Do you know what you want?"

"Crab cakes." It's an iconic Maryland cuisine.

"You're the first middy I've seen since before Christmas. Do you live in Annapolis?"

"No," Charlie answered. "I came back early."

"What?"

"Yeah, I know. It's a long story."

"Well, come back and tell me sometime."

"Okay," Charlie said with a smile. She was flirting with him. He flirted back while struggling to cope with this alternate reality.

"The waitress smiled again. "Be back in a couple of minutes."

When his order arrived, Charlie sat alone in this quiet venue savoring two crab cake sandwiches. He could hear WPGC playing on the radio from behind the bar. Many of the songs were unfamiliar. He had heard little music since June.

Later, Charlie wandered without direction through the quaint fishing town. His walk took him through unfamiliar neighborhoods. The atmosphere was eerily still after midnight.

For Charlie, the freedom was exhilarating. Walking gave him an opportunity to think. He walked for hours in the dead of night.

By four a.m., Charlie had walked through many of the lesser-traveled side streets. Returning to Church Circle, he reacquired his bearings. With no other place to go, he turned toward the Naval Academy. The air had become warmer. A front passed through causing thick fog to cover the city. He had only the streetlights and signs to help him navigate.

Rather than take Maryland Avenue, Charlie decided to try College Avenue, a parallel street. Though it looked familiar, he couldn't remember the street. Had he never passed through it?

He continued down College Avenue for several blocks. He passed rows of narrow brick townhomes built long before he was born. The architecture of most included wooden front porches, now in a delicate state of disrepair.

Charlie crossed another street. A neatly trimmed hedgerow on his left replaced the townhomes. It seemed to stretch for the length of several blocks. He looked across the hedge into the fog beyond. In the thick mist, he could see what appeared to be an institution of some sort.

Charlie tried to see more deeply in the darkness. Fog shrouded and blurred the lighting in the distance. Charlie felt something, nonetheless—a feeling he could not identify.

Halfway down the block was a sign standing next to a brick walkway. It identified the entrance to St. Johns College. Charlie stopped. He had heard of the college, remembering it to be a progressive liberal arts college that shared Annapolis with the Naval Academy. The college and its students were the butts of numerous jokes by his fellow midshipmen. Its student body was liberal—the antithesis of his midshipmen counterparts.

Charlie stopped and looked down the wide brick walkway that disappeared quickly in the fog. In the distance were more lights barely twinkling in the haze.

The walkway seemed to welcome him.

Charlie stepped tentatively on the campus. Immediately, he felt drawn to continue and walked further into the campus. He could see little now but made a point to come back to the college in daylight.

Returning to the Academy main gate, he saw the sky glow over the Severn River. The sun would rise soon.

Charlie decided to try breakfast in the mess hall. Only two tables were set, cordoned off in the west wing of the gigantic mess hall. It was here that the men left behind had breakfast. Today, only three other midshipmen were at the table. They looked at Charlie curiously—a newcomer.

"You don't need to brace up, man," a second classman said to him. "We, the derelicts of society, don't stand on formalities. What's your name?"

"Charlie, sir."

The Second Classman leaned over the table and extended his hand.

"Bill."

The other man, a Third Classman, shook hands with Charlie as well.

Charlie looked around. Most of the mess hall was unlit, quiet and dark. The same surrealist feeling returned to him.

"It's like an alternate reality, isn't it?" Bill said. "Who'd think that, in another four days, the place will again hold four thousand guys."

"It is," Charlie answered. "I'm trying not to think about it."

"That's for sure," Bob said. "In four days, January 2nd, this place will revert to its former status— the armpit of the world."

"I assume you're here on restriction, Charlie."

"Actually, no. I came back early."

"You what?" Bob almost spilled his coffee.

"Long story."

Charlie helped himself to platters of grits, biscuits and scrambled eggs as he related his experience over the last thirty-six hours. His new friends were the first to hear his story. It felt good to get it off his chest.

"Sounds like you hail from a family of dicks; your dad and brother, I mean."

"Your brother must be Frank McDaniels then," Bob surmised.

"Yeah, he is. Do you know him."

"I know of him," Chuck said. "His reputation matches your story correctly. Would you like us to break his legs or something?"

Charlie laughed at the offer. "No, but thanks anyway. Why are you guys here?"

"I told a Firsty to go fuck himself. He seemed offended."

Charlie laughed heartily—it was good therapy.

"What prompted you to say that?"

"He tried to pull rank on me. I mean, what the hell, I've been here two and a half years. It was chickenshit."

"What about you, Bob?" Charlie asked.

"Honor violation," Bob answered. "I accidentally looked at someone else's paper during an exam. I wasn't looking at his paper. He just thought I was…my word against his. They couldn't prove it so I didn't get kicked out."

"*Were* you looking?"

"Of course! I need all the help I can get."

Charlie laughed again. He liked these guys. While they seemed normal now, Charlie knew they would revert next week.

❋

Charlie could use the pay phones whenever he wanted. He had to call his mother to let her know he was all right.

Nervously, he dialed the number. His mother answered immediately. Somehow, she knew it was Charlie calling.

"Charlie?" her voice was hushed.

"Hi, Mom. Is Dad home?"

"No. You picked a good time. How *are* you?"

"I'm fine, though still a little shocked," he answered.

"You and I both. Your father didn't tell me you were gone until the next morning."

"Don't be upset, Mom. I feel terrific. I stood up to him for the first time! I told him bluntly about how I feel, made him mad enough to throw me out."

"What do you mean, he threw you out? He said you left voluntarily."

"That's not true."

"I didn't think so."

Charlie could tell his mother was holding back a lot of anger.

"We never had that talk, did we, Mom?"

"It can wait a little longer, Charlie. I want a proper venue."

"Can you come here?"

"Not with him around. I don't want him to know. Let's give it a little more time."

Charlie and his mother talked and laughed for another hour. His spirits rose with each chuckle. Things will work out.

"Remember, Charlie, I *agree* with everything you said about the war. I'm on your side; know that."

"Thanks, Mom."

"You and your father are cut from a different cloth. Maintain your resolve. Break away from this insanity and follow your heart. All things work for the best."

"Thanks, Mom. I understand."

"Try to have a Happy New Year, Charlie."

❋

Today was the last day of 1969. Tomorrow, a new decade would be ushered in. The direction of Charlie's life hinged on events and decisions that he would be forced to address in the next month. How could he utilize these free days?

He had the opportunity to do further research on Vietnam. With three full days ahead, he could dig even deeper into the Vietnam War. Charlie wanted to know more about this war than any other and vowed to become an expert in case anyone tried to judge him. Knowledge had given him the upper hand with his father. It would serve him here as well.

He returned to his room and put on his overcoat. He hoped Nimitz Library was open. Snow still covered the ground. It was a cold and breezy day as Charlie walked along Stribling Walk toward the library.

As he reached the top of the steps to the library, a sign on the door said it was closed and would not reopen until January 2nd. Disappointed, he shrugged and turned back down the stairs.

Suddenly, it occurred to him.

St Johns would have a library. Here's an opportunity to see that place in the light of day anyway.

He called the college from a nearby pay phone. On the third ring, a cheerful female voice answered.

"Good morning, St Johns College."

"Hi. I was calling to see if your library is open over the holidays."

"It is," she answered. "From nine to three this afternoon. We close early today for New Year's Eve. Are you a student?"

"Student?"

"Yes. A student at the college."

"Oh, of course. Sorry. No, I'm not. Are non-students permitted to use the library?"

"Sure. Greenfield is the main library at St. John's. It's open to everyone."

"Thanks for the info," Charlie said politely and hung up.

❋

St. John's University was the other institution of higher learning in Annapolis. It was a respected college of liberal arts with a reputation for graduating free thinkers. The University occupied thirty-six picturesque acres only a few blocks from the Academy.

Charlie had never visited the campus. He only knew about St John's and its students through the snide unflattering comments from his fellow midshipmen. They considered the college a breeding ground of hippie communist liberals—scorned and ridiculed by those who felt superior to those with liberal philosophies.

St John's had little interest in athletic abilities or military aptitude. Rather, the college sought open-minded young men and women seeking an education beyond a traditional curriculum.

❋

The entrance to St. John's was a mere three blocks away. In minutes, Charlie again stood hesitantly at the wide brick walk that led to the center of the campus. The sun shone and illuminated a campus every bit as beautiful as that of the Naval Academy. Charlie sensed a feeling of peace, wisdom, and stability—from the stately brick buildings to the beautifully maintained grounds.

He was grateful that the college was as deserted over the holidays as the Academy. His uniform would draw attention. He didn't think the university received many visitors from the Navy.

Charlie paused at the entrance and stepped onto the brick walkway. Taking a deep breath, he moved on to the campus.

At the intersection with another walkway fifty yards in, Charlie found what appeared to be a map of the campus. He brushed off the snow and ice and found Greenfield Library, located directly to his left.

There was no sign of any activity on the campus—not a soul in sight. Charlie sauntered in the direction of the library while taking in the ambiance of the campus.

A feeling of envy began to swell like a building wave. It washed over Charlie with a peaceful energy, enveloping and welcoming him. The energy grew stronger as he stood outside the library, looking at the massive portico adorning the entrance.

Charlie meandered up the wide, circular steps to the library and opened one of the solid wood doors. It felt warm and hospitable inside. He stood quietly to get his bearings.

A stately brass chandelier hung above a grandly decorated foyer. Beyond the foyer was a bright and cheerful environment that beckoned Charlie inside.

Its main floor looked like any other library—rows of card catalogs and bookshelves everywhere. Some study tables were in the central area.

To his right was an ornate circular stairway leading to more floors above. Charlie looked up and could see more books and desks on the second and third floor.

He approached the main desk. A lone female librarian stood behind the counter. Her eyes widened slightly at the sight of his uniform; she followed Charlie as he moved toward her.

"May I come in?" he asked.

The librarian greeted him with an engaging and welcoming smile.

"Of course! Just sign in," she answered. "We don't discriminate against the Naval Academy, you know."

Charlie laughed. "That's good. It's pretty obvious where I'm from, isn't it?"

"Doesn't matter. You're more than welcome here," she said warmly. "My name's Becky, by the way."

"Hi, Becky. I'm Charlie. Are you a student here?"

"I am. I work here under a scholarship program. Do you want a card?"

"Yes, please."

Charlie filled out a couple of forms and received a library card of his own. It would allow him to check out books if he wanted. He took the card with a smile and placed it carefully in his wallet.

"Thanks," he said.

"Anything, in particular, you're looking for?"

"Vietnam."

Becky grabbed a pencil and paper. "What about Vietnam?" she asked.

"I'm looking specifically for information about our use of chemical weapons in Vietnam."

"Napalm?

"Yes. And Agent Orange."

"Don't they teach you about military weapons systems, including chemical ones?"

"The Navy's version is that it's justified. I'm looking for a more objective, rational insight into our use of such weapons, one not sugar-coated."

"Sounds like you're not a supporter of our war tactics."

"No, not particularly."

"So what are you doing in the Navy then?"

"Good question. I'm taking a lot of heat for my position against the war."

"I bet you are." Becky laughed.

"All I want is the truth."

"Check out the opposing views expressed in the magazines and newspapers then," she said. "We subscribe to most. All of the editorials have come out questioning the war…like you."

"You think I should start there?"

"Yeah, for sure. Make yourself comfortable, Charlie. You can use the study area by the windows. It's near our collection of periodicals. You can go through them all. We'll have a few students coming in and out. I doubt they'll be any bother…although you may get a few strange looks."

"I imagine so. Thanks again, Becky. I appreciate your help."

Charlie walked to the huge magazine section. Becky was right. Current editions of all mainstream publications were stacked neatly in piles with the most up-to-date issue on top.

Many of the magazines and periodicals featured the same gruesome pictures on their covers. Charlie grabbed several and found a table by the window. He lay the magazines and his midshipman cap on the table. Before sitting, he removed his jacket and hung it on the back of the chair. He knew it was against regulations to be out of uniform in a public place

Screw it. Who's going to see me?

Charlie picked up *Newsweek* and began to flip through the pages. The facts reported were similar to those published in Time although presented from different perspectives.

Charlie began to focus on the editorials. Virtually every magazine he opened began with indictments against the government and its war policy. He skimmed each and went back for more.

The information he absorbed was disturbing.

He read the interview with Sgt. Michael Bernhardt who was with the platoon that committed the My Lai atrocity.

"I walked up and saw these guys doing strange things… Setting fire to the hootches and huts and waiting for people to come out and then shooting them… going into the hootches and shooting them up…gathering people into groups and shooting them.

"As I walked in you could see piles of people all through the village… all over. They were gathered up into large groups.

"I saw them shoot an M79 (grenade launcher) into a group of people who were still alive. But it was mostly done with a machine gun. They were shooting women and children just like anybody else.

"We met no resistance, and I only saw three captured weapons. We had no casualties. It was just like any other Vietnamese village-old papa-sans, women and kids. As a matter of fact, I don't remember seeing one military-age male in the entire place, dead or alive." Charlie put his head in his hands and closed his eyes.

The only defense given by the soldiers that did the shooting was that they were only following orders. Officers told them that day to destroy everything in My Lai village.

Including the children?

Charlie read on in another magazine.

An unnamed helicopter pilot landed near the platoon on the day of the massacre. According to Bernhardt, the pilot screamed at Calley to stop. He threatened to report what he was seeing.

A week later, the pilot died in battle. His story died with him. The Army subsequently dropped the investigation due to insufficient evidence.

Charlie questioned as he read.

There had to be other officers and enlisted personnel aware of the killings. Why did the incident conveniently go away?

Charlie read further, going from one source to another. He found that the cover-up would have been successful, were it not for a Ronald Ridenhour, was a staff photographer traveling with "C" Company that day. Ridenhour was the company photographer, assigned to capture and preserve military operations. He was issued a camera that took pictures of the action in black and white. The Division's public affairs office confiscated his film each day.

Didn't anyone in Americal Division look at his pictures?

However, Ridenhour secretly carried his own color camera. Both cameras recorded the horror at My Lai. The Army confiscated Ridenhour's military camera, unaware that he had captured the chilling and damning images on his own camera. Ridenhour kept the pictures for a year and a half before delivering them to the press and members of Congress. These images opened a Congressional investigation into the atrocities.

Whatever happened to Ridenhour's official black and white photographs? Could the evidence have been suppressed?

Charlie's research went from My Lai to the ideology of this or any war in general—how the U.S. Army struggled to defeat an enemy it could not see or differentiate from civilians.

No longer did he care what his father and brother thought about My Lai. Their ignorance was apparent and their opinions ludicrous. Instead, Charlie's anger centered on the deceptions, the cruelty of the war. He went deeper into the U.S. oversight of military operations.

❋

Charlie worked undisturbed for the next several hours. After a while, he stopped reading and rubbed his eyes. Looking at his notes, there was every reason to justify his disillusionment over the politics and conduct of this war. How could others not see?

He put his pen down and yawned. He was sick of reading about war. It was depressing.

As Charlie took a break, three women students entered the library, chatting in hushed whispers. They formed in a small circle near the librarian's desk. Charlie turned briefly in their direction before returning to his notes.

One of the young women noticed Charlie sitting alone in the distance. His dress code caught her attention.

Who wears long sleeve white shirts anymore? With cufflinks?

Her attention was drawn to the navy blue jacket hanging on the back of an adjacent chair. A white cap with a black visor lay at the end of the table.

That guy's a middy. What could possibly bring a middy to our library? Shouldn't he be on Christmas break with the rest of them?

She could see only the back of his head from her vantage point. His blond hair was trimmed neatly and closely. He reminded her of someone. She was curious.

She removed her hooded parka and tossed it casually over a nearby chair. She shook deep chestnut hair that fell down her back and shoulders.

"You guys go on," she said to her friends. "I'm going to hang on the first floor for a while."

Her friends nodded and walked toward the circular stairway.

She carefully approached Charlie who remained oblivious to her curious stare. He shifted slightly and lay down his pen. The chair squeaked and his weight moved. The sound reverberated through the silence of the large room.

She continued to stare at Charlie, curious what it was about him that seemed so familiar. Ostensibly, he looked like just another handsome uptight middy, dressed stiffly and conservatively—clean-shaven, spit-shined shoes.

I need to see his face. What is it about him that reminds me of someone?

She navigated around row after row of neatly placed books looking for a vantage point. Charlie remained unaware of her attention. His head stayed down as she slowly and quietly circled him.

She was now directly in front of his table remaining concealed, waiting for him to look up. After a minute, she became impatient and moved directly toward his table. He would have to look up eventually.

Charlie leaned forward to grab another magazine. As he did, he saw her approaching him. His eyes were down so the first things he saw were tattered jeans and Nike running shoes. He looked up to acknowledge her presence.

"Hello…" he started. Then his eyes grew wide and disbelieving. He froze.

It was her—the girl from the bus station!

Charlie stood so quickly, he nearly fell over. Suddenly, he was looking directly into brilliant green eyes staring back inquisitively. Instantly, her clear eyes danced brightly with recognition.

Kacie Mitchell was looking back at Charlie with equal surprise.

She found her voice first. "Hey, you're the guy from the bus station, aren't you? The guitar player."

Charlie nodded, struggling to find words. He blushed and smiled awkwardly, "And you're Kacie."

"Yes, you remembered," she answered softly. "Why were you running down New York Avenue? Were you chasing us?"

"Sorry. It was spontaneous insanity. I'm sorry."

"Don't be. I'm glad you did."

Kacie was at once captivated by Charlie. His awkward and unassuming smile charmed her. The softness in his eyes and the quiet confidence in his voice attracted her at once.

"What's *your* name?" she asked.

"Charlie. Charlie McDaniels."

Kacie pointed to one of the empty chairs at his table. "May I?"

"Of course." Charlie moved the chair back for her.

"Tell me," she said easing into the chair and turning towards him. "I'm curious. What were you doing at the bus station at four a.m. in the morning? You looked like you were giving a concert to the homeless."

"I was. It was a spontaneous performance. It was a family of three who came over while I was strumming. We sang Christmas songs."

Kacie smiled at the image of Charlie singing *Frosty* to a family behind the bus station. "Are you any good?"

"I must be. The little girl offered me a quarter."

Kacie laughed. "You didn't take it, did you?"

"I did take it. I plan on saving it."

"You didn't answer my question. What in the world would draw a middy to the Greyhound bus station at four in the morning? Did you spend the night there?"

He grinned. "Yeah, I was waiting for the seven o'clock bus back to Annapolis. It was a long wait."

"I don't get it. You look like a plebe. Are you?"

"I am."

"And you decided to come back early?"

Again, Charlie nodded, knowing he would have to explain.

"Why would you do that? Don't you have a home?"

Charlie sighed. "I do. I'm just not welcome there."

"How come?"

"It's a long story."

"I've got time if you don't mind sharing personal stuff, that is. Just tell me."

"Sure. I don't care."

"I don't know—I'm curious, that's all. May I sit with you a little bit…or do you want to be alone?"

"Of course," he whispered. "No, I don't want to be alone."

"I hope you don't think this is rude," Kacie whispered back easing into a chair opposite him, "But really? What the hell are you doing here in the Johnie's library?"

Charlie saw her eyes twinkle with humor as she spoke.

"Your library has better books. Besides, ours is closed."

"Maybe so, but I thought you guys liked to read about guts and glory, you know, the military stuff?"

"I'm researching the Vietnam War," he whispered back. "Your library has much more on that subject. Certainly more objective at least."

"Now I'm *really* curious," she said leaning in. "Here's this good-looking guy, trained at a military school, without a home who wants to know more about Vietnam. I know there's more to this story."

"Yeah, just a little."

"You're not a war junkie I hope?"

"No!" Charlie countered defensively.

"That a relief. Now tell me the story."

"It's a long story though. You probably don't have time."

"Listen," she said grinning. "I sense you're procrastinating. Look, it's Christmas vacation. I've got plenty of time. Go ahead."

Charlie shrugged his shoulders. If Kacie's anything, she is *persistent*. He liked that.

"There's not *that* much to tell really. My dad threw me out of the house that night I was at the Greyhound station. I had no place to go but back here…to Annapolis. I was killing time waiting for the next bus back to Annapolis."

"Hold on. Your dad threw you out? A dad with a son in the Naval Academy…and he kicked you out into the cold night? What on earth did you do?"

Charlie relaxed more. Her light and airy manner fascinated him. Her eyes communicated everything.

"I didn't do anything. I hate the Vietnam War. I told him so."

"So what. You're not alone. Everyone at St. Johns hates it," Kacie said.

"Well, my dad's a general. He loves it."

"A general? Like in the army?"

"Marine Corps."

"So you told him you didn't like the war. So what? A lot of people don't like it. It's not a crime for god's sake. You must have done something else."

"Well, I did stand up to him. He doesn't like to be challenged… particularly by a wayward son. We got into a big argument when I told him what I thought of his war—My Lai, Napalm, Agent Orange. I said all of it is a disgrace to this country."

"It *is* a disgrace!" Kacie's voice became even more animated. They were both becoming louder. There was no one in the library to mind.

"Listen to this. When I pushed him on My Lai, he said Lieutenant Calley is a hero and should get a medal! I couldn't help myself—I *couldn't* leave that alone."

"What? A hero?" she asked, her tone rising. Becky looked towards them with a finger on her lips. Kacie gave her an apologetic wave.

"You *can't* be serious, Charlie!" she stared back in disbelief. He green eyes were fixed on his, conveying astonishment. She waited for some kind of denial. Finally, "you are, aren't you?"

Charlie nodded glumly.

"Who *wouldn't* stand up to that crap?"

"Yeah. I told him that we're destroying that poor country. God, we've lost 50,000 lives, thrown everything we have at the Viet Cong, and *still* can't beat them."

"I bet that's when he threw you out."

"Yes," Charlie said. "He wouldn't even give me a ride to the bus station. I had to hitchhike."

"Don't you have friends you could stay with?"

"Not really; not with something like this. It was late anyway.

"I decided to come back here early to spend my time digging deeper, getting more facts to support my position."

"How many more facts do you need? Tell your old man to look at the pictures."

"I don't need to prove anything to him, Kacie. He *is* wrong and I don't care what he thinks. However, I do have to coexist with a lot of junior warmongers who know how to make life miserable. I need facts to rebut should my shipmates accuse me of being soft on war."

Kacie stared at him for a long time. Charlie sensed she was sizing him up. He knew at that moment she would either get up and walk away or remain with him. He waited.

"I can help you if you want," Kacie said finally. Her eyes were soft and questioning. "But what's the point? How many facts do you *need*?"

He shrugged. "Who knows? Maybe I'm just killing time."

Kacie laughed. Her smile weakened him. "You guys don't know how to kill time. Let's find something for you to do that won't take you to the depths of depression. You don't really want to spend the rest of your vacation in our library reading about how awful the war is…although I'm glad you came."

"So am I," he answered putting away his notes "Okay, I'm open to anything. What would you suggest to keep me occupied?"

Kacie's smile was animated, her spirit bright and confident. He was beginning to understand the instant attraction he felt for her. It grew with each word she spoke.

Kacie paused again, thinking. She liked Charlie. He had a kindness about his persona. She could see right away that he wasn't the military type. So many of the midshipmen she observed were like robots—fully brainwashed and sanitized, ready to take on whatever battle their superior officers sanctioned.

This man's different.

Suddenly, Kacie's eyes sparkled with an idea.

"Can you really play that guitar?" she asked.

"A little. The homeless loved me. Why?"

"Where is it?"

"Back at school waiting to keep me company. Why?"

"Go get your guitar," she told him excitedly. "Let's jam…if you have time, that is."

Charlie stammered. "Of course. Do you play?" It was a dumb question.

"A little," she mimicked. "if you have the time. I don't want to take you away from your mission."

"I can manage," Charlie answered with a grin.

Kacie flashed him her brilliant smile and rose. "Good!"

"When are you free?"

"In about fifteen minutes. I have to run out and do a couple of things first—I'm free after that."

"Really?" Charlie was almost too flustered to think. "I don't want to cut into your New Year's Eve plans," he offered lamely.

"Look, if you're not all that good, it'll be a short session," she said trying to look serious.

"Okay. You're really serious, aren't you? Why would you want to jam with *me*? Don't I represent the antithesis of your ideology?"

"Don't try to talk me out of it," she answered with a foxy expression. "Listen, Charlie. You don't strike me as the Navy type. You look like a nice guy who's stuck—a square plug in the wrong hole, or whatever."

"Thank you."

"I like that you're fighting back, too" she continued. "You don't seem afraid to challenge the edicts from *within* the military establishment. Maybe someday you can make a difference in your own way."

"That's kind of you to say."

"Sure, I mean it," she answered with a wink and turned abruptly to leave.

Charlie watched her walk away. The intensity of her presence raced through him. He knew he could no longer concentrate on anything else.

He stood and put on his jacket. Life was about to present him with choices. How he responded would mold and shape the remainder of his life.

He left to get his guitar.

❋

Charlie skipped down the steps of Bancroft Hall holding his guitar case firmly in his right hand. He was elated. This could be a good Christmas break after all.

Slow your role, pal. She'll forget you after Christmas break.

It was foolish for a plebe to become infatuated with anyone, let alone a "Johnnie". Plebe Year is not the time to be lovesick. Yet, in spite of his self-admonitions, he couldn't help it. She radiated such a soft and warm energy that it was impossible to be realistic.

He had to accept that Christmas leave would be over in a few days. His brief insight into this wholly different academic reality would go dark when classes started next week. He was too restricted at school to start a relationship.

Face it, man. It won't work. Will she put up with the long absences?

Hardly.

He shook off the negativity. Five minutes later, he returned to Greenfield Library.

Becky was still behind the librarian desk when he returned to the lobby. "Hi, Charlie. Back for another round?" she asked glancing at his guitar case. "Or are you going to play for us?"

"Can't here—I'm way too noisy," he answered smiling. "Besides, shouldn't you be getting ready for New Year's Eve?"

"I'm here until the library closes…which is in forty-five minutes. You'd better hurry."

"I'm finished with the research, Becky," Charlie said. "It's too depressing. I don't *want* to know anymore."

Becky smiled in grim acknowledgment. "I sure understand that. Does that mean you're not coming back?" she asked. "We were just getting used to having a Middy in our midst."

"It's been a real eye-opener to be on your campus, Becky. I appreciate your taking in a stranger."

"Well, you're not a stranger now so come back whenever you can."

"Deal."

"You and Kacie seemed to hit it off well."

Charlie blushed. "I'm out of her league, Becky. She's been terribly kind to me despite the uniform and all."

"I think Kacie's a good judge of character—regardless of where you come from. If she likes you, she'll do anything to help you."

"You have good people here it seems to me. I feel sorry that your student body is the butt of a lot of jokes at the Academy."

"It's all right, Charlie. Maintain your God-given principles. In the end, character and compassion will form the gist of your mettle."

"Wise words, Becky. Thanks."

Charlie smiled and returned to the same table. He sat with his guitar propped against the table and waited nervously.

As he waited, Charlie let his eyes wander to admire the beautifully ornate library. It had an entirely different feel and personality than Nimitz Library. He sensed that in these walls lived students who favored peace and tolerance over the war. It was an institution where students were encouraged to ask questions and express their feelings in an environment of open-mindedness and understanding.

Charlie couldn't help his envy.

It wasn't long before he heard Kacie's voice from the library's foyer. His heart quickened as a feeling of eagerness rushed through him.

She entered the library carrying a well-worn acoustic guitar case, similar to his own. Charlie stood immediately and waved. She waved back and ran towards him.

Looking at the well-worn case beside him, she stated, "Wow! Your case looks as old as mine does. How long have you had it? Where on earth has it been?"

"All over," Charlie answered. "It was my mom's. She toured a lot when she was younger."

"Really?"

"Yeah. Mom quit when she met my dad."

"That's a shame. I bet he didn't approve, did he?"

"No. I never knew how much she sacrificed."

"Open the case. Let's see it."

Charlie opened the case to reveal a beautiful mahogany Martin, carefully preserved over many years of play. Though the surface was worn in places, its character aged like a fine wine. Every scratch and nick had a story behind it.

Kacie felt the guitar's texture with reverence. "A Martin; *Nice.*" She stopped, and her eyes grew wide. "Holy cow! Is that Joan Baez's signature?"

"Yeah. She and my mom were friends. Let's see your guitar."

Kacie opened her case. She also had an old and worn Martin guitar as well. "Good God," he said. "They're practically twins."

"They do look alike, don't they? Let's see how they sound together."

"Here?"

"No, silly. Let's go to the music center. It'll be empty now. We'll find a room to play and talk without having to whisper all the time."

"I'll have to put on my jacket and overcoat if we go outside. You won't be embarrassed to be seen with a Midshipman, will you?" Charlie asked with a grin.

"Screw it; I don't care. Let's go."

Charlie put on his uniform jacket and overcoat. He struggled to find the armhole in the thick blue coat. Kacie moved to assist.

"My goodness. This thing weighs a ton!"

"Yeah. It's even heavier when it's wet."

"Good. Then you're strong enough to carry mine, too. Follow me."

When back in uniform, he said, "Lead the way."

Together, they left the central library, each carrying a guitar case. They waived to Becky as they walked by the front desk. She smiled and waved back. Charlie had to admit that they appeared every bit the odd couple, Charlie in full uniform and Kacie dressed in tattered jeans and a St John's parka. The only thing each had in common was the guitar by their side.

As they walked, Kacie looked up and smiled at this handsome albeit confused young midshipman. She sensed his integrity and grace despite obvious sacrifices. His was not an easy life for sure. Yet, below his navy blue exterior was a kind heart and good soul. She decided to try to know him better.

Outside, a brilliant afternoon sun glistened through oak branches that cast crooked shadows across the frozen lawn. The wind had diminished and the temperature moderated. A cloudless deep blue sky signaled great weather for fireworks later in the evening. Charlie almost forgot that it was the last day of the decade.

Kacie pulled up her hood and zipped up her parka. Together, they strolled across the campus following a network of brick walkways.

The more Charlie saw of the university campus, the more envy he felt. He fantasized that he was a student here also. It was a painful, bittersweet fantasy. Perhaps it would have been possible for him to attend an institution similar to St. John's had it not been so important to measure up to the standards of others. He shook off the regret.

The language center was across campus from the library. The short walk enabled Charlie and Kacie to converse without the constraints of the library environment. They laughed and talked comfortably along the way.

"Tell me something about yourself, Kacie," Charlie. "Where are you from?"

She spoke about growing up on a farm near Charlottesville, Virginia. "It was just the chickens and me mostly," she said. "I started by singing to the animals. It calmed them and made them easier to control." Kacie had a practical and objective view of life. Unlike Charlie, she knew what she wanted. She loved animals and once thought seriously about becoming a veterinarian.

They each shared stories from their short time as adolescents. Charlie told Kacie about his frequent moves and troubled high school years. He had enough escapades to go on for hours. She laughed hysterically as he described his night in the Kaneohe Detention Center.

"God, Charlie. With your high school record, how'd you ever get into the Naval Academy? No offense, but I thought they were after high achievers, not beatnik musicians with attitude problems."

He laughed. "Nobody knows, and *nobody* was more surprised than I was."

Kacie watched Charlie carefully as they walked. Intuition told her that he was smart, personable and competent—not the delinquent he described. She suspected that he could do anything he wanted with the right motivation. It was sad to see him waste his talents in a place that didn't appreciate him for who he is.

Charlie changed the subject. "How long have you been an activist, Kacie?" he asked. "What drives your passion?"

"I don't know. I've always felt sorry for the underprivileged. The compassion I feel for animals carries over to disadvantaged humans, I guess. I hate to see people treated as if they don't matter."

"So were you going to a demonstration in DC the other night?" he asked.

"There was a small, early morning peace rally that day. I spent a few hours with a lot of other anti-war demonstrators, waving my sign and shouting," she answered.

"Was that your boyfriend with you in the bus station?"

"Ignacio?" she laughed. "He *thinks* he is; thinks he owns me. He's just a fellow activist and no more. Never was anything but."

Charlie smiled inwardly with relief. He doubted *anyone* could own Kacie.

The language and music center was a staid old brick building that exuded charm like the rest of the college. A concrete plaza with a central fountain and cherubic statutes framed the entry. Charlie held the glass entry door open for Kacie and followed her into the main lobby.

The interior had been recently renovated, reflecting a modern and practical motif. Walking down the aisle, Charlie saw a number of large rooms, some paneled in rich oak with built-in bookshelves and modern furniture. In these chambers, all forms of music were taught and performed. It was a setting that encouraged creativity.

"Let's try this one," Kacie suggested opening a door halfway down the corridor. She preceded Charlie into a room that contained groupings of sofas, tables, and comfortable chairs. It could accommodate an orchestra or a duet comfortably. The room was acoustically designed for sound.

"Normally, this place would be full of students. For now, we have it to ourselves. Pick a place that looks comfortable and let's get started."

Charlie set his case gingerly on the closest table and removed his overcoat and jacket. He opened the case and removed his guitar.

"May I?" she asked.

Charlie handed her the guitar. She held it with reverence.

"How old is this thing, Charlie?"

"At least thirty years. Mom taught me how to play when I was ten. She used to be quite good."

"She must have been to be friends with Joan Baez. Are they still friends?"

"Not for a long while. My father has a somewhat negative view of musicians. Mom said she stopped playing professionally soon after they were married. She and I always played together alone—whenever my dad and brother weren't home."

Kacie shook her head in disbelief. "Has your father ever heard you play?"

"No. He believes music is a foolish pastime—thinks musicians are uncouth and dirty."

"Why am I not surprised?" she mused aloud. "Did she teach your brother, too?"

"No, he's more like my dad—tone deaf and disdainful of the music we played, especially music with a message, like folk or bluegrass."

"How can you be related to those people?"

Charlie shrugged his shoulders. "What about you?" he asked.

"Both my parents thought I might be musically inclined from the beginning. They bought me a ukulele when I was a toddler. I played it all the time.

"When I was six, they encouraged me to take lessons. I became good enough to perform. I've given a fair amount of concerts in Charlottesville as a teenager. Mom wanted me to apply to Julliard when I was seventeen."

"Did you?"

"No. I said I wanted a less specialized institution, one where I could expand more on my own. Both parents went along and so, here I am."

Charlie smiled at her. "I, for one, am glad they did."

"Me, too."

"Okay, Charlie, we've talked enough," Kacie said as she grabbed her guitar. "Let's see what you got, boy. You may be good enough for the homeless; but are you ready for prime time?"

"Let's find out," he said sliding the guitar strap over his shoulder. "What key?"

"I prefer D Major. Is that okay?"

"Sure. Play me your E string."

Charlie tuned his guitar effortlessly by ear. He turned and nodded to Kacie. "Sounds good. Requests?"

"I love Bob Dylan," she said. "Can you play his songs?"

"Sure," he answered. "Which one?"

"*Don't Think Twice*?"

"Sure. Do you want to start?" he asked.

"No. You go ahead. I'll jump in after you set the tempo."

"Okay. I'll do the intro and first verse. You do the second verse, and we'll do the chorus together."

Kacie nodded as she adjusted her position.

"Ready when you are."

Charlie took a deep breath and paused. He flexed his left hand and began to play. His fingers flew across the frets effortlessly as he picked the introduction. Kacie's smile expanded while her eyes flashed enthusiastically.

Charlie began to sing the first verse.

Well, it ain't no use to sit and wonder why, Babe
Even you don't know by now
And it ain't no use to sit and wonder why, Babe
It'll never do somehow

Charlie's eyes were on Kacie the whole time he played. She closed her eyes and began to sway with his rhythm. When her turn came at the second verse, she looked at Charlie with a big smile.

So it ain't no use in calling out my name, gal
Like you never done before
And it ain't no use in calling out my name, gal
I can't hear you anymore

Charlie almost stopped when he heard her for the first time. She was fantastic, every bit his equal…or better. He beamed as her voice resonated with a unique tone and timbre. She was a professional—he hoped to compliment her talent.

At the end of the second verse, he closed his eyes and began to strum softly.

They sang together as if they were seasoned practitioners, each voice in a natural and effortless blend of harmonies. Something about the combination of their voices was captivating. Each complimented the other flawlessly. The effect grew as they sang; each quickly realized that this was a special combination.

I'm a-thinkin' and a-wond'rin' wallkin' way down the road
I once loved a woman, a child I am told
I give her my heart, but she wanted my soul
But don't think twice, it's all right

Their harmony was pure and flawless as if they had played together for years.

When they stopped at the end of the song, each looked at the other with an expression of astonishment. Then, they laughed with joy, unable to find the right words. Instead, they looked at each other and mouthed softly, "wow!"

"Kacie, you're incredible! I had no idea. It's a joy to play with you!"

"Thank you. Your mom taught you well. Who would have thought a lowly plebe could have such ability?"

"Let's keep going!"

A tentative knock on the door interrupted their euphoria. Kacie looked up and answered, "Come on in."

Behind the door, five or six students had gathered to listen. The door opened, and they filed in with incredulous looks.

"Kacie, that was awesome," one of them said, "you guys harmonize beautifully!"

Kacie stood and said to their small audience, "Did you guys like it?"

"Like it?" another answered. "We loved it!"

"Who's your friend, Kacie?"

She looked somewhat embarrassed at Charlie and answered, "This is Arlo. He's a friend I met over the holidays."

Charlie looked at her grinning. His shirtsleeves were rolled up past his elbows; no one could identify him as a Midshipman. He stood and shook hands with each student.

Arlo? Really?

"You two have just met? Come on. Have you guys never played together?"

"First time," Kacie answered.

"Go on. That sounded way too good for impromptu."

"It's true. Want to do another one, Arlo?" she asked him.

"Sure. Why not."

"You guys want to hear another?" Kacie asked.

The group shouted together, "Yes!"

"Do you know other Bob Dylan songs?" Kacie asked Charlie rhetorically.

"Most of them," he replied unassumingly.

"Okay, let's do *Blowing In the Wind*. I'll start, and you come in whenever you're ready."

Charlie nodded and watched Kacie begin the intro. Like Charlie, her fingers moved effortlessly across the frets. Music was unquestionably one of her callings.

How many roads must a man walk down
Before you call him a man?
How many seas must a white dove sail
Before she sleeps in the sand?
Yes, how many times must the cannon balls fly
Before they're forever banned?

Charlie joined her in the chorus.

The answer my friend is blowin' in the wind
The answer is blowin' in the wind.

Together, they completed the song brilliantly. It was a special moment for each of them. Charlie had never experienced perfect vocal harmony like this. He was as surprised as Kacie.

Others from outside joined the growing audience. Charlie was stunned, spellbound by their reaction. He knew at their first note together that Kacie was a perfect accompaniment for him. However, he was as surprised as Kacie at the group's reaction. Neither realized the effect their harmony had on others.

As the applause grew louder, more students entered the room.

Charlie and Kacie played an impromptu concert for the next two hours. The tones of their voices were so unique and complimentary. It was a once in a lifetime union for them both.

At the end of their performance, the room was nearly full. Applause echoed down the hallway.

"You guys should do a concert," someone suggested. "I'll bet you could fill our auditorium."

"Okay," Kacie answered, "We might just do that, guys."

Later, after their audience reluctantly left, Charlie looked at Kacie. She was grinning with happiness. His fingers ached from lack of practice.

Charlie understated the obvious. "That went well, didn't it?"

"For sure. You're an amazing singer, Arlo, and you know how to use that guitar."

"Thank you. And you, as well."

Charlie's face became serious. "But a concert?" he asked. "We barely know each other."

"I'm game if you are," she said confidently.

"Absolutely! But we need to rehearse, don't we?"

"From what I just heard, not much. Let's see if I can get the auditorium next Sunday, say, around 2 in the afternoon."

❋

Charlie's fingers throbbed. He hadn't done a sustained concert for six months. While they were putting the guitars away, Charlie paused and looked at his watch. It was almost six.

"I bet you have a New Year's Eve party tonight?" he said playfully.

"Are you kidding? I don't mix well with intoxicated frat brothers. Do you have time to go into town?"

Charlie looked slightly uncomfortable.

She knew why and said with a smile. "How much money do you have, Charlie?"

"About eighty dollars; I can afford dinner."

"Bullshit. We're going Dutch. And don't give me that crap about men always paying."

Charlie was uncomfortable at first but agreed. "Thanks. It's all the money I have to my name."

"So I guess your old man didn't hand you a fat check on your way out?" she said with a crooked smile.

Charlie laughed at her suggestion. Kacie could find humor in his predicament. He liked that.

"Hardly," he grinned back.

As he focused on her dark green eyes, they danced playfully. She could banter like a pro. She was perfect for him.

"Let's put the guitars away. I can keep yours with me in the room if you trust me."

"Of course. I'm much more comfortable leaving it with you than hiding it under my bed."

"Good. I can show you where I live."

❋

Hand in hand, they left the music hall and walked toward Kacie's dorm. Colonial lampposts illuminated the walkway in the darkness of late December. Charlie marveled at how the day had transformed him. This morning, he was but a single plebe looking for some way to prove he was right. Now he was with Kacie, mystery woman from the Greyhound Bus station, holding her hand and walking toward her dorm.

The freshmen dorm was a more modest building on the other end of the campus. Few windows had lights on. That would change in a few days. Kacie led Charlie up the steps and into a small lobby. A large bulletin board occupied one wall. On the opposite wall were two payphones framing a well-worn couch.

"Wait for me here," she said. "I'll put the guitars away and be right back."

When she returned a few minutes later, Charlie noticed she had dressed up slightly. The trace of makeup she now wore accentuated her beautiful face even more.

Kacie slipped her arm through Charlie's as they walked into the cold night. Charlie thought he would burst with joy.

They strolled around town looking in search of an inexpensive restaurant. Excited partygoers filled the streets in anticipation of the start of another year, another decade.

At the end of College Avenue on Church Circle, they found a cozy but crowded tavern, still with a few empty seats.

They took a small table near the front next to a window. The atmosphere was charged tonight with the prospect of the arrival of a new decade. A jukebox blared from somewhere in the back. No one would miss the sixties. It had been a decade of tragedy and upheaval.

They ignored the crowd around them as they focused on the menu. All each could talk about was the prospect of doing a concert next weekend.

"Let's put together a song list," Kacie said. "We have all day tomorrow to rehearse. We'll be ready. What time can you get out next Saturday?"

"Around twelve-thirty," he said.

"Alright, we're on. I'll schedule the auditorium at two and put up some posters. Word gets around here fast. The whole student body will know about our impromptu concert. We'll have a good turnout."

Their eyes shined with excitement and enthusiasm. For each, performing live was the ultimate experience.

"You know, Arlo, we'll have to take requests. Some of our performance may have to be ad lib. You think we can pull this off?"

"Of course," he answered. "But tell me, where does 'Arlo' come from? Is it like Arlo Guthrie?" he asked.

"No. I made it up, goofy. Arlo will be your stage name. It comes from three letters of your first name. She spelled the letters, "c-h-*ARL*-i-e. See? 'ARL'."

"What about the 'o'? Where does that come from?"

"My imagination," she said with a wink. "Don't be difficult."

"Okay. I'm Arlo," he grinned. "You have to have a stage name, too. What's your middle name?"

"It's Elizabeth. Why?"

"Well, there you go. '*Eli and Arlo*'. What do you think?"

"Has a nice ring. I've never been called 'Eli' before."

"Well, you will always be Eli to me, then."

After dinner, they strolled through downtown admiring the Christmas lights along Main Street. Charlie ached to hold Kacie's hand but knew he would be reported if any officer should recognize him. Kacie laughed when he told her about the Reg Book and all the actions for which demerits would be given. One was "Public Display of Affection" which included holding hands on the sidewalk. She didn't care; she was happy just to be with Charlie, regardless of his limitations.

The inner harbor and marina were particularly crowded. This was the city center and hub of the New Year's festivities. They were fortunate to find an unoccupied bench with a partial view of the fireworks. The celebration and festivities provided a special background as they focused primarily on each other, laughing and bantering through the evening.

The fireworks over the Severn River were excellent. The city of Annapolis was a tourist mecca and had plenty of money to fund events such as this one.

Half an hour later, the show ended. Soon the crowds began to thin. By one a.m., the hard-core party people were back in the bars and the streets nearly empty. Reluctantly, Charlie and Kacie stood to begin walking back to the University.

When they returned to St. Johns, they stood near the entrance sign. Though quite late, time no longer mattered.

Kacie stood to face Charlie. Her eyes glistened; her expression gentle yet urgent. He felt overpowered by the force of energy that acted upon him. Each felt a unique force drawing them closer.

Charlie put his hands on each side of Kacie's face and kissed her gently. The touch was like an electric shock. She threw her arms around him and returned the kiss passionately. Time stopped. Through closed eyes, each experienced a brilliant light show in their consciousness and hearts, swept away to a place of incredible peace and joy.

Life was a gift—a beautiful gift, sacred and fulfilling despite the pain and suffering it was capable of inflicting.

Charlie kissed her again with all the passion stored since he first saw her at the bus station. It would be a memorable new year.

"It's two o'clock, Charlie. Why do you have to go back now?"

He shrugged. "I have no place else to go."

"Yes you do. My roommate's gone. You can stay here."

❋

The first day of 1970 began magnificently—best ever for each. Their lives faced the symbolic beginning, a time to shed old habits and feelings, a time to forge ahead with a new resolution.

Charlie's eyes fluttered open just before noon. Lying on his back, the first thing he saw was an unfamiliar ceiling in an unfamiliar room. Quickly, memories returned, and a surge of warm energy flowed through him. Kacie was still asleep on his right shoulder. Her long dark hair covered half his chest.

He never wanted this to end. He lay quietly letting his mind replay the amazing events of the last two days. In six hours, it would be over. He wanted time to stop.

Kacie moved ever so slightly against him. She was waking up. He turned his head towards her, and their eyes met.

With a groggy voice, she whispered, "Hey. Don't I know you?"

"Barely," he whispered back with a grin and moved his free arm around her neck. She turned towards him.

He was on fire.

CHAPTER SEVEN

Eli and Arlo

Present Time

The old man crawled on his hands and knees searching for every pill scattered across the dirty floor. One by one, he retrieved them while gasping with the exertion. He strained to reach those that fell behind the toilet. When he had them all, he struggled to stand. Exhausted by the effort, he fell back on the floor and bumped his head on the toilet bowl. The blow stunned him and the pills fell again to the floor.

Angrily, he swept up as many handfuls of the pills he could reach and slammed them into his mouth. With a mouth full of deadly pills he cupping his hand to scooped enough water from the toilet to wash them down in a single gulp.

There. It's done. The suffering is finally over.

He closed his eyes and waited for the tunnel of light that would take him home.

1970

A hazy sun infiltrated the fabric of the curtains. The sounds of laughter and conversation filled the room. Students were returning from the holidays.

Charlie and Kacie had fallen asleep again.

Kacie opened one eye and punched him gently. "What time is it?
Charlie looked at his watch. "Three o'clock. We've slept through most of New Year's day. Hey, where's the bathroom, by the way?"

"Down the hall," she giggled. But you have to put *something* on before you leave the room. We're liberal, but not *that* liberal."

Charlie laughed. "This is what's called 'out-of-uniform' in public—to the extreme."

She continued to giggle while he struggled to get his pants on.

"Is it a men's room?" Charlie asked warily.

"No. You have to go downstairs. However, you're free to use ours. I would advise knocking first before you go in."

Charlie just shook his head with an embarrassed smile.

"See you in a couple of minutes."

When Charlie returned, Kacie was sitting at her desk wearing a flannel bathrobe.

"Cute," he said with a wink. "Flannel becomes you."

"Hey, you're wearing government-issued underwear. No fashion judgments from you, plebe."

Charlie laughed and kissed the top of her head.

Charlie looked at her. His pulse quickened.

"Tell me last night wasn't a dream."

"No. Because it wasn't. This is reality, Charlie. Get used to it."

"I'm afraid to. I have to be in Bancroft Hall this evening."

"You have memories, don't you?"

He smiled and nodded.

"Go there whenever you need to."

"I will. Should we rehearse anymore?"

"We're good enough. Besides, my fingers are sore."

"Mine, too," she said. "Charlie, all you have to do is show up next Saturday. Believe me; we're ready."

"You're right. I'll be here."

"Let's make posters tonight. They'll be all over the school in a few days."

For the remainder of the afternoon, they sat at Kacie's small table.

They talked and laughed about the silliest things. Each minute brought them closer.

Nothing is forever, however. The Brigade would return this evening. Six o'clock was the deadline to be back.

By five, Charlie stood fully dressed in uniform. "How do I look?"

"Like you're from another world!"

"Do I pass inspection?"

Who is this person? Kacie thought. *He's going back to the Navy. How do I let him go?*

"I'll miss you," she answered, looking into his eyes. "Keep out of trouble. I want you back."

"Aye, aye, sir."

Kacie ran into his arms and held him. She had no words.

As the afternoon light grew dim, they lingered in each other's arms, lost in each other's energy as long as possible. In a few minutes, Charlie would have to don his cap and head back to Bancroft Hall.

At five, Kacie walked Charlie downstairs and outside. Most of the student body had returned. Charlie ignored the odd looks.

They walked slowly down College Avenue toward the academy's main gate. On the other side of the wall, they could see Midshipmen everywhere, returning with suitcases and duffel bags.

Charlie stopped just outside the gate and looked at Kacie with such sadness. He was surprised to see tears in her eyes.

"I'll be back Saturday, he said. "It won't be the same, but I'll still be with you. I'll be ready for the concert."

She nodded absently and placed a gloved hand on his arm. "Will you call me?"

"Whenever I can. Plebes don't get to the phone booths very often."

She smiled. "You'd better go."

Charlie nodded and bent to kiss her gently on the lips. "See you, Saturday, Eli."

"Bye, Arlo.

He turned towards the gate and disappeared into the darkness.

⁂

Saying goodbye to Kacie was heartbreaking. Charlie turned to wave goodbye from the other side of the gate. She was still standing across the street, dimly lit from the glow of a nearby streetlamp.

How desperately he wanted to run back to her. Instead, he had to face reality.

He walked slowly across the Yard and joined a larger throng of Midshipmen in Tecumseh Count. Entering the cold and unfriendly walls of the Rotunda was like a time warp. It slapped him harshly across his face. He was back.

He had the memories, though. They would have to sustain him.

⁂

An energy of doom and depression flowed through the maze of hallways in Bancroft Hall. No one in the Brigade wanted to return to the inflexibility of the military doctrine—other than, perhaps, those who would aspire to be admirals one day.

Charlie was not one of those.

For the first time in ten days, he assumed the braced up position and marched briskly down the center of the passageway.

His roommates were waiting for him when Charlie arrived. Neither had any interest in telling each other how good Christmas leave was. Neither wanted to think about it now.

Charlie went through the motions. He was a plebe now and was required to act like one. Still, it was an emotional effort to stand in that first formation before the evening meal.

As he stood, Pete came over and looked into his eyes.

"Did you have a good Christmas, Mr. McDaniels?" he asked.

"Yes, sir."

That was the end of the dialog.

The mess hall was hushed that evening. Christmas was over—no one at Charlie's mess table felt like talking. Even Harry stared sullenly at his plate. Charlie appreciated the lack of attention—he remained quietly to himself knowing it would not last.

✵

Breakfast the next day was also relatively quiet. Pete didn't ask about the news nor did anyone have much interest.

Classes resumed today. Semester exams were less than three weeks away. Charlie had fifteen minutes to prepare for class. He checked his schedule and his appearance in the mirror.

Just as he was about to head for the door, his brother appeared in the entrance. He waved at Charlie's roommates to carry on.

Charlie stared at him. He said nothing.

"Jesus Christ, Charlie," Frank began judgmentally. "What the hell did you say to dad to get him so riled up? He told me you walked out on him."

"That's not the truth. I didn't walk out, Frank. I was *ordered* to leave—thrown out of my home!"

"What the hell did you do?"

"We were talking about My Lai that night. I expressed my opinions, and he apparently didn't agree. He got pissed. He was drunk."

"Shit, man. No one challenges him on military stuff. What got into you?"

"The *truth.* That's what's 'got' into me, Frank. You and the old man need to take off your blinders and look at what's really going on in Vietnam."

Frank shook his head slowly allowing the full impact of his condescension to glow. "Boy, you've got a lot to learn."

Charlie paused. His eyes bore into Frank. "And where in the hell were you? I could have used a little brotherly support, you know… or were you too afraid to intervene?"

"I was asleep," Frank answered somewhat lamely.

"Bullshit! You weren't home yet; I *know* it."

"You don't know shit, Charlie."

"I know you're an accomplished liar. *You're* going to be the next Brigade Commander, someone who can't even be honest with his own brother?"

"Easy, man. I outrank you."

"Don't pull that rank shit on me! I was here by myself four days! You never even bothered to call? Why not?"

Charlie knew he was losing control. There was much anger to express.

"Dad told me not to contact you," Frank said. "He wants you to grow up on your own."

"I don't believe that either. I no longer trust either of you."

Frank's face was red. He was losing control, too. "Listen," he said, "you'd better shape up fast, man. Stop being so goddamned critical of everything!"

Charlie's voice lowered. "This place could use a little critical thinking. I'm not a robot. I'm not accepting a Goddamned thing without understanding it. The Vietnam War doesn't make any sense!"

"Christ, Charlie. Hold your voice down! Your attitude is going to get both of us in trouble."

"My attitude's fine, Frank," he said calmly. "It's the ignorance I see from you and everyone else here that fries me. Open your eyes for god's sake!"

Frank's clenched his fists. "Watch it!"

"Watch what?" Charlie said sarcastically. "Some brother you are. You've always been like that, sucking up to the old man like there's no tomorrow! That's probably how you got to be brigade commander."

Charlie's two roommates wanted to crawl into their lockers. They were astounded to see a First Classman and Plebe arguing so bitterly.

"Listen, I *earned* everything I have," Frank retorted. "Unlike you, I support our country."

"You don't even know what I'm talking about, do you, Frank?"

Charlie said. He gave up and returned to his locker. There was no further point in explaining.

"Listen, you jerk. I'm a First Classman. You're a fucking plebe. You can't talk to me like that around here!"

"Get out of here, Frank. Don't come back until you're ready to talk like a man."

Frank's face reddened. He looked at Charlie's stunned roommates menacingly. He had to lash out at somebody, to prove his authority.

"Eyes in the boat, you two," he bellowed. "Drop for fifty."

"Why, for Christ sake, Frank? They didn't do anything."

"That includes you, too, mister!" Frank said furiously to his brother. His temper was making him irrational.

"Fuck you, Frank. Get out of here before I throw you out!"

Frank hesitated. He was weaker than his younger brother was. His reputation would suffer should he lose. No one should see a plebe throw out a first classman.

"I'll go," he said bitterly. "But, you're in really deep shit now, Charlie! You don't *know* how deep!"

"Go," Charlie said quietly.

Frank turned on his heel and stormed out. Charlie's roommates stood and looked at him in disbelief. They had never heard a plebe yelling at a first classman before—especially the new Brigade Commander. Charlie waved them off with a shrug.

"He's my brother. We fight a lot."

Charlie grabbed his books and headed to class.

❋

The following days were a whirlwind of meaningless activities. Charlie had no chance to talk with Pete Hartwick and no chance to use the payphones.

In the mess hall, Charlie felt all but ignored. No one asked him about Vietnam. No one seemed to care. Even Harry kept to himself.

Charlie wondered why Pete hadn't addressed him at any meal. The brigade had been back for two days. They had barely spoken at the mess table.

It was later Wednesday afternoon when Pete Hartwick paid Charlie a visit as he spit-shined his shoes. He held his left dress shoe, polishing the toe with his right hand until he could see his reflection.

Suddenly, the sound of chairs scraping against the floor interrupted Charlie's meditation.

"Attention on deck!" Bob called out.

Charlie looked up to see Pete standing in the doorway. He waved everyone to carry on and looked at Charlie.

"Mister McDaniels," he said as he entered the room. "How have you been the last three days?"

"Good, sir."

Pete nodded. "Come by my room this evening during study period. I want to talk with you. Don't bother getting dressed. Come as you are."

"Aye, aye, sir."

Charlie wondered what was on his mind. His roommates suspected he was in trouble but said nothing.

Halfway through study period, Charlie slipped on his Navy-issue bathrobe. "I'm off to see Mr. Hartwick, guys."

"Good luck," they mumbled.

"Thanks," he answered unenthusiastically.

Charlie walked the short distance to the end of the second wing, one he had traveled many times. He knocked softly on Pete's open door.

"Request permission to come aboard, sir."

"Come in, Mister McDaniels."

Pete asked his roommate to allow them some privacy. Obligingly, Dave stood and departed quietly. Charlie expected the worst. He knew it must be about Frank.

Charlie watched Pete slowly enter his field of view. He braced for impact.

To Charlie's surprise, Pete extended his right hand.

"Call me Pete," he said smiling.

Charlie grabbed his hand and shook it tentatively.

Charlie had been "spooned."

"Sit down, Charlie. Carry on."

"Thanks," Charlie answered befuddled. He had assumed he was in trouble. He was not. Something was going on, however.

"Charlie, your brother came by yesterday. He said you were insubordinate and disrespectful to him."

"It's a long story, Pete," Charlie said.

"He's thinking about reporting you. That could have you restricted for the rest of the year."

"What! Really? That can't be!"

Pete nodded. "You want to tell me what happened? I don't want to pry into your personal life but I'd sure like to hear your side of the story."

"I was thrown out of the house over Christmas. I had no place to go and was forced to come back here four days early."

"You were thrown out? By your brother?"

"No, my father."

"The general?"

"Right."

"Why, if you don't mind me asking?"

"No. We got into an argument over Vietnam."

"Uh-oh. I assume you expressed yourself candidly," Pete said with a wry grin.

"I told him the war is immoral, a travesty. My Lai is an embarrassment. He, however, thinks those guys from Charlie Company are heroes! He said Cally should get the silver star."

"No kidding!" Pete could only shake his head in wonder.

"Yeah. I'm probably the first in the family who ever rose their voice to him."

"Gutsy, huh?"

"I don't know. No one's probably ever called him on Vietnam—or anything else. I told him we're indiscriminately killing not only poor peasants, barely able to survive but also hundreds of species of wildlife and vegetation. We've lost fifty thousand men over there and only made things worse."

"Your points are valid, Charlie. Doesn't he want to hear opposing views?"

"He a general; I'm a nineteen-year-old Plebe. Do you think he wants *my* opinion?

"Well. I know you and your disdain for sugar coating what you believe to be the truth," Pete replied and paused. "I assume this has something to do with your fight with Frank the other day."

"It does. Frank spent four more days at home, probably having a great time and never once made any effort to contact me. He never called, never checked on my welfare."

Pete frowned. "Some brother," he mumbled. "Okay, so what did you say to him when he came to see you?"

"I told him to go fuck himself."

Pete laughed heartily.

"No wonder he was so upset...and this happened in front of your roommates?"

"He was in *my* room He started bullying my roommates to assert his authority."

Charlie hesitated for a moment and said, "He *lied* to me, Pete. Said he didn't know I had left until the next day. He said my father ordered him not to call me."

Pete shook his head. "I hear you, Charlie," he said. "And see your point. However, you can't be in a fist fight with a firsty, whether he's your brother or not."

"You're right, Pete. I should have handled it privately."

"Some things are justifiable. In some situations, anger *is* appropriate. Lying *never* is."

"Thanks, for understanding, Pete."

"Sure. Look, I told Frank to lay off you for a while. However, since he's going to be the Brigade Commander in a few weeks, he can't have Plebes disrespecting him in public. He's thinking about reporting you—could be a Class-A. You should be careful."

"Thanks, Pete. I will. I've cooled off. There'll be no more scenes."

"Good. You don't have the luxury of telling a superior officer to go fuck himself—not in a military environment anyway."

"I understand," Charlie answered with a humble smile.

Pete moved on to his main subject. "Do you want to talk about Vietnam a little?" he asked. "I'm keenly aware of your anti-war attitude and worried about your reputation here, Charlie. I feel responsible as the one who got you started. I didn't know you'd *obsess* and become an expert, though."

Charlie laughed. It *was* an obsession.

"Listen," Pete continued. "I've followed your reports on Vietnam every morning. You've done an outstanding job, Charlie. The whole table has a different perspective on the war now, thanks to you. You followed orders. Am I right?"

"Yeah, I did; I kept going deeper and deeper," Charlie answered. "When I learned from my Chem professor what was in Agent Orange, I was shocked. It was the beginning of my tipping point"

Pete grinned. "You asked your Chemistry professor? What did he say?"

"He said we're using an extremely dangerous poison—one of the most deadly known."

"That bad? Really?"

"Yes. There's no honor in what we're doing to those poor peasant people over there," Charlie continued. "I can't reconcile that kind of warfare with *anything* that I've learned here."

"I hear you. It's obvious to me, Charlie, that this affects your motivation. I can almost *see* your attitude change daily. Do you want to keep doing the reports? Believe it or not, some at our table find them helpful."

Charlie smiled. "Really? Sure, I'll keep going."

"I know that My Lai has affected us all, Charlie. Most of us are withholding judgment until more facts come out. Nevertheless, as an officer, you can't diminish the efforts of our guys over there. The vast majority are doing the best they can."

"I know that, and I certainly don't judge their efforts. I would like to know, however, what would drive a bunch of guys to *do* something like that massacre? And why was it covered up for a year and a half?"

"We may never know, will we?"

"Not if we remain silent."

"So what are you going to do then?" Pete finally asked. "It's counterproductive and self-defeating to be against the war while training to become an officer and military advocate."

"I can't be hypocritical—but I want to get through plebe year. I wouldn't want anyone to say I couldn't take the hazing."

"Okay. But what's your conscience telling you?"

"To quit. Look, I know I'm not cut out for military life. I don't have the aptitude, skills or desire for it. I'll never be what my dad wants—or match my brother's accomplishments here. I want to show them that I'm not a quitter, though—despite my inadequacies."

"Hold on, Charlie," Pete said abruptly. *"Nothing* about you is inadequate. You want to dance to a different song, that's all…and you're not afraid to say it."

Charlie nodded slowly and smiled.

"Thanks, Pete. That means a lot."

"I guess the best advice I can give you, Charlie, is to follow your heart. Take stock of your true abilities and allow them to flourish. In the end, no one will criticize you for that. Just try not to create too much of a ruckus here in the process. In spite of some bad apples, the majority of us want to serve with honor."

"I agree. Behind all the rigid exteriors are a great group of guys. I know that."

"I know you do, Charlie. I'll support you as best I can. Listen, I *admire* your character, regardless of whether or not I share all your views."

Charlie sensed the conversation was over and stood. Pete stood as well. The two men shook hands again. "Thanks so much, Pete. I'll remember your advice."

"You're welcome, Charlie. Go do the right thing—for you."

Charlie smiled as he walked back to his room. He *would* remember Pete's advice for the rest of his life.

❋

At last, on Wednesday afternoon, Charlie had an opportunity to use the pay phone. Though he had tried every free moment he had, upperclassmen always occupied every booth—always ahead of him. The frustration was infuriating.

When at last he saw an empty phone booth, he sprinted towards it. He quickly slipped inside and slammed the folding door behind him.

Nervously, he dialed her number.

Please answer.

He heard the receiver click.

"This is Kacie."

"Kacie?"

She gasped when he said her name. Her eyes open wide.

"Charlie! God, I've been worried! Are you all right?"

"Hanging in there. I've missed you. Tell me again you're for real."

"Yes, yes, I am," she cried. "I miss you, too, Charlie."

"I've been trying to call all week. The phones are always in use. Upperclassmen get priority."

Kacie laughed. "It must suck to be a Plebe."

Charlie laughed back. "Sometimes. How are you doing, Kacie?"

"I'm lonely but otherwise fine. Listen though. Word's gotten out around campus about how good we sounded the other day in the music hall. We'll probably have a full house in the auditorium Saturday."

A fearful thought crept into Charlie's mind.

What's Frank going to do? Is he going to have me restricted here for insubordination?

I wouldn't put it past that little ass kisser.

Charlie brushed away the thought. "Really? A full house. That'll put some pressure on us."

"Nah, we're as good as anyone else I've seen on that stage."

"Okay. I'm ready."

"I can't wait to see you again," Kacie said. I'm missing you terribly."

"Me, too, missing you."

Kacie paused. Something was missing in the tone of his voice. "You sound hesitant. Is anything wrong?"

Suddenly, there was an angry thump on the glass door of the booth. Charlie's time was up. A frowning first classman stared at him.

"I've gotta go, Kacie. Some upperclassman wants the phone. I'll try to call you later. Otherwise, I'll meet you Saturday on the Quad. We can do a final rehearsal then. Bring my guitar."

"Okay, Arlo. And you bring your best stuff."

"You know I will…bye, Kacie."

Charlie wanted to slam the phone down in its cradle. He wanted to grab the jerk who was pounding on his booth. He was in too much trouble to do either. He opened the door and slipped out into the hallway.

Kacie held the phone in her hand for a long time, as if it held a small piece of Charlie's energy still within. She wondered about him. She hoped he would call again before the weekend.

❋

The following morning, Charlie sat at his table patiently waiting for the large silver platter of eggs passed around by rank. Exams loomed in the near future. It was the beginning of what was called

"The Dark Ages"—the most difficult and darkest time of the year. It would last until April.

"Okay, Charlie," Pete said, "bring us up to date on the status of the war. What happened over the holidays?"

Harry's head snapped up. He looked angrily at Pete.

"Charlie?"

"Come on, Pete. Don't tell us you *spooned* this guy?"

Pete ignored him.

Harry looked back at Charlie with a menacing sneer.

"Go ahead, Charlie," Pete said.

"Sirs, the Philippines, and Thailand have announced that all their troops will be withdrawn from Vietnam. President Nixon announced the planned withdrawal of 50,000 troops by April of this year and Secretary Laird pronounced a corresponding reduction in draft calls by 25,000. Congress has refused to approve any appropriations for ground forces in Laos and Thailand."

"That's good news," someone stated.

"On the surface, sir. However, another one hundred U.S. soldiers died during Christmas leave."

"What about My Lai?" another asked.

"Sir, the Americal Division reported killing fifty-three enemy soldiers. Sergeant Davis Mitchell is charged with the premeditated murder of thirty civilians at My Lai."

The table was silent for a moment. Finally, a third classman asked Charlie if he thought others would be charged in the massacre.

"Yes, sir. The massacre has been covered up for over a year and a half. There *has* to be more about My Lai that we don't know."

Harry looked across at Charlie with a deriding snicker. "Are you a fortune teller, McDaniels? Your opinions don't matter here."

"Yes, sir."

When breakfast was over, Charlie ran back to his room to get ready for classes. With a full schedule, he had little free time. Nevertheless, he decided to make room for a visit to his brother on the way to class.

Pete was right. He should apologize. He had been unreasonably upset the other day. Frank was still his brother, after all.

He tapped gently on Frank's door. "What do you want, Charlie?" he asked curtly.

Frank was alone now. Charlie entered and stood at ease.

"Hey. I just wanted to say I'm sorry for lighting into you the other day. It was personal and disrespectful. I shouldn't have done it in front of my roommates."

Frank said nothing. He stared at Charlie for a long time and shook his head sadly. "Just remember, man, you brought this on yourself."

"Brought what?"

"I called Dad and told him about you little tizzy-fit—word for word. He was furious as you might expect."

"Why'd you tell him? It was between us."

"We don't keep secrets in this family, Charles."

"Your call to the little general was a secret to me," Charlie said.

"So what?" Frank mimicked.

"All right, whatever. I only came to apologize, Frank. Whether you accept it or not, it still stands."

Charlie turned to leave and then froze at his brother's next sentence.

"I have no choice but to put you on report."

Charlie turned angrily. "What do you mean you have no choice?"

"Dad told me to. He said it was a direct order. I have to."

"What do *you* want to do, Frank."

"Doesn't matter, Charles. I have to follow orders." He shrugged with a self-satisfied smile."

"Frank, you spineless fuck," Charlie whispered. He had nothing to lose now. "When are you going to learn to think for yourself."

"Get out of here."

Charlie left quickly and ran back to his room. He grabbed his coat and books and left for class. It seemed his world was spinning too fast. He was losing control.

✵

After morning classes, Charlie ran through Bancroft looking hopefully into every phone room on his way.

In the next room, there it was—an empty phone booth. He looked at his watch. He had fifteen minutes before noon formation. He was cutting it close. He didn't care. He had to talk to Kacie.

He listened to the phone ring.

Come on!

She answered on the third ring. "Hello?"

"Kacie, it's Charlie!"

"Goodie. You found a phone booth!

"Yes, thank God. I only have a couple of minutes."

"We're still on Saturday, right?"

"Yes. But I need to tell you something, though."

Kacie's pulse quickened. "Go ahead."

"My brother and I got into a big fight Monday. He's threatened to put me on report for insubordination. I'll tell you the details later."

"Your own *brother*? What are you going to do, Charlie? Will you be restricted?" There was a grave concern in her voice.

"I don't know. I think Frank's pissed; I damaged his ego. I just have to wait, I guess."

There was a long pause on the other end. Charlie looked at his watch.

"Kacie?"

She was holding back tears.

Finally, she said, "I'd sure like a chat with your brother—and your old man. I'm telling you, you can't be related to them!"

"I'd like to think that. Anyway, I had to tell you. It wouldn't be right to keep it from you I don't want you to worry, though."

"Thanks, Charlie. I knew something was bothering you when we talked yesterday."

"The concert is a go for sure, Eli. I'll see you Saturday."

PARADOX

On Friday morning, Charlie sat behind his desk watching his roommates preparing for classes. He was thinking about tomorrow. Liberty Call would commence immediately after noon formation. By twelve-thirty, he'd be with Kacie again. At two, they would begin their concert.

The words of each song in their playlist ran continuously through his mind. He performed each in his imagination.

He looked once at his roommates and started humming one of the songs.

His roommates looked at him and grinned. They had heard him sing in the shower.

Charlie looked at them questionably.

"Go ahead, man. Anytime. You're good."

Charlie sang softly—Blowing in the Wind.

A moment later, the door swung open.

Charlie and his roommates rose to attention.

It was Harry, on watch duty today in battalion headquarters. He had a sheet of paper in his hand and a very self-satisfied smile on his face. If Harry was happy, it surely meant bad news for Charlie.

Harry looked at Charlie. "Were you singing one of those fucking peace songs, McDaniels?"

"Yes, sir."

"Doesn't belong here. Shut the fuck up!"!"

"Aye, aye, sir."

"Do you want to know why?"

"Yes, sir."

"It's a *peace* song." He spat the word angrily. "Oh, that's right, I forgot, you're a peacenik shithead, aren't you?

Charlie said nothing. He stared ahead.

"You probably love that song, don't you?"

"It's one of my favorites, sir."

Harry shook his head in disgust. He would have gone on with the peacenik thing but had something far better. He handed Charlie the paper he was holding in his hands.

"Read this, dickhead. You're in deep shit! I knew it was only a matter of time with you, McDaniels."

Charlie took the paper from Harry and looked at it. It was a particular form—one designated for Class-A offenses.

"Your own fucking *brother* Class-A'd you, you poor miserable shit."

Harry laughed heartily and left with his self-satisfied smile.

Charlie read the form. There it was—"gross insubordination." Frank followed through on his threat.

Dad would be so proud, he thought bitterly.

⁂

Charlie stopped by Pete's room on his way out. He showed him the Class A.

"Who would Class-A his brother, for god's sake?" Pete asked in disbelief. "If it goes through, this could restrict you until June Week!"

Charlie said nothing.

"Your dad's a general, right?"

Charlie nodded.

"Boy, you've got your tit in a wringer big time, don't you?"

"Yeah, you could say that. I seem to have an affinity for trouble."

"Maybe so, but you have facts and the truth going for you. I have a feeling you know how to handle trouble."

Charlie smiled. "Yeah, I have some experience with it."

"Okay. Let's see how you handle this. There'll be a hearing first. Look for a notice next week. You'll go before the Honor Board and be given the opportunity to defend yourself. I'll put in a good word for you."

"Thanks, Pete."

"That's a tough one, Charlie—hard not to take personally, huh?"

"Yeah. I tried to apologize. That's when Frank told me that my father ordered him to put me on report."

Pete said nothing. He was angry, too.

Finally, he shook his head and said, "Regardless, I'll back you any way I can. Keep me posted, okay?"

❋

That afternoon, Charlie found a letter from his mother waiting on his desk. He opened it slowly, hoping for the best. She told him that his father had shipped out for Vietnam and is gone for the next thirteen months."

She wrote about his alcoholism—how it had affected her and everyone around him. She confirmed her desire to talk to Charlie in person as soon as possible.

Charlie couldn't help the anger he felt towards his father as he read her words. He hoped he would be able to call her. In case he couldn't, he wrote a long letter to assure her he was okay. He wrote to her about Kacie—how he met her and how they came together. He told her about the planned concert at St. John's.

❋

Twenty-five minutes before reveille, Charlie stood in the dim hallway outside Pete's room. He opened the *Baltimore Sun* and began to scan the headlines.

There was usually a story about Vietnam on the front page along with accounts of how many Americans died each day and week—merely statistics on the surface: seven soldiers here and another thirteen somewhere else. It was a never-ending string of tragedies. Each death robbed a young man of his life—robbed him of his past and robbed him of his future. It made no sense.

Nixon's promise to withdraw all troops this year was another political promise, a way to garner support. President Thieu announced today that, without ongoing military assistance, his government would collapse. How much more does America have to do for this insignificant little country on the other side of the world?

How could anyone still claim that the sacrifices were worth it?

Turning to the second page of The Sun, Charlie read another article about My Lai. According to the *Sun*, a private and sergeant were accused of murder and "sexual offenses" in the area near My Lai.

Charlie felt sick. Killing civilians during the heat of battle could be reconciled with the shoot-or-be-shot mindset of deadly combat. But rape?

Charlie closed the newspaper in disgust and dropped it carelessly on the linoleum deck.

Later, at breakfast, he sat in his usual chair waiting for whatever harassment and hazing would come his way.

"Charlie, what's going on today?" Pete asked.

"Sixty-five Americans were killed last week in combat action. No report yet on VC kills. The Army has charged two more soldiers with murder and sexual offenses related to Song My and My Lai."

"What do you mean by sexual offenses? Are you talking about rape?" Pete's roommate asked.

"There are no details reported as of this time, sir."

Charlie's table became unusually quiet. He knew the shock of alleged rapes would shake anyone's patriotism. To murder was deplorable; rape was beyond deplorable.

❋

Saturday arrived at last. In a few hours, Charlie would be free to again leave the confining walls of the Academy and return to Kacie. Last week was a nightmare. He was grateful it was over. He sat through classes in the morning, unable to concentrate on any lecture. All he could think about was Kacie and their concert.

At twelve-thirty, the sound of "Liberty Call" rang through the hallways of Bancroft Hall. Charlie was one of the first out. He walked through the Rotunda and bounded down the front steps.

He was free!

Charlie hurried across the Yard, past the bandstand, the chapel. He was close to running as he passed through Gate Four.

Five minutes later, he stood at the entrance to St. Johns. There was Kacie, waiting for him in the Quad. He ran to her with open arms. She ran to him as fast as she could while carrying both guitar cases. When he reached her, Kacie put down the cases and ran into his outstretched arms. Charlie picked her up joyfully and twirled her around.

"Charlie, Charlie! Thank God. You're safe here." It was all she was able to say.

"I've missed you so much, Kacie."

"Oh, me, too." She hugged him fiercely.

Charlie hugged back in wanton disregard for the rules concerning public display of affections. Screw it. He was safe here.

When she, at last, pulled away, the first thing she asked was about the pending Class-A. "What's going on with your brother?"

"He *did* put me on report," Charlie answered glumly. I have a hearing next week. I'll know more then."

"What will happen if you're convicted? Does that mean I won't be able to see you again? Or do any more concerts?"

"Who knows?" Charlie answered hesitantly. "All we can do is wait. Let's not talk about it now."

"Okay," she said, trying to shake off the anger. "Are you ready? We're on in an hour, you know." Her green eyes danced all over him.

"Absolutely," he said. "Let's go set up."

Charlie took the guitar cases and followed Kacie to the FSK Auditorium. Kacie opened the door and held it for him.

Inside the lobby was an atrium filled with exotic plants. They thrived happily in their artificial homes under expansive skylights.

Kacie opened another door that led into the empty auditorium. Charlie looked in and whistled.

"Nice venue!"

It was an enormous theatre filled with hundreds of seats and decorated in a modern motif. Charlie admired the setup. Careful attention had been given to acoustics. Charlie recognized all the strategically placed sound-deadening devices on the walls and overhead. He looked at Kacie and smiled.

"This should work."

They walked down the aisle on the right and stood at the base of the stage.

The stage featured a curved front that wrapped back to the stairways on either side. An ebony piano sat in the rear behind the opened red curtains.

Charlie walked to the front of the stage and surveyed row after row of red seats extending across the majority of the auditorium.

"Ready?" she asked.

"You bet! This is perfect! Let's go."

She smiled and took her guitar while leading Charlie up the stairway on the right side of the stage. Together, they walked across the maple platform and stood at the center looking out.

"What do you think, Arlo?"

"Nice. The acoustics are awesome—no echoes at all."

"We'll sound as good as we can, for sure."

Kacie went backstage and found the lighting panel. She flipped on the house lights, flooding the area with a soft glow.

Kacie turned off the house lights and flipped another switch to turn on the stage lights. "Close your eyes. It's bright."

She was right. Charlie was momentarily blinded.

"Sorry," she said. "I'll turn on the spotlights." The harsh lights disappeared, replaced by a soft cone of light that formed a small circle of light in the center of the stage.

"How's that?"

"Better," he said.

"Okay, grab one of those old stools over there. I'll get the other."

They positioned the two stools in the middle of the spotlight.

"Arlo, sit on one of the stools so I can adjust the spotlight. Watch your eyes again."

Kacie adjusted the light so that it just illuminated Charlie's and her stools.

"Perfect," she said while picking up two mike stands and placing them between the chairs. "How does that feel?"

He placed his feet on the stool's footrest. "Good."

"I'll get the mikes," Kacie said disappearing somewhere in the darkness behind. In a minute, she returned with two mikes, each with a cord that led to an invisible power supply. She handed one microphone to Charlie and placed the other on the mike stand. Charlie did the same and lowered it to pick up the guitar. The other would amplify their voices.

Each had done this before. It was strictly business now.

"Ready for a sound check?"

For several more minutes, they adjusted and fine-tuned the volume of each mike so that their voices amplified clearly.

When satisfied, they looked at each other and smiled. "I think we've got it. Let's do a number to be sure."

Charlie started the first verse, Kacie accompanied softly in the background. At the second verse, she joined in. The same beautiful harmonies came through the sound system. Their instruments were as if made for each other.

The reverberations of their voices transcended mere harmony—their voices blended magically, almost spiritually.

After completing the opening number, Charlie leaned over and shook Kacie's hand. "Sounds good to me. I think we're ready."

"Bravo!" A voice suddenly rang from behind. Maria Wilkes walked from behind the stage applauding enthusiastically. Kacie introduced Charlie to the head of the Music Department. She held a copy of the poster advertising the concert.

An Afternoon of Folk Music by Eli and Arlo

"I hear good things about you two," Maria said. "My students love you guys. This concert should be a memorable event."

"Thank you, Miss Wilkes."

"Maria."

Charlie smiled. "Maria."

"You guys keep practicing," Maria said. "I'll be back just before two to introduce you."

For the next half hour, Kacie and Charlie reviewed the playlist one more time. At a quarter to two, Kacie heard the voices in the atrium; the audience was arriving.

They rested the guitars on the stools and exited to a small waiting area offstage. Here, they remained until Maria returned to introduce them.

"Can you take off your jacket, Arlo?" Kacie asked. "And your tie, too?"

"May I leave my pants on?"

Kacie laughed and punched him playfully on the arm. "Be serious. This is no time for your goofy humor."

"Okay. Sorry. I'll take off the coat and tie. This is a performance and I need to play the role. I need to fit in with the ambiance."

Charlie knew he might be walking a narrow edge. The moment he removed his jacket, he would be out of uniform in public. Nevertheless, he felt safe in the middle of this beautiful college. He was surely the lone midshipman on campus.

As they waited for the auditorium to fill, Kacie said. "The word's out. I'm expecting a big crowd. You won't get stage fright, will you?"

He laughed. "Every time I do this I get the butterflies. It'll pass quickly. I'll be okay," he answered. "What about you?"

"Same." She answered with a confident wink.

As they waited backstage, Charlie asked Kacie casually, "Are you sure Ignacio's doing okay with all this?" he asked.

"Not completely, I'm afraid. I told him who you were and that you and I are a couple now."

"You told him I was a *midshipman*?"

"I'm sorry. I was only trying to be honest. He would find out soon anyway. Ignacio didn't take it well—still thinks I'm his girlfriend. I never was. Don't worry. I'm sure he'll get over it."

Her words echoed hollowly in Charlie's mind. He hoped she was right. He was in a vulnerable public venue. He didn't need any trouble.

At two o'clock, the auditorium buzzed and hummed with anticipation. The lights dimmed and the spotlight directed attention to the center of the stage.

Charlie was uncharacteristically nervous. He felt a lot of pressure—it was as if the future of his life depended on it.

CHAPTER EIGHT

ONI

Present Time

The old man waited for death to absolve him of his inadequacies and self-loathing. He knew it would happen quickly and painlessly.

And then, in a moment of self-pity, he realized that he didn't want to be found dead on his dirty bathroom floor. Others would laugh and think it fitting that he met his maker beside the toilet. They would mock him even in death.

No. He had to get up and return to his bed.

He was cold, colder than he had ever been. He struggled to pull himself upright as the darkness began to overcome him. He staggered down the short hallway gasping for breath; his body didn't want to move anymore.

An overwhelming tiredness fell upon him as he reached his bedroom. Ahead, was his old and dirty bed. He lurched towards it as the lights went out. The last thing he remembered was the softness of the mattress surrounding him, welcoming him one last time.

1970

Maria looked out briefly from behind the curtain. "Looks like you might have a full house this afternoon."

Kacie smiled. "I did a little bit of advertising this week."

"I know. I've seen the posters you made. 'Eli and Arlo'—has a nice ring, don't you think?"

The chatter from the audience grew louder. It was now 1:55. Maria hugged them both, wishing good luck and harmony. "I have a feeling this will be a special concert."

Charlie and Kacie stood just behind the curtain to the left of the stage. As the lights dimmed, Maria walked out to address the assembled students.

"Good afternoon, ladies and gentlemen," she said, picking up one of the mikes, "welcome to an afternoon of folk music from the last decade presented by our brand new duo, Eli and Arlo. Anyone who's heard these two play knows what a treat the next two hours will be."

The auditorium was silent; a sense of expectation pervaded the atmosphere. Everyone focused on the two guitars resting on respective stools.

"Without further ado," Maria said loudly, "I bring you, Eli and Arlo!"

Polite applause greeted Charlie and Kacie as they walked to the center of the stage. Charlie's tie and jacket were gone, his white shirtsleeves casually rolled up his forearms. Kacie had thought to wear white so they would blend as a couple.

They smiled and bowed before settling onto the stools. Simultaneously each grabbed a guitar and secured the strap around their shoulders. Kacie looked at Charlie with a wink. He nodded back with his crooked smile.

With that, Charlie took a deep breath. He fingers effortlessly began the intro to *Blowin' in the Wind.*

The audience recognized the song immediately and began to applaud in support of the song and its anti-war message.

As Charlie sang, the audience listened attentively with quiet expectation. With each note, he could hear a low-key, excited buzz. When Kacie joined him in the second verse, many began to applaud. Most, however, remained in spellbound fascination.

Eli and Arlo were magic together. The rush each experienced from the live performance only accentuated their feelings and emotions as they played. Their excitement pushed them on to even higher levels.

When the first song ended, the audience remained quiet for a few seconds. For a moment, Charlie feared the performance had not gone well. Then, the entire student body was on their feet, applauding enthusiastically. He looked at Kacie with a huge grin. She smiled back and stood to bow with Charlie.

In the last row of the auditorium, however, one student sat uncharacteristically silent. Ignacio focused on Charlie with a look of contempt. Since the house lights were still on, he dared not get too close to the stage for fear of being recognized.

However, Ignacio congratulated himself for having the foresight to bring a pair of binoculars with him. Carefully, he raised the glasses to his dark, angry eyes.

So that's the dude Kacie dumped me for. He looks vaguely familiar. Where have I seen him?

He left after the opening song. No one noticed him leave nor heard him slam the outside door.

Ignacio refused to accept having his "girlfriend" stolen—not without a fight. He had a mean-spirited personality and an ego crying for revenge. He decided to find out what he could on this Arlo fellow. He had to bring him down if he wanted Kacie back.

For the next two hours, the duo of *Arlo and Eli* covered all the popular protest songs of the era. Many students sang with them.

They were an unqualified hit. The combined tones of their voices brought a powerful harmony that accentuated the lyrics and stirred the audience. It was a fairy-tale moment.

❋

Completing their second encore, Charlie and Kacie felt

emotionally exhausted.

Maria was the first to congratulate them. "You two were unbelievable!" she said.

"Thanks, Maria!" Kacie said. The excitement in her eyes burned with feeling. Charlie was likewise overwhelmed by the crowd's reaction. It was by far, the most enthusiastic audience for whom he had played.

"And," Maria continued with a glance at Charlie, "this young man is a keeper, for sure, Kacie. You make a beautiful couple. And, Charlie, don't *ever* let her go."

"No, ma'am. Not on a bet, I won't," he answered with a wide grin.

Eli and Arlo stood together for a half hour chatting and basking in the warmth and joy of their accomplishment.

Finally, the auditorium was empty.

"That went well," Charlie said. His understatement brought a smile.

"We were terrific, Charlie. I could do this every day."

"Me, too. Should we do another?"

"For sure."

Charlie kept careful track of the time and began looking at his watch. He had to leave no later than 5:45 to be in Bancroft Hall by six.

It was 5:40.

Charlie looked at Kacie sadly. "I need to go," he said.

"I know," she said sadly. "You're coming back tomorrow?" Kacie asked.

"After the chapel service," he answered wryly.

"Really?" she smiled. "You didn't tell me you were religious."

He gave her his crooked grin. "I'm not. It's a command performance—mandatory that all midshipmen attend a church of their choice. A lot of tourists line up to see us march into the chapel. It's a great image for freedom and democracy—the PR office here milks the shit out of it."

Kacie rolled her eyes. "Forced religion is freedom?"

"Yeah, funny, huh?" he answered. "But, I'm free afterward, say around noon. We should meet somewhere other than St. Johns. Being seen with you marks me as Arlo. I don't want anyone to connect Arlo with the Naval Academy."

"Yeah. We need to keep you under wraps around the campus. Your uniform would tip everybody off. Probably best if your identity is confidential at first."

"Where should we meet?"

"I'll wait for you on State Circle. Look for me on one of the benches around the Governor's mansion."

"Deal."

*

After the chapel service Sunday morning, Charlie changed uniforms and returned to town. He had five hours of freedom. He felt as if he were walking on air. His head continued to swim with the exhilaration he felt. It was a beautiful feeling.

Maryland Avenue intersected State Circle a few blocks away. It was the residence of the Governor and kept meticulously maintained. Even in January, the gardens and trees brought peace to each visitor. He could only imagine what this place will look like in the Spring.

Kacie was waiting for him on a bench secluded from visitors by a tall hedgerow of Arborvitae. It was a small but private park in the middle of town. Charlie looked around. They were out of sight. He bent over and gave her a quick kiss.

The weather was relatively mild and sunny. They sat on the bench undisturbed for several hours, holding hands and reflecting on the concert and each other.

"I never knew this place existed," Charlie said. "It's perfect."

"Yeah, people will walk by occasionally. I doubt there'll be any of your kind, though."

Charlie grinned. "*My* kind? You make me sound derelict."

They talked for an hour in relative privacy. Charlie made a quick trip to find bagels and milkshakes. Other than that, they were together all afternoon.

They reminisced about the concert yesterday.

"I can reserve the auditorium again in two weeks. Want to give it another go?"

"Sure. Why not? Exams will be over for both of us by then."

"How 'bout a program?" Charlie asked.

"No sense arguing with success," Kacie said cheerfully. "We can keep the basic theme—just vary it with a few different songs. Otherwise, I'm ready."

"Okay. If I had any time to rehearse, I'd go for a completely different program," Charlie said. "I don't have that luxury, though."

"You don't need much rehearsal, Arlo…but, since you can't even touch your guitar until the concert, the same program is probably best."

The conversation paused.

"We have to talk about the elephant in the room," Kacie ventured finally.

"You mean in the garden, don't you?"

She smiled and punched him playfully. "Whatever. Don't evade the issue."

"There's not much more to say until the hearing is over. It'll be next week sometime. I'll let you know as soon as I know. The outcome will determine whether or not there'll be another concert."

"What's wrong with your brother?" Kacie cried. "Why would he do this?"

"He takes all this way too seriously. Plus, he thinks he's a big shot because he's about to become Brigade Commander."

"I hope I get the chance to confront him some time."

Charlie laughed again at the image in his mind. "He'd turn and run, I'm sure."

"Seriously, though, Charlie? What's the point? The Navy doesn't seem to suit you a whole lot."

"No, it doesn't. We're in complete agreement there."

Tears filled angry green eyes. "Damn it, Charlie! You don't *belong* in the military!"

"I know, and I agree. I'd just like to get through plebe year."

"And endure another five months of this bullshit, maybe on restriction to boot? Why?"

Charlie had no answer. He looked down at her hand in his.

He turned to her with a deep sigh. "I hear what you're saying, Kacie. Give me just a little more time, okay?"

"Of course, Charlie. But you and your sense of honor are only wasting time. What *is* the point?"

"It's not that simple, Kacie. If I quit now, I'd have no money, no place to live and no job. I'd be just another homeless person."

She thought of him panhandling on State Circle and shook her head to dismiss the thought.

"Couldn't you stay with your mom since your dad's not there?"

"I could. It's an option…not a good one for me though. I'll be twenty next September. I can't be living with my mother. I have no skills, no education, and no experience. I *need* to be in college, or I'm eligible for the draft."

Kacie pulled her head off his shoulders and kissed him tenderly.

"Figure out where you're going. I'll wait. I'll always be here regardless of what might happen."

The shadows lengthened across the lawn. Charlie stiffened. She knew it was time for him to leave.

Kacie stood reluctantly.

"Walk me back to school."

❋

Charlie arrived at the steps of Bancroft Hall seconds before the deadline. He raced up the steps and into the rotunda. He didn't have time to clean up. He just made it to his place in the evening formation. Charlie looked at his scuffed black shoes.

He fell at attention, praying to be left alone. Sunday evening formations were usually lax. Everyone was depressed. Another week of classes began tomorrow.

Charlie heard a small commotion further down the line. It was the click of the shoes of an upperclassman as he made his way down Charlie's row. He was inspecting plebes. He knew it was Harry by the sound of his voice.

Shit!

Harry sidestepped smartly to Charlie's front. He surveyed his uniform with dark eyes and a cruel smile.

"Ah, Mr. McDaniels," he said. "I'm certain I can find something wrong with *you*. Let's see, where should I start? Oh, I know, what's for dinner tonight?"

"I'll find out sir," Charlie answered. He'd had no time to memorize the menu.

Harry glared at him. He had to whisper so Pete wouldn't hear him. "You don't sweat anything here do you, McDaniels? You think this is all a game, don't you? Are you having fun?"

"No, sir. Yes, sir!"

"You think you're special, don't you, because you're cozy with Pete and our table?"

"No, sir."

Harry began to inspect Charlie's wrinkled uniform. Before Harry got to Charlie's shoes, the company commander announced, "Fall in!"

Harry raised his head and glared back at Charlie with feigned indignation. "Come around, you oversized piece of shit—and bring me a Form 2," he whispered.

"Aye, aye, sir," Charlie responded. He knew he was woefully unprepared for dinner. All he wanted was to be left alone.

ONI

❋

Monday, brought a substantial snowstorm to the Annapolis area. When Charlie arose at five in the morning, he could see snow swirling and dancing outside his window. He had two classes this morning and dreaded the prospect of tramping through the snow toward classrooms a quarter of a mile away…to listen to subjects in which he had no interest. He forced himself out of a warm bunk and prepared for the day.

Shortly, he made his way down the hall to Pete's room. He picked up the newspaper beside his door and scanned the headlines. It was the same depressing news. The ground war continued with the persistent reporting of dead U.S. soldiers and Vietnamese. Charlie could only shake his head sadly. On the third page was another short article on My Lai. Two more U.S soldiers charged with murder and sexual offensives.

This is insane.

The halls were empty. Reveille would not sound for another half hour. Dejected and feeling very alone, Charlie returned to his room to prepare for the day.

The snow stopped by mid-morning. Several inches covered the Academy grounds. Charlie's footsteps crunched on frozen walks on the way to a Naval History class.

In the afternoon, Charlie tried to call Kacie but was unable to get through. He bought postcards from the Midshipman Store. He missed her terribly. His depression mounted.

There was no news about the pending Honor Committee hearing. It was just a matter of time.

Now, a half hour before evening formation, Charlie dressed and prepared for his come-around at Harry's room. It seemed his life here was stuck like a broken record. The same dreary routine repeated itself day after day.

❋

When the clock in the hall read 1800, Charlie knocked on Harry's half-opened door.

"Request permission to come aboard, sir."

"Get in here, pussy," Bruce commanded.

Charlie took two steps into the room. He remained at rigid attention and waited.

Harry's roommate, Bruce Pascal, snickered as Charlie stood at attention in the doorway.

There were others in the room—Harry's band of brothers who knew of Charlie's left-leaning opinions. They formed a half circle formed around Charlie, ready to gang up on him.

"Start running in place, plebe," Harry commanded.

Charlie ran in place, a relatively slow, relaxed pace.

"Pick it up, you commie pinko!"

Charlie ran faster. He didn't care what any of them thought—he would remain calm, casual and answer the questions fired at him as best as he could.

Above all, keep your cool.

"Recite the Pledge of Allegiance," someone shouted.

Charlie did as commanded.

"Again. Run faster."

"Aye, aye, sir," Charlie responded. He would soon be at a sprinting pace. He cited the Pledge again. His words became labored.

Charlie repeated the exercise five more times, each faster than the previous one. Although in good shape, sprint running in place drained his oxygen quickly. His breathing became labored, his words hoarse.

"That's enough," Harry said at last. Sweat was pouring down Charlie's face. His legs ached. "Brace up against the wall," Harry commanded.

"Aye, aye, sir."

Four men surrounded Charlie and looked scornfully at him.

Each took their turn.

"What's the greatest country in the world?" Joe asked.

Charlie remained silent, breathing laboriously.

"Answer my fucking question, plebe!"

"I'll find out, sir." Charlie had no intention of answering.

"What? We're talking about your *country*, asshole!" Joe yelled indignantly. The circle around Charlie grew tighter.

Charlie said nothing. His silence said it all.

"Shove out, ass-hole," Harry commanded.

Charlie slid down the wall until his upper legs were almost parallel to the deck. He knew he would remain there until he answered the question. It was a bit of a predicament. Charlie would not respond to the question to their satisfaction. However, he knew he would not be allowed back up until he did.

To Charlie's extreme relief, the PA system reverberated through the hallways. Evening meal formation was in five minutes.

"Get up you miserable traitor!" Bruce ordered. His shrieks of anger sounded false and insincere—almost comical.

Charlie rose unsteadily, resuming his prior position of attention.

"Get out of here! Clean yourself up. We'll see you again same time tomorrow."

As Charlie limped out the door, he overheard one of his antagonist's comment, "Tough little bastard, isn't he?"

He smiled. It made his day.

After dinner, Charlie sat at his desk massaging strained muscles. Exam week was coming. His roommates buried themselves in textbooks. Abruptly, a plebe on watch duty appeared at the doorway.

Charlie looked up.

"For you," he said. "Good luck, man."

Charlie looked at the small note. He knew what it was.

The Battalion Honor Committee is meeting tomorrow afternoon at 1600 to consider charges against you by Midshipman First ClassMc-Daniels. Report at 1545 to defend your behavior.

"Thanks," he replied with a sigh.

⁂

The following day, Charlie stood at attention outside the battalion office. His appointment with the Honor Committee was in five minutes. He wore dress blues; his appearance overall was spotless. Precisely at 1600, he entered the office and faced the first man he saw.

"Midshipman fourth class McDaniels reporting as ordered, sir."

"Have a seat over there until they're ready," a Second Classman said flatly.

"Aye, aye, sir."

Charlie waited quietly, lost in thought. Ten minutes later, his trance was broken as he heard the words, "You can go in now, McDaniels."

Charlie walked over to the conference room door and knocked loudly.

"Request permission to come aboard, sirs."

"Come in, Mr. McDaniels" a voice inside ordered.

Charlie opened the door and stepped in smartly. Facing him, the Battalion Honor Committee, seated in a row, stared back. The committee consisted of five upperclassmen—two senior midshipmen, and three juniors. Its duty was to investigate and evaluate reported honor violations and other gross misconduct. The decision they would shortly render was to determine Charlie's fate at the Academy for the rest of the year.

Charlie remained at attention and stared ahead at the dull green wall. He waited while the committee reviewed the particulars of his case.

"Mr. McDaniels," the board president said, "we have a Form 2—a class-A offense submitted by your brother, Midshipman first classMcDaniels."

"Yes, sir."

"He claims you were grossly insubordinate and threatened him on 3 January 1970. What have you to say?"

"Sir, I admit my insubordination. Midshipman McDaniels and I argued over a personal incident that happened during Christmas leave."

"Do you care to share the incident?"

"My father told me to come back here four days early. My brother offered no support."

"Wait a minute. You were thrown out of your own home during Christmas?"

"Yes, sir."

"What did you expect your brother to do?"

"Stand up for me, sir. Check on me to see if I was okay…"

"And he didn't."

"No, sir. He was afraid to anger my father."

"*You* obviously angered your father," one of the Second Classmen stated.

"Yes, sir. He told me Lt Calley should receive the Silver Star."

No one on the Committee spoke for several seconds. It was as if they were collectively not sure that they correctly understood Charlie. The president stared at Charlie. His eyes narrowed.

"He *said* that?"

"Yes, sir."

"Does your brother believe Calley's a hero?"

"He believes whatever my father believes," Charlie replied.

"Okay," the President said. "Let's not get sidetracked by My Lai." He looked again at the typewritten charges against Charlie. "Do you have any explanation for your conduct, Mr. McDaniels?"

"Sir, we're brothers; we've had many fights in the past. That's no excuse, I know. However, I would never act that way to anyone here other than my brother. I was angry that he abandoned me at a time I needed help. I have since visited my brother to apologize."

"Very well," the president answered and looked for comments and questions from the board. The majority of the Honor Committee knew Frank McDaniels by reputation. None liked him. They knew him to be an opportunist with a big ego.

"McDaniels, your record here is not what I'd call sterling. It indicates a lack of respect and enthusiasm for the system you've pledged to support. Specifically, there is a comment in your aptitude review regarding a negative attitude toward our war effort. Is that true?"

"Yes, sir. One of my duties every morning is to report on the war to my tablemates in the mess hall. Recently, the papers have reported a lot about the My Lai massacre. I have tried to remain objective in the reporting of facts despite the negative feelings this incident engenders."

"Well, that makes a difference if you were acting under orders," the president said.

"Yes, sir."

"Do you sympathize with the anti-war movement, Mr. McDaniels?"

"Sir, I am against the atrocities at My Lai and our widespread use of chemicals that may permanently damage the ecology of parts of Vietnam. To that extent, sir, I sympathize with the anti-war movement."

"Okay, that's your business", the president answered. "I assume you're smart enough to keep these thoughts to yourself."

"Yes, sir."

"We won't discipline you for an opinion, Mr. McDaniels. Our purpose this afternoon is to evaluate your insubordination, to determine if you should be Class-A'd for gross misconduct."

"Yes, sir."

After several additional questions, Charlie was told to wait outside while the board discussed his case.

"Aye, aye, sir," Charlie answered with a smart about-face. He opened the door and returned to the main battalion office, standing awkwardly at attention. Someone finally said to him, "Hey man, you can sit if you want."

"Thank you, sir."

Charlie had no sooner sat than the door opened and the Committee President stuck his head out. He nodded toward Charlie and motioned to return to the conference room. Charlie rose immediately and walked into the room to stand at attention before the Committee.

"Mr. McDaniels," the president began, "the Board had considered your behavior and believe that, since MidshipmanMcDaniels is your brother, it mitigates the disrespect you have shown him. Your apology, whether or not accepted, further indicates good faith on your part.

"Nevertheless, you have set an extremely poor example by conducting yourself in such a way before others, specifically your roommates and anyone else that may have overheard your remarks."

"Yes, sir. I regret my lack of discretion."

"The conclusion of the board is that you are not Class-A'd for insubordination, given the circumstances you have described. However, the next time you want to lay into your brother, find a private place."

"Aye, aye, sir."

"We must also caution you, however, that your pejorative attitude about the war will not make you any friends here. You *need* friends if you want to make it through Plebe Year. You already have a fair number of people watching you. I'd keep a low profile if I were you. Is that clear?"

"Yes, sir."

"This hearing is over. Dismissed."

"Thank you, sir." Charlie did another about-face and left the room. The Battalion office personnel on watch looked at him expectantly. He said nothing; his smile said it all.

No phones were available. There was a waiting line as well.

On his way back to his room, he stopped to see Pete. When he knocked on the door, Pete had his head buried in books. He looked up when Charlie knocked.

"Charlie!" he said. "Come in. What happened?"

"Just a warning; no Class-A," Charlie answered with a smile.

Pete stood to shake Charlie's hand. "Congratulations. I think that's fair. He *is* your brother, and you tried to apologize."

"I accept the responsibility. My temper got the best of me."

"It's a good lesson, Charlie. I hope you take it constructively."

"I will."

"Okay, buddy, keep after it. I'll see you later tonight. And congratulations again."

"Thanks, Pete."

Charlie went from Pete's room back to the pay phones. There was an open booth.

Charlie stepped in quickly and dialed Kacie's number. The phone rang several times.

Please answer, Kacie!

He was about to hang up. Suddenly, he heard the distinctive click.

A sleepy voice answered, "Hello? Charlie?"

"Oops, I woke you, didn't I?" he said.

"Just a nap. God, it's good to hear from you. Any news?"

"Yes! The Honor Committee dismissed the charge! They rejected Frank's claim. I'm *not* restricted."

He could hear her sigh with relief. "That's the best possible news you could give me! How's he going to take it?"

"Frank? Not well. He's vindictive like the old man."

"Well stay the hell away from him. He could be gunning for you."

"I'm not going near his wing. He no longer exists as far as I'm concerned."

"Good. You coming back Saturday?" she asked.

"Absolutely. Same time, same place?"

"I'll meet you in the Quad around twelve thirty."

"Can't wait to see you!"

"Me, too…uh oh, I have to go, Kacie. Some jerk's banging on the door to the phone booth."

"It's okay. I miss you. See you Saturday."

Charlie walked to his room. Waves of relief flowed through him. On his desk was a stack of textbooks. Exams would start next week.

I really should be studying.

❋

Pete nursed a cup of coffee at breakfast the following morning. He said little while deciding if Charlie should speak about the war this morning. Every day, he could see Charlie's attitude weaken.

Pete knew Charlie was not a military person. To convince him otherwise would be a disservice to both him and the Navy. No, Pete wanted what was best for Charlie—even if it brought things to a boil.

He put his coffee down and looked at Charlie carefully. "Charlie, tell us more about Agent Orange."

"The antiwar movement just sued Dow and Monsanto," Charlie answered.

"For what?"

"Sir, the movement wants to disclose the manufacturers' relationship with the U.S. Government. The lawsuit relates to the use of Agent Orange and its long-term effects on the people."

Harry's head snapped up. "Who the fuck cares about Agent Orange? This is a war, dufus. We want to know about the *war*."

Pete held up his hand.

"Gentlemen, I ordered Charlie to research Agent Orange. Don't blame him for his findings. What do you know about Agent Orange, Harry?"

"It's a powerful defoliant used to expose the VC trails and tunnels."

Pete knew he was creating tension at the table. He forged ahead. "What *are* the long-term effects?"

"Agent Orange contains a variant of dioxin known as TCDD, 2,3,

7,8-Tetrachlorodibenzo-p-dioxin. It's the most deadly of any chemical ever produced. Four million Vietnamese have been exposed to it."

"So what," Harry shot back. "War's a dirty business. People get hurt." No one argued that despite the harm being done to US troops as well.

Charlie clenched his fists under the table. He was amazed at both the insensitivity of this man and the ignorance his friends displayed.

"Sir, Dioxin not only destroys jungle foliage, but it also destroys crops and farmland—people's livelihood. It remains in the soil and the body for years, potentially causing god knows how many birth defects in future young children. The U.S. *knew* these collateral effects of Agent Orange yet continued using it. Over twenty million *gallons* have been sprayed since 1961, stripping eight thousand square miles of jungle and cropland."

"And your point, Mr. McDaniels?" a second classman asked while others nodded in agreement.

"It's a chemical weapon sir, a violation of the Geneva Conventions. It is my understanding that our government abides by a moral code of conduct in war, especially if it chooses to invade a foreign country unilaterally."

Charlie sensed the anger his editorial comments were creating. He was angry, too, however, and couldn't tone down his comments. He was telling the truth.

"McDaniels, how many American lives has Agent Orange saved do you think?" a second classman asked belligerently. "I would say a lot, wouldn't you?"

Charlie was losing control—he couldn't help himself. "That was the same argument our country used when it dropped nuclear weapons on Hiroshima and Nagasaki. That was the greatest terrorist attack ever perpetrated by one country on another."

Pete held up both hands. "Okay, Charlie, that's enough for today. Good report."

No one responded. They were all looking at Charlie angrily.

Pete observed the tension he had started by asking Charlie about

Agent Orange. Charlie was going to take a beating for reporting about Agent Orange the way he did. If Pete let Charlie pursue the line of chemical warfare, he wondered how long it would take before Charlie reevaluated his priorities.

Charlie sure as hell won't dance around the facts. I just hate to see him suffer because of stubbornness.

He decided to let Charlie continue to speak as candidly as he chose amidst a surmounting tide of anger.

It would take guts. Pete respected that.

❋

Word infiltrated the ranks of Charlie's company that he was critical of the war tactics. He became the subject of intense scrutiny at every formation. Each upperclassman who stood before him searched for any minor infraction that might be cause for discipline. Charlie had the unfortunate distinction of being the focus of attention.

He was hazed, ridiculed, insulted and demeaned. Charlie knew by now it was a game. They were pissed—that's all. They were duty-bound to make Charlie change his mind, to convince him of the honor brought by defending democracy.

Charlie knew too much. He wouldn't relent.

❋

Thank god for the weekends! Charlie thought. Five hours of liberty each Saturday and Sunday—not much, but enough. His relationship with Kacie grew stronger. He knew they had something special and would do anything to keep it

Their time together was like a brilliant flash in an otherwise gloomy existence. Their time together flew by quickly. They rehearsed, laughed and were grateful for the time they had.

Their next concert was Sunday, February 1st at two.

Kacie showed him the poster she had designed. Charlie loved the graphics. He noted in the footer she added: "Kacie Mitchell and Arlo McDaniels." Something told him that it would be better to keep his last name anonymous.

"I love it, Kacie," he said. "Although, couldn't the use of my real name get back to the Academy?"

"Yeah, I suppose…if anyone knew you're from the academy. No one does. I think you're safe."

"Okay, if you think so."

"Come on; we need to rehearse."

"What about lunch?" Charlie's crooked grin was back.

"Come on. I'll buy you a candy bar on the way."

Ignacio seethed as he read the poster he had snatched off the bulletin board in the dorm.

Another fucking concert!

He was determined to find out who Arlo was. He had little to go on. He was pretty sure that Arlo was not a student at the college. Still, there was something about his clean-shaven look that reminded Ignacio of someone.

Then he remembered.

That nut-job middy in Washington—the one who ran after us. He had a guitar. He was playing when we arrived at the station!

If this asshole is from the Naval Academy, I can find him. I have his last name!

He scratched his curly dark beard and simmered again at the thought of a midshipman interfering with his personal life. It occurred to Ignacio that the Naval Academy would be reluctant to condone one of its own participating in a folk concert on a liberal campus. Did the Academy know Arlo participated in an anti-war demonstration?

Okay, "anti-war" was a bit of a stretch—but he was playing anti-war songs. I wonder if he had permission from the Naval Academy.

The seeds of his revenge sprouted into a plan. He looked again at the bottom of the poster.

Arlo McDaniels.

What if I reported—better yet, complained about a midshipman disrupting our campus?

Ignacio opened the Annapolis phonebook and found the number of the academy's information office. He dialed the number and waited.

"Good morning. U.S. Naval Academy information office," a female voice answered politely. "How may I help you?"

"I wish to file a complaint against a midshipman," Ignacio said in his heavy Latino accent.

"Yes, sir. The nature of your complaint?"

"This midshipman led an anti-war demonstration on our campus on St Johns recently. Can't you control your people? I'm a student at St. Johns and support of the war. I'm very offended."

"One moment please."

Ignacio held for several minutes. He felt power and control again. It was a good feeling.

A male voice came on the phone. "This is Commander Wilson. Please state your name, sir."

"Ignacio."

"Last name?"

"I prefer to remain anonymous, please," Ignacio answered.

"Okay. However, it will be more difficult to establish your credibility without a full name."

"Let's just say I'm a student at St Johns College."

"Very well. Are you claiming one of our midshipman led a peace movement at your college? Do you have a name?"

"Yeah, it's Arlo," Ignacio answered. "Arlo McDaniels."

"Do you know what class or company he's in?"

"Nope. Sorry."

There was another long pause as the officer checked the master roster. When he returned to the line, he said, "We have a Charles McDaniels. There is no Arlo McDaniels registered here, sir. Are you sure about the name?"

"Of course I'm sure!" Ignacio responded sharply.

"All right, sir. I suggest you put your complaint in writing. I promise you the academy will do everything in its power to investigate. Here's the address."

Ignacio hastily searched for a pen or pencil. He found one in his pocket. "Go ahead," he said.

❋

Ignacio's hand-written letter reached the Academy two days later. Commander Wilson read it skeptically. The charges were implausible at best. Wilson's first thought was to throw the letter away. The man was probably a kook, his claim preposterous. He couldn't take the chance, however, and reluctantly decided to open an investigation.

He searched the Brigade roster and found the two McDaniels, a first and fourth classman.

Of course. McDaniels is the new Brigade Commander. No way would it be him.

Wilson wanted to talk first with the brigade commander before referring the matter anywhere else. He called to the plebe on duty, "Have Mr.McDaniels report to me ASAP."

"Aye, aye, sir."

Wilson's office was in the Admin Building adjacent to Bancroft Hall. Ten minutes later, Frank McDaniels stood before him.

Commander Wilson asked Frank outright if he was involved in a peace movement on St Johns Campus recently.

"No, sir. I've *never* been on that campus and certainly would not demean our war effort in public or anywhere."

"Very well. Do you know the other McDaniels here?"

"Yes, sir. Charles McDaniels is my brother."

"Does he ever go by the name 'Arlo'?"

"Not that I know of, sir."

"Do you think your brother is capable of such a blatantly outrageous and traitorous act?"

"Yes, sir. I regret to say that he could."

"Really? That's a hell of an accusation. He *is* your brother."

"I know, sir and I know how much against the war he is."

The commander sighed. "Okay, see if you can find a guy named 'Ignacio' over there at the St. John's. Get me more information on what the hell's going on."

"Aye, aye, sir."

"Dismissed."

⁂

It wasn't hard to find Ignacio. He was the only one at the college with that name. When Frank called, the operator put him through to the men's dorm. A masculine voice answered on the first ring.

"Men's dorm. This is Jason."

"Hello," Frank said. "May I speak with Ignacio, please?"

"Gonzales?"

"I'm sorry. I don't have a last name."

"Hang on."

Frank heard the sound of a shrill whistle in the receiver. "Somebody see if Gonzales is here," Jason yelled down the corridor.

After a pause, Frank could hear the sound of flip-flops running across the floor.

"This is Ignacio," the voice answered gruffly, slightly out of breath.

"My name is McDaniels. I'm a Midshipman First Class at the

Naval Academy. Are you the one who reported that one of our men led an anti-war concert recently on your campus?"

"Yes. Are you Arlo?"

"No. I'm investigating the incident. Can you answer some questions for me?"

"Go ahead."

"We have no Arlo at the Academy. Might you be referring to *Charles* McDaniels instead?"

"Look, all I know is that the guy goes by the name Arlo McDaniels. If it's not you, it's gotta be him."

"All right."

"You should watch your people more closely," Ignacio began to rant. "That asshole sang anti-war songs at our school!"

"I regret the incident, Mr. Gonzales."

Ignacio assumed a tone of feigned indignation. "Did you know that he was out of uniform? He disrupted our quiet environment with his anti-war chants."

"Anti-war chants?"

"Yeah, songs mostly. You know, the anti-war songs."

"If anyone from my school is doing such things, I shall take immediate steps to investigate the matter thoroughly."

"Thank you." He paused. "I bet you don't know he's doing it again, do you?"

"Doing what? Another demonstration?"

"Yeah."

"No. When?"

"Two o'clock Sunday. In our auditorium."

"This Sunday?"

Frank knew that if Arlo was indeed Charlie, he would have to be caught in the act if the story was to be believed.

"We'll monitor the situation closely, sir," Frank answered.

"I don't want you to *monitor* it, goddamn it. I want you to fucking *stop* him! You hot shits think you have all the answers, don't you?"

"No, sir. I'm only trying to help. I'll have to report this to my superiors."

"Yeah… okay. Sorry."

Ignacio hung up. He felt giddy with smug satisfaction. He hoped they would lock Arlo up for the rest of the year.

After putting the phone down, Frank immediately tracked down Commander Wilson to report what he had discovered.

I have his smart ass this time. Dad will have a shit fit when hears about this one!

❋

Standing at attention in Commander Wilson's office, Frank relayed the information he obtained from Ignacio.

"Next Sunday, sir," Frank reported stiffly. "My brother will be leading another 'demonstration' in the St Johns Auditorium at 1400 under the fictitious name of 'Arlo'."

Wilson shook his head slowly. "Tell me, Mr. McDaniels, is your brother that crazy to do something like that? He's only a Plebe, for Christ's sake."

"I know, sir. He's never had a good attitude about anything."

Wilson jotted down the date and time of the next concert before asking, "You're absolutely positive? We don't train our people here to demonstrate against us."

"Yes, sir, I know. My brother and I have had unpleasant encounters in the past, sir. We don't agree on much."

"I imagine not," Commander Wilson said. "Very well. Thank you for the information, Mr. McDaniels. You're dismissed."

"Aye, aye, sir. Thank you, sir." Frank answered crisply. He did an about-face and left the office.

Wilson watched Frank leave with a sad expression. If this story is true, it should go directly to the Commandant. A midshipman demonstrating against the war at a local college would be an embarrassment to both the Naval Academy and the Navy. It had to be investigated right away.

Commander Wilson shook his head slowly. He wondered what kind of brother could rat on his sibling so quickly. He picked up the phone and dialed a special branch of the Office of Naval Intelligence. The office investigates major infractions of Academy policy and security.

"Office of Naval Intelligence, Annapolis Division. Lieutenant James speaking."

"Lieutenant, this is Commander Wilson, Brigade Admin. I have an unusual report that I would like to have investigated. Do you have someone available Sunday? Let me give you the details."

❋

The first day of February was a gray and gloomy Sunday. It was 1:55 and the auditorium had filled with eager students and faculty. Backstage, Charlie peeked out at the crowd with an unsettled feeling. Though he tried to shake it off, it persisted nonetheless.

"What's the matter, Charlie?" Kacie asked. She knew him well enough now to recognize if his attitude shifted.

"It's nothing, Kacie," he answered. "Probably a little stage fright again."

"Well, you'd better get used to it; you're a bit of a celebrity around here now."

"Celebrity is gonna make it hard to keep my cover."

Kacie smiled and squeezed his hand tightly. "Don't over think it. Focus on the performance."

Charlie smiled. "You're right. I'm ready."

The auditorium lights dimmed and the audience hushed. As before, a single spotlight cast a glow around two stools at the front of the stage. Two perfectly tuned acoustic guitars stood waiting in holders next to the stools.

Maria Wilkes walked to the front of the stage to introduce Charlie and Kacie.

"Good afternoon, everyone," she began. "I see we have a full house again. Back by popular demand is the duo of 'Eli and Arlo' to serenade us with more folk music from the last decade. Many of you were here for their first concert two weeks ago. It was the talk of the campus. We have every reason to believe this one will be equally exciting. Ladies and gentlemen, Eli and Arlo!"

When Charlie and Kacie walked through the curtains into the spotlight, they received a standing ovation. Charlie was a little overwhelmed to see such enthusiasm. He and Kacie smiled and waved back. They bowed and assumed their positions on the stools again. The auditorium became completely quiet.

When the lights dimmed, two uniformed naval officers entered the auditorium quietly and stood together in the deep shadows of the back. They were Navy lieutenants sent by Naval Intelligence to observe the concert. Their orders were to remove Charlie from the scene in the event he encouraged *any* anti-war activities. Both officers began to take notes.

In the glare of the spotlight, Charlie and Kacie could not see that they were under observation. Kacie spoke into the microphone, thanking the audience and announcing their first song: *Where Have All the Flowers Gone* by Bob Dylan. They took and deep breath and began to play with every bit the grace and style as before. Maria watched them from backstage. She knew this was a unique duo.

At the chorus, Kacie invited the audience to sing with them. The full house responded enthusiastically. The auditorium exploded as the lyrics reverberated from every mouth. Their voices echoed the song's appeal for peace.

When the song ended, the two lieutenants looked at each other and nodded. The crowd's enthusiasm was strongly against the war, so much so that the Lieutenants concluded that the event *was* a peace demonstration.

The officers separated. Each walked smartly down the aisle on either side of the audience. As they drew near the stage, angry voices shouted at them.

"Hey, sit down! Down in front!"

Charlie squinted his eyes and searched in the darkness for the source of the disturbance. It was then that he spotted the Lieutenants on each side of the stage, walking up the stairs. He glanced at Kacie. She looked back with a puzzled expression.

Charlie put his guitar down. The audience went crazy, yelling expletives at the two officers and throwing whatever was handy at them. The atmosphere became riotous.

Ignoring crowd reaction, each officer walked up onto the stage. Charlie put his arm around Kacie to protect her from any flying missiles. He quickly led her offstage. "Is there a back door?" he asked.

"Yes. Hurry!"

One of the officers ran towards Charlie and grabbed his arm.

"Midshipman Charles McDaniels?"

Charlie stopped. "Yes, sir. I am."

Kacie stood between Charlie and the first officer. "None of your fucking business. Where's your warrant?"

The other officer tried to pull her aside.

Kacie's face darkened with anger. She faced them defiantly as she sought to free Charlie's right arm.

"What do you goons think you're doing?" she demanded. "This is a private school!" She had to shout over boos from the crowd. "You have no right to interrupt this concert!"

"This is a security matter, ma'am," one lieutenant said and looked back at Charlie. "Mr. McDaniels, we're apprehending you for leading an anti-war gathering and for being out of uniform. Get your hat and coat. You're coming with us."

"Sir, this is a concert in a private school, not a peace rally."

"Sounds like one to us. Let's go!"

Charlie knew better than to resist. He accompanied the officers backstage and retrieved the rest of his uniform. Kacie followed shouting and pounding on each officer's back.

"One moment, please. I wish to speak briefly with my partner."

"Go ahead. Get her off of us and make it fast!"

Charlie pulled her over to one side and put his arm around her. "Someone set us up, Kacie, someone who knew the concert was today. Can you find out who did it? Start with Ignacio."

"That sonofabitch! It *had* to be him."

"Time's up, buddy. Let's go."

Charlie's captors led him backstage toward the back door leading to the main hallway.

Kacie ran after him, struggling with the first officer, trying to extricate Charlie from his grip. As she began pounding again on his back, he pushed her away roughly. Kacie stumbled and went to one knee.

Charlie stopped and shook himself free. He looked at the officer squarely in the eyes, figuring, at this point, he had nothing left to lose.

"Do not touch her, sir!" he shouted angrily. *"Ever!"*

Charlie's eyes looked deadly serious, even menacing. The officers backed away for a moment before pulling out their handcuffs. "Don't fuck with us, kid. You're in *way* over your head."

By now, the audience had left the auditorium and swarmed into the hallway, blocking the officers and threatening them with raised fists. The crowd formed a wall of resistance at every exit of the building, effectively holding the officers in place.

One of the officers pulled out a walkie-talkie and spoke into the receiver as loudly as he could. "We're in a dangerous situation. We need back up!"

Within a minute, sirens sounded in the distance.

Kacie stood hopelessly in front of Charlie. "What can I do?" she cried. "How can I help?"

"I'd better go peacefully. Take my guitar," he shouted over the noise of the angry crowd. "Find out who tipped the Navy off. I'll call you as soon as I can. You'd better get out of here. Can you find another way out?"

"No, Charlie. I'm staying with you!"

"It's okay, Kacie. I can't resist arrest."

"No talking, mister!" The first officer commanded.

In three minutes, the Shore Patrol wagon drove onto the campus and across the grass. It stopped in the Quad. Six armed enlisted personnel with dark blue insignias around their upper arms jumped out of the wagon and pushed their way through the crowd. They were big, burly and mean. They forcefully pushed students aside in an attempt to clear a way for Charlie and the lieutenants.

Students showered the Shore Patrol with drinks, food—anything available to express disapproval.

The Lieutenants pulled Charlie through the crowd roughly. In the process, he lost his cap; his uniform became stained from flying debris.

A black sedan waited at the curb. On its side were the words, *Office of Naval Intelligence*. The officers opened the back door and pushed Charlie's head down as he entered the vehicle. He sat quietly, waving at the crowd with cuffed hands.

With the assistance of a police escort, the sedan eased down College Avenue toward the Naval Academy, leaving a very angry group of students behind. As it entered the main gate, the police cars peeled away and the sirens stopped.

The sedan continued through interior streets in the Yard and up to a pedestrian walkway. It drove into Tecumseh Court and stopped at the foot of the steps into Bancroft Hall. One of the lieutenants opened the back door for Charlie while a crowd of curious midshipmen and tourists watched a handcuffed midshipman exit the sedan.

Flanked by a lieutenant on either side, Charlie walked briskly up the marble steps and into the Rotunda. To the left was the main watch office. Charlie entered the office and was led to a door at the very back. "Officer of the Day" was stenciled on it in gold letters.

One of the lieutenants opened the door and instructed Charlie to enter. He stepped into the office of the senior commissioned watch officer.

ONI

❋

Major Garrett looked up at Charlie as he entered. It was a small office, sparsely decorated. A picture of Richard Nixon hung on one wall, the American flag and coat rack on another.

The major's desk was spotless. It held a clean blotter, black phone, and small desk lamp. Beside the desk was a window overlooking Tecumseh Court.

"Here he is, Major," one of the lieutenants said as he shoved Charlie closer to the desk. "Mr. McDaniels was out of uniform in public, singing anti-war songs. We'll follow his apprehension with a complete report."

"Thank you, gentlemen," the Major said. "I'll take it from here."

Charlie stood at attention, waiting for the door to close behind him. He knew of Major Garrett. He was the 2nd Battalion Officer, known for his friendly, laid-back manner. He had a reputation for no-nonsense strict military behavior. He could be a powerful ally or a feared enemy.

The major looked at Charlie for a full minute. His brown eyes traveled from top to bottom. The trace of a smile started above his square jaw.

"Singing anti-war songs in public? What in the world were you thinking, Mr. McDaniels?"

"I have no excuse, sir."

The major leaned back in his chair. It intermittently squeaked as he stared intently at Charlie—still sizing him up. "Don't give me that "no excuse" bullshit. What were you thinking?"

Charlie's eyes shifted down to his. "Sir, we were singing traditional folk music. There was no intent to demonstrate or publicly criticize the war."

"Then who the hell said it was an anti-war demonstration?"

"I don't know how that happened, sir."

"What were you doing over there?"

"It was an encore performance, sir. St Johns wanted us back."

Major Garrett looked up with wide eyes. "You've done this before?"

"Yes, sir. Two weeks ago. I have a friend at St. John's who I met on Christmas leave. She and I formed a duo and were asked to give a concert at the college."

"Asked by whom? And why would St. Johns College want a midshipman singing on their campus?"

"The staff at St. Johns asked, sir, at the request of the students. No one knew where I was from."

"The staff? I bet they're more than a little pissed off that we interrupted."

"Yes, sir. The students were very angry."

"Singing folk music with the Johnnies is not a big deal. Unusual? Yes. However, it could have been a positive thing for both schools… before ONI stormed the place."

"Yes, sir."

"Why is ONI involved anyway? Seems like a waste of resources to me."

"Sir, I believe one of the students complained after our first concert."

"A student from St. Johns?"

"Yes, sir."

"Wait a minute. Let me read the rest of this report."

Several minutes later, the Major closed the file and laid it to one side.

"You're right. There's a handwritten letter from a Mr. Gonzales complaining about an Arlo McDaniels leading a peace demonstration of some sort. Is that you?"

"Yes, sir. Arlo is my stage name."

The major couldn't help smiling. "You have a stage name?"

"Yes, sir. Kacie gave it to me."

"Kacie's your musical partner, I assume."

"Yes, sir."

"Sounds to me like a vocal performance, not a peace demonstration."

"That's correct, sir. Kacie and I were sitting on stools on the stage.

We each play the guitar. We sang contemporary folk music—Bob Dylan, Pete Seeger—there was no demonstration or intent to express discontent."

"St. Johns College is a pretty liberal school. Why would this fellow Gonzales make such an outlandish claim?"

"I don't know, sir. I suspect he was jealous."

"Jesus! Are you telling me we got involved in a goddamned love triangle of some kind?"

Charlie grinned. "Probably, sir. Gonzales thought Kacie was his girlfriend."

Major Garrett laughed. "Do you have any idea how this thing became so fucked up? St. John's is probably upset and it's likely the press will be involved."

"It's all a misunderstanding, sir."

Major Garrett threw the folder back on his desk. "According to this file, it was your brother who spoke with this fellow Gonzales after he first complained."

Charlie looked dumbfounded. He struggled to maintain his composure.

"I wasn't aware of that, sir."

"He didn't brief you or ask you about it before he went to Commander Wilson?"

"No, sir."

"Why not?"

"We don't speak much, sir. I have reason to think that he's upset with me."

"I guess so. Your brother told Commander Wilson that you would be leading a peace demonstration. Would he really think that of you?"

"Yes, sir."

"Wow. It was on the basis of your brother's claim that Commander Wilson called ONI."

"His assertion was inaccurate, sir."

"You know, I have a younger brother, too. I wouldn't dream of doing that to him."

"No, sir."

The major shook his head and, to Charlie's surprise, chuckled. "I'm a big fan of a lot of folk music, too, Mr. McDaniels. However, I don't consider myself a pacifist, in the pejorative sense, that is. I just like the music. Do you consider yourself a pacifist, Mr. McDaniels?"

"I'd rather have peace than war, sir. Depends on the circumstances, I suppose." "What about the war we're in now?"

"I don't support it, sir. I would gladly serve, even risk my life—but not for the political interests and actions of this war."

"Really? You don't seem shy about expressing an opinion, do you?"

"No, sir."

The major couldn't help smiling at Charlie and the dilemma in which he found himself. He liked this young man, still a teenager, who spoke openly and candidly—not afraid of the truth.

"Sit down, Mr. McDaniels. Relax for a while."

"Thank you, sir."

"I want to look at your official file."

The major picked up the phone and asked Personnel to bring him Charlie's complete file. It was on his desk in less than three minutes.

"They keep these folders under lock and key. If you don't mind, I'm curious about yours."

"No, sir. I don't mind."

Major Garrett restated what he was reading. "Your father is GeneralMcDaniels? Commander of Fort McNair?"

"Yes, sir."

"And your brother is Frank McDaniels, the Brigade Commander?"

"Yes, sir. He's fourth generation."

"You're in a bit of a shit sandwich, aren't you?"

Charlie flashed his crooked grin. "Yes, sir. Kind of."

"So what the hell happened to you? I doubt either your brother or father ever performed at St. Johns. What was it that caused you to stray from the family legacy?"

"I don't know, sir. I'm just different, I guess. I don't fit the military mold according to them."

"Then, if the Navy isn't the gig for you, what keeps you here? Surely, you have other options."

"I have no other options, sir."

"You don't?"

"No, sir. My father is a Marine general, sir. He pressured me to come here as my brother did three years ago. I was surprised when I found out I was accepted. However, it gave me a chance to prove to them that I had what it takes to survive plebe year, too."

"Okay, you have something to prove. Tenacity is a good thing as long as the objective makes sense."

"Yes, sir."

The major smiled. "Does your father know of your judgments about the war?"

"Yes, sir, he knows."

"What does he think of them?"

"Not much, sir. He threw me out over Christmas when I expressed them."

"Jesus."

Major Garrett said nothing for several minutes. Charlie could tell that he was thinking. Finally, he looked directly into Charlie's eyes and said, "You know, Mr. McDaniels, on the one hand, I admire your dedication to the truth, although I doubt you have the whole story."

"Yes, sir."

"It takes courage to speak your truth when so outnumbered as you are here. It's a quality in young officers I don't often see. On the other hand, however, the military, as a group, is a collection of the very finest in my opinion. We want to build both character and military efficiency in the men who choose to come here."

"Yes, sir," Charlie answered, "I understand and respect that."

"It doesn't accommodate dissenters very well."

"No sir, it doesn't."

There was a long pause before the major's next comment.

"As far as I'm concerned, your politics and opinions are yours personally. You're entitled to them in a free country."

"Thank you, sir."

"This thing with St. John's is over and done with as far as I'm concerned. It should never have happened in the first place. I bear no grudges, and you should not feel guilty about performing in public. I think the only thing you should have done was call the Public Affairs Office. They'd probably want to take pictures."

Charlie sighed with gratitude. "Thank you, sir."

"Carry on while I go through the rest of your file."

Charlie remained seated in a wooden chair facing the major's desk while he read Charlie's file.

"I see you have a fair number of demerits," he said. "Your brother tried to report you, for insubordination?"

"Yes, sir."

Major Garrett shook his head and continued reading. When he came to the end of the folder, he read a letter, the first entry in Charlie's file.

Charlie watched the major. He looked surprised. He reread it, stunned.

"Is something wrong, sir?"

"Do you know the chairman of the Joint Chiefs of Staff?"

"I've never met him, sir."

"Really?"

"No, sir."

The major changed the subject without elaborating. "You know, once this incident with the Johnnies gets out, you'll have a huge target on your back."

"Yes, sir."

"I think you can assume word of what happened this afternoon will spread here quickly."

"Yes, sir."

"You dodged a bullet today. It could have gone very badly for you. There are some here that would want to lock you up. I assume you know that if you leave based on unsatisfactory military conduct, you could go directly to the fleet as an enlisted man."

"No, sir. I didn't know."

"In fact, I wouldn't be surprised if your father would facilitate that for you in such a case."

"Yes, sir. I *know* he would," Charlie said with his crooked grin.

"Stay away from your brother. He'll come after you, too."

"Aye, aye, sir."

Major Garrett paused and turned to look out the window. Charlie wondered what he was thinking.

Finally, he looked Charlie directly in the eyes and asked an unexpected question. "Do you think you really belong here, Mr. McDaniels?"

Charlie paused to think. "Sir, it's a stretch for me, for sure. I don't have the military aptitude that my brother and father have. I don't know how I got in here in the first place."

"Have you considered resigning?" It was a suggestion with no overtones of judgment.

"Yes, sir. Several people I trust have suggested that option."

"And…"

"I would like to finish Plebe Year."

"Oh, that's right," the major said sarcastically, "So you'll just gut it out to prove you can do it?"

"Yes, sir." Charlie's response was weak and wavering.

"I get that—the pride aspect. However, if you resign voluntarily before the end of Plebe Year, you'll simply go back to the civilian world. Of course, you'd be eligible for the draft."

"Yes, sir. May I ask what would happen if I quit *after* Plebe Year?"

"The Navy…and your father… would be a lot less forgiving. You cost the taxpayers a lot of money."

Yes, sir. I know that. I'd still like to show them that I have what it takes here, sir."

"Show who?"

"My father…and my brother, too, of course."

"Really? The brother who just fucked you over and the father who threw you out of your own home?"

The major smiled. "And what about you?"

"Sir?"

"What's best for you? Stay here and maybe win a few points with your dad—or stop the charade and take charge of your own life?"

Charlie had no answer.

"Okay, Mr. McDaniels. Go back to your company and search your conscience carefully. Regardless of your personal views, you're either with us or against us. There can be no middle ground, no compromise in a military environment. No one has the right to tell you how you should think. However, you can't live a charade here as I suspect you're finding out. There's no dishonor in disagreeing with the majority. *You* are the only one able to decide what's best for you."

"Yes, sir. Aye, aye, sir."

The major stood signaling the meeting was over. Surprisingly, he extended his hand in friendship. "Do the right thing," he said. "Do it for yourself *and* your sense of honor. It's your call."

Charlie returned the handshake with a wide grin.

"Thank you, sir."

Charlie did an about face and exited the office. Questioning eyes followed him as he walked back into the rotunda.

CHAPTER NINE

Decisions

Present Time

It was like a dream. All feeling gone; all remorse washed away.

A few final thoughts mocked him as the tunnel of light grew wider and closer.

"I held the world in my hands once only to let fear and insecurity snatch it away. Why?

"She and I were a team. I left her for another with more suitable, more conventional credentials just to further a military career and lifestyle that didn't suit me.

"I had so many gifts and talents. I threw them away for the sake of approval by others _ approval of a family that never mattered— a family that no longer exists."

Without family or friends, there would be no one to miss him.

His passing would go unnoticed. Unless...would she come to his funeral? Would she even care?

1970

The major's words had affected Charlie. Their wisdom reverberated through his mind as he walked back to his wing.

Sunday afternoons are fairly quiet and relaxed in Bancroft

Hall. There should be open phone booths available to call Kacie—to let her know that he was all right. A little over an hour remained before evening meal formation. He had lots of time.

Charlie raced to the nearest phone room where wall-to-wall phone booths surrounded him, most empty. He went directly to the first open booth and eased onto the seat.

Closing the folding door halfway, Charlie stopped. Here was an opportunity to sit in relative silence, to think, to organize his thoughts. He had the rare luxury of an arguably semi-private place to allow him time to think through what Major Garrett had said to him. Only an occasional muffled voice from a nearby booth broke the silence.

Charlie looked inward and asked for the strength to be honest with himself, to see beyond his need to procrastinate. With complete honesty, every thought coalesced into one.

It was then that he understood.

Disapproval of the war served merely as a cover to hide the *real* reason for wanting to quit—it was fear.

Fear of his father, fear of appearing weak, fear of what others might think if he decided to leave.

The "others" would say, "I told you so." They would say his admission to the Naval Academy must have been a mistake. In their eyes, Charlie would return to being the screw up he had always been.

For Charlie, it was easier to gut through Plebe Year than to return home to face the shame of his failure. Many would react to his resignation with disapproval and judgment.

Judgment comes easily from detractors. Criticism is cheap—it comes readily from the ignorant, those who had never walked in his shoes. They would never understand, and Charlie could never explain.

So why bother? Why worry about explaining to anyone?

It takes more courage to leave than to stay. Staying was the coward's way out. *He* was the coward if he stayed.

Make a choice from your heart, damn it, not your head. Screw anyone who judges you.

He slipped a dime into the slot.

Charlie sighed as he waited to connect. It rang twice before Kacie answered breathlessly.

"Charlie? Is that you?"

"Yes!" he answered. "How are you holding up? Are you okay?"

"Oh, I'm fine," she said. "But, what happened to *you*? I thought they were going to put you in *jail*!"

"So did I."

"You don't sound upset. Where did they take you?"

"Back to the Academy. We drove right into Tecumseh Court—right to the front steps! The two lieutenants escorted me inside Bancroft Hall to the duty watch officer."

"Who or what's that?"

"Senior commissioned officer on duty. It's a twenty-four-hour watch duty that rotates between the company and battalion officers. The officer on duty today was a Major Garrett. I was taken directly to him."

"Shit! Another Marine. That's all you need, Charlie."

"Fortunately, Major Garrett turned out to be a decent guy—talked to me like a real person; like I mattered."

"What did he say? Was he angry?"

"No. He thought the whole thing was ridiculous. He was angry at ONI and the Shore Patrol for storming your campus...said our concert could have been a good PR event for both schools."

"Wow. Are you in trouble then?"

"None, Kacie! Major Garrett shook my hand and said to do the right thing for myself. I was free to go."

"Really? Thank god. Did you understand about doing the right thing for yourself?"

"I did and I'm going to. I've decided to resign. I'm done."

"Leaving the Academy?"

"Yeah. After talking with Major Garrett...and Pete, of course, I can see it makes no sense for me to stay here."

Kacie sighed heavily in the phone. "Really?" Her tone strengthened and became more animated. "I'm so grateful, Charlie; I don't know what to say."

He could tell Kacie was crying softly. He pictured the tears on her cheeks.

"I hope those are tears of joy," he said.

"Of course, silly. It's just such a *relief*!"

"For me as well. I don't know where I'll go or what I'll do. I know I'll figure out something."

Charlie paused and continued. "There's something else though."

"Really? What else?"

"Major Garrett told me someone from St. Johns complained that a midshipman was leading a peace demonstration. That's how Naval Intelligence became involved."

"What? That's crazy!"

"I know, but the Academy had to investigate if they thought one of their own was involved in such a thing."

"Shit! It must have been Ignacio who complained," she snapped back. "He wanted revenge! I'm sorry for the trouble he caused you, Charlie and I'm sorry for using your last name in the program."

"Forget it," he said. "It was a beautiful flier. However, the flier gave Ignacio a name to use when he complained. There are only two 'McDaniels' in the Naval Academy right now."

"You and the Brigade Commander."

"Right. No one would think the Brigade Commander would lead a peace demonstration. That left me."

"Don't tell me!"

"Yeah. Frank got involved because he had the same name. He was probably questioned about Ignacio's complaint. I bet he and Ignacio communicated because Frank told the Academy that I was the midshipman demonstrator."

"How could he?"

"He's capable. If the two did get together, Ignacio would have told Frank about our planned concert today. Frank reported it back to headquarters, I assume. ONI was told I was leading some kind of peace demonstration on your campus. It's like Frank and Ignacio conspired to have me busted."

"I am truly *stunned,* Charlie. And Frank never talked to you about it before he ratted on you?"

"He never said a word to me."

"God, Charlie. That's bullshit! We weren't doing anything to warrant that kind of attack. We just sang some popular songs that discouraged war."

"Yeah, I know, but it all turned out well."

"If it changed your mind about resigning, I would *definitely* agree."

"It did. I only hope we haven't offended the college."

"Are you kidding? We're heroes around here, Arlo."

"I'm thankful for that and just want to put it all behind me and move on—somewhere."

She wiped a tear away. "Wherever you go, I want to be with you."

"Same here."

"Thanks, Eli," Charlie said. "I love you."

Kacie's voice collapsed with emotion as she replied, "I love you as well, Charlie. Be careful."

The decision was a catharsis. He could finally let go.

❋

He needed to call his mother next for advice.

He had the phone booth, another half hour and a few more quarters left. It was an opportunity to let her know what he was doing.

He dialed her number.

She answered on the second ring.

"Hello?"

"Hi, Mom. It's Charlie."

"Charlie! It's so *good* to hear your voice!" she answered. "How are you?"

"I'm doing great. I wanted to tell you what I've been thinking."

"Of course. How were exams?"

"Okay, I guess. I passed—not as good as Frank's grades, I'm sure."

"Stop comparing yourself, Charlie."

"I have stopped comparing, Mom," he replied. "I wanted to tell you I *know* I don't belong here. I'm going to resign. I've decided to follow my heart."

"Really? You know I support you, Charlie—if that's what you think is best. I knew from the first that you weren't compatible with the military lifestyle."

"Thanks, Mom. I knew you'd understand."

"I worry about your father, though. The man is crazy and capable of anything. Does your brother know?"

"No. We haven't talked for over a month. I'm sure he'll find out somehow. I don't care."

"As soon as he does, he'll tell your father. You'll be facing two powerful adversaries."

"I know. I'll keep my head down."

"Charlie, you *have* to be careful! I'm serious. Your father is a dangerous man. I'm not exaggerating. He's capable of hurting, and he's going to try."

"I'll be careful. Once I'm a civilian, I'll be free and out of range of his influence."

Melinda wasn't convinced. She changed the subject.

"I always knew you didn't belong there, Charlie—not with your talents and abilities. It broke my heart when you gave them up to please your father. It takes maturity to find your path. You're growing up. These are the choices reserved for adults."

"Thanks, Mom."

"Is there anything I can do for you?"

"Not at the moment, thanks," he replied. "How are you doing in that big house all by yourself?"

"Are you kidding? I love it!"

Charlie laughed. She sounded so cheerful and relaxed, like her old self.

"Are you still leaving him?"

"Yes. I'm mailing him the papers as soon as I finish cleaning out the bank accounts."

He laughed again. "You'd better be careful, too."

"Tell me about Kacie," Melinda said. "When do I get to meet her?"

"How about if we come visit you."

"That would be *wonderful*, Charlie! Are you allowed to leave Annapolis?"

"I don't know what my status will be until I submit the resignation papers."

"Perfect. I'll send you some money. Rent a car and bring Kacie with you."

"Thanks, Mom, we'd love to. I have to get my civilian stuff, too."

"Come anytime—spur of the moment, if necessary. Feel free to stay if you want."

"I'll call you as soon as I know."

There was a pause on the other end.

"Mom? You still there?"

"I'm still here, Charlie." Melinda's tone was heavier, more serious. "Charlie," she said, "I have some important things to say to you, things you should know. It's time."

"Time for what? Sounds serious."

"It is. Let's talk about this in person, though. Do you know Kacie well enough to share something profoundly personal?"

"Of course. You're making me *very* curious."

"Just get down here whenever you can."

Charlie's voice cracked with emotion. "Okay, Mom. I'll shoot for this weekend if Kacie's free."

"Wonderful!"

"Uh oh, I'm running out of quarters. I have to hang up soon."

"Keep me posted. I'm genuinely happy for you, Charlie."

"Thanks. That means everything. Love you."

"I love you, too, Charlie. Be careful."

Charlie hung up and looked at his watch. He'd been in the phone booth over forty-five minutes. He still had time to see Pete. He had to give him a heads up on the concert and tell him he was leaving.

❋

Charlie knocked softly on the door. Pete looked up from shining his belt buckle. "Charlie! How was your weekend?"

"Exciting. That's why I'm here. You should be the first to know, Pete."

"Okay. Know what?"

"Word's gonna travel fast."

Pete pushed the buckle aside and stared back. "Tell me, for chris-sake," he laughed.

"Okay. A friend and I were doing a folk music concert at St. John's College yesterday."

"I didn't know you were a musician, Charlie. But why St. John's of all places?"

"My friend is a student there."

"Oh? You're dating a Johnnie?" There was no condescension.

"I am."

"When you say folk music, do you mean like Joan Baez or Bob Dylan?"

"Yeah, exactly."

"So what's the deal? Probably good PR for both schools. I assume you performed inside, out of the general public's eye."

"Yes. We played in the auditorium. It's a free concert and very popular. I did one two weeks ago."

"Okay. So why do you feel the need to tell me all this?"

"ONI raided the concert this afternoon and hauled me back here in a paddy wagon."

"What?"

Charlie nodded.

Pete eyed Charlie cautiously. "Go on."

"Two lieutenants from ONI stormed the stage after our first song and took me off the stage."

Pete's jaw dropped. "Holy shit! Naval Intelligence? What the hell for?"

"Someone reported that I was leading a peace demonstration… against the will of the student body."

"What? For playing Bob Dylan and Joan Baez?"

"That's right. It was a full house. You can imagine how the audience reacted."

"Jesus, Charlie."

"I know. Crazy, huh?"

"So what happened to you?"

"ONI took me back to the Duty Watch Officer. Major Garrett was on duty today."

"What did he have to say about all this?"

"He was pissed that ONI stormed a civilian college for no reason."

"I don't blame him. But, why in the hell did Naval Intelligence get involved in a concert at St. Johns?"

"It was reported that I was going to lead an anti-war demonstration at the college."

"Reported by whom?"

"My brother."

"Jesus!" Pete was on his feet, knocking his chair over in the process.

"Yeah. Someone from St. John's contacted the Academy with a false claim. I don't know all the facts yet. Major Garrett told me that Frank was the one who confirmed that I would be leading a demonstration, though."

"That son of a bitch."

"Yeah. Anyway, you'll hear about it soon. The facts will likely be distorted, so I wanted to tell you first hand."

"I appreciate that, Charlie."

"Anyway, Major Garrett told me I hadn't done anything wrong and let me go."

"Thank God for that."

"Yeah, we had a good talk in his office…about what keeps me here if I'm against the war. He said essentially the same thing that you did."

"And that is?"

"I'm crazy to subordinate my interests and skills to prove how tough I am. You were right. I'm going to do what's best for me, not my father."

"Does that mean you're going to leave us?"

"It does."

"That takes guts, man. I'd be sorry to see you go, Charlie, but I genuinely believe it's the right thing for you."

"I appreciate all your advice, Pete. I'm starting the paperwork tomorrow."

The bell rang announcing evening meal formation. "Stop back later," Pete suggested. "I'll tell you how the resignation procedure works."

"I will. Thanks."

❋

On the way to formation, Charlie stopped at the Battalion Office and asked for the forms necessary to initiate his resignation. A second classman on duty gave Charlie a dirty look.

"Hang on. I have to find them."

After rummaging through a nearby file cabinet, the man produced a single sheet of paper. "Here you go."

Charlie looked at the paper. *Notice of Resignation.*

"Is that all, sir?"

"Yup. Fill in your name, the reason and whatever else you want to say. Sign it and bring it back here."

"Thank you, sir."

He folded the form and placed it inside his coat.

DECISIONS

❋

As Charlie stood in evening formation, he could hear and feel an energetic buzz of conversation. The word had spread at lightning speed. Everyone wondered who the midshipman was that ONI picked up this afternoon from St. Johns.

Charlie prayed to be left alone. It was too late. Harry suspected immediately.

"McDaniels, are you this Arlo fellow by any chance?"

"Yes, sir."

"Hey everybody," he yelled. "This is the guy! I found him."

"Fall in, Harry," Pete ordered. "We need to go."

Charlie could hear the muffled drone of excitement as he marched with his company to the mess hall.

He had been found out. His tablemates would try to eat him alive tonight. Though he had the resignation form in his coat pocket, Charlie was still a plebe. He had to keep acting the part until the form was accepted. Regardless of the criticisms, he would act with integrity.

In the mess hall, Charlie moved quickly and silently to his table. The rest of the men in his company followed him with anger and curiosity. He could almost *feel* the cold energy from his tablemates. Harry would have a field day.

"Hey everybody," Harry announced as he arrived at his place, "let's all sing a few verses of *Blowin' in the Wind*. Our boy, McDaniels here knows *all* the words, don't you pussy?"

Two Second Classmen at the end of the table thought that was a very good idea. "McDaniels, get out in the central aisle and start singing your peace songs."

Pete stood abruptly. "Hold it guys. Let me talk to him first."

He grabbed Charlie's arm and said quietly, "You don't have to do this. Tell them you're resigning. They'll leave you alone."

"That's okay, Pete. I'm a plebe until my resignation is accepted. They're pissed; they don't know the full story. For me, this is the higher ground. I'll give Dorfman what he wants. I don't care."

"Okay. I sense this is something you want to do."

"It is."

"Eyes in the boat, shit-head," Harry yelled. "Pete's not going to bail you out of *this* one."

Charlie ignored the anger. He looked at Harry with a subtly superior smile and winked. "Aye, aye, sir."

He was on his way before a stunned Harry could react.

Charlie squeezed between the next two tables and walked to the middle of the main aisle. Those in his company booed. Others stopped talking and watched Charlie stand.

He looked around and saw that roughly twenty tables, over a hundred men, were staring, waiting. Filipino stewards moved about him pushing carts filled with entrées of steaming chicken and vegetables.

He stood at attention, facing his company. Many already knew about the concert and Charlie's role.

Harry stood up and yelled, "Start singing ass-hole. What are you waiting for? Now!"

Charlie began slowly, barely audible in the angry growling around him.

"Louder!"

He tried to sing over the noise. It was useless. No matter how loud he sang, his classmates shouted him down.

Nevertheless, Charlie stood at attention, doing his best to comport with Harry's wishes.

Suddenly, men began hurling mashed potatoes and sauerkraut at him. He fended it off easily and continued to sing.

Pete watched carefully as Charlie deftly waved off the airborne attack. At the beginning of the second verse, a half-full milk carton hit him from behind. The force of the blow staggered him, spilling milk all over his uniform. Everyone was laughing.

Pete raced into the main aisle and addressed his company. The food stopped. Pete put his arm around Charlie's shoulders and yelled back to his company, "Stop it! The next person who throws something will be put on report. None of you know the facts!"

Charlie stopped singing and turned to look calmly in the direction of the attack. "I'm okay, Pete. I'll finish the song."

"No you won't," Pete said. "You gotta get out of here! I'll bring you a sandwich later."

Pete escorted him to the nearest exit and said, "I'm protecting you from yourself. We have to get you through this week without *any* controversial incidents. It could screw up your resignation."

He's right. Best thing to do now is walk away.

Showing no fear, Charlie walked straight ahead with his head high. Pete opened the double doors that led to Bancroft Hall.

"You did well, Charlie. *That* took balls!"

"Thanks, Pete."

After a long, hot shower and change of clothes, Charlie relaxed at his desk. He hoped the incident would relieve some of the tension with his classmates. Tomorrow, it would no longer matter. He would sign and submit his resignation. It would be over.

Men were returning from the mess hall. When his roommates entered, they looked at him incredulously.

"Good God, Charlie," Bob said. "I wouldn't want to be you right now."

Charlie didn't answer. Neither of his roommates wanted anything to do with him.

A minute later, Pete knocked on the door. Charlie's roommates stood. Pete signaled them to carry on. He looked at Charlie.

"Are you all right, Charlie? You just took a hell of a beating. Here, I brought you a sandwich."

Pete's protection brought Charlie close to tears.

"Thanks, Pete. I'm all right." Charlie's voice was dull and flat.

No matter how uncomfortable Charlie felt, he knew he had a true friend in Pete.

❋

Breakfast the next day started awkwardly. Charlie stood behind his chair and endured a spattering of insults. He ignored them and continued to act like just another plebe.

Accordingly, he sat stiffly on the edge of his seat, ready for any challenge.

When Pete arrived, he looked at Charlie. "How are you holding up? Takes guts to come back after the beating you took last night."

"Thanks. I'm fine…really."

Harry glared at Charlie from across the table.

"What's on the menu, puss?" he asked.

Charlie looked directly at Harry and recited the menu flawlessly.

"Keep your gutless, fucking eyes in the boat, dumb ass!"

"Calm down, Harry," Pete commanded. He was clearly angry. "You don't know enough to judge Charlie for anything!"

Harry looked as if he had been kicked in the stomach. He started to argue but never got the chance.

"Come, on, Pete," Bruce whined. "Are you going to defend this jerk after what he did yesterday?"

Pete looked at Bruce. He'd had enough. "Do you *know* what happened yesterday, Bruce? Or are you just repeating rumors."

"Jesus, Pete. He was leading a peace demonstration!"

Pete looked at the entire table, "Is that what you think, gentlemen?"

Most nodded cautiously. "Everyone knows what he did," Harry whined.

"No, you don't," Pete lashed out angrily. "He was giving a concert; the student body *invited* him to play for them. Someone falsely reported Charlie was leading a demonstration. There was no demonstration!"

"But, we don't associate with the Johnnies," Bruce stated.

"Why not?" Pete shot back. "You think you're better than them?"

"I don't like their politics," Bruce replied. "They're all a bunch of hippies as far as I'm concerned."

"Did you know it's harder to be accepted to St. Johns than it is here? Those 'hippies' you mock are smarter and brighter than a lot of you. The college is one of the best schools in the country."

"Every one of you owes Charlie an apology for jumping to conclusions based on rumors. What he did was good for both schools."

No one spoke.

Pete looked at Charlie. "Can I tell them?"

"Sure."

"Charlie's resigning this week. You can stop acting like jerks and treat him like an equal for a change!"

No one said a word to Charlie after that.

⁂

Later, Charlie stopped by Pete's room to thank him for standing up for him.

"Forget it. You'd do the same for me. What's the deal with your resignation?"

"I just submitted it."

Dave looked up at Charlie. "Really?"

"Yes, sir."

Dave extended his hand. "I'm going to be sorry to see you go, Charlie. You're one of the good guys."

"Thanks, Dave."

"Okay," Pete said to Charlie, "do you have a minute to talk about the resignation process?"

"Sure, if you do."

"After your resignation is approved, you'll be separated from the Brigade without prejudice. That means you do so voluntarily and not for disciplinary reasons. You'll have to spend some time at the Personnel Office. They'll guide you through the various steps. Some officers, including the chaplain and battalion officer, will interview you.

"Once your resignation papers are in the Admin office, you'll be given a receipt. You'll be placed on administrative leave until the process is complete. Administrative leave means you can come and go anytime or place you choose. All that's expected of you is to sign in at Battalion once a day and remain in uniform in public.

"You're still welcome to sit with us in the mess hall as usual—without bracing up. It's my hope that the men at the table will treat you respectfully."

Charlie nodded. For a split second, some part of him would miss this place. The bonds and friendships he had made over the last eight months were unique.

❋

That evening, Charlie sat at his regular place in the mess hall. He was permitted to carry on and was treated cordially by everyone, including Harry. After so many months, he still felt a little awkward. Nevertheless, he resolved to act with dignity.

As the platters of food passed from man to man, Pete tapped the side of his water glass for attention. When the table was quiet, he said, "Gentlemen, as I told you yesterday evening, Charlie is leaving us."

"Anything you want to say, Charlie?"

Charlie hesitated. He wanted to leave on a high note. He thought for a moment. The words came precisely and evenly.

"I know many of you consider me a coward or, worse, a traitor for my feelings about Vietnam. I have spoken candidly, but more often judgmentally. I understand your anger. I never intended any disrespect. Rather, in spite of my comments and actions, I have gained much respect for the Navy—all the military in fact.

"My decision to leave is not based on the war in Indonesia. I have to stand up to my values and pursue a course in which I can do the most good. Most of you know I have little aptitude for the military. Of that, I am not ashamed. I have other skills.

"It was fear of failure and disgrace that was keeping me here. I no longer worry about that.

"I have the greatest respect for those who serve our country with conviction. Of course, that includes every one of my tablemates here."

The table was silent. A few plebes applauded softly, followed by louder applause from the whole table.

"Nicely put," Pete said. "I, for one, respect your decision and the guts it takes to go against the grain."

Charlie nodded in appreciation.

CHAPTER TEN

St. Johns College

Present time

The old man's eyes were glued shut. No amount of effort now could open them.

Soon, there was no feeling left. The darkness was complete. His breath came in labored gasps as he struggled for air. It was too late to reconsider. It was over.

A whirlwind of last-minute emotions begged for attention. He couldn't feel them now; they had no effect. The darkness on the other side of his closed eyelids grew denser. He stopped breathing.

1970

Charlie was no longer required to attend classes. He was free to leave the academy grounds at will. He remained a midshipman and required to be in uniform in public. Otherwise, he had little restrictions.

While others rushed to class, Charlie walked out the main gate and turned toward the college. It felt odd to be so untethered. No matter. Kacie was waiting for him.

Through the crowd of students, Charlie saw her at once. Kacie ran to him and hugged him as if they hadn't been together in months.

Unexpectedly, she grabbed his arm and directed him across the Quad to a nearby small and secluded garden. Once they were safely out of sight, Kacie dropped her textbook and came to him like wildfire. Charlie met her with equal passion.

Kacie pulled back and looked up at him breathlessly. "Wow! You kiss pretty well for a plebe. Who taught you that?"

"Must be Arlo's alter ego," he said with a grin. "You're not too shabby yourself, Eli."

Taking a deep breath, she said happily, "God, Charlie. I thought I'd never see you again after the Navy busted up our concert!"

"We owe the college another gig. It's the least we can do."

"You sure you want to do another?"

"Sure. As soon as I'm a civilian."

He tilted her chin up with one hand and kissed her tenderly. "It's all behind us now."

"Come, let's talk some." Kacie grabbed his arm and led him toward the student center in the Quad. It was warm enough to sit outside today.

A single cafe table was available. Charlie grabbed it and held the chair for Kacie to sit. They held hands across the table and stared at each other with the exhilaration that comes from freedom.

"What was it that changed your mind?" she asked. "You were pretty stubborn about finishing the year?"

"I owe Pete and Major Garrett everything, Kacie. They both knew I didn't belong in the Navy. It was about what *I* wanted to do, not what I wanted people to think."

"Have you had time to think ahead yet?"

"A little. I will have choices. For now, I'm going to listen to my inner self and wait for those choices to come forward. I don't want to rush anything."

"Understood. Let's let things percolate for a few days. Have you told your mom yet?"

"I called her yesterday. We hadn't talked much last month because my father was still around. He's gone now."

"There not much he can do to you from there."

"I don't see how."

"I told Mom about you and the concerts and my decision to resign."

"Will you see her soon?"

"I thought I'd drive down to Fort McNair this weekend. She has all my civilian clothes. Want to come?"

"Sure. Where are you keeping your wheels?"

"I can rent something in town."

"Okay. I'm ready when you are."

"She's anxious to meet you, Kacie. She also said she has something important to tell me."

"Important? How important?"

"I don't know. She sounded pretty serious on the phone. Said it was heavy stuff—personal."

"You sure she'll want me around?"

"She doesn't care as long as it's okay with me. I told her sure, Kacie knows everything I know."

She squeezed his hand. "Okay. Your call."

"What about your old man? Does he know you're leaving?"

"I mailed him a letter yesterday. It should be in Danang in a few days. He won't be happy—I'm sure the response will be interesting."

"Are you nervous?"

"Surprisingly not. I only wish I could tell him in person."

"What about your brother?"

"He doesn't know yet. I'll stop by to say goodbye, of course."

"I wonder how he'll take it."

Charlie smiled. "Who knows? There is one thing bothering me, though."

"And that would be?"

"I need to apologize to the school for the disturbance. I know it wasn't our fault, but I still feel responsible."

"Sure. If you really think so. I know the dean would like to meet you. All the staff would, in fact. I'll see when I can get you an appointment. She's hard to pin down sometimes."

"Thanks. Just let me know when."

As they talked, others in the Quad recognized Charlie with Kacie.

"Are you Arlo, the musician?" they asked.

Many were glad to see him back and surprised to learn Arlo was a midshipman. Nevertheless, the responses were universally good.

Charlie could have spent the rest of the day—the rest of the week, in fact, there in the Quad holding her hand. However, he worried about her missing too many classes.

"Listen," he said. "I don't want you to get behind. Don't skip classes for me. We have a whole weekend coming up."

"Let's get your appointment with the Dean set up first. That won't take long."

They walked through the campus to the administrative office and made an appointment with Dean Williams at nine o'clock the next day.

❋

Charlie wiled away the afternoon walking through the Yard, relishing the peace that allowed him to think about what lay ahead. To have free time to himself was a luxury he had not known for a long time.

He had a couple of interviews scheduled later in the day with department heads and staff. One included the battalion officer, Major Garrett at 1400.

That afternoon, Charlie stood next to the major's door. On the frosted glass were the words, "Second Battalion Officer." He knocked softly.

"Come in," the major yelled from within.

Major Garrett recognized Charlie immediately. He stood and welcomed Charlie warmly with his outstretched hand.

"So, you've decided to stand up for your personal beliefs, Charlie?"

"Yes, sir. I have."

"I had a feeling you would. You strike me as the type not afraid to go his own way. I wish you luck wherever life leads you."

His comments were genuine. The major liked Charlie.

"Thank you, sir. I'd like to thank you again for the advice you gave me Sunday. Your words had a profound impact on me."

"My pleasure, Charlie. Have you made any plans yet?"

"No sir, I haven't."

"What about St Johns?"

"Too expensive."

"It is that but an outstanding school nonetheless. By the way, I hear glowing reports about your first concert. If you decide to do more performances, let me know. My wife and I would like to come."

Charlie's eyes lit up; he grinned. "Yes, sir, I will. Thank you, sir."

"By the way, call me Don. I don't stand on formalities with civilians."

"Thank you, sir…Don."

"Okay, I won't keep you. I've signed off on your resignation. It'll be over at Brigade Admin tomorrow. Let me know if I can be of any help."

Charlie stood and shook hands again.

"Keep in touch."

"Aye, aye, sir," Charlie answered with a broad smile.

❋

The next morning, just before nine, Kacie was waiting for Charlie in front of the building that housed the administrative and admissions facilities. She saw him instantly, although he was hard to miss in uniform. She ran to him; he hugged her tightly,

"God it's weird to walk in and out of that place anytime I want."

"I love it! Let's go."

She took Charlie's arm and led him down King George Street

in the direction of the administrative offices. They paused briefly at their destination.

"This is the Carroll Barrister House," she said as they stood before a small colonial-style building facing King George Street.

Directly across the street were the grounds of the Naval Academy, specifically senior officers' quarters and the parade field. Charlie couldn't guess how much of his life he had spent in that field.

They turned and proceeded up the wood steps to a small portico protecting the main entry. Charlie opened the door and stepped into a cheery and stylish foyer. A fire in an old fireplace blazed warmly on the opposite wall.

Charlie followed Kacie across the foyer to a large corner office. At precisely nine, Kacie knocked on the door and entered. Inside, the Dean waited behind a simple mahogany desk. She stood to greet them with a warm and friendly smile.

"Emilee, this is Charlie McDaniels."

The Dean was a kind, cheerful middle-aged woman with stylish bifocal glasses and graying auburn hair. She looked up at Charlie with an engaging smile while extending her hand.

"Charlie, it is *indeed* a pleasure to meet you! You know, you're somewhat of a celebrity around here." She said. Her eyes sparkled with playfulness.

Charlie liked her at once. Her cheerful demeanor put him at ease instantly.

"Thank you, ma'am. I'm honored to meet you as well."

"Take a seat, you two. Coffee?"

"Nothing for me, thank you," Charlie answered. "Thanks for seeing me on such short notice, Dean Williams. I wanted to let the college staff know how sorry I am about the Navy's intrusion last weekend. I never intended to create such a mêlée."

"Mêlée? Whatever it was, you didn't create it. And please call me Emilee."

"Thank you, Emilee."

"Someone from the Academy has already contacted us, accepting complete responsibility and apologizing for the actions of all involved. So, you didn't do anything, Charlie. We're all just sorry your performance was cut short. A lot of people were looking forward to it."

"That's a big relief."

"Will you and Kacie be planning any more concerts? We'd love you to come back—this time preferably without the Shore Patrol."

Charlie laughed. "Thanks, Emilee," he said glancing at Kacie's smiling eyes. "We'd love to perform again, anytime at all."

"Well, as a Plebe, I know your time is limited."

"Charlie has resigned from the academy, Emilee," Kacie announced. "He's going to be a civilian in a few days."

Dean Williams looked at Charlie with surprise and sadness. "It's such an honor to go to the Academy, Charlie. It is an opportunity that would open many doors for you in the future. Are you sure that's what you want to do?"

"I am. It's taken a while to reach my decision—it wasn't easy," he said and added, "I have little military aptitude. I've been wasting my time and the Navy's money."

Emilee smiled. "They can afford it." She looked affectionately at Kacie. "Did she sway you in any way?"

"A little. However, I have two terrific friends at the Academy who encouraged me to go my own way. I shall always be grateful for their advice."

"I first met Charlie in the library, Emilee. He was researching Agent Orange."

Charlie nodded. "My disdain for the war was a contributing factor to my resignation from the military."

"As you might expect, Charlie, this campus is universally against the war. We're a small group, though, but, like you, deep in knowledge. In fact, we have a course here that analyzes our military and political conduct from 1960 to the present. Anyone who takes it comes out thinking like you. We encourage our students to ask questions, to challenge politics and ideologies critically. You should be proud to have done it on your own."

"Thank you, Emilee."

"What are your plans now, Charlie? Do you have a family who will take you back?"

"Sure. My mother would. However, it's time to be on my own. I'll find a community college somewhere and restart my life. My time at the Academy has not been wasted. It's taught me to work harder than I ever expected."

Dean Williams nodded. She remained quiet, apparently deep in thought. She looked at Kacie for a brief moment and then said slowly, "Have you ever considered becoming a student here, Charlie?"

Charlie's jaw dropped. He looked confused at first before a gleam of enthusiasm appeared in his eyes. He wasn't sure how to respond. He looked at Kacie whose eyes sparkled. He looked back at the Dean with a surprised expression.

"I would be honored, Dean Williams. I don't know what to say. I would *love* to be a student here, but I'll have virtually no means of support. I could never afford the tuition."

Emilee paused again, weighing thoughts in her mind.

At last, she spoke. "We might be willing to offer you a music scholarship—if the Board concurs, of course. Full tuition and board. We'd put you to work, though. Your lessons at the Academy would serve you well here because you'd have to earn your keep. We need help in the kitchen badly. That's where you'd start. I promise you; St. John's will work your ass off—as much as the Naval Academy."

Charlie was speechless. He glanced at Kacie whose mouth was open in surprise before breaking into a wide grin. "I would do anything, Emilee."

"We want you and Kacie to continue with your act—there's no telling how you each might grow in the right environment. It would be an outstanding experience for the college as well—a sound investment, I think. Each of you can give lessons and participate in a number of our music study programs. From what I see and know already, you'd be an asset for us."

"Of course, I would accept your offer in a heartbeat, Emilee. I'm honored. I don't know what to say or how to thank you."

"Thank us by becoming a Hall of Fame student. I have a strong gut feeling about you. Call it an educator's intuition. I think you have potential."

"You will have my utmost cooperation and enthusiasm! I know I can meet your expectations."

"Great. However, before you two start celebrating, I need approval from our Board and Admissions Committee. You'll need to write an essay, of course. It's part of the process. We want to see how well you write—how well you communicate your thoughts. Our next meeting is Friday. Can you be ready by then?"

"Certainly! But it will take a while to get all my transcripts."

"We don't care where you've been or how much or how little you've accomplished before. If the Naval Academy took you in, that's good enough for us."

Charlie felt a strong twinge of guilt, knowing his high school record wouldn't get him accepted anywhere.

"Thank you," he answered weakly.

"You'd be on provisional probation at first. As long as you perform the way I think you can, the scholarship will continue."

Charlie was dumbstruck, as was Kacie. Before he could say anything further, Dean Williams stood and offered her hand, indicating the end of their brief meeting. Charlie rose immediately and shook it enthusiastically. His eyes sparkled with gratitude and happiness.

"You have my word, Emilee."

Kacie shook Dean Williams' hand as well. "Wow! You sure have made *my* day!" she said. "We're both honored by your confidence."

"Forget it, Kacie. Just keep playing the music. It represents our college so well."

When they returned outside, each was numb. Kacie put her arms around Charlie and hugged him fiercely.

"Charlie! We could become classmates! Is that awesome or what?"

"I sure didn't see that coming," Charlie said.

"Me either. Dean Williams apparently sees something special in you—as I do. I know Maria Wilkes has been a big fan of our act… and of course, all the students. The Dean pays attention to these things. She wants what's best for the college, too."

"What do you know about the admission essay?" Charlie asked.

"The standards are extremely high—only the best of the best are accepted. Hope you write well. I can help you. Any idea what your subject will be?"

"I'm thinking of writing about my experience at the academy and how the Vietnam War changed my attitude about serving."

"Good choice."

Charlie and Kacie continued to talk excitedly for another hour. As evening approached, they shared a pizza at a local Italian restaurant. To be able to converse without looking at the clock was such a treat.

Charlie stood. He knew Kacie needed time to study.

"I'll look into renting us a car this weekend," he said. "Can you go early Saturday?"

"Of course."

Charlie hugged Kacie again before heading back to the Academy. He planned to visit his brother and tell him his decision as a courtesy. He'd love to tell his father in person as well. The airmail letter he wrote him would have to suffice, though.

❋

Walking across Tecumseh Court and up the marble steps to the rotunda, he felt a tug at his heart. Could this be regret? He had been a midshipman for almost ten months. If he stuck it out for three more months, the hazing would be over; he would no longer be a plebe; it would be easier then.

Charlie shook off the pangs of indecisiveness. He stopped at the central office in the rotunda to check on the paperwork regarding his resignation. A Second Classman was on duty behind the desk. "I need a name and ID," he answered.

"McDaniels, Charles. Service Number six nine one zero zero three." He took out his military identification card and gave it to the Second Classman.

After a reading Charlie's card carefully, he stood and went into a back room. He returned with his file.

"Looks like you're all set."

Inside the file were his resignation papers. It appeared that everyone had signed the necessary documents. The effective date of his resignation was midnight, Tuesday.

"Thank you," Charlie said as he closed the file. "May I take this file with me?"

"Absolutely not. There're kept under lock and key all the time. After graduation, they're destroyed. Of course, in your case and others who leave early, their files are destroyed as soon as you're gone."

Walking through the corridors of Bancroft, he felt self-conscious, not bracing up as he moved from wing to wing. Occasionally, there would be a challenge from an upperclassman. Charlie conveyed his status and was left alone.

Back in his room, he found his roommates busily shining shoes and de-linting uniforms for the next formation.

"Hey, Charlie," Brian greeted him. "How's the process going? We'll miss your colorful remarks in the mess hall."

He smiled. "Going good, thanks. I leave Tuesday."

"Oh, by the way, there's a telegram waiting for you at the Battalion Office. Just came in."

"Okay, thanks," Charlie said taking the notice. He instinctively knew who sent the telegram. Charlie felt that familiar pang, again—fear of punishment and comparison.

"I'll go down right now to get it."

Walking towards the office, he changed course, deciding to see his brother first. He wanted that over and out of his mind.

As he walked across the bridge to Frank's wing, he thought about his father and the telegram waiting in the Battalion Office. He knew what to expect.

How pissed is my father? Will I ever be able to make things right with him? Perhaps someday he'll understand.

Charlie knocked on Frank's door. Inside, a couple of plebes were doing pushups. Frank was fully dressed for the evening meal, sitting behind his desk with his feet up. He looked at Charlie passively.

"What do you want?" Frank asked indifferently.

"I'll be gone next week. I've resigned and thought you should hear it from me. I'm here to say goodbye."

Frank looked up at Charlie in disbelief. "Do you have *any* idea what you're doing?"

"Some. I'd like to part as friends, though. I know you were the one who ratted on me about St. Johns. I'm letting it go."

"Hey, some Mexican guy told me you were disrupting their school. What was I going to do?"

"Talk to me first."

Frank stood up and walked over to Charlie. "You're a real dumb-ass. The shit's going to hit the fan when Dad finds out, you know."

"Yeah, I know. There's a telegram waiting for me at the Second Batt office. Most likely from him."

"For sure. He'll figure out a way to rip you a new one all the way from Danang."

"Listen, Frank, I don't care what he, you or anyone thinks. This is *my* choice—no one else will influence me ever again. Not you, not dad, not *anyone*!"

"Okay, man. It's your life. Personally, I think you've fucked it up. Good luck, dude."

"Can we at least part as friends, regardless of our differences and petty jealousies?"

Frank shook his head and returned to his seat. His message was clear. Charlie sighed and turned quickly to leave.

At least I tried.

Returning to his wing, Charlie stopped to pick up the telegram waiting for him in the in the basket.

After retrieving the yellow envelope, he stood in the corridor leaning against the wall and ripped it open. With a nervous smile, he unfolded the letter. He expected the worst.

His father's message was concise and brutally descriptive.

Coward! Stop. *Do not call me father*. Stop. *You are no longer my son.*

Charlie crumpled the yellow paper and strolled back to his room. Men were racing down the stairs to form for the evening meal. He sidestepped to make way.

Returning to his empty room, he took off his jacket and sat solemnly behind his desk. Regardless of their differences, the general was still his father. In the space of five minutes, he understood that half his family was gone—a part of his soul ripped away on ideological differences.

He wondered who the *real* cowards were. Anyone can go *with* the grain; he had simply chosen to go against it. Abandonment is a harsh judgment. Charlie would have to remain alone with his truths.

For once, he felt totally on his own— free from the shackles of parental authority, free to determine his own identity and value. It was a good feeling.

A small smile crept from the corner of his mouth.

I will overcome this.

❋

Later that evening, Charlie began the essay that would determine his provisional acceptance to St. John's.

Were he accepted, this college would challenge his intellect rather than his endurance. Charlie looked forward to a radically different academic philosophy—a place where there are more questions than answers. St. Johns would give him the ability to explore and communicate with like-minded individuals, those who ask questions and challenge the dogma.

The essay gave Charlie a chance to crystallize in writing the awareness that turned him against the war, an awareness that created an advocacy for peace. As he wrote, a stream of repressed consciousness flowed. His Navy-issue ballpoint pen raced across the yellow legal pad.

He wrote with passion and conviction, transforming thoughts of shame and inhumanity into love and light. His objective was optimism, not blame. He wished that all cultures throughout the world could coexist in harmony and respect for each other. Was it possible or a hopeless dream?

Charlie's subject allowed him to express his views and opinions about Agent Orange, Napalm, and My Lai. Charlie was free to write critically about U.S. terrorism through chemical warfare—warfare indiscriminately applied for the sake of defeating a contrary ideology. He questioned the wisdom of entering a foreign conflict against a culture with strong nationalistic pride.

Charlie wrote about foreign policy in an era of both fear and nationalistic exceptionalism. He denounced the use of chemical defoliants containing *known* carcinogens. These chemicals had destroyed over eight million acres of forest and half a million acres of peasant cropland.

He grieved for the pristine rainforests that might never recover. He grieved for the local inhabitants whose culture and way of life had been lost for generations—indifferently taken away. Many indigents found themselves forced to live in hastily built refugee camps. He questioned a national war policy that disrespected the lives and livelihood of so many.

The United States declared Agent Orange safe for humans and animals while *knowing* it was the deadliest of poisons. Nevertheless, the defoliation program continued while American citizens remained ignorant of its potential long-term consequence.

Charlie suggested that politicians and special interest groups ignored the danger of using dioxin. They knew it to be deadly;

that it would remain in the body, passed to future generations of Vietnamese children.

Charlie started a new paragraph to describe Napalm, the terrorist cousin of Agent Orange. Napalm is a combination of gasoline and naphthenic acid. It creates an incendiary gel that sticks to the skin that burns at 2000° F.

Eight million *tons* of Napalm bombs fell over the rural Vietnamese countryside by high-speed US bombers. Civilians and wildlife in the way died in intolerable pain.

On a new page, Charlie wrote of the atrocities committed in My Lai on March 16, 1968. He described how U.S. soldiers lined up and executed hundreds of women, children and old men with no regard for the sanctity of human life.

Where are honor and integrity, he asked, of a system that would allow such things to happen? Could it happen again in the future? Will this generation of anti-war activists grow to become an influential voting alliance, a moderating influence over man's lust for war? Will future leaders permit callousness in the name of a "just" war?

Charlie wanted to write so much more than his two pages would allow. Charlie *had* to include the thoughts of Dr. Martin Luther King, Jr., ardent supporter of Lyndon Johnson and The Great Society.

Dr. King deplored how the Vietnam War crippled Johnson's bedrock program of social justice, diverting resources and young men to a political undertaking with no end in sight.

Charlie knew little about Dr. King when he died. His outspoken criticism of the war in Southeast Asia was a powerful ally of the peace movement. Charlie now understood how devastating the loss of this great man was.

Charlie concluded his paper with the words of Mohamad Ali, world heavyweight boxing champion, in 1966. Ali refused to serve in Vietnam because of religious convictions. The government arrested Ali and stripped him of his heavyweight title. The government ignored his self-proclaimed status as a conscientious objector; the government tried to shame Ali for refusing to serve.

Charlie thought Mohamed Ali's quote a fitting summary of the words on his paper:

"Man, I ain't got no quarrel with them Viet Cong. Why should they ask me to put on a uniform and go ten thousand miles from home and drop bombs and bullets on brown people in Vietnam while so-called Negro people in Louisville are treated like dogs and denied simple human rights?"

When he had finished, he reread the pages of handwritten notes. The essay had become an indictment of his own country. It was a sad conclusion. Charlie took no satisfaction from his thesis.

Tomorrow he would fine-tune the essay. He hoped with all his heart that it was good enough to impress the St. Johns Admission Committee.

⁕

The next morning, Charlie called Kacie early. He walked down the hall and found an empty phone booth. Perhaps Kacie could help him find a typewriter.

He dialed her number. She answered immediately.

"That you, Arlo?" she asked hopefully.

"Sure is, Eli. How are you doing?"

"Good. You coming over?"

"Of course. I've been working on the essay. It's just about finished, but I need a favor. I need a typewriter."

"That's no problem. Bring your scribbles with you, and we'll polish it."

"Thanks. When are you available?"

"I have two classes this morning and two more this afternoon. While I'm in class, I'll set you up with a quiet place to type. You know how to type, don't you?"

"No, but I can hunt and peck my way through it I suppose."

"Don't worry," Kacie said. "My roommate is certified typist. She's good and can guarantee a professionally proofread and formatted document."

"Really? That would be wonderful!"

"Don't mention it. She's a big fan of yours. We all want to support you."

"Thanks, Kacie."

"Any word on the resignation process?" she asked.

"Tuesday at midnight—four days."

"Getting close. Are you nervous?"

"Not really. However, there's a feeling I can't shake, you know like maybe I've forgotten something."

"I'm not surprised. For you, it's a leap of faith into a chaotic future that's hard to imagine."

"I guess so. I'll get through it, though."

He purposely avoided mentioning the telegram over the phone.

"You'll be fine, I know. When are you coming?"

"I can be there at noon. Wait for me at the Quad—you can't miss me. I'll be wearing navy blue."

Charlie returned to his room with a feeling of elation. He read and reread his essay, making tweaks and changes as necessary. He was satisfied with his conclusions.

❋

An hour later, there was a knock on the door. The hall monitor, another plebe on watch duty, handed Charlie a Special Delivery letter from Twenty-Seventh Marines in De Nang. He signed for the letter with an uncomfortable feeling.

Charlie scanned the official-looking envelope decorated with the airmail red, white and blue border. The return address was the Fleet Post Office. It could only be from one person.

With a deep sigh, he opened the envelope and retrieved the single-page handwritten letter. It was brief.

Charles,

There are no words to express my disappointment in a son turned traitor. Your cowardliness is an affront to both me and the Navy. You should be ashamed.

My only salvation is in knowing that you are not my biological offspring and thus, I blame your mother and her boyfriend for the way you have turned out. I never told you this in the hope that I could mold you into a real man.

I gave you the opportunity of a lifetime. You have thrown it away.

CoronelMcDaniels III

Battalion Public Affairs Officer, 27th Marines

Charlie stared at the letter in disbelief. He read it repeatedly, noting the idiosyncrasies of his father's penmanship. Unquestionably, he was the author.

He thought about crumpling the letter and discarding it. However, he wanted to show it to his mother first. She should know exactly what he said.

That's the reason she wanted to talk.

However, Charlie felt no emotion, no sense of rejection. Rather he celebrated his genuine and unquestionable freedom. He felt happy!

If the general's not my birth father, fuck him.

He had expected an ugly response and received just that. However, it had no more impact than if it had come from a stranger.

No longer did his differences matter. To have no genetic ties to the man who bullied him so badly opened a new reality. The need to compare favorably vanished.

At that moment, his hidden demons jumped ship. He had never felt better.

But…who is my real father? Mom knows. I have to see her right away!

He walked quickly to the phone room.

❋

Charlie waited for Kacie in the Quad, relaxing on a bench beside the brick walk. The weather was moderating and the sun shining. February could be uncharacteristically warm. It was a good opportunity for him to collect and reshape his thoughts. He no longer felt self-conscious about the uniform.

He knew her schedule by now—when she was free and when she had to be in class. She was late.

Then he saw her, running across the grass waving at him. She flew into his arms breathlessly.

He grabbed her, spinning her in a full circle.

"You're looking pretty chipper today, if I may say so…or are you just glad to see me?"

"Obviously that. But there's something else. You should sit down for this one."

Kacie's smile vanished. "That serious?" She knew to expect the worst from the Academy.

"Don't worry. It's good news. I'm still trying to absorb it all—my mind's spinning all over the place on this one."

Kacie dragged him by the arm to the nearest bench. "Here. Sit. Tell me."

Charlie reached into his overcoat pocket to retrieve a single sheet of crumpled paper.

"This came by Special Delivery this morning."

He handed Kacie the letter. He waited while she read it.

Suddenly, she looked up at him. "What the hell? He's not your father?"

"Not according to him. Actually, I'm pretty happy about it."

"I bet you are! Me, too. Your gene pool is looking a hell of a lot better, you know."

Charlie laughed. "Thank you."

"What's this about your mom and her so-called boyfriend? Are they responsible for you? Frankly, I think you turned out fine — even if you're not the general's son. Probably better."

"He has a different set of values."

"No shit...but aren't you curious about your real dad? Who and where he is?"

"I talked to Mom before I came here. I told her about the letter. She confirmed it. Wants to see me right away."

Kacie sprang from the bench and grabbed his hand. "We have to go now, Charlie! Have you found a car?

"Yeah, but you have classes. What about the essay?"

"Screw the classes. Let me read your essay now, right here."

"Sure."

"Then we have to see your mom. Today, if possible. Let's get a car and see her this afternoon if we can. You can't leave *that* fruit hanging from the tree!"

Kacie picked up Charlie's legal pad. "Is that your masterpiece? May I?"

"Sure."

Kacie frowned as she looked at his handwritten.

"Is this in code?"

"No. Can't you read? It's in *perfect* English."

"Perfect for you maybe. You're going to have to help me decipher this."

As she progressed through the first page with Charlie's frequent help, she read faster.

Her struggle continued through the second and third pages. When Kacie was at the end, she reread it more fluidly.

"You put it well, Charlie!" she said. "While it's an old argument, you present it passionately and with such conviction. You write beautifully, I might add."

"You're serious?"

"*Yes*! I'm serious. Do you think I'd blow smoke up your skirt?"

"Wait. I'm trying to picture that in my mind."

She punched him softly on the arm. "It's an expression."

"I know. But seriously, do *you* think it's good enough?"

"I do. I'll ask Jen to type it while we're gone. It'll be on Dean Williams' desk by noon tomorrow. Let's go see your mom."

Charlie called the car rental place to see if he could take the vehicle now. He had reserved an old De Soto at the lot near the bus station.

In fifteen minutes, Charlie and Kacie were in the car lot

The owner of the lot was an old gentleman who sat in a small, dingy office inside a tiny building near the center of the lot. He looked up suspiciously when they walked in.

"My name is McDaniels. I called yesterday about reserving a car."

"You twenty-one?"

"No. I told you that yesterday."

"Okay, I'll make an exception for a middy." He winked at Kacie while Charlie reached into his wallet and produced a twenty-dollar bill and his driver's license.

"When are you bringing it back?"

"Later this evening."

"We close at nine."

"That's fine. I'll be back by then."

Charlie signed a few papers. The old man stood with the assistance of a cane and pointed his finger in the direction of the lot.

"It's the blue De Soto. You know how to drive stick?"

"Sure."

"Okay. Here are the keys and my card. Call if you have any problems."

Charlie took the keys and slid them into his pocket. "Thanks."

He opened the door for Kacie, and they walked into the lot. The De Soto was unlocked. Kacie jumped in the passenger seat.

Charlie slid behind the wheel and put the key in the ignition. The De Soto started immediately. Charlie put the car in first gear, and they were off. Soon, they were headed south on the Baltimore-Washington Parkway.

In forty-five minutes, Charlie crossed the South Capitol Street

Bridge and took the first exit into Fort McNair. He produced his ID card at the gate and received a smart salute.

"I've never been on a military base before," Kacie commented.

"I practically grew up on them."

Kacie looked out the window as Charlie turned on First Avenue. "Is that the Potomac?"

"Yeah, my room used to look across to it."

"Will you show me your room?"

"It's not mine anymore."

"I bet it is while your mom's here."

"Here we are," Charlie said. He turned the De Soto into the driveway and parked.

As they climbed out of the car, Charlie saw his mother running down the front steps.

"Hi, Mom!" he said giving her a big hug. "This is Kacie."

"Kacie! So nice to meet you. Call me Melinda."

They entered the front door and turned into the living room. It was exactly as Charlie remembered it the night he left. He and Kacie sat together on the sofa.

Kacie looked around the living room. There was a picture of Charlie in uniform on the table beside the couch. On the opposite side was a picture of his brother. She studied Frank's photograph curiously. She saw no family resemblance.

"I was so excited to hear about a possible scholarship at St. Johns, Charlie. When will you know?"

"Within a week."

"Well, I'm crossing my fingers. What can I get you, Kacie?"

"Just coffee or tea, thank you, Melinda."

"You want a beer, Charlie?"

"Yes please." He needed something to remove the edge.

When Melinda returned a few minutes later, she served the drinks and took the chair opposite the sofa.

"Let me see his letter, Charlie."

She read it once, looked up at him, and read it again.

"God, Charlie. Did he have to tell you like this? It's disgraceful. I'm so sorry. I had planned to tell you myself."

"Then it's true?"

"Yes," Melinda answered and looked at Kacie. "Are you comfortable with this story? It's a little personal and messy."

Kacie returned the gentle smile. "Of course. I've read the letter. Nothing matters. I feel like I've known Charlie forever."

His mother nodded and looked Charlie straight in the eye and began.

"You were born six months after Buzz returned from Europe. He was worried when I went into labor. He thought you were early," she said with a twinkle.

However, when you weighed in at nine pounds, seven ounces, he knew something was not right.

Kacie put her hand to her mouth, trying not to smile. Charlie snickered.

"He waited a few months before confronting me. I confessed. He would have divorced me on the spot were it not such a black mark on his ambitious young career. Instead, he made me swear never to tell *anyone* and to agree to perpetuate my role as the adoring and charming Marine wife.

"To his credit, he adopted you as his own. He *had* to maintain the deception of our 'stable' Marine family."

Melinda stopped and looked at Charlie. "Are you okay?"

"I'm still trying to process this. My first reaction is relief and the second is anger."

"I understand, Charlie. He treated you poorly. He thought he could force his way of life on you. He believed he could mold you as he did Frank. He couldn't. He had the wrong set of tools.

"When you pushed back as a teenager, he took the gloves off. That was the hardest part. The terms of our "agreement" forbade me from interfering with his form of discipline."

"I get it now—why you never came to my assistance when he was ragging on me."

Melinda nodded sadly.

"Who *is* my father then?"

"He's used to be a musician," she answered. "I knew him when he played cello with the Washington Symphony. He was unmarried; I had to let him go when Buzz returned. We've not communicated since."

"Do you know where he is now?"

Melinda shook her head. "You may be too young to understand this, Charlie, but when you fall in love with someone—and I mean really in love, you believe it's a once-in-a-lifetime opportunity. To walk away is an incredibly difficult thing to do. I had to do it to keep you."

"So Dad…or "Buzz" blackmailed you?"

"He did. Because of the infidelity, he knew he could win custody of you in a divorce settlement. I didn't have much choice. I traded him an ostensibly happy Marine Corps family for you. You were more than a fair trade," she added with a warm smile.

Melinda paused to recollect her emotions. She was close to tears.

"What was his name, Mom?"

"David Hunter," she answered. He was an awesome, fun guy and an unbelievably gifted musician. You're very much like him, Charlie. He would be proud to see how you've grown up.

Kacie squeezed Charlie's hand. She said nothing.

"So the general never found out who my real father was?" Charlie asked.

"No. He tried. I refused. It's one thing I would *never* do," Melinda said. "In the end, he gave up. He took his anger and resentment out on me instead."

"So you stayed with him for me?" Charlie had never felt such respect for his mother.

"Buzz's first love was the Marines. His career path couldn't handle a messy divorce—not in those days. He needed charming wife by his side, and so I played the part. I can't tell you how many boring cocktail parties I've endured."

Charlie smiled. "I know you hated them. You told me so yourself."

"I did, didn't I? Well, I can tell you I won't be attending anymore. Now that you've left the roost, nothing holds me here."

"And so now you're free of all that."

"Yes. However, we both have to be careful. Buzz can be vindictive when his ego's bruised. His deployment to Vietnam gives me the perfect opportunity to do this on my time and terms." She chuckled. "Maybe I'll send *him* a telegram."

"The perfect squelch," Kacie snickered.

"All I want is to slip away without any further contact. He can handle the divorce. You're over eighteen. He can't take you away from me, Charlie."

Kacie put an arm on his shoulder. "It worked out for the best, Charlie," she said. "Otherwise, I would never have met you."

Charlie hugged her. "Yeah," he said. "If he hadn't thrown me out, I wouldn't have been at the Greyhound bus station that night."

Melinda smiled. "The twists and turns of life are unpredictable, aren't they?"

Kacie and Charlie both nodded wholeheartedly.

The conversation shifted to St. Johns College and Charlie's tentative scholarship.

"The Dean loves him, Melinda. They met a few days ago. The Admissions Committee is meeting shortly to consider accepting Charlie mid-term on a scholarship basis."

"I'm so proud of you, Charlie. You have the strength to stand up for what you believe and choose the path that suits *you*, not your brother, not your father, not anybody."

"Thanks, Mom. Your support means everything."

Melinda smiled in appreciation and turned towards Kacie. "Now, tell me about yourself, Kacie. I've heard so much from Charlie. You can imagine my curiosity."

As soon as Kacie began to talk, he could see the instant connection between these two women. It felt good that his mom believed he had chosen wisely. Charlie sat quietly, waiting for the right moment. He patiently delayed so as not to interrupt the flow of their dialogue.

Charlie said nothing for a long time. He struggled to put his mother's story in context. His heart went out to her. Where he once thought her to be weak and subservient, he now saw her as a woman of enormous strength. She had to endure so much silently—all for him.

As they were about to leave, Melinda grabbed an envelope from the nearby desk. "This is for you, Charlie," she said. "It's a check for ten thousand dollars. Put it in a bank and use it as you see fit. I don't want you having to worry about money while you transition."

Charlie looked back with wide eyes. "I don't know what to say, Mom! This is a lot of money. What about you?"

"Don't worry about me, Charlie. There's a *lot* of cash in the bank accounts. I'll be fine."

Charlie hugged his mother emotionally. He had no words. Melinda knew. It was a wonderful feeling to support her son in a way neither she nor anybody else had done before.

❋

The trip back to Annapolis was relatively quiet. Charlie's clothes and eclectic guitar were in the back seat. Kacie would safeguard them until his resignation was final.

As they headed north on the BW Parkway, Kacie turned to Charlie and said, "I'm glad we went today, Charlie," she blurted. "Your mom is awesome! It was a hoot talking with her."

"She's changed so much, Kacie," Charlie answered. "There's a sparkle in her eye I've never seen before."

"There's no question she's behind you one hundred percent. Must feel good after all you've been through in your life."

"Yeah," Charlie answered. "For sure. Let's hope the last few days of my time in the Navy go as well."

It was well after dark by the time Charlie pulled into the used car lot on West Street. The old man was still there.

"How'd she run, boy?"

"Like a charm."

"They don't make 'em like that anymore."

After walking Kacie back to the dorm, he kissed her goodbye and returned to Bancroft Hall. They planned to meet tomorrow. Charlie's essay would be typed and in the hands of the Dean and the Admissions Committee tomorrow.

*

The following day began the weekend. Charlie met Kacie early, well before Liberty Call. He wanted as much time with her as possible while the streets of Annapolis remained relatively quiet.

"Jen's finishing up your essay, Charlie. She's probably done by now. Let's go see her."

In a few minutes, they were back in Kacie's dorm room.

"Jen, this is Charlie or Arlo as you know him," Kacie said as they entered her room.

Jen looked up and smiled. She had long, dark hair and wore thick glasses. She smiled warmly and extended her hand. "Nice to meet you. Shall I call you 'Charlie' or 'Arlo'?"

"I respond to both," Charlie answered. "I can't tell you how much I appreciate your helping me with the essay."

"You're welcome, Arlo. My pleasure," she said. "It's excellent, too. You write very well and put an interesting twist on the years of political misconduct."

Kacie beamed. "See, Charlie? Jen is one of our best and brightest. If she likes it, you're going to do fine!"

"It would be so awesome if you became a student here," Jen said. "Everyone's pulling for you."

After thanking Jen again, Charlie and Kacie left the dorm and headed for the Admissions Office.

Charlie looked at the two neatly typed pages. "Wow. This looks beautiful. Jen did an excellent job."

"Let's drop it off at the Admissions Office. I can run it in."

Charlie waited outside while Kacie delivered the essay to the receptionist.

"Done," she said, rejoining him. "Emilee said she would pick it up later in the day. She'll read it and make copies for the Admissions Board. You're all set!"

"Awesome! Let's relax for a bit and walk into town. I want to find a pizza place."

"Pizza? At ten-thirty in the morning?"

"Yeah. For me, it's a delicacy. I haven't had good pizza since last June. Call it a celebration, of sorts."

The local pizza shop on Green Street was reputed to be the best in town. They walked into a fairly quiet and empty restaurant and selected a table of their choice. As with most businesses and restaurants in Annapolis, it's quiet and peaceful until the Brigade is let out. Liberty Call is what supports a majority of small commercial establishments in town. Had the Brigade been in town, they'd be waiting for a table for over half an hour. Instead, they were able to talk and banter for over an hour. It was that wonderful time of courtship when everything was funny—everything was delightful. Charlie was so grateful for how events were flowing so smoothly.

Afterward, they walked along the docks, watching the fishing boats arrive with their catch.

Charlie spotted a florist across the street. "Come with me, Eli," he said. What kind of flowers does Jen like?"

"Don't know. I've never given her any. Why?"

"I want to thank her."

"Really? You're just too gallant for words."

"Stop trying to embarrass me. It won't work. I'm going with roses."

Charlie bought a small floral arrangement and a single yellow rose for Kacie.

The evening shadows fell across the streets and buildings as they strolled through Annapolis and back to the college. This moment became one of Charlie's best memories.

"Have we been out here all day?" he asked.

"Didn't you notice all the Middies milling about? It's been Saturday afternoon for some time now."

"I only saw you."

Kacie smiled happily. "Corny, but nice, thank you."

They returned to St. Johns and sat in the Quad for several more hours, listening to music from all parts of the campus. The more Charlie interacted with Kacie, the closer he felt. His heart ached with joy.

CHAPTER ELEVEN

Drafted

Present Time

Darkness enveloped him. It was over. His last thought was of the one he left foolishly behind.

1970

Charlie returned to Bancroft Hall late. With a free pass, nobody questioned him; nobody cared any longer. As soon as he entered the central rotunda, the feeling of anxiety returned. The cold green walls towered above him, seeming to taunt and ridicule him. He would be glad when Tuesday arrived.

In his room, Charlie's roommates greeted him briefly though they were too busy with other matters to spare him much attention.

Charlie sat down at his desk and instantly saw an official envelope with his name on it.

"What's this?" he asked.

"Came while you were gone," Bob ventured. "Must be important for a Saturday delivery."

Charlie froze when he saw the return address. It was from the Selective Service System. Charlie picked up the manila envelope gingerly as if it might explode. He looked warily at the official date and time stamps indicating a tracked correspondence. His hands shook while a shiver ran down his spine. He slowly opened the envelope and removed a single page official document.

The first thing he saw was his name and address followed by a brief order:

"You are hereby directed to present yourself for an Armed Forces Physical Examination at The Naval Academy Hospital 0800 on Wednesday, February 11th, 1970."

Shit! Charlie couldn't believe what he was reading. This must be some kind of joke. It wasn't.

The letter continued:

"If you fail to report, you will be declared delinquent and ordered to report for induction into the Armed Forces. You will also be subject to fine and imprisonment under the Military Service Selective Service Act of 1967."

He ignored his roommates who looked at him questionably. It was implausible—how could he be called for duty while technically still in the Navy? Wednesday, however, he wouldn't be in the Navy anymore, he'd be a civilian.

He remembered what his mother had said about his "father's" power of influence. He acknowledged that the general was indeed powerful but couldn't believe he was able to pull strings like this.

He shivered. This was more than mere coincidence. Only he and the personnel office knew the exact timing of his departure. That information was confidential, unavailable to anyone without a proper authority.

Charlie immediately thought of his brother. Frank had to be complicit in some conspiracy to frighten him with the notice from the draft board. Only a commissioned officer could review the folder, though. How could Frank pull rank and lie about some need to see Charlie's resignation papers?

In an instant, he knew. Frank must have told his father who set up the physical.

Mom was right. Don't underestimate him.

Again, they continued to manipulate Charlie's life. Nothing

changed. Could he be drafted?

He needed to find Pete. Taps was in ten minutes. Charlie grabbed his coat and hurried out the door.

⁕

He tapped on Pete's door and looked inside. Charlie found him behind a stack of books.

"Hey, Pete, may I interrupt for a couple of minutes?"

"Sure, Charlie, come on in."

Charlie said hello to George before sitting on the edge of Pete's bed.

"So, what's up?"

"Who has access to my files and records here?"

"No one. Our records are classified. Why?"

"How could anyone find out the date and time I'm leaving?"

"They couldn't unless you told them. Who knows you're leaving?"

"A few people...but, *no one*, other than Kacie and you, know the exact date and time I'll officially be a civilian."

Pete's eyes narrowed, "Are you going to tell me what this is about? Taps is in five minutes."

"I just received a notice to report for a draft physical."

"What? That's impossible. You're already *in* the military."

"I won't be Wednesday morning. My resignation is effective 2400 Tuesday."

"Is that the notice?" Pete asked looking at the paper in Charlie's hand.

"May I?"

"Sure."

Pete scanned the brief notice shaking his head. He looked confused.

"I don't know how this could happen. Okay, *technically* you have to report. You'll be a civilian then and eligible for the draft like anyone else. However, your resignation is no reason to have you drafted. The system doesn't work that way."

"I didn't think so."

"I'll admit that the timing of the notice is suspicious," Pete said. "Have you talked with Frank recently?"

"No."

"Does he know the effective date of your resignation?"

"No. Could he have looked at the processing papers?"

"Not without your permission. Those records are confidential and kept under lock and key."

"I know. However, he's the Brigade Commander. Maybe he pulled some strings or looked over someone's shoulder."

"It's possible, I guess. But think of the risk he'd be taking," Pete said. "That information is confidential. If he relayed it to anyone else, he'd be guilty of disseminating classified information. People go to jail for that."

"What if my father ordered him?"

"Doesn't matter. We're not obligated to follow knowingly illegal orders."

Charlie frowned. "So I have to report for the physical. I have no choice, do I?"

Taps sounded.

"If the notice is legit, you have to go. We're out of time. Let's sleep on it and talk more tomorrow."

Back to his room, Charlie's mind race as he continued to try to make sense of the notice.

He decided to tell Kacie in person tomorrow rather than by a late-night phone call.

❋

The following day, as they sat on a bench on the campus, Charlie pulled out the letter from the Selective Service System and handed it silently to Kacie.

She read it slowly, unable to comprehend at first as a tear ran down her cheeks.

"Charlie. Everything was going so well. What have you done to deserve this?"

"Someone knows that I'll be out on the street in two days. I'm nineteen and fully eligible for the draft."

"Someone must be watching your every move. Someone knows exactly when your discharge is scheduled," Kacie said hoarsely. "It *has* to be your brother. Have you talked to him about it?"

"I'm not going near him. He wouldn't tell me the truth anyway."

"So what happens next?"

"Let's say I pass the draft physical Wednesday. I'll be classified 1-A. So what? I'll become one out of millions of other guys hoping my number won't be called."

"Yeah. But not too many of them have a dick for an ex-father."

"No, not likely," he snickered.

"What about the draft lottery? Do you know your number?"

"Yes. It's high—top ten."

"So you would be drafted soon, one way or another. It's just a matter of time."

"Yeah. If 'Buzz' has enough influence to order this physical, he could just as easily accelerate my draft…like the next day."

Kacie was on her feet. There was eagerness and determination in her voice. "You have to get a student deferment!"

"I don't have time, Kacie. I have to wait until I'm accepted to the college first…*if* I'm accepted. Then, I suppose there would be other requirements before the scholarship would be official. We're talking weeks, I'm sure."

Kacie wiped another tear away as she searched for a solution. He was right. Time would run out and he would be helpless to resist.

Neither said a word for what seemed like a long while. Slowly, the seeds of an idea germinated. Charlie looked at her expectantly.

"I have a special relationship with the head of the music and philosophy department. Maria Wilkes. She introduced us at the concerts."

"Sure. I remember."

"She and I often jam together, so we're pretty close. I know she raved about the concerts. She thinks we both have real potential, especially since we're a couple."

"Okay…"

"Charlie, she's *on* the Admissions Committee!"

"Okay, that's good. But how does that get me a deferment? Even if they accept me, I wouldn't become a student overnight."

"Why not?"

"There'll be all kinds of conditions I'd have to fulfill. They can't be waived. Who would do that on *my* behalf?"

"Don't underestimate yourself, Charlie. I know this school's philosophy pretty well now. If they see someone they want, they can make it happen."

"But they don't even *know* me."

"Several have met you. The rest know *of* you. Believe me, they know more than you think."

"Well okay, but, don't you think I should cancel the resignation to give us time?"

"No! That would give *him* more time, too."

"Okay. Tell me what you're thinking."

"You have to be accepted and *admitted* as a student before Wednesday."

"But how?"

"I'll see Maria first thing Monday…in fact, I may even call her at home. I know it's Sunday, but this is an emergency."

"Yeah…but, still. How?"

"Let me handle it, Charlie. Sometimes you have to go on faith."

❋

General McDaniels sat behind his desk and looked out the lone window in the Commander's office. The harbor of Da Nang provided a peaceful backdrop in the distance. He watched small fishing boats come and go in the distance and smiled with smug satisfaction.

For the past three days, he had been in continual communication by phone with his son, Franklin. A simple phone call was all it took to obtain Charlie's exact discharge date.

Using his network of associates, it was easy to arrange the scheduling of the Selective Service physical. The general congratulated himself nonetheless.

If Charles applied to another school, General McDaniels knew it would take weeks before any college would accept him formally. In that window of time, the kid was vulnerable. Without a student ID, he would be unable to obtain an immediate student deferral, unable to dodge the draft as so many others had before him. If the general moved quickly, Charlie was screwed.

The minute after he passes the physical, he'll be drafted by special order—his.

The general chuckled to himself.

Wait'll he finds himself in Marine boot camp. He'll wish he was back at the Academy.

The general would follow Charlie from boot camp to his first overseas deployment. He could pull more strings to have him sent anywhere.

❋

On Monday morning, Charlie returned every item the government had issued him over the past eight months. At a respectable time, he called Kacie. He knew she would be up early today. The sound of her voice helped shake off his worry.

"Hi Arlo," she answered cheerfully. "Guess what?"

"Don't keep me in suspense. I'm a nervous wreck. Haven't slept all night."

"Emilee loved your essay, Charlie. She said it's remarkable!"

"She *said* that? Wow! Thanks, Kacie. What happens next?"

"I asked her what the college's policy was on waiving the other admission requirements like transcripts and what not."

"Yeah?"

"She said it's never been done before; highly improbable. However, she said if we want to give it a shot, you'd have to appear in person for an interview by the department heads. Emilee scheduled a meeting with them—they're the Admissions Board, for one p.m. this afternoon."

"Wow!" Charlie exclaimed in disbelief. "You are unbelievable, Miss Eli."

"Also," she continued, "I met with Maria Wilkes. She's on board with waiving all pre-admission requirements. She said that, as far as she was concerned, you could start here tomorrow."

"Kacie, I don't know what to say."

"Say you'll be the same guy I know and love. You'll need to be every bit that guy and more at the interview. The college has never given special treatment to anyone. You have to earn it. I've seen you under pressure—I believe in you."

"I promise not to let you down."

⁕

That afternoon, at five to one, Charlie stood outside the door to Dean Williams' office, ready to subject himself to the most important interview in his life. His uniform was impeccable—as if that mattered here.

Kacie stood next to him. They had done everything they could. There was nothing more, it was up to Charlie now and the strength of his spirit. His real character would have to shine beneath the facade of his persona.

Charlie looked at Kacie one more time before knocking on the door. She kissed him on the cheek and whispered, "I wish I could go with you."

"Me, too. Wish me luck," he said knocking on the door.

"Come in, Charlie," Dean Williams' familiar voice sounded from inside.

"Good afternoon, Emilee," he said cheerfully opening the door.

"Hi, Charlie. How are you doing?"

"A little nervous, otherwise, great."

"I can imagine. Let's talk for a bit before we address the Admissions Board. They're almost ready."

"Sure."

"First, Charlie, I must say that your essay is one of the best I've ever seen. Your passion jumps out from the first paragraph. You write beautifully, and your research is excellent."

"Thank you, Emilee," he replied. "It's easy when the words come from the heart."

"Well, it shows. Maria and I chatted a few minutes ago. She is adamant that we accept you on the spot. She said, and I quote, 'Don't let this one get away.' She really likes you."

Charlie smiled and began to relax. "The feeling is mutual. She's an awesome person."

His self-confidence was back. He was ready.

"Any other questions before we go in?"

"No. I'm ready."

Emilee smiled as she pushed her chair back. "Okay, Charlie. Let's do this."

Dean Williams pointed to a door to her right. A simple brass plaque on the door said "Conference Room."

Charlie knocked on the door. From inside, a male voice responded, "Come in." Emilee preceded Charlie into the boardroom and introduced him to each member. She showed him where to sit.

The Admissions Board consisted of three women and two men.

They looked back at him politely, concealing their skepticism. A copy of Charlie's essay lay on the conference table in front of each member

Charlie saw Maria and smiled. He sat at the head of the table and nodded to each committee member as Emilee introduced him. He thanked the Naval Academy for teaching him to react calmly under pressure.

"Ladies and gentlemen," Emilee began, "this is Midshipman Charles McDaniels. He is resigning from the Naval Academy. I've offered him a full scholarship here subject to your concurrence."

Rick Abrams looked at Charlie with a welcoming smile. He was the head of the science department. "Charlie, it's good to meet you. I speak for all of us in thanking you for your musical contributions here."

"It was my honor," Charlie answered. "I couldn't have done it without Kacie, though."

"Kacie is one of our most gifted students. You're fortunate to know her," Sally Owens said with a wink. Sally was the head of the Philosophy Department.

Charlie nodded with a shy smile. He could feel himself blushing.

"So, Charlie," Sally began. "I understand you want the Admissions Committee to accept you solely on the basis of your essay and musical abilities. That's a tall order without your transcripts and teacher recommendations."

"I realize that, Sally, and am deeply grateful for your consideration."

"We don't normally even *consider* applicants without a complete review of their academic credentials. Moreover, you ask us to make an exception to our admission standards to avoid the draft. I'm a little uneasy about that. On the other hand, it would be tragic if we lost you to the war. Too many good men have had their lives ruined because of the draft."

Maria spoke next. "Charlie is a most talented and gifted musician. He and Kacie have performed two live concerts here in the auditorium. The house was packed. Those who haven't heard them play are missing out on a real treat."

"But, Maria," Rick interrupted, "there are many talented musicians in this world. What is it that you think makes Charlie special? Why should we break policy for another talented musician?"

"I've been at the college almost ten years," Maria answered. "Never in all my associations with these wonderfully gifted student artists, have I heard anyone play with more style and more passion. Charlie is pitch perfect. His harmonies with Kacie are very, very special. There is no question in my mind that Charlie would be a wonderful addition to our student body. To lose him to another school or, God forbid, the military, would be a formidable loss—one I believe we would eventually regret."

Maria continued. "Charlie has already received notice from the Selective Service to report for a physical Wednesday morning, his first day as a civilian."

"That quickly?" Sally asked. "Is that how the Academy treats those who resign?"

"That's only a physical, Sally. It doesn't mean he'll be drafted," Jeff Ratcliff stated. Jeff was head of the Language Department. He turned back to Charlie. "When's your birthday? How vulnerable are you to the draft?"

"September 14," Charlie answered.

"Ouch!" Jeff winced. "If I'm not mistaken, that's a pretty high number."

"Yes, I'd be one of the first in line at the next draft call."

"But what difference does that make, Jeff?" Emilee asked. "Besides, the war is supposedly winding down. There may not be another draft call."

"I'm trying to establish the urgency in his request. How do we know how great a risk he faces?"

"We can't?" Sally said. "However, the timing of Charlie's notice is suspicious. The government seems to have him in its sights."

Dean Williams stepped in. "Charlie believes that the timing of his notice from the Draft Board was no coincidence."

"Really?" Rick asked skeptically. "Is this normally what the academy does to those who don't care for their program?"

"No," Charlie responded. "The Naval Academy is not vindictive. Over a third of my classmates have resigned for various reasons without consequence."

"Charlie believes his father has something to do with the coincidental timing of his notice," Emilee said.

"Is your father *that* powerful, Charlie?" Sally asked.

"He has a lot of connections, Sally," Charlie replied. "He's been in the service for over twenty-five years. He's currently serving as commander of the 27th Marine Division in Da Nang."

"But you have no way of *proving* that, do you?" Sally asked.

"No, I don't."

Charlie could see that Sally was not convinced. He braced himself for her further questions.

"Here's my problem, ladies and gentlemen," Sally continued. "I don't doubt that Charlie would be a credit to our school. But we know so little about Charlie as a man. Granted, the endorsements of Emilee and Maria are extremely influential; however, beyond a very well-articulated essay, we have little on which to base a decision—one way or the other."

"How would *you* address that, Charlie?" Rick asked.

"You have to decide on instinct and faith. I accept your conclusion, for or against."

"Show us right *now*, without your guitar, what you'll bring to our college."

Charlie smiled at her reference to the guitar. This was not the time to be humble.

"I have many intellectual curiosities, Sally. One of my greatest frustrations at the Academy is the limitation to only one field of study. I'm a self-starter with a passion for the *truth*. I've read and researched the Vietnam War thoroughly and believe I now know its truth. I want to learn other truths and believe I have the ability to discern fact from propaganda—regardless of the subject."

"We've all read your essay, Charlie," Rick said, "multiple times in fact. I think I speak for all of us when I say this is one of the most professional and well-documented essays in support of withdrawal from Southeast Asia we have yet to read." Each member nodded in agreement.

"How were you able to assemble so many compelling facts in such a short time?"

"I've been studying the war on my own since September. The more I read, the more I realized that I wanted no part of it. The incident at My Lai broke my spirit completely. I've spent a lot of time researching that incident."

Charlie spoke for the next five minutes without interruption. Each member listened to his story intently, evaluating his presence—how he carried himself. They saw that Charlie was a natural speaker who articulated as well as any student they knew.

As he described his life, each member of the committee listened intently, looking deeply into Charlie's eyes. He communicated a stature and maturity well beyond his years.

Charlie gave the performance of his life. The soft honesty of his eyes gave added credibility to his words. When he finished, the room was silent. He waited.

At last, Emilee spoke. "Ladies and gentlemen," she said, "I believe we have someone special in Charlie. He is the perfect fit for our student body and has the potential to do great things here. I, for one, wholeheartedly endorse an exception to our admission policy and recommend that he be admitted immediately under a full scholarship."

Charlie watched the committee as Emilee and Maria spoke. Several nodded ever so slightly; others remained stone-faced.

"Does anyone have any other question for Charlie? Otherwise, we should vote now," Rick said.

"I agree; let's consider this and vote," Jeff responded. The others nodded in agreement. "Charlie, will you excuse us, please. We will discuss your case among us. Dean Williams will give you our decision later today or tomorrow."

Charlie rose and looked at each member again. "I want to thank every one of you for considering me for a special exception. I promise you that I will be worthy of and grateful for your acceptance." With that, he turned and left the conference room, passing through Emilee's office and out the door.

No sooner had he closed the door to the Dean's office, than he saw Kacie waiting for him. She ran to him with a big expectant smile. "What do you think?" she asked.

"It's hard to say, Kacie. Emilee and Maria were on my side. I can't say about the others. They asked some tough questions."

"When will you know their decision?" she asked.

"Probably later today or tomorrow."

"So what now?"

"I guess I should get back and start packing. I have to return all my uniforms and other books and gear. The Navy will give me back the civilian clothes in which I first arrived. I'll be free to go tomorrow at midnight. I can walk out as a free man."

Kacie hugged Charlie intensely. "Whatever happens, I want to be with you. Let's pray that we can always be."

"Me, too." Charlie knew he had fallen for Kacie in a way never before experienced. He asked the guiding hand that was steering him to help him find his real purpose.

❋

For the rest of the day and into the evening, Charlie packed all his uniforms, books and other issued gear. Tomorrow he would return them back to the Navy.

Later, he joined his tablemates in the mess hall for the last time. At first, he felt awkward, relaxing in his chair while his plebe classmates remained stiffly in their chairs. Pete wanted to put Charlie at ease for this last time. He tapped his water glass with a butter knife and stood at the head of the table.

"Gentlemen," he began, "in spite of our differences, I want to wish Charlie well in whatever endeavor he chooses to pursue. Acceptance, regardless of personal views, is one of the true tests of manhood. I hope you will share my sentiments and wish Charlie Godspeed."

Slowly, each man at the table rose. Pete gave the plebes permission to stand as well. The second classman at the other end of the table raised his water glass. "Gentlemen, a toast to Charlie. May he find the joy and happiness God planned for him."

Charlie looked at each. His emotions prevented him from saying anything. With tears running down his cheeks, he acknowledged the toast gratefully.

"Thank you," he said at last. "You may not believe this but, honestly, I'll miss each of you. I shall always have the greatest respect for all of you."

❋

After dinner, Charlie stopped by the battalion office to check on paperwork and any other requirements of him before he left. Entering the door, he looked at the man on duty.

"Charlie McDaniels," he said, "I'm checking to make sure everything regarding my resignation is in order."

The third classman behind the first desk looked bored and disinterested. He moved slowly to an overflowing in-basket and looked for recent notices. Finally, he extracted a paper with the name "McDaniels" written on the front in bold letters.

"Here you go," he said, handing the notice to Charlie. "These are your discharge papers. You can go anytime Wednesday."

"Thank you."

Charlie wanted to shout from the rooftops. Instead, he walked calmly back to his room. On the way, he looked at the papers. Beneath the cover was a letter on Naval Academy stationery addressed to him from the Commandant of Midshipmen. It stated that effective 0001, Wednesday, February 11, 1970, Charlie was honorably discharged from the Navy *without* further obligation.

Charlie knocked on his door and stepped inside. Bob and Jim looked up at him from their studies.

"Hey, Charlie. Are you a civilian yet?"

"Wednesday. Mind if I still spend the night here until then?"

They laughed. "Boy, if it were me," Bob said, "I'd be in the nearest bar at the stroke of midnight tomorrow."

Charlie stopped and looked at the file sitting on his desk. "What's that?"

Brian shrugged. "I don't know. Major Garrett dropped it off while you were gone."

"Major Garrett?"

Charlie looked at the file. He had seen it once before —Major Garrett reviewed it in his presence a few days ago. In it was every piece of information about him from the date of his original application. He knew he wasn't supposed to have access to this file and wondered why Major Garrett had left it for him.

He opened the folder cautiously. His eyes were drawn to the inside front cover. Handwritten in pencil was a short and somewhat cryptic note: *"Look at application. JCS? Return file to my office and place on the chair."*

Charlie scratched his head and started thumbing through his file. The Academy was right to keep these records confidential and destroy them whenever a midshipman either leaves voluntarily or graduates. Every man deserves a clean start. It was a time-honored tradition.

Charlie was not supposed to see this file. Why had Major Garrett left it for him?

"Look at Application?" I don't get it.

Charlie flipped through the file. His original application to the Academy should be at the very back. He found it quickly.

Stapled to his application was a sheet of linen stationery addressed to the Academy Selection Board. He carefully removed the staple and stared at the letter skeptically. It was from the Chairman of the Joint Chiefs of Staff, highest ranking of all who served in the armed forces. Charlie had no idea how or why such a letter from the military's most senior officer would be in his file.

The body of the letter contained two paragraphs about Charlie, both of which were highly complimentary. He was stunned as he tried to comprehend the absolute absurdity of what he held in his hands. Yet, there it was, just as if he and the admiral were good buddies and went way back together.

I never knew the Chairman of the Joint Chiefs. He's a five-star Admiral. How could he possibly recommend me in such glowing terms? Why would he lie to the Selection Board?

Below the body of the letter was an original signature. Fleet Admiral Hyman Lemnitzhour had personally signed this letter of recommendation using an ink pen. Charlie studied the signature's twists and turns of pale blue ink as it flowed across the bottom of the page.

Fuck!

It was evident what Major Garrett wanted him to see. It must be why he asked him if he knew the Chairman. He read and re-read the glowing references to him—his fitness for military service, his character, and love of the sea.

This is bullshit. The Admiral didn't know me from Adam. He wouldn't make up things about me, would he? No, of course not. That's impossible!

Suddenly, Charlie grabbed the sides of his chair. Then he understood. The Chairman couldn't possibly have written the letter; someone else had...but who? What could be worth stooping to such a level?

The question resurrected the façade of his former father. Charlie knew he worked for some hot shots in the Pentagon around the time of his application. Perhaps he had some influence with the Joint Chiefs. Yet, he was just a coronel at the time. It's inconceivable that he would ask the Chairman to lie on his behalf.

He studied the signature again, looking at the distinctive swoops and dives of each letter. Something about it looked familiar. Even though hastily scrawled, there were elusively familiar characteristics in it. He'd seen this handwriting before. He didn't want to think about the implication.

He needed another sample of the Admiral's signature for comparison. He flipped hastily through the pages following his application. He didn't have to go far to find the Xeroxed welcoming letter from the Chairman. A copy was placed in his file and probably those of each new plebe after they were sworn in.

Charlie ripped the copy out of his file and place it side-by-side with the signature on his recommendation.

They were close, but not the same. Certain letters and flairs didn't match. One of the signatures looked like a forgery.

Then it hit him like a brick. His father had forged the Admiral's signature! It was the only plausible explanation.

It took a moment for the enormity of his father's transgression to sink in.

This was how his father had obtained an appointment for him to the Naval Academy. This was how he created the "fantastic opportunity" he so often bragged about after Charlie had been accepted.

He closed the file. One of his roommates asked him if he was all right. "Yeah, I'm okay," Charlie answered. "Just looking through my file."

"How'd you get that?"

"I don't know. Maybe we're supposed to get it when we leave."

Charlie tried to remain calm despite a smoldering anger expanding in his consciousness. The man he thought was his father manipulated and forced him into an environment for which he had no aptitude.

Unable to control himself, Charlie slammed his fist hard on the file folder, so hard, in fact, that a burning pain shot up his arm and into his shoulder. Both roommates looked up in surprise.

"Hey, man, what's going on?" Bob asked with alarm.

"Sorry. It's nothing," Charlie responded. "I'm fine now. Keep studying."

Charlie carefully folded the forged recommendation together with the other copy of the Chairman's signature and slipped them inside his jacket. The forgery was a powerful document—one he knew could bring his father down.

After erasing the note on the inside cover of the file folder, he left his room to return the folder to Major Garrett's office. The office was dark inside. Charlie quickly slipped in and placed his file on the seat behind the desk. Back in his room, he sat deeply in thought trying to imagine how his ex-father had created the deception.

March 1969

General McDaniels knew Charlie could never get into the Naval Academy on his own. The general took it personally. His inability to convince Charlie to follow his standards of conduct frustrated him. Moreover, he knew as well as Charlie that the acceptance of his application was virtually impossible.

The general decided to intervene on Charles' behalf. He had to influence the decisions of the admission committee. He had a plan.

In 1969, General McDaniels, then a colonel was the Chief of Staff to the Chairman of the Joint Chiefs of Staff, Fleet Admiral Hyman Lemnitzhour.

The general decided to use his connection with the Joint Chiefs to influence the Academy selection board—make them think Charlie was worthy of a favorable look.

One night, after the Admirals, Generals, and staff had left the Pentagon, General McDaniels feigned working overtime. In the silence of the dimly lit secretary's office, he searched through the office supplies surrounding her desk.

At last, he found what he was looking for—the Chairman's stationery. He carefully removed one of the linen sheets from her shelf. He looked at it and smiled.

Fine gold print displayed the emblem of the Joint Chiefs embossed at the top. Below were the words: *The United States Joint Chiefs of Staff, Fleet Admiral Hyman Lemnitzhour, Chairman.*

The general placed the linen stationary in the secretary's typewriter. Sitting at her desk, he carefully typed a short letter to the Naval Academy Selection Board. He wrote as the Joint Chiefs Chairman, asking the board to look favorably at the application of a young man named Charles Andrew McDaniels. The general espoused many fabricated military virtues that, despite Charlie's record to date, "warranted special consideration," the general wrote. "He will make a fine officer and is uniquely qualified for admission."

He included Charlie's address. At the letter's signature line, he typed the Chairman's name. Several ink pens lay on the desk. He removed the cap and carefully forged the admiral's signature. It was not a good forgery, but good enough to get by. It was the letterhead that mattered. He knew that any correspondence directly from the Chairman's office would receive immediate attention by the Selection Board.

On his way out to the parking lot, he quietly slipped his forged letter into the outgoing mail. It would be in the hands of the board in two days, less than a week before the final appointments.

Five days later, the Chairman received a letter from the selection board addressed directly to Admiral Lemnitzhour. Coronel McDaniels typically reviewed and prioritized the Admiral's incoming correspondence. He looked for anything from the Naval Academy.

There it is!

Colonel McDaniels removed the letter from the selection board and included it in the stack of mail he would review. Later, he slipped the envelope in his uniform coat. He waited half an hour before getting up.

"I'm on my way to the head," he told his secretary. "Be back shortly."

Sitting on the toilet, in the relative privacy of one of the stalls, he opened the letter.

"Dear Admiral Lemnitzhour," it began. *"Thank you for your recommendation of Mr. Charles McDaniels. Your support of his candidacy is, of course, grounds for immediate acceptance. A letter awarding him an appointment will be sent to the address you provided."*

"*Yes!*" the general exclaimed while flushing the toilet. He had done it!

✵

Early Tuesday morning, Charlie woke with a feeling of optimism. He could barely wait to call Kacie. Everything rode on this one chance. If St. Johns declined his immediate admission, he would have no place to go.

He skipped breakfast, sitting in his room gathering thoughts and planning for whatever lay ahead.

At nine thirty, the plebe on floor duty knocked on the door and placed a pink note on Charlie's desk. "You have a phone call," he said apathetically and turned to leave.

Charlie grabbed the message. It was from Kacie.

He ran down the hall to the nearest bank of phone booths, most of which were empty at this time of day. Hastily, he jammed a dime into the slot and dialed Kacie's number. She answered on the first ring. She knew it would be Charlie.

"Hello? Is this the commander?" Her voice was lighthearted. Charlie could hardly speak.

"Tell me, *please*!"

"Charlie, you made it!" she said excitedly. "You're accepted and can join the student body tomorrow!"

"My God," he almost shouted into the phone, "What a relief! You can't imagine."

"I'm so happy, Charlie, I can hardly stand it! Emilee called me first thing this morning. She said Maria was the dominating influence in their decision. One member had to sleep on it. They liked how you carried and presented yourself."

"I'm still speechless, Kacie. I just want to dance with joy."

"Well, come on over, then. I'll dance with you. We have a lot of administrative stuff to do. We'll get you a student ID card and a letter of acceptance from Dean Williams. That should be enough to have you classified 2-S—Student Deferment. We should mail the deferment application today."

"No kidding. I'm on my way, Kacie. See you in fifteen minutes."

❋

Kacie was waiting when Charlie arrived at the Quad. She saw him immediately and stood. They hugged each other with joy and relief.

"You must have a remarkable guardian angel," she said. "Sit with me, and I'll fill you in."

They found an empty table. Charlie went to the café nearby and returned with two coffees. "Okay, fill me in."

Kacie removed the plastic cap from the Styrofoam cup. Steam rose in the chilly morning air.

"I talked a while with Dean Williams after she told me the good news. You know what? They accepted you not for your musical talents nor your essay, although both certainly helped. Each member of the Committee wanted you here because of you!"

"How do you mean?" Charlie asked.

"I can't describe it," she answered, "other than they sensed in you a potential by your demeanor and persona. They knew you would be a perfect fit."

"I don't know what to say. I need to see Dean Williams and thank her right away—each of the other members of the board."

"There's a powerful force guiding you, Charlie. When the path is correct, the obstacles fall away, don't they?"

"So far," he answered tentatively.

"Okay," Kacie continued. "Let's take care of the administrative stuff now. We have to find you a room in the dorm and get you enrolled as a freshman. And, most importantly, your student ID card. That and the letter you'll get from the Committee will be all the proof you need. You're a bona fide member of the St. Johns student body!"

"Awesome!" Charlie answered. He paused and looked down at his half-empty coffee cup. "Before we go, though," he said, "I want to show you something."

He reached into his jacket pocket and pulled out the forged letter to the Selection Board. "My ex-father forged a letter to get me in the academy."

"What?"

"Yeah. Look at this," he said handing her the letter.

Kacie opened the letter and scanned it. She looked back at Charlie with surprise.

"Wow! This admiral, the joint chiefs guy, really likes you!"

"I've never met him."

"What? You don't know him? Then, how…"

"Someone else wrote and signed it."

Suddenly, it dawned on her. "Are you saying this letter might not be authentic?"

"Yes. It's a forgery. That's not the Chairman's signature. The bastard forged his signature."

"How do you know?"

"I recognize aspects of his handwriting. There are subtle giveaways," he said. Then he handed her the welcoming letter. "When you compare that signature with this one, the differences are more pronounced."

"How can he get away with this? Forgery is a felony."

"No kidding. At first, I was just *really* pissed. However, after I cooled down, I realized that the letter could bring him down if I made it public."

"Would you?"

"Of course."

"Let's stop by the library and check out Maryland law on forgery before we do anything."

"Yes. Let's find out if what would happen to the old man if this letter got out."

Kacie thought about the implications of such a deception. "Could he have done the same thing for your brother?" she asked.

"That's a good question," Charlie responded. "If he knew, Frank would wonder about *his own* acceptance to the academy. He could be dismissed for fraud."

"So what are you going to do, Charlie?"

"Nothing for now. If they both stay out of my life, I'm going to let it go."

Kacie nodded. "Let's hope that's the case. Let's still look at what the law says about forgery."

⁂

They walked up the steps to Greenfield Library. Kacie led Charlie to the legal section where she found a thick book on Maryland law. Searching the index, she found the articles on forgery and fraud.

They studied the definition of forgery carefully. "Forgery," it said, "must be of legal significance and false," it began.

"The prosecutor must prove that the defendant took action with regard to a false document with the specific purpose of defrauding someone or some organization or government entity."

As they read the definition, each knew that General McDaniels had indeed committed a felony—a serious felony. The crime would ruin him if exposed.

Kacie closed the book and returned it to the shelf. Charlie stood and joined her. As they walked out of the library, Kacie said, "This knowledge *is* a powerful hammer, Charlie. Let's put the letter in a safe place."

"Yes. Can you keep it? I don't even want to take it back there."

⁂

It took several hours for Charlie and Kacie to go through the orientation process. They stopped at the dean's office first. Emilee looked at them with a broad grin. "You guys must be pretty happy," she said.

"We sure are! Thank you so much for your support, Emilee," Charlie said.

"My pleasure, Charlie. We had some dissenters at first. I could see them soften, however, when you spoke. Your articulation was superb. We discussed how it would affect the school's policies and the precedent this would set. That was the big hurdle. We weren't unanimous until this morning."

"I'm drafting a letter," she continued. "It confirms both your acceptance and the terms of your scholarship. You'll be a busy man, here."

Charlie grinned and said, "Bring it on. I can't wait to start!"

Charlie later returned to Bancroft Hall bursting with pride and confidence. The draft physical was no longer of concern. His request for a student deferment was in the mail by registered letter. The deferment would be automatic with the included copy of his student ID. He had proof of his status as a bona fide student.

Charlie lay comfortably in his bunk with hands behind his head. He stared at the ceiling with gratitude in his heart. He had done the right thing—and was rewarded for his courage.

Tomorrow morning, he would walk out of Bancroft Hall and become a member of the St. Johns student body.

The selective service physical tomorrow, although an inconvenience, was not a big deal. Charlie would hand over his student ID, letter of acceptance and copy of his deferment request. That should be sufficient to postpone any induction process.

He couldn't help smiling as he wondered what his ex-father

and half-brother would think when they found out. He didn't care. They would be furious that he had circumvented their strategy to have him drafted.

❋

Word of Charlie's acceptance and scholarship quickly spread around the campus. Most students were pleased though surprised. All, however, universally accepted Charlie as a beneficial addition to the student body.

He planned to attend his first class at St. John's Wednesday morning after returning from his physical appointment.

Ignacio sat in his dorm room Tuesday with clenched fists. He, too, had learned of Charlie's acceptance. It was not what he had intended. His efforts to have him expelled backfired. He had to move quickly—maybe there was still time.

He picked up the phone to call his "friend" at the Academy.

❋

The weather had turned unseasonably warm for February. Formation, usually inside over the winter, was outside today. It would be Frank's first chance to display his command presence at the center of Tecumseh Court. He relished the recognition and respect. He pictured himself standing with his staff behind him, each man with swords drawn. He hoped there were tourists outside who would take his picture.

Frank received notice of Ignacio's call just before noon formation. The message said it was urgent and that the caller would stay on the line. Though pressed for time, he took the call in the Battalion office on the way to formation.

"Midshipman McDaniels here."

"This is Ignacio," the caller answered in a strong accent.

Ignacio paused for a moment before relaying the bad news. "I have just learned that St. John's College has accepted your brother on a full scholarship. He starts tomorrow. Do you know about this?"

"What?"

"You heard me. I thought you had this under control."

"How the hell does someone get accepted with a scholarship in only two days?"

Charlie could have a student deferment if this man were telling him the truth. How could he report this development to his father? Is there more he should have done? Had he let his father down?

"Can you come here immediately?" Frank asked with authority. "We need to call my father right away. He may want to talk to you."

"Yeah, I can do that," Ignacio answered. "But I don't know how he got accepted either."

"I don't care. Meet me at the Visitors' Center in twenty minutes if you want any hope of having Charlie inducted into the service."

❋

For Frank, his first outside noon meal formation had lost its rosy glow. He wanted to get it over. Immediately after the brigade marched off, he raced to the visitor's center. The room was empty. He looked at his watch and waited in anguish.

Ten minutes later, Ignacio walked in.

Frank looked questionably at the somewhat disheveled and bearded man sitting alone on one of the sofas.

"Are you Ignacio?" he asked politely.

"Yes. Are you Frank?"

The two men shook hands and sat to talk.

Frank got directly to the point. "Tell me again," he said with authority. "How in the hell could Charles become instantly accepted at your school? He didn't have any time to provide the data needed for admission. His grades sucked. What kind of place takes someone on the spot like that? There must be a fraud of some sort going on that would allow that little punk to hide behind the skirts of a liberal institution?"

"I don't know. Maybe he paid someone off."

Ignacio started to say that he wasn't running the "institution," He was irritated with Frank's condescending manner.

"We need to notify my father about this latest development," Frank said. "We can't let him evade the draft based on a sham."

Frank stood and paced back and forth, trying to decide how to tell his father of this development. The general would be pissed, for sure. He picked up a courtesy phone by a sofa and dialed the number that would eventually connect him with his father.

"Stay here while I make this call," Frank commanded. He was upset that he would miss lunch.

❋

It took several minutes for the call to connect with the Twenty-Seventh Marine Regimental Headquarters in Danang. Frank sat nervously holding the phone to his ear. He refused to make eye contact with Ignacio during the wait.

Frank knew it was early morning in Danang; he also knew his father wouldn't care under the circumstances.

"McDaniels," the groggy voice answered angrily.

"Dad, it's Frank. Sorry about the time. I need to talk to you right away. It's about Charles."

"What about him?"

"I have with me a student from St. Johns College that claims Charlie's been accepted there. He starts tomorrow with all the paperwork necessary for him to apply for a student deferral from the draft. That will postpone his deployment to Vietnam."

"What the hell?" the general yelled. Frank cringed and moved the phone away from his ear. "I thought you were watching the little fucker!"

"I am, Dad. I don't know how he did it, Dad. I'm sorry."

"Did you talk to that Latino guy?"

"Yes, I did. He just informed me. He's with me at the moment if you want to speak with him."

"Put him on!"

Frank handed the phone tentatively to Ignacio. He took it and answered. "This is Ignacio. Who are you?" A trace of disrespect laced his accent.

"General McDaniels here."

"Buenos Dias, general. How is the war going for you?"

The general, with considerable restraint, asked, "What is the source of your information, Mr. Ignacio?

"Ignacio is my first name."

"Then what's your *last* name!"

"My last name is not your business."

The general clenched his fist. "How do you know that Charles was accepted to your school?" He spit out the word "school" as if it were sour wine.

"The whole campus knows about it," Ignacio answered. "The Admissions Committee accepted him. It is very unusual. Maybe there was a bribe involved. I do not know."

"Well, find out then. Are you capable of that?"

Frank cringed. He could hear the conversation. He wished his father would tone down the sarcasm.

Don't piss him off, Dad!

Ignacio paused for effect before answering. "Listen, amigo. Do not fuck with me. I am not one of your war toys."

He then hung up.

Frank sprang from his chair and yanked the phone from Ignacio's hand. "Hello? Hello? Dad?"

The line was dead. Feverishly, Frank redialed the number to reconnect with his father. As he waited, he looked at Ignacio apologetically. “Sorry man. He’s just upset.”

“Whatever,” Ignacio said as he stood to leave.

“Don’t go yet!” Frank pleaded.

Ignacio shrugged his shoulders and walked back into the Rotunda.

⁂

Fifteen minutes later, Frank was able to reconnect with his father. He was grateful for the lapse in time, hoping it would give his father time to cool down.

Without salutation, his father ordered, “Go over to that place and find the Dean of Admissions. Find out everything you can. I wouldn’t take a whole lot of stock in what your Spanish friend says.”

“I have classes all afternoon. I’ll be put on report if I leave the Yard now.”

“Just go, goddamnit! I’ll cover your ass.”

“Aye, aye, sir.”

The phone went dead.

The general slammed the phone down. It was three in the morning. He was fully awake now. His mind raced; he was desperate. He had to find a way to prevent Charles from obtaining that draft deferment.

He had gone to considerable effort to arrange for the physical tomorrow morning. If that school accepted Charles, he had only one option.

Time to call in a few favors and perhaps make some friends in the process.

⁂

As it turned out, the general had a friend in the Selective Service

Board—a classmate of his at the Academy.

Bruce Fargo. I wonder if he's still there. We never were the best of friends. Who cares? I outrank him now.

He woke up his aide and instructed him to find his friend, Captain Bruce Fargo at the draft board. "Tell him it's an emergency!"

Captain Fargo, who was in the Navy, struggled to advance along the career path. A succession of desk jobs minimized his chances for advancement. He desperately needed a combat command to obtain the coveted first star on his collar. The general knew this. He could offer help.

Surprisingly, the connection occurred quickly. In a matter of minutes, Captain Fargo was on the line.

"Bruce!" the general began. "Frank McDaniels here. How are you, you old fart?"

"Doing good, general. What's up with you? Heard you're in Nam now."

"I sure am, Bruce. I love it! Nothing like combat to bring out the best in you. How are you coming in getting *your* combat command?"

"Not well, Frank. I'll probably be stuck in this dead-end job for the rest of the war."

"Maybe I can help, Bruce. But first, I need a favor."

"Sure. I'll try."

"I need you to intervene in the system. Have my son apprehended. I want him to have duty in Nam. Get him in the Marine Corps as fast as you can. Make up whatever story you have to. Just get him to the nearest recruiting office."

"Jesus, General! I can't do that! If I'm caught tampering with the system, they'll have my ass. Politically, the draft board is serious shit these days."

"I know, and you fellows are doing a top-notch job over there."

"Thank you, sir. We try. But tell me what's going on? I don't understand why you can't go to your son directly."

"We don't see eye to eye, Bruce. He won't listen to me. Charles is a plebe at the boat school and he's quitting. He's become a pacifist,

I'm afraid."

Captain Fargo had no idea what the general was saying. "Okay," he said. "he's a pacifist. I'm sorry about that. But if he's at the Academy, why the hell do you want to have him drafted?"

"Long story, Bruce. The little fucker just quit yesterday. I want to show him what happens to quitters."

"That's a hell of a lesson, don't you think? If you force him into the Corps, he could wind up in Nam, you know."

"Exactly. That's the point, Bruce. He needs to have his snotty little nose rubbed in it—hard!"

"I'm sorry, general. I have two sons myself—both solidly for the war thank God. Maybe they could talk some sense into him."

"No time, Bruce. This job needs to be executed immediately by an experienced and capable officer like yourself."

"I appreciate the compliment. Tell me about the job."

"Now listen carefully, Bruce. I've arranged for him to be called in for what he thinks is a mandatory selective service physical."

"How'd you do that?"

"Doesn't matter, Bruce. *He* thinks it's for real."

"I still don't get it, General. Hang on a minute. Let me get his file."

General McDaniels waited patiently while Charlie's thin file was retrieved. He used the time to chat pleasantly with Captain Fargo…to butter him up.

"Okay. I have it. Hell, general, the kid has the highest possible number. He's a cinch to be drafted. Why not wait for the inevitable?"

"The little fucker's applied for a student deferment."

"Does he qualify?"

"Yes." The anger in the general's voice betrayed his attempt to act nonchalant and innocent.

"Oh, I see. You think he can avoid the draft altogether?"

"I'm afraid so, Bruce. It's a gut-wrenching disappointment."

"Okay. Where do I fit into all this, then? It doesn't sound like there's much I can do if he has a deferment."

"He'll be in the Academy hospital tomorrow at 0800 your time. I want you to have a couple of your toughest guys pick him up. Take him to the nearest Marine Corps recruiting center. "Convince him to sign up."

"Jesus, I can't do that! You *know* that, general. The kid has rights. You're asking me to circumvent policy and break the law. I could be court-martialed for doing something like that. Hell, your son could *sue* me."

"It's a personal favor, Bruce. Besides, once the kid's in boot camp, no one's gonna listen to him. Don't worry about the repercussions. I'll cover you on that."

Fargo hesitated. "How you gonna do that? You're ten thousand miles away for chrissake."

"Have I ever let you down, Bruce? We go back a long way."

"I know we do, General, but this is breaking the law for chrissake! I'd like to help, but that's asking *way* too much."

General McDaniels paused. Fargo could hear him sigh in the silence.

"Bruce, relax. Think of this as an opportunity. Do you remember that time ten years ago when I covered for you when we were on duty at Charleston—when you snuck off watch for half an hour to see your girlfriend for some nookie?"

"That was a long time ago, General," Bruce replied guardedly.

"Doesn't matter, Bruce. There's no statute of limitations on deserting your post."

"Come on, general. That's crazy!"

"You do this for me, Bruce, and I'll get you that combat assignment you need to make general. I used to work for the Chairman of the JCS, you know."

"The Joint Chiefs?"

"Yeah, Lemnitzhour and I are pretty close. We can get a lot done together. A good word from him will *guarantee* that combat assignment."

The line was silent for some time. With a deep sigh, Bruce finally answered, "Okay. I'll see what I can do."

"Thanks, Bruce. You won't regret this. I owe you."

Captain Fargo stared at the phone after the disconnection. He slammed it into its receiver.

The son of a bitch!

⁂

Wednesday morning began a new chapter in Charlie's life. For the last time, he was jarred awake by the ear-splitting reveille bells.

He rolled over and sat up, watching his roommates rush around in nervous anticipation of another formation. Charlie tried to stay out of their way.

Charlie said goodbye to his classmates as they ran out the door. He could hear the sounds of footsteps as his company formed for breakfast in the hallway. The formation lasted fifteen minutes. When his company marched off to the mess hall, the silence was a welcome relief.

The administrative department had returned the clothes and suitcase he brought with him last June. Slowly, he stood and put on his "civies"—a sports coat with white shirt, tie and dress pants. Even the pennies in his old loafers were still there.

With one last look around at this room he had called home, he picked up his suitcase and walked out into the long hallway. Everyone was at breakfast. It was a good time for him to make his exit.

He stopped at the main office and picked up the discharge papers that were waiting for him. After signing one more form, he was free to go.

"Good luck, buddy."

"Thanks. You, too."

I'm a civilian!

Walking out the main door and down the wide marble steps, Charlie breathed in the morning air, savoring the feeling of complete freedom.

He walked across the cobblestone court for the last time and paused in front of the statue of Tecumseh. Dawn revealed another cloudless sky, a continuation of February's unseasonable weather.

He had another half hour before he was to meet Kacie at the main gate. He sat on a bench along Stribling Walk and watched the brilliant sunrise over the Severn River.

Kacie insisted on accompanying him to the hospital for the physical. She wouldn't relax until Charlie had the student deferment. They were to meet at the main entrance at seven-thirty.

Charlie stood and strolled casually toward the Academy entrance. Rounding the chapel entrance, he saw Kacie waiting for him. She walked towards the main gate.

They met near the guard post. Charlie hugged her with all his might.

"She's with me, Corporal," Charlie yelled over to the Marine guard.

"Who are you?" the guard asked. Charlie no longer had any identifying uniform.

Charlie showed the guard his notice to report for a physical. He scanned it briefly.

"Do you know where the hospital is?" he asked indifferently.

"Yes, I know," Charlie answered.

The guard gave them an apathetic wave through.

"You're a civilian!" she said happily and paused. "We *definitely* have to find you some new threads, though. You look like a yuppie!"

Charlie laughed and hugged her. He whispered in her ear, "I *am* a yuppie."

"Don't get used to it. I'll help you get over it."

Charlie chuckled at the image he presented. His father had insisted he dress up for the induction last June. "These are the only clothes I have with me."

Charlie grabbed Kacie's hand, and they proceeded down Maryland Avenue and through the Yard. The hospital was on the other side of Spa Creek.

"Don't fool me. You have a whole box of jeans and sweatshirts back at the dorm. Let's get this over with so I can dress you properly."

Kacie looked around as they walked down College Avenue to Decatur Road. The hospital was on the far side of the academy yard on a lone hill by the cemetery. It was a fifteen-minute walk.

"Nice place," Kacie commented as they walked hand and hand through the grounds. "I've never been on your campus before."

Charlie laughed despite his nervousness. "You've never been here?"

"Are you kidding? Never. I must say, however, it would be an excellent place for our next demonstration."

Once they crossed the small bridge over Spa Creek, the Naval Academy Hospital could be seen atop a hill overlooking a small cemetery.

They across an asphalt circular drive at the entrance and stepped into the hospital lobby. At the main desk, Charlie showed the nurse on duty his papers. He waited while she looked them over.

"Down that hall," she said. "Last door on the left."

"Thank you," Kacie answered sweetly.

Sure enough, a gray military-styled door, inset with frosted glass, read "Induction Physicals."

Charlie held the door open for Kacie. They walked across the small room. It felt cold and unfriendly with its drab linoleum floor and bare walls. They approached the desk together. Charlie rang the little bell on the counter for service.

While they waited, they looked around the room. Several other young men waited nervously on the worn and scratched wooden benches. They eyed him curiously.

At either end of the row of benches sat two uniformed Chief Petty Officers dressed in the uniform of the Shore Patrol—white spats, billy clubs and braided arm brands. Each looked to be well-seasoned and powerful.

A chill ran up Charlie's spine. Kacie sensed that something was not quite right. The clerk arrived behind the desk. She looked up at Charlie with a questioning look.

"McDaniels," Charlie said as he handed her the papers.

At the mention of his name, the two uniformed men stood and flanked Charlie and Kacie on either side. "Are you Charles McDaniels?"

Charlie nodded slowly, attempting to understand what was happening. Kacie moved closer to him and put her arm through his.

"I am. Why do you ask?"

"We have orders to transport you directly to the nearest induction office. Your physical has been waived. You're 1-A and going straight to boot camp."

Charlie looked back scornfully. One petty officer rested a hand on his billy club while leering aggressively at Kacie. She gave him the finger and moved even closer to Charlie.

"The hell I am!" Charlie answered, attempting to control his anger.

Who sent these guys. How did they know I'd be here?

The other petty officer spoke disdainfully, "Listen, buddy, you can come peacefully, or you can come in handcuffs. Doesn't matter to us."

Kacie shot back at them with intense anger. "Hey," she said. "You goons can't just abduct a law-abiding citizen. What about due process?"

They ignored her as one pulled out a set of handcuffs and dangled it in front of her. "Forget it, sweetheart. Your boyfriend's back in the Navy. We can do whatever we want."

"Who sent you here? How did you find out I'd be here?" Charlie asked.

"We're not here to answer your questions, buddy." He said with a scowl as he deftly slipped the handcuffs on Charlie's right wrist. Kacie began to scream.

"Okay fellows. Wait a minute. I'll come peacefully if you allow me a minute with my friend."

The senior petty officer looked at Kacie. She was lovely, even in anger. His stare told her what he was thinking.

"Okay," he said looking at his watch. "Sixty seconds." He released the cuffs from Charlie's wrist.

Charlie pulled Kacie to the far end of the room. He whispered urgently in her ear, "The forged letter," he whispered. "Copy it and show it to my brother. "Tell him it can have his old man put in jail and have him thrown out of the Academy!"

"How do I find him?" she whispered back.

"He's the Brigade Commander—only guy with six stripes on his sleeve. He's short with dark curly hair. Ask for him at the main desk. Room 2306. Tell him it's urgent. Tell him it's about me—anything to get his attention. Make a copy of the letter and give it to him if he agrees to see you. Otherwise, mail it to him with a note."

"Do you think he's behind this?" Kacie asked.

"I *know* he is."

"Time's up, fellow. Let's go."

Charlie hugged Kacie tenderly and whispered in her ear. "Everything's going to be okay. I love you, Eli."

"I love you back, Arlo. We'll get to the bottom of this."

At that point, a burly petty officer grabbed Charlie's arm roughly. They pushed him out the door, leaving a bewildered, sobbing Kacie behind holding Charlie's suitcase.

❋

Kacie watched Charlie disappear around a corner. She ran back to the lobby. He was gone. A black sedan squealed around the drive and vanished into the distance.

What's with the Navy and black sedans?

She collapsed on the nearest bench and put her head in her hands. She felt helpless as if they were fighting the U.S. government, itself. She needed to think—she knew she was Charlie's only hope.

Finally, she stood slowly. The lobby was a blur. A test of will brewed inside her, gathering momentum with each breath.

Kacie sprinted back to campus. When she arrived, her composure was back. She thought about what Charlie had asked her.

Find Frank! You bet I'll find that son of a bitch!

The admin office could make a copy of the forged letter. First, Kacie had to find Ignacio, though. He *had* to be the source of information for Frank and the general—the enabler who broadcast the date and time of their concerts and Charlie's accelerated acceptance by the admissions board. It was obvious.

She looked to the Arts Building. Ignacio was probably in class—Wednesday morning was Philosophy. Kacie had skipped this class today.

She looked at her watch. Eight fifty-five. Classes changed on the hour.

Kacie ran toward the Arts Building. The bell rang as she raced down the hall. Students began filing out into the hallway.

Kacie spotted Ignacio with his new girlfriend. She took a deep breath and moved to confront him.

"I need a minute with Ignacio, please," she spoke calmly to his friend while blocking their exit from the building.

"What do you want?" he asked rudely.

"I know you're behind this, you son of a bitch!" she challenged. "I know you've betrayed Charlie…and me as well."

"I don't know what you're talking about," he answered. His dark brown eyes told her he was lying.

"Bullshit!"

"Hey, don't blame me, Kacie. He's the one who broke the rules. He got himself in over his head. He should have known better."

"Listen, asshole; you don't want *me* for an enemy here. I know your dirty little secrets. I can have you deported back to whatever little banana republic you came from."

Ignacio began to sweat and wiped his palms on his pants. With one last contemptuous glare, she turned away and ran to the exit.

Kacie was completely calm and knew precisely what to do next. She picked up the nearest phone and dialed the number.

The information center answered her call on the first ring.

"United States Naval Academy," the voice on the other end answered.

"MidshipmanMcDaniels, please," she asked politely. "It's urgent!"

"Please hold, ma'am."

After several minutes of waiting, the voice on the line returned. "I'm sorry. Mr. McDaniels is unavailable. Would you care to leave a message?"

"No, thank you," Kacie replied and hung up. She looked at her watch. It was eleven thirty. She needed to make some copies.

She patted the letter in her coat as she ran to the main office. St. John's had recently purchased a Kodak's Verifax copy machine—a huge expense for the college. She prayed that the staff would let her use it.

Bursting through the office door, Kacie approached the counter. She was out of breath. A young woman looked up from her desk. She was a fellow scholarship student.

"Hanna, I need to make a copy. It's an emergency!"

"Kacie, you *know* I can't do that."

"I'll pay for it! I'll *never* tell a soul. Can you *please* make an exception? It's an emergency."

Hanna looked at the sheet of paper in Kacie's hand. "Just one?"

Kacie nodded.

"Don't you *dare* tell anyone!"

"I swear!"

Hanna took the letter and disappeared into the back. Shortly she returned with Kacie's copy.

"Thank you! Thank you!"

Kacie ran down Maryland Avenue toward the main gate. The same corporal was still in the guardhouse. She ignored him and ran through the entrance. He could challenge her if he wanted. He didn't.

Inside the Yard, classes had just ended. Midshipmen hurrying toward Bancroft Hall surrounded her. Some tried to get her attention. She ignored them, continuing to run toward the main entrance of Bancroft Hall.

Dodging and weaving across Tecumseh Court, Kacie ran to the top of the marble stairs. She turned once and saw a gathering of tourists near the statue.

Midshipmen surrounded her. "Hey! Any of you guys know Frank McDaniels?" she yelled as loudly as she could to anyone who would answer. A small circle of men began to form around her.

"He's the Brigade Commander," someone close to her said. "If the formation is outside today, he'll be the head guy with six stripes and a sword. He'll be right in front of the tourists. You can't miss him."

"What's a formation?" she asked.

"We assemble in the courtyard at noon. You can watch it from over there," he said pointing to the tourists.

"Thanks."

"What's your name?"

She ignored the question and moved into the crowd.

He's in that building somewhere.

Kacie followed more midshipmen into the Rotunda. To her left was an official-looking office. As she turned toward it, men began running by her in the opposite direction. They passed her with appreciative looks, hurrying toward the courtyard and their assigned position.

What the fuck is going on?

She walked toward the office while continuing to dodge midshipmen going out. A plebe behind the front desk looked up with a smile. "How may I help you, ma'am?"

"I need to see one of the guys here immediately," she said. "It's very urgent."

"Is this an emergency?" he asked.

"Yes. Please hurry!"

"Stand by, please." The plebe was unsure how to handle a report of an emergency. He turned to the second classman in the desk by a window.

"Mister Rogers, sir, I have an emergency."

Rogers looked toward the desk and then at Kacie. He stood and approached her with a charming smile while straightening his tie.

"What is the nature of the emergency, ma'am?" he asked.

"It's personal," she answered. Frustration darkened her eyes. "I have to see MidshipmanMcDaniels immediately!"

"May I have your name please?" he asked. She suspected he was flirting with her.

"No!" she yelled back. "Where is he?"

Rogers stepped back defensively. He turned to look out one of the windows overlooking Tecumseh Court. Midshipmen were filling the courtyard, morphing into perfectly structured rows of white caps on heads staring straight ahead. Perfectly aligned companies of men stood in complete silence. The brigade had assembled for noon formation.

"If you step in here, ma'am, I can point him out to you."

Kacie joined him at the window overlooking the entire formation. "That's Mr. McDaniels," he said pointing out the window.

"Where?" Kacie asked.

"See the statue of Tecumseh?"

"Yeah."

"Look straight down into the court from there. He's at the head of that triangle of six men standing near the visitors."

Kacie followed his extended arm and saw Frank at once.

"At the very head, the one with all the stripes?"

"Yeah. That's him."

"Thank you," she said and hurried back to the rotunda.

"You can't go out there now, ma'am," Rogers shouted behind her. She ignored him.

The massive double doors to the rotunda were swinging slowly shut. They would remain closed for the duration of the formation. Two midshipmen stood on either side like guards.

"Wait!" she cried.

Kacie grabbed one of the men's arms pulling him away just long enough for her to slip through the doors. One tried to grab her but missed.

"You can't go out there now, lady!"

"Go fuck yourselves!"

She looked around. Several thousand men now occupied the court, standing at attention in perfect formation. Beyond, were over a hundred civilian tourists taking pictures from a roped off area at the entrance to the court.

She ran down the stairs with Rogers in pursuit.

"Stop!" he yelled.

She ignored him

Kacie couldn't see much from the back of the formation. She plowed ahead towards the tourists.

Rogers was scared. This ceremony was sacrosanct—some crazy woman going after the commander could not interrupt it.

"Shit," he said to himself and ran after Kacie. She looked over her shoulder and saw him gaining.

He grabbed her right arm. She shook him off and pushed away. She darted between companies of surprised and delighted midshipmen, always on the lookout for excitement. Many began to laugh and point in her direction.

Kacie pushed through row after row of men who stepped aside so she could pass.

When she finally reached the front of the formation, Kacie looked back at thousands of men following her curiously. She didn't care. To her left were the regimental staffs; ahead the Brigade Staff, each standing at attention facing the tourists.

Rogers stopped the chase, figuring Kacie was going into the visitor section. All he wanted was for her to go away. He desperately wanted the silent dignity of the ceremony restored.

Kacie looked at the very front of the formation. There he was—dark and barrel-chested as Charlie had described. Frank stood at the head of the triangle, looking proudly toward the visitors. Flashbulbs went off. He loved that sound—the sound of tourists capturing the Brigade of Midshipmen in another time-honored tradition. He was at the head of it all.

Suddenly, he heard Kacie's screams behind him.

What the hell?

Frank turned to see Kacie pushing her way through the regimental staffs. He looked surprised and unsure of what was happening. The young girl appeared to be heading directly toward him. Tourists started taking even more pictures. They sensed something unusual was going on as the odd scene unfolded before them. Flashbulbs popped incessantly.

As she approached him, Frank yelled at Rogers, "Call security! Get her out of here!"

The tourists were confused. For those familiar with the ceremony, this was most unusual. The buzz of excited conversation accompanied the popping of flashes. Every midshipman turned to follow Kacie running at full stride. A cacophony of whistles filled the air adding to the confusion.

Kacie reached the brigade staff and stopped breathlessly. She stood head to head with Frank, looking at him with contempt.

"Are you Frank McDaniels?"

"Ma'am, you have to leave at once!" he said pleadingly.

"Fuck you!" Kacie answered loudly. Her voice echoed through the court. "We know what you and your slimeball father have done. We will take you down with the information we have."

Frank tried to shush her. "Please, ma'am, lower your voice," he said desperately. "We can't talk here; you're disturbing the ceremony. If you leave quietly, I'll meet you at the statue of Tecumseh in ten minutes."

Kacie pointed to Tecumseh. "That one?"

"Yes."

Then Kacie saw the Shore Patrol coming after her.

"You'd better be there!"

She quickly ducked under the barricade while pulling the hood of her sweatshirt over her head. With dark sunglasses, Kacie was able to disappear into the crowd.

Every civilian looked at her as she tried to blend in with the crowd. "Sorry, everyone," Kacie said.

They moved to shelter her.

A single older man with a camera strapped around his neck was smiling at her. He was carrying a thick brown overcoat. She moved toward him and said softly, "Please put your coat around me. Pretend you know me. I need to hide."

The man was delighted at the specter of intrigue with a beautiful young woman. He obliged at once.

Security walked behind the tourists looking for Kacie. The crowd loved it.

"Fan out! She may be headed for the gate."

The shore patrol ran away from the statue of Tecumseh and disappeared behind the landscaping.

By now, the formation of midshipmen had settled down. The incident was over quickly. Badly shaken, Frank knew this had something to do with Charlie. He had no doubt whatsoever that this young woman was capable of drastic measures. He couldn't afford to blow her off.

It was time for the brigade to march into Bancroft Hall. The ceremony had run overtime.

Frank raised his sword and barked the command that would set the brigade in motion. What would normally be an impressive military command voice broke; it sounded like a loud croak. Regardless, companies began to move smartly towards Bancroft Hall, following the brigade staff into the building and wings beyond.

The incident had passed although it would become a story passed from class to class.

Frank felt embarrassed and disgraced. He *had* to meet this woman. He hoped she was bluffing. What information could she possibly have that would affect him and his father? He had to be sure she posed no threat.

As soon as he and the brigade staff were inside, Frank broke ranks and changed direction.

"Where are you going, Frank?" someone asked.

"I have some work to do," he answered. "I'm skipping noon meal today," he replied while heading back to the Rotunda. He passed through the massive doors and out into the sunshine.

Tecumseh Court was deserted now except for a few lingering tourists roaming about the large, empty space. Frank walked down the steps and across the court. He headed directly towards the giant bronze statue. The visitors recognized him; several took his picture. He wasn't in the mood anymore.

He saw her at once. Kacie was sitting alone on one of the benches facing toward the court. She observed him as he approached. Frank stopped and addressed her directly, "All right, I'm here. Now tell me what you want."

Kacie stood slowly and faced him. Before she spoke, she studied Frank's face and eyes. She saw that he was handsome, by most standards, but looked little like Charlie. He lacked the softness of Charlie's eyes, the gentleness of his manner.

Standing a mere foot from his square-jawed face, she glared at Frank menacingly. "What kind of man are you to do that to your own brother?" she asked coolly.

"I don't know what you're talking about. Who are you, anyway?"

She ignored the question and shoved the forged letter in front of him.

"Are you aware that your father forged this letter? He defrauded the United States government to get Charlie accepted to this place. I assume you're mindful of the fact that forgery is a felony."

"That's ridiculous! My father would *never* commit fraud for Charlie or anyone."

"Really? Take a closer look at the signature. Tell me that's not your father's handwriting over the Admiral's name."

"You're crazy!"

"Really? Here, you can have it. Take it back with you and look hard. Then tell me how crazy I am."

Frank took the letter and read it carefully. He had seen the Chairman's signature many times before. It was unique and uncharacteristically flamboyant. This signature did not belong to the Chairman. He quickly recognized elements of his father's handwriting. He began to sweat; his hands started to shake.

He remembered his father bragging about how he had to pull strings to get Charlie admitted. He had no idea that his father had done something dishonest. The color drained from his face. This girl could have his father court-martialed.

"You could have created this letter yourself. How do I know this is for real?"

"You don't," Kacie answered. "You could have it investigated, I suppose. You have neither the time nor the balls to take that chance, do you?"

"Now listen, goddamnit. You don't talk to me like that!"

"Fuck you…again."

Something about the look in Kacie's eyes told him not to play games with this one.

Regaining his command composure, Frank asked gruffly, "So what do you want?"

Kacie ignored his question. "Do you think there might be a similar letter in *your* file?"

"I wouldn't know," Frank stammered.

"Of course you don't. However, maybe your old man forged one for you, too. Perhaps, it's buried in the back of your file—unknown and soon to be destroyed. *Unless* that is, *this* letter is made public. Not only would your father face a court-martial, but your acceptance here would be under false pretenses. Do you think you'd be allowed to remain here?"

"I don't know what would happen."

"You'd be kicked out of here, that's what would happen! What a shame… since graduation is less than two months away. Come June, you could be on your way to the fleet—not as an officer, but a lowly enlisted man."

Frank felt his knees buckle and sat unsteadily on the bench. His hands were badly shaking as he stuffed the letter into his pocket. "What do you want?" he asked.

"Have Charlie released and never, *ever* try to interfere or otherwise control him again. If you do, we'll send the letter to the proper authorities."

"All right, all right. I'll see what I can do."

"I don't care what you *see, goddamnit. Do* it!"

"Okay! I have to call my father," Frank pleaded.

"Whatever. If Charlie's not back at St. Johns by midnight tonight, this letter's going public."

With that, Kacie stood and turned to leave.

Frank watched her walk away. He was going to be sick. He walked behind the statue of Tecumseh and threw up. Wiping his mouth on his gilded sleeve, a curious tourist snapped a picture of him.

❋

Frank hobbled back into Bancroft Hall. The brigade was still in the mess hall. He walked slowly through empty hallways and bridges toward his room in the fifth wing.

Inside his room, he removed his sword, cap, and white gloves and threw them angrily on the bed. Then he looked at himself in the mirror. His face was ashen—a few vomit stains remained on his sleeve where he had wiped his mouth.

He retrieved the letter Kacie had given him and reread it. She was right. His father's handwritten signature had every aspect of forgery. Had he committed fraud to get Charlie admitted to the Naval Academy? It explained how someone with Charlie's lack of credentials was able to gain entrance in a very competitive field.

Did dad do the same for me? How would I find out? Perhaps it's better if I not ask until after I graduate.

He had to call his father immediately. He believed the woman who confronted him to be quite dangerous and a clear threat to his career.

After sitting on his bunk for a few minutes, he felt somewhat better. He needed to get to a pay phone right away.

⁂

Calls to Da Nang could be unreliable at times. Frank prayed that his call would go through. After several minutes of suspense, a voice finally answered. "Twenty-Seventh Marines Headquarters, Sergeant Balks speaking."

"Sergeant, this is Frank McDaniels calling—General McDaniel's son. I need to talk to him immediately. It's an emergency."

"I'm sorry, sir," Balks responded. "The general is in the field for the day—won't be back until later this afternoon."

"What time?"

"Hard to say, sir. Probably around 1500. The general never misses Happy Hour at the club, you know."

Frank ignored the attempted humor. "What time would that be here—on the East Coast?"

"0400, sir. Can I leave him a message?"

"Just tell him I called, please. It's important."

In an act of frustration, he slammed the receiver down on its cradle. He needed to think.

There wasn't time to talk with his father.

I'm fucked and alone on this one. I can't afford to call the girl's bluff? But I don't even know where Charlie is or who has him.

Shit!

He remembered his father bragging to him on a recent phone call. He proudly claimed that he had "browbeat" the head to the Draft Board—made him circumvent the system to have Charlie picked up immediately. It was only yesterday when the two had a good laugh about it at Charlie's expense.

It wasn't funny anymore.

What was the guy's name?

Frank struggled to remember the name of the officer his father mentioned.

Fargo, Captain Fargo! That's it!

He was sure what his dad would do—cover his ass. The general had long ago perfected the process. His forgery had to remain covered up. If exposed, he would face an embarrassing investigation and possibly a court-martial. Frank imagined himself saving him.

He picked up the phone again and asked for directory assistance. He was able to obtain the number of the Selective Service Board. He dialed the number and waited anxiously.

"Selective Service Board. How may I direct your call?"

"Captain Fargo, please."

"I'm sorry, sir. Captain Fargo is in a meeting. May I have him return your call?"

"No! Please! It's a matter of grave importance."

"Who may I tell him is calling?"

"General McDaniels," Frank lied. "It's an emergency."

"Of course. One moment, General."

The captain was not pleased to receive another message from Buzz McDaniels. His face darkened. He stood up angrily and excused himself.

"I'll take it in my office," he told the messenger.

Captain Fargo entered his office and slammed the door behind him. He was still furious that his old friend had blackmailed him.

What else does this asshole want? I did what he asked, for chrissake!

He feared the general would continue to blackmail him over a mistake he had made long ago. He picked up the phone and snarled, "What is it now, General? I did what you wanted. Your son's in our custody."

"Sir, this is the general's son," Frank said uneasily. "I'm calling on my father's behalf. He's in the field and asked me to call you."

The captain's face darkened with rage. "What the hell's going on with you two? I can only take so much of this bullshit."

It felt good to vent some anger.

"Sir, my father asked that you belay his previous order and have

Mr. Charles McDaniels released immediately."

"How do I know you're the general's son? I'm on thin ice here and need to know for certain who you are."

"I understand, sir. But, how else would I know that you had my brother apprehended? Sir, all I can do is give you my word."

"That's not enough! I don't trust anyone with the name 'McDaniels.'"

"Sir, if you call the Naval Academy, you can verify who I am. I'm the Brigade Commander."

"I don't give a shit who you are. I'm not going to take this crap anymore. I did him a favor yesterday. As far as I'm concerned, our debt's paid in full. Tell your old man I won't be pushed around or blackmailed. I'm finished with you guys!"

The phone went dead in Frank's hands. He looked at the receiver as if it had bitten him. He hung his head; he was going to be sick again.

He didn't know what to do.

⁂

Captain Fargo looked at his phone with a smug smile. It felt good to tell this little snot to go to hell.

The general will soon understand that no one pushes me around—particularly by some kid claiming to be his son. I need proof!

Of course, if I did release his kid, I could claim it was a mistake to apprehend him in the first place. That will get me off the hook with the Board if the kid complains. Sure, the general would be pissed; but, hey, it was his son who relayed his direct order.

But then, why wouldn't the general call me himself? Something stinks here. I should stay the hell out of it.

Fargo shrugged his shoulders and returned to the meeting. He had no interest in doing anything for anyone with the name McDaniels.

❋

The Shore Patrol wagon's engine stopped after a forty-five-minute ride. Peering out the small window at the back of the wagon, Charlie looked out on a large, empty parking lot.

There was a bang on the door. One of the burly Shore Patrol ordered Charlie out of the wagon. He stood uncertainly on the asphalt pavement. Both petty officers flanked Charlie and ushered him across the parking lot. Ahead was a Marine recruiting office that occupied a small space in a nondescript strip center off Security Boulevard.

Surely, they don't think they can force me to enlist?

Charlie felt his anger intensify. He couldn't escape this ongoing interference with his life.

Charlie continued to protest to the Shore Patrol. He had rights.

This is kidnapping. What about due process? This is bullshit!

In the vice-like grip of his abductors, there was no chance to escape.

Stepping over the curb, Charlie looked at the glass storefront ahead. A large poster featuring the picture of a proud Marine occupied the entirety of the window. Charlie read the large lettering below the photograph.

"Marines. The Few, the Proud."

The Shore Patrol opened the door and shoved Charlie inside. He stumbled on the threshold. Staggering to regain his balance, he glared at his captors. A Marine Gunnery Sergeant sat behind a sleek metal desk and watched Charlie enter with some amusement.

He was in a small lobby partially visible through the outside window. Four small desks and chairs occupied the lobby. Posters and pictures depicting the marine way of life decorated the walls. American and Marine flags framed the front of the lobby. The ever-present slogan, *Semper Fidelis,* was proudly displayed.

On the opposite side of the room, the spotless desk of the Sergeant faced the "interview area." Here, young men, many of them still teenagers, were sold the Marine Corps and all its glory. All the necessary paperwork required to enlist sat waiting on each desk.

The sergeant ordered Charlie to sit at the empty desk away from the door and out of sight of the window. His paperwork, neatly prepared with all his personal information waited for his signature. The Shore Patrol Petty Officers lounged at the other desks.

Charlie surveyed the room and his situation.

Somebody wants to make sure my induction is swift and unnoticed.

He *had* to think this thing through critically.

No one will even know I'm missing other than Kacie. Will she call the police? Will she call Mom?

He shuddered involuntarily at the next thought.

Are they in danger? Would someone try to silence them?

A small kernel of fear crept up his spine. Whoever's behind this has no concern for the law.

I need to figure a way to get out of here!

Charlie sat in a squeaky wooden chair and looked at the papers in front of him. The Shore Patrol, with their feet on the desks, observed him carefully. He looked passively at the documents before him. With a few quick signatures, he would "voluntarily" become a new marine recruit.

Charlie looked up at one of his petty officer guards and said, "You know, I'm being abducted, against my will."

One of the petty officers answered with a smirk, "I don't know what you did, fella," he said, "or who you pissed off, but our orders are to have you enlisted ASAP. You'll have to whine to someone else. Nobody's going to believe you anyhow. You've been designated as a special case—Captain Fargo's orders."

"Who the hell is Captain Fargo?" Charlie asked.

"None of your fucking business, kid. Let's just say you picked the wrong guy to fuck with."

"I haven't fucked with anybody!"

"Someone thinks you have."

"What happens if I refuse?" Charlie demanded.

"You can't refuse," the Gunnery Sargent interrupted. "We take a dim view of deserters."

"I don't give a shit what you think, Gunny!"

"Maybe some time in the brig will change your mind, kid. That's where we take the deserters, you know."

"I can't be a deserter if I don't enlist, for god's sake."

"We have ways to fix that technicality. Now shut up and start signing the papers."

Charlie shuffled absently through the papers while he thought. He knew that nothing signed under duress could be held against him. That wouldn't help him now.

To the dismay of his captors, Charlie pretended to read each document slowly and carefully. When he finished the set, he started over.

"Come on, kid. We don't have all day."

"Do I get to make a phone call?" He had to let either Kacie or his mom know where he was.

"No."

Less than four hours ago, he was on top of the world—he was a civilian holding hands with Kacie as they walked happily towards the Naval Academy Hospital.

Feeling victimized isn't going to help.

Charlie stood up and looked around. "Hey, I've got to pee. I can't concentrate. Where's the head?"

The Gunnery Sergeant looked at him contemptuously. "Goddamnit, kid. You're on thin ice. Don't fuck with us!"

"I said I have to pee, goddamnit. I'm not signing anything until you show me where the head is...or I can piss on the floor. Your call."

"Get up!"

Charlie stood, pretending to dance in discomfort. A strong arm grabbed his shoulder and turned him around. Charlie shook the arm off with equal strength.

"Down the passageway," the sergeant pointed. "You have two minutes!"

Charlie sauntered down the short hall, stopping to read various notices on the wall. Behind him, he could feel the attentive and angry eyes of his captors.

Standing in front of the door marked "Head," he stopped and looked back.

"Is this one for men or women?"

"There *are* no heads for women here, kid. Get in there."

"Hey! You know, that's discrimination, don't you?" Charlie said sanctimoniously. He *wanted* them angry…and distracted. Anything to help his chances.

One of the Shore Patrol began to curse loudly. He came toward Charlie with a bully stick in hand. Charlie ducked quickly into the bathroom and slammed the door.

He barely had room to turn around. The small bathroom contained a dirty sink and toilet. There was no window. As quietly as he could, Charlie locked the door behind him.

He looked in the mirror. His clothes were still in relatively good shape despite his treatment. Charlie decided to wait for them to come after him. It wasn't much of a plan. It would at least buy him some time.

In the meanwhile, he read with some amusement the childish graffiti covering the walls.

After a few minutes, there was a loud thump on the door.

"Times up, buddy."

"I just need a few more minutes. Don't you ever clean this place? It's filthy."

"Get out here! Now!"

"Is there a fan in here?"

Someone began kicking the door.

"Hey, that's government property you're destroying."

The kicking persisted more aggressively.

Charlie could tell the weak lock wouldn't hold back much force. He grabbed the mop. It was about four feet in length, long enough to act as a barricade once the door opened. He propped one end of the mop against the wall opposite the door and waited.

Another kick on the door—louder than the first. Charlie ignored it. Soon, he could hear the sound of feet trying to bust the door. He held the mop securely in place.

"I have a key," the sergeant said to someone. "Wait here."

In a minute, Charlie heard the key unlocking the door. It swung only a few inches before stopping as it made contact with the mop. Charlie held the mop securely. An arm tried to reach behind the door vainly trying to reach the obstruction.

"Get a power saw," the sergeant said. "There's a hardware store a few doors down."

Charlie waited. He couldn't keep the smile off his face.

Might as well have a little fun. Anything to buy time.

It took over an hour. The hardware store was closed for lunch. The petty officers returned. He heard someone ask where the nearest electrical outlet was. It took another fifteen minutes to purchase an extension cord. Charlie finally heard the sound of a power saw cutting through the hollow steel door. Sparks flew at first. He watched the blade travel slowly up the door, looking for the obstruction. When they got close, Charlie slid the mop head away.

However, the steel door quickly dulled the saw's blade. They had to stop.

"Goddamnit!" Sargent's voice admonished from outside the bathroom. "You can't cut steel with a wood blade, dummy. Go back and get another blade—the *right* one, goddamnit!"

Charlie bought another half hour.

Finally, after numerous passes of the saw blade, the door began to give. It had lost its structural integrity and collapsed into the room. Charlie dodged a furious petty officer who fell inside with the crumbling door. The party was over.

They dragged Charlie down the hallway and shoved him back in his chair. He stood defiantly while the Gunnery Sergeant screamed at him as if he were a recruit at boot camp. With a lightning-fast move, Charlie hit the sergeant's chest with an open palm. He staggered back and nearly fell.

"All you guys can go fuck yourselves," Charlie screamed back. "Now let me out of here!"

The sergeant walked back to Charlie rubbing his chest. He feared the noise they made might draw the police. "Gag him and get him out of here," he ordered evenly.

This was routine work for the Shore Patrol. Charlie was cuffed and gagged with duct tape.

The Shore Patrol wagon pulled in front of the recruiting office and idled by the curb. The driver opened the rear door and stood by. When the outside walk was relatively clear, Charlie was hustled rapidly into the wagon.

The Gunnery Sergeant yelled something to him about the destruction of government property. Charlie smiled behind the duct tape. He raised his cuffed wrists as a symbol of defiance and extended a middle finger.

"You want to play games, fucker?" the lead petty officer yelled from the front, "We're going to have your ass locked up! After a few days in the Navy Brig, you'll be *begging* to come back and sign those papers."

❋

It took an hour to get from Security Boulevard to the brig. Charlie could see the traffic become heavier, slowing their progress. He guessed they were in the city.

The Shore Patrol wagon finally stopped in front of a one-story brick building in a seldom-visited area of Baltimore. The building was on a side street and completely fenced with triple concertina barbed wire. It had no windows or doors on the street side. Graffiti covered the buildings on either side of the brig.

The wagon stopped at a gate at the end of the street. Thirty seconds later, the gate slid open with a groan. They were inside the compound. The engine stopped. Charlie heard footsteps on the gravel drive. The rear door opened and a petty officer unceremoniously dragged Charlie off the back of the wagon. His wrists were bruised from the handcuffs; the duct tape uncomfortable across his mouth. After checking the handcuffs and placing ankle shackles around his feet, the duct tape was ripped off his face in a single painful moment.

Charlie grimaced. It was his only response and his eyes glared at his captors while one padlocked his wrists to the side of the van.

"Is all this really necessary, fellows?" Charlie asked. "I didn't *break* anything back there. *You* did."

They waited, ignoring him as if he wasn't there.

Five minutes later another man exited the brig and unlocked the handcuffs.

"You guys can go," the man said. "I've got it from here."

"He's all yours, Mac. Careful; this one's a pain in the ass."

He released Charlie from the wagon and ushered him inside.

Charlie's new friend, Mac, pushed a button beside the steel door that activated two-way speakers. After a brief identification, Charlie heard bolts unlatching the door. It slid open with a loud hiss.

Down a dark corridor, heavy steel doors lead to a bank of small cells. A faded stenciled sign overhead identified it as the custodial facility.

Mac removed Charlie's handcuffs and took his personal effects. After the check-in process, Charlie was led down the hallway and into the first cell on the right.

The brig was sparsely populated. A few cellmates looked over at Charlie but said nothing.

After removing his ankle braces, Mac closed the cell door with a loud bang that reverberated down the hallway.

Charlie sat on the dirty bed and closed his eyes. He could hear occasional sounds from the front desk. Otherwise, it was silent. A harsh overhead light shined down from the ceiling.

He closed his eyes. Somehow, he would get through this.

DRAFTED

❋

Charlie eased down on the dingy cot and closed his eyes. He waited for hours in hopes that his nightmare would soon end. He slept for several hours before waking with a start. For a moment, he didn't know where he was. Quickly, however, the awful reality of his situation came back. Nothing had changed. He was completely alone.

A few prisoners glared unpleasantly at Charlie. No longer in possession of his watch, he could only guess at the time. He looked around. A piece of bread and glass of water had been delivered at some point during his nap.

The phone in the front office rang occasionally. Charlie was able to make out parts of the conversations from his cell. They were administrative in nature and uninteresting. Otherwise, there was complete silence.

He looked down at the dirty concrete floor rubbing wrists still sore from the cuffs. He had lost all concept of time. He waited, fighting an immense depression born from helplessness.

This must be hell.

The phone rang again. Charlie eavesdropped to ease the monotony. He had a feeling the conversation was about him.

"Gunnery Sergeant Mac Davis, speaking. How may I help you?"

"Yes, he's here," the sergeant continued shortly.

Charlie looked up.

"By whose orders?" the sergeant asked. He nodded and continued, "I need to speak with him personally. My orders must come directly from him."

The sergeant waited patiently. He was apparently on hold.

Suddenly, the sergeant stiffened in his chair. "Yes, sir," he responded. "I understand. Aye, aye, sir."

The call ended. The brig was still again. Nothing happened for a while. He concluded the call was not about him after all.

Charlie tried to hang on to hope and faith in Kacie. Time passed.

Suddenly, Sergeant Davis entered the room and unlocked Charlie's cell, looking at him with a somewhat bewildered expression.

"You're free to go, McDaniels. I suggest you get out of here ASAP before someone changes their mind again."

Had Kacie done it?

Charlie returned to the reception desk where his personal effects waited for him in a small basket.

"Can I get a ride back to Annapolis?" Charlie asked the man behind the caged area.

There was no answer. A loud buzzer sounded, triggering the entry door to unlock. When it opened, Charlie was unceremoniously pushed out the door.

It was dark outside. He had his watch back and saw that it was eight fifteen.

How long was I in there?

The last twelve hours would haunt him forever—a nightmare he could never forget.

Standing outside in in the chilly air, Charlie remained on guard. He knew he couldn't relax until he was safely within the walls of St. Johns.

He looked around to get his bearings. He was near downtown Baltimore, close to one of the poorer neighborhoods. A white guy in a sports coat was not what he wanted to be in this part of town.

He saw a bus approaching two streets over. He sprinted to the bus stop on the next block and waved his arms. The bus driver slowed to pick him up.

"Thank you," Charlie said to the driver as he boarded. The driver looked back. He was an elderly black man with soft eyes. He wore an *Orioles* baseball cap.

"Where are we?" Charlie asked. He grabbed an overhead rail to steady himself.

"We're on Green Street going south."

"I have no money," Charlie told the driver. "I just want to find out where I am."

The driver looked at him. Something in Charlie's pleading eyes told him it was all right.

"I'm going to the ballpark. I'll drop you off there."

❋

Frank remained nervously alone in his room. He skipped afternoon classes and visited St. Johns College as his father ordered. He stood uncomfortably on the campus, watching students travel to and from classes. From a distance, several students mistook him for Charlie.

"Hey Charlie," someone yelled. "Welcome to St. Johns!"

Frank waved him off. "Where's the Admissions Office, buddy?"

"Sorry, man. I thought you were Charlie," he called. "It's that white building on Saint George Street."

Without responding, Frank turned and ran toward the Admissions Office. He burst through the door and looked around. Only the sound of a crackling fire broke the silence.

Where the fuck is everybody?

"Anybody here?" he called loudly.

A moment later, a student appeared in the hallway.

"Yes? Do you need assistance?"

"I need to see the dean of admissions right away!"

"Is it an emergency?" she asked with a trace of alarm.

"No."

"Why are you *yelling* then?"

"Where *is* he?" he said more quietly.

"The Dean is a 'she' and she's in a meeting. I can't interrupt her meeting if it's not an emergency. She'll be out for an hour or so if you don't mind waiting."

"It *is* an emergency," Frank corrected himself.

The student looked at him strangely. She was not a fan of the Naval Academy. Frank wasn't endearing himself much now.

"Who are you and what do you want?" There was a tone of irritation in her tone.

Frank tried to calm himself and be more ingratiating. "Please forgive me. My name is FrankMcDaniels. I need to find my brother, Charles."

At the mention of his name, the student excused herself. She knocked gently on the conference room door.

"Come in," Emilee called back.

She opened the door and peered in.

"What is it, Becky? Is it important?"

"Yes," she whispered.

"Come in."

Becky closed the door behind her and nodded at the department heads.

"Are you all right, Becky?' Emilee asked, somewhat alarmed.

"I'm so sorry to interrupt. I think it's important."

"Okay. Tell us."

"There's a middy in the lobby who claims to be Charlie's brother. He wants to know where he is."

"Charlie's brother? The one who screwed up his concert?" Sally asked.

"Yes."

"Tell him we don't give out that kind of information to the public. Ask him to leave. If he doesn't go right away, call security or the police."

Becky nodded with a smile. She left the room and closed the door.

Frank was pacing in the lobby.

"Well?" he asked with a trace of rudeness.

"I'm sorry. We can't give out personal information about the students."

"What do you mean? Damnit, I *told* you he was my brother!"

"Hey, keep your voice down."

"Listen, honey. I want to know where my brother is. Somebody better find him now!"

"Please leave. I can't help you."

"Bullshit! I'm not leaving until someone tells me where my brother is."

Becky turned and walked into another room. She picked up the phone and dialed the number of the Annapolis police.

❋

The police left Frank at the bottom of the steps to Bancroft Hall. The driver turned off the flashing red light. "Okay, buddy. This is where you get off. Stay away from the college. We won't be so lenient next time."

Frank slinked out of the police car. Afraid of being observed, he almost tiptoed up the steps and into the Rotunda.

He had failed his mission.

Back in his room, he sat on his bunk trying to figure out what to do.

As evening approached, a soft knock the door interrupted his worry. A messenger entered with a note in his hand.

"You have an emergency phone call, sir."

Frank stood and grabbed the message from the plebe's hand.

"Thank you," he said gruffly.

It was from his father. It was the call he dreaded but looked forward to at the same time. He grabbed his coat and ran to the nearest bank of phones.

Please tell me I did the right thing, Dad!

Fifteen nervous minutes later, he heard his father's voice on the other end of the line. "What's going on, son?" the familiar voice echoed.

"Dad! Charlie found a letter he said you forged—the one that got him accepted here."

"What are you talking about? I didn't *forge* anything."

"It's what the girl said. She showed it to me."

"What girl? You're not making any goddamned sense."

"She showed me the letter from the JCS recommending Charlie. Is that how he got in the academy?"

"Where'd she get that fucking letter?"

"From Charlie. I guess they gave him his file when he resigned."

"Bullshit! They don't do that. Files are classified."

"I saw the letter, Dad. Charlie's girlfriend gave me a copy."

"Girlfriend? And you believed her!"

"I *had* to, dad. The stakes are too high." Frank tried to keep the whine from his voice.

"Stakes? There are no stakes. No one can prove anything."

"Dad, you *forged* the letter. There are handwriting experts that could have you indicted."

The line was silent for a long time. The general had assumed that the letter of recommendation would never be seen. Had Charlie not accepted the appointment, it would have been discarded.

"How the hell did he get that letter? No one ever goes into those files. All details of *anyone's* admission to the Naval Academy are secret. They're held until graduation or resignation and then destroyed."

"I don't know sir. All I know is that Charlie has the letter you forged. After he was taken away, his girlfriend confronted me and gave me a copy. She threatened to make it public."

"So? I've signed tons of letters for the Admiral. It was part of my job at the Joint Chiefs. Don't worry about it. I can handle that one."

"Did you forge one for me, too?"

"You didn't need it. You weren't the screw up that Charles was."

"That's a relief. The girlfriend said that if you had, it could get me expelled."

"Listen; let me handle all this stuff. I have many friends. This is nickel-dime stuff. Just forget about it, ignore the girlfriend."

"I was afraid, Dad. I didn't know what to do so I called Captain Fargo and told him you had changed your mind. I told him to release Charles."

The line was silent for what seemed a very long time. Frank winced as he white-knuckled the phone with shaking hands, waiting for his father's response.

Finally, a steely calm voice answered. "Are you telling me you countermanded a direct order...one from your father, no less?"

"Yes, sir. I'm sorry, sir."

The phone went dead.

Kacie sat nervously in the student center. It was eleven p.m., and she had heard nothing yet. She stared into the darkness beyond the large plate-glass window. Hope drained from her heart with each tick of the large wall clock.

Kacie *had* to face reality. She knew they were facing a formidable opponent in General McDaniels. His mom was right. They had no idea what they were confronting.

At 11:30, tears filled her eyes with growing sorrow. She thought of what might have been. She and Charlie were capable of *anything*.

Were it not for an angry and narcissistic father who wanted to destroy their dreams.

She had looked forward to telling Charlie about her adventure in Tecumseh Court. She pictured him laughing uproariously at her story. Charlie's not here, though. There is no one to listen to that story.

At 11:45, she buried her head in her arms and began to softly sob as grief overcame her.

By 11:55, she looked up one more time into the darkness beyond. There was nothing. Kacie was giving up. The student center closed at midnight. She would have to leave shortly.

She buried her head in the crook of one arm while putting the other over her head.

The click of a door latch broke the silence. The door opened with a swish. Her head jerked up from folded arms. A cry of delight and surprise escaped her.

"Charlie!"

Standing in the doorway was Charlie. He looked like he had been through hell. She jumped, knocking over her chair, and ran to him with such joy and love. Kacie fell into his outstretched arms and gripped him fiercely. He kissed her with a powerful and unstoppable passion.

"You did it, Kacie. I'm free!" Charlie cried. The words rushed out of his mouth. "You're amazing. I thought I was done, on my way to boot camp. When I didn't cooperate at the recruiting office, they took me in the brig, gagged and handcuffed."

Kacie was shocked. "That's outrageous! How can they get away with that?"

"It's scary. The right people with power can do anything."

"How did you get out?"

"Bizarre. I was lying in a cell when I heard the phone ring down the hall. A little later, a guard opened the cell door and said I was free to go!"

"I did what you told me, Charlie. I don't think your brother likes me very much, though."

"Sit with me and tell me all about it," Charlie said.

Kacie's eyes were shining with excitement. Tears of happiness replaced bitterness.

"This place is about to close. Come to my room. I'll tell you there."

CHAPTER TWELVE

Present Time

The old man was gone.

His soul wept in bitterness for what might have been. It sobbed deeply in dismay; silently shaking in the darkness...shaking and shaking.

Home

"Arlo, wake up! You're having a bad dream."

He was trembling and disoriented. Charlie opened his eyes and saw her, sitting on the edge of their bed. She looked concerned.

She was as beautiful as ever. The years were gentle with her, even though she was over seventy now.

"Kacie?"

"Arlo, you've had a bad dream. Shake it off. Come back."

He sat up and reached for her. She came to him and hugged him tightly. He hugged back, afraid to let go.

Kacie held him and stroked the back of his neck. She whispered in his ear, "You want to tell me about it?"

"It was the worst nightmare I've ever had, Eli...so real, I was there."

"One of those lucid dreams, huh? They're the scariest."

"No shit. I dreamed I was a lonely old man living in a dirty trailer. I was so sad, I killed myself. You brought me back."

"Hey look around. Does this look like a dirty trailer to you?"

Charlie smiled and shook his head. Tears filled his red and swollen eyes.

None of it ever happened.

Eli held him tightly. She felt his fear and waited until it dissipated. Finally, she drew back and looked deeply into his eyes. "I love you, Arlo. And I love everything about you, everything you've done. It was a dream!"

"I know. It really shook me up, though. Let me wake up and I'll tell you all about it."

"Okay. Whenever you're ready. I'm going to get you some coffee. You look like you need it."

"Thanks," he said as she stood. "And, Kacie?"

"Yes?"

"I love you, too."

She smiled back with those same deep green eyes. "Don't go anywhere. I'll be right back."

THE END

Made in the USA
San Bernardino, CA
11 January 2018